W9-BHM-371

Praise for Lynda William's
Previous Books

"Handsome cover and a very nice look ... a lovingly detailed world." - David Brin, author

"An exhilarating and enjoyable read ... enthusiastically recommended reading for dedicated and discerning science fiction fans." - Library Bookwatch

"... you may find yourself caught up, as I did, by a complex and richly-imagined story. Like a Shakespearian tragedy ... (it) leaves you with almost as much sympathy for the "villains" as for the "heros." ..." - David Casperson

"...one of the most original and fascinating works of fantasy I have ever read... marvellous world-building, and a genuine page-turner of a plot." - Marie Jakober, author

"... this is a novel about people and cultures, honor and duty, and love and hatred. Featuring gunfights and swordfighting, rodeo-quality spaceship manuevers and murderous nobles ... an enjoyable stand-alone read..." - Dru Pagliassotti, reviewer

"I was captivated by the possibilities of living in that time and impressed with Williams' visions of the future and her ability to successfully weave in cultural differences in sexuality and love. I look forward to the next volume." - T.M. Martin, reviewer

"I recommend this book highly... (it) has intrigue, mystery and a wealth of history imbedded in a futuristic story setting.... Maybe I am just being selfish, but I am betting that most of you will love this book ... and those that don't ... well there is no accounting for taste." - Stephanie Ann Johanson, Neo-Opsis, reviewer

"The story delves into two very complex societies, explaining a very involved caste system, and proves that a lot of thought went into the world building for this series.... If you like a good Science Fiction/Fantasy, give (it) a look." - Lisa Ramaglia, Scribes World

"This book is truly, simply put, amazing. Set in the universe of Okal Rel, I found myself awestruck and lured in by the meticulously thought-out galaxy and characters. Oh, the characters! Electric, brilliant characters, both unique and full of life, grab hold of your affection (and sometimes hatred) and don't let go. And of course, to accompany all this, is a wonderful plot, brimming with adventure, seductive romance, politics and more then the characters' fair share of hardships.... This is indeed one of my favorite books of all time!" - Brianna Thomas, reader

Part Two of the Okal Rel Saga

RIGHTEOUS ANGER

a novel by Lynda Williams

EDGE SCIENCE FICTION AND FANTASY PUBLISHING
AN IMPRINT OF HADES PUBLICATIONS, INC.
CALGARY

Righteous Anger
copyright © 2006 by Lynda Williams

This is a work of fiction. Names, characters, places, and
incidents are the products of the author's imagination or
are used fictitiously and are not to be construed as real.
Any resemblance to actual events, locales, organizations,
or persons, living or dead, is entirely coincidental.

Edge Science Fiction and Fantasy Publishing
An Imprint of Hades Publications Inc.
P.O. Box 1714, Calgary, Alberta, T2P 2L7, Canada

In house editing by Richard Janzen
Interior by Brian Hades
Cover Illustration by David Willicome

All rights reserved. No part of this book may be reproduced,
scanned, or distributed in any printed or electronic form
without written permission. Please do not participate in or
encourage piracy of copyrighted materials in violation of the
author's rights. Purchase only authorized editions.

EDGE Science Fiction and Fantasy Publishing and Hades Publications, Inc.
acknowledges the ongoing support of the Canada Council for the Arts and the
Alberta Foundation for the Arts for our publishing programme.

Library and Archives Canada Cataloguing in Publication

Williams, Lynda, 1958-
    Righteous anger / Lynda Williams. -- 1st ed.

ISBN-13: 978-1-894063-38-8
ISBN-10: 1-894063-38-4

I. Title. II. Series: Williams, Lynda, 1958- . Okal Rel saga.

PS8595.I5622R53 2006   C813'.6   C2006-906099-1

FIRST EDITION
(s-20061108)
Printed in Canada
www.edgewebsite.com

Dedication

To my mother, Monica Williams
1915-2006
Cymru Am Byth

With special thanks to Craig Bowlsby, a Western Canadian fencing champion, for his expert advice on the fight scenes in Righteous Anger, Alison Sinclair for her input and friendship, and the people at EDGE who make dreams come true.

Other Books In The Okal Rel Saga

The Courtesan Prince
Part One

Righteous Anger
Part Two

Throne Price
Part Four

PROLOG

The End of the Nesak War

164 Americ Calendar

Ships cluttered space surrounding the barren moon-base of Cold Rock in Red Reach. Enough ships to tear reality.

Battlewheels hummed in place, drives engaging just enough for *skim*-telemetry to reveal the firefly tracts of *rel*-ships on their *nervecloth* displays. All around them, in ever-changing arcs, buzzed hoards of small, spherical *rel*-fighters manned by highborn pilots — the living weapons of the medium. Emotions soaked the medium in which they traveled: grief and anger, and a pale hope held out against the horror of a final, soul-numbing battle, if their leaders down on Cold Rock could not find a way to end the war that was destroying them all.

Vrellish clans had met on Cold Rock for a thousand years, coming from all across Red Reach to settle their differences by the sword, because swords were safer than space wars and habitat was far more precious than any cause that might inspire battle. This was the great truth of *Okal Rel*. But Sword Law required shared courts of honor. And the Vrellish shared no liege with their enemies.

Di Mon, of the Green Vrellish, did not know what the defeated Nesaks planned. Maybe a duel to save face, or a bargain to negotiate a safe withdrawal. Perhaps even some treachery with hidden weapons, meant to kill the Vrellish leaders.

He had talked his side into this meeting on the Cold Rock challenge floor in the hope that the Nesak survivors were as sick of grief and mad destruction as he was.

The Nesaks had sent three representatives to negotiate. Behind them were witnesses drawn from their battlewheels, all of them wearing their swords with pride, as if they had never participated in space-side massacres.

The inhabitants of Cold Rock filled the rest of the seats around the challenge floor, seated on thick rugs with children on their shoulders or in their laps. Both sexes managed the children and both dressed the same, right down to the swords worn at their sides.

Di Mon had been chosen to speak for the Vrellish cause. Beside him, young Vackal Vrel fingered his sword. Hangst Nersal of the Black Vrellish stood large and menacing, backed up in space by the best standing fleet in all Sevildom.

The warrior, priest and princess facing them were members of the Nesak ruling family — or so Di Mon had been told. He understood very little of Nesak political structure.

The princess had wide, green eyes, long hair that fell to her shoulders, and a floor-length gown worn beneath a bulky cloak of plain velvet. Neither she nor the priest wore a sword. That meant only one of the Nesaks was equipped to parley, under Sword Law.

"I am Prince Kene," said the Nesak warrior, as he drew his sword. "I speak for my people. Who speaks for the Vrellish?"

"I do." Di Mon cleared his own sword with equally formal intentions. "I am Di Mon, liege of Monitum."

Kene frowned at Monitum's sextant crest embroidered on the breast of Di Mon's silk shirt. "I would rather not negotiate with the Monatese," he declared. "Hangst Nersal is our kinsman, descended from Prince Nersal Nesak. Let him speak for the Vrellish."

Hangst's jaw muscles clenched. Di Mon considered graciously conceding, but he was not feeling diplomatic at all. His heart hurt for the pilots he had lost. His blood boiled as hotly as Vackal's, with a lust for vengeance that he had to fight to control. Hot sweat trickled between his shoulder blades, heated by his skin despite the cool air in the cavernous chamber. They were all over-flown. Vackal was agitated, Hangst was grim, and Di Mon was feverish with anger at the waste and stupidity of it all.

The silence grew so brittle that it had to break, soon, or draw blood.

Then Hangst Nersal stepped forward. "Well met, in honor, Prince Kene," he told the Nesak prince. "*Ack rel*."

Ack rel. People said it in grief and in parting. They said it in triumph, to mitigate the sting of an enemy's defeat. Most of all, they said it to remind themselves that the duty of all living souls was to preserve the potential for life in the universe for the sake of the Waiting Dead.

Ack rel, Di Mon repeated silently to himself, and felt the great pressure of his own hatred relax in his chest. Never had he wanted more desperately to believe the dead could live again, or felt more bitterly the isolation of his doubting nature.

The phrase worked its magic on the Nesaks, as well.

"*Ack rel*," said Kene. Turning to the robed man beside him, he said, "This is Zer Sarn, a priest, representing *Zer-sis* Ackal and his council."

Di Mon knew Hangst had Nesak ancestors, but he had never felt the truth of it until then. Hangst and Kene were both big, wide-shouldered men, while he and Vackal were lean, with sharper features. He felt momentarily insecure, and immediately regretted it.

I do not doubt you, brerelo, Di Mon silently promised his comrade and mentor, drawing strength from the word *brerelo* itself, which meant someone you trusted to stand with you in a common cause.

"Both sides have lost too many lives," said Kene. "Survivors need time to grow strong again. How will we settle our differences with honor, to conclude this war?"

"This is my reach!" Vackal cried, pushing forward. "I'll fight the duel!"

"Not a duel," the priest spoke up, in a booming voice of command. He waved the Nesak princess forward. "Marriage."

The Vrellish in the audience hissed and shouted. Di Mon clapped a hand on Vackal's wrist to stop him charging.

"Vrellish do not marry!" Vackal roared, struggling to break free of Di Mon. "I do not even pleasure female cattle like that one!" He spat in the princess's direction.

For an instant, Prince Kene was too astonished to attack Vackal, and in that instant his sister laid a restraining hand on his shoulder.

"It is Hangst Nersal," she said, looking at him swiftly and immediately dropping her wide, green eyes to the floor, looking flushed. "To whom I am betrothed."

"Hangst then!" Vackal spat. "It makes no difference."

Hangst Nersal stared, stony-faced, at the Nesak princess as she made herself look up again and meet his eyes. She wore a modest dress of light blue beneath her velvet cloak. Her long black hair was bound in ribbons that became her green eyes. She was not entirely grown up, but promised to be full-figured. Not at all like a hard-muscled Vrellish woman.

"You are my destiny," the green-eyed princess told Hangst Nersal, with the certainty of a religious zealot. "And I am yours."

"Really," Hangst said coldly. "How so?"

The priest answered. "It is her duty to restore the lost souls of the San line to us, through you. When we began this war, we believed that your ancestor, Nersal Nesak, had been reborn among our warriors. But the new *zer-sis*, Ackal, has seen that his soul is still bound to the Nersallian line. We cannot prevail in our goal of uniting all eternals while a great soul stands against us, blinded by the influence of childhood."

Their new zer-sis *is clever*, Di Mon decided, his hand still clamped harshly on young Vackal's arm. *How better to explain the failure of a priest-inspired war, than by discovering a spiritual miscalculation in one's predecessor? And not only that, but one that needs a generation to be put right again. Which is exactly how long they think they need, in order to prove, once again, that Nesak wives can breed warriors faster than we can restock ourselves with highborns.*

Vrellish of both genders were warriors and Vrellish women bred with difficulty. Di Mon was afraid the Nesaks were right about the breeding differential, and resented it.

"Fool priests!" Vackal cried. He snapped free of Di Mon's restraining grip and sheathed his sword in a contemptuous gesture. "Give Hangst your plump princess! Vrellish women are generous! I am sure his *mekan'stan* will share him, provided you throw in her brother to give us a fair crack at soul-stealing in the opposite direction!"

Vackal's speech whipped up cheers among his followers, accompanied by more than a few obscene gestures.

The Nesak princess averted her bright green eyes while Prince Kene moved to shield his sister from Vrellish mockery. Nesaks thrust fists into the air, shouting insults about Vrellish sexual habits.

Seconds short of mayhem, and to Di Mon's complete astonishment, the priest broke into song.

Zer Sarn had a powerful set of lungs. The words sounded as if they might have once been English: a dead tongue that Di Mon 's years of scholarship had required him to master. The song calmed the agitated Nesaks and astonished the Vrellish observers.

As the audience settled down, Di Mon turned to Hangst.

"Will you do it?" he asked. "To buy peace, without blood, will you marry?"

Hangst took his time to think through the ramifications. "They will expect a true marriage," he said finally. "I will be

unable to sire for vassals or to keep up *mekan'stan* relationships and that will offend the *kinf'stan*."

Di Mon wet his thin lips, wondering how he could feel
disappointed when moments before he had felt murderous.
Mood swings were a symptom of *rel*-fatigue, he decided. He
wanted to see the green world of Monitum again; to ride his
favorite horse at his home estate of StableHome. He wanted
to spend time in Green Hearth, deep within the barren
world of Gelion where the Demish ruled the Ava's court. He
would even be glad to sit through some interminable
Demish recitation of everyone's ancestry, if only he could do
it without dreading the next update of losses, in a war that
was consuming lives he held dear and threatening human
habitat that, by its rarity, had to be even more precious than
lives to a space faring culture.

"What if it was temporary?" Di Mon asked his *brerelo*.

Hangst looked at him, hard, and Di Mon had the eerie
sense of sharing the same thoughts. Hangst, too, wanted to
go home: not fight one more insane battle in space, perhaps
destroying Cold Rock in the process.

Hangst decided, and pushed forward.

"I accept," he told the Nesaks. "I will honor the terms of
marriage as you understand them, but only until your
princess has produced three children. Then she, and the
children, will return to the Nesak world of SanHome."

The Nesak princess gave a small cry of joy and threw
herself at the feet of her predestined husband.

The priest conceded with a nod. "So be it. Do you,
Hangst Nersal, so bind yourself by oath?"

"I do," said Hangst, looking as grim as Di Mon felt.
Hangst would be challenged for this betrayal of Vrellish
culture.

"Rise, Beryl," *Zer* Sarn told the princess. She tried, but
her gown and her trembling impeded her. Kene's jaw
clenched, but he stood firm. It was Hangst who reached

down to help his controversial bride. She rose and stood beside him on her own, looking much steadier.

"Beryl Nesak," the priest addressed her, "in the name of the *zer-sis* and all the Waiting Dead who are your ancestors, I name you married to Hangst, liege of Nersal. Take no man to your bed, but him, and bear him children. Manage the keeping of his home estate and keep his faith strong. Love as life demands us love each other, but remember that only the soul is immortal and no life more important than the soul's right to be cleanly reborn."

The girl looked up with tears in her wide green eyes. "Do not fear for me, uncle, nor you, Kene. I will not fail in my mission."

"Take good care of my sister, Liege Nersal," said Prince Kene. "You may lack respect for our women because they do not fight like your Vrellish she-animals, but you have the soul of a great man. One of ours. I know that you can love, and so, because I know her, I know that you will learn to love Beryl. Treat her well while she is with you. And when the third child is old enough to leave home, send for me, and Beryl will return to SanHome with the children. She will always be your wife, but this will free you from your side of this bargain."

Part I

The Third Child

11 Years later (175 Americ Era)

Beryl Nesak knelt to buckle a sword on her four-year-old son and sat back on her heels with a worried look. "Must you take him, Hangst?" she pleaded. "He is frightened."

Horth looked up at the large man dressed in a long, admiralty cloak. He liked the red dragon that clawed at Hangst Nersal's collar and swept down one side of his body, embroidered in russet and crimson. The dragon's tail went all the way around the back, ending near the tip of his father's sword.

Mother felt firm and sheltering, standing behind Horth. He resisted the urge to back up into her skirts and hide there. He was fearless at sword practice, according to his trainer, Hara; and his brother, Zrenyl, who had taken him up in a *rel*-ship a few times, said he took to it so naturally it was irksome.

But what he faced now was neither swords nor ships — it was a court reception.

"Horth's biggest risk," Hangst told Beryl cheerfully, "will be dying of boredom, listening to the Ava's heralds recite every one of baby Amel's Demish ancestors." He grinned. "I suspect they'll leave out the dash of Red Vrellish in the child. I am surprised they haven't dyed Amel's hair blond and found a way to make his eyes blue instead of gray." Father was amused by his own cleverness.

"There will be too many people there," Beryl insisted.

"Branst will keep an eye out for him," Father promised her. "And so will Zrenyl."

He did not mention Hara, but Horth was not surprised by that. Father had given up talking about his retainers and staff in front of Mother, because Mother didn't like anyone who wasn't highborn. Hara belonged to the nobleborn challenge class, which meant that in Mother's terms, she wasn't Sevolite enough to qualify as an "eternal."

Mother's hands began to dig into Horth's shoulders. "Let me keep Horth apart, to myself, Hangst! Please. Just Horth. He isn't suited to the sly ways of your Ava's court. Horth is too honest!"

"Honest?" Father laughed the way he did when he felt more threatening than threatened: a rough, aggressive sound. "How would you know, Beryl? Does he talk to you more than he talks to us?"

"I know his soul," Mother insisted.

"Neither his life, nor his soul, will be in any jeopardy today, I promise," said Father. "It is just a genotyping, even if it is an imperial one. Your own Nesak priests test children to confirm how Sevolite they are! You have told me that yourself."

"Priests are not *gorarelpul*," said Beryl. "*Gorarelpul* practice Lorel arts."

"We won't settle our differences on this or other matters today, my Nesak," said Hangst. "Nor in our next dozen lifetimes should we be doomed to spend them together, as you insist we are." He pulled her away from Horth into his arms. "But I like arguing with you," he said, smiling at her worried expression as he stroked her heart-shaped face with one large hand.

She let herself be held a moment before grief distorted her features and she pulled back, shaking with hard emotion. "Go," she said. "Take him! And go please your Vrellish sluts!"

Father sighed. "Beryl, so far it has only been the one. And it's political. I've explained that."

She listened in stony silence. Horth, like his brothers, was perfectly aware how she felt about Father resuming a sexual relationship with Tash Bryllit, an important vassal.

Father put out his hand. "Horth, come."

With a last glance at his mother, Horth left her side to take his father's hand. It was a good, strong hand. It filled him with confidence. He was afraid, yes, but he would conduct himself with honor because his family was there, to watch. It was a family that extended backwards and forward in time, spanning the living and the dead, with the living ones merely the happy few riding the curve of the *rel* symbol's S-shaped arc between the barbed hooks that symbolized birth and death.

There was a *rel* symbol, like that, embroidered on Horth's shirt. Mother did it herself. She used dyes from the plants that she raised in her special garden inside the nursery's greenhouse: the one with the real Nesak soil in it, that she had brought with her from SanHome. That was the only soil, she said, that would grow special plants. Magic soil that connected her soul to her ancestors. Horth stroked the symbol with his finger once, for courage, remembering some of Mother's maxims. *Your soul is older than your memories,* was one. *Lorels use the truth to tell lies* was another one she liked a lot, and *A clean soul is better than a bad life.*

He had memorized many of her sayings, even if he never spoke them aloud. But as usual, he could not decide how to apply even one of them.

Horth and his father left the nursery and passed down the connected rooms of the Throat, which ran the length of the family residence, called Black Hearth.

Hara stood waiting in the entrance hall, a sturdy looking woman who headed up the house guard of nobleborns known as knights errant, or simply errants, because they were on loan from vassal families. Hara disliked Horth's mother as much as Mother disliked Hara, but she was fiercely loyal to Father and generally fond of his hearth-children, despite the abnormality of Horth and his brothers being raised in Black Hearth. Horth knew all about that because it was constantly talked about. He knew that the hearth-children of a male liege were supposed to be the children of his sisters or aunts. A marriage, like that of Horth's parents, was not Vrellish at all — it was Demish. Or, even worse, Nesak. And the Vrellish resented it — a lot.

Horth's brothers, Zrenyl and Branst, were waiting with Hara and her errants.

"We're bringing Horth?" exclaimed Branst, aged seven.

"What's it look like, dummy?" answered Zrenyl, who was ten years old.

"Branst, I expect you to look after Horth," said Father.

"Can't Zrenyl, for once?" Branst protested. "Everyone's going to be there!"

"You mean everyone as in Tessitatt Monitum?" said Zrenyl, well aware of his younger brother's obsession with the girl next door, at Green Hearth. "She'll never like you, stupid. You're half Nesak."

"Stupid yourself!" cried Branst.

"Simmer down, boys!" ordered Hara, setting her thick arms akimbo and grinning at them. "Horth doesn't need looking after when he's got a sword!"

Horth was used to her joking like that. Hara liked to show off what she called his instinct for the art of fencing by encouraging older children to take him on. Horth liked the challenge, but the experience had made him acutely aware of size and age disparities in any serious bout.

Hara ruffled Branst's hair. "As for you, my randy one — what will we do with you? Only seven and pursuing a woman twice as old!"

Branst ducked out from under her affectionate razzing. "It's not like that," he muttered.

"Then it might be Horth who has to protect you from Tessitatt," Hara continued to tease Branst, "if you keep bobbing about her heels like a silly Tarkian farm puppy, when you aren't equipped yet to follow through on promises."

"I said it isn't like that!" said Branst, quite thoroughly red in the face now.

"That's enough, all of you," said Hangst. "Branst, you will keep an eye on Horth. Is that understood? I promised your mother someone would, and I will need Zrenyl with me."

"It's not fair," Branst complained, as they followed Father out. "Just because Zrenyl is older, he gets to do what he wants."

"Nothing's fair in life except a witnessed duel," Hara told him. "And Zrenyl isn't merely older. He is better at most things than you are. But cheer up! With those good looks, you'll be popular with all the women once you grow up."

"I don't want all the women," muttered Branst.

"Hush," Hara admonished him more harshly. "Stop sounding like a Nesak."

The reception lay beyond the big double doors that opened onto Fountain Court. Horth waited breathlessly for the family heralds to swing them open, dreading the moment when they would have to go out and face the crowd. There were so many Demish at court! *More than there were Vrellish people in the entire universe*, Horth often thought. But it wasn't merely being outnumbered that bothered him. The trouble with the Demish was that they talked and talked.

Fountain Court was an eight-sided courtyard with eight grand doors leading to the eight hearths that served the empire's ruling families as residences when they were at court under the Ava's eye. The fountain at its center was white marble. Usually, the court felt still and cool. But today it brimmed with food and noise and decorations.

Horth had been hearing for days about all the Demish people arriving from across the empire to witness baby Amel being genotyped. The Demish men stood about, stiffly, in costumes that proclaimed their ancestry. Their women also wore braid patterns worked in embroidery, but not in ways that interfered with being fashionable. Horth was bewildered by their hair styles and long, elaborate dresses, with great flows of hanging tassels at their waists and shoulders. The Demish women did not wear swords, but it would have been virtually impossible to fight in such clothes, even if they had.

The few Vrellish in the crowd wore short vests decorated in the distinctive patterns of their house braid. Under the decorative vests they wore plain shirts and tightly fitted pants that had enough stretch for complete freedom of movement. All the Vrellish wore swords — regardless of their sex — and the women were as likely as the men to sport liege marks to show that they led their clans.

"Demish sheep," Hara muttered, as a group of Demish women flocked about the entrance to Blue Hearth where the Ava was making his entrance.

Ava Delm was a dazzling figure, his cloak studded in jewels and lined in less showy, but more valuable, cat fur. Horth thought the Ava looked silly, but most of the Demish in the room were pulled in his direction like iron filings to a magnet.

Horth noticed that a sculpture of baby Amel's head had been inserted into the fountain that Fountain Court was named for. The face was colored to look realistic except for its exaggerated size. The water splashing down over the child's dark curls troubled Horth. If the baby were real, he would be cold. He decided it was monstrous to put a huge, severed head in the fountain like that. It made no sense to him at all; nor did the other decorations and arrangements, like the animals made of a sweetened protein paste that were being cut up and distributed by an army of giggling, female Demish children, dressed as servants, who were very ineptly serving the treats to their families. *Real servants would have done the job much better*, Horth thought.

Other Demish children fished for things in the fountain with ridiculous little stick toys; and a commoner choir sang play songs and lullabies, as if the severed head in the fountain could hear.

The only meaningful part of the whole scene was the genotyping apparatus set out near Green Hearth and manned by *gorarelpuls* from all the houses present, so they could check each other's work.

Green Hearth's *gorarelpul* would take blood cells from baby Amel, then run them through the gene reader of Lorel manufacture that looked more or less like a big metal box when it was all closed up. Then each *gorarelpul* would repeat the process until all were satisfied with the outcome.

"Hangst!" A dark-haired man knifed through the crowd from the direction of Green Hearth, next door.

"Di Mon," Father greeted the newcomer, and clasped sword arms. Father used his right arm and Di Mon his left one.

"You brought them all this time, I see," Di Mon said, with a nod in Horth's direction.

"I considered what you said about letting Beryl isolate him," said Horth's father, "even if it is not hard to understand why she is protective. He never spoke, except to Branst in baby grammar, and now he does not even do that much anymore."

"Horth has a Vrellish look about him," said Di Mon. "He will talk when he's sure he has something worth saying."

"Exactly my feeling about it, Liege Monitum," said Hara. "All that silence is a good sign, not a problem! Horth understands more than he says — I know!"

"All the more reason why you shouldn't let his mother monopolize him, then," Di Mon told Hangst.

"Beryl is entitled to her opinions," said Father.

"*Nesak* opinions," Di Mon objected.

They were interrupted by the arrival of a teenaged girl dressed in Di Mon's colors. She had brown hair, which was unusual in Sevolites, but her sword and clothes preempted the possibility of her being a servant. She wore the same house crest as Di Mon, and her braid proclaimed her a member of his family.

Branst was immediately riveted.

"I understand congratulations are in order, Liege Nersal," said the girl, who Horth knew was named Tessitatt. "Rumor has it that Horth is no longer your youngest child."

"Liege Bryllit's child has genotyped as mine," Father acknowledged. "Yes. I... owed her one."

"The gift child is an encouraging sign," said Di Mon. "But it has been four years since the term of your marriage expired. When are you planning to send for the Nesaks?"

"Marriages don't expire!" put in Zrenyl.

"Mine did," Hangst told his son, curtly. "When Horth was born."

"Then why haven't you sent Mother back to SanHome?" Branst wanted to know, his eyes bright with the threat of that looming betrayal, and the hope of its denial.

"It's a good question, Hangst," said Di Mon.

Horth listened very hard, as intense about the question as his brothers. It kept coming up, but Father never answered. It was no different this time.

"Still, it's good news, right?" Tessitatt said brightly. "About Liege Bryllit's baby."

"Mother doesn't think so," muttered Zrenyl.

"She didn't say everyone thought so!" Branst defended his idol to his brother.

"Tessitatt," said Di Mon. "Why don't you take Horth and Branst to fish for trinkets in the fountain. Silver Hearth's ladies-in-waiting made a great production of the children's entertainment. It would be a good thing to show them that Vrellish children can play just like Demish ones do."

"I'm not a child," Branst objected.

"Fine then, stay here," Tessitatt told him and put out a hand to Horth. Her hand had the hard-muscled feel of all Vrellish adults who studied the sword.

"He doesn't talk," Branst explained, catching up to them a moment later.

"Maybe you've never kept quiet long enough to let him!" said Tessitatt.

By now they had reached the fountain where a peppering of blond children, ranging in age from toddlers to teenagers, were plucking brightly colored packages out of the water with the stick-toys that Horth had seen earlier. The painted sticks ended in hooks used for catching a loop on the packages.

"This is so dumb," said Branst.

Tessitatt thrust one stick into his hand and another into Horth's. "Afraid you'll be shown up?"

"Me?" said Branst. "A baby could snag one of those!"

Tessitatt gestured for him to demonstrate. Branst frowned and thrust himself between a couple of girls in flounced dresses, startling them.

"Hey!" One of the Demish boys grabbed Branst by the shoulder.

Tessitatt pushed herself forward. "Pick on someone your own size, blondie."

"That's right! Get your big, mean Vrellish sister to rescue you!" the Demish boy mocked.

"She's not my sister!" cried Branst.

"How do you know?" the boy hurled back. "Vrellish women sleep with anyone!"

Tessitatt hit the Demish boy square in the mouth. He reeled, and staggered into waiting arms.

"Not quite anyone," said Tessitatt, grinning at her victim with a look of unrepentant sexual confidence. "He has to look like he'll be worth the trouble."

One of the blonde girls went white and swooned, collapsing a whole raft of her friends as she went down. The next moment, anxious mothers and angry Demish men descended followed by Di Mon.

"Sorry, Uncle," Tessitatt greeted him, looking abashed.

Di Mon helped the injured boy up and began negotiating terms of an apology, from Tessitatt, with the offended adults.

Horth put his stick down and turned to face the mass of people that filled Fountain Court — all talking at once.

For a moment the sound was a single roar. He fought down panic and was ashamed to be afraid of mere talk. He decided he would cross the floor on his own, just to prove that he could.

He had to concentrate to prevent the babble of voices from disturbing him, which was why it was possible for a woman to startle him by touching his arm.

"Oh, look! It's a Vrellish child!" she cried aloud.

A couple of her friends scurried up beside her. Horth held his ground.

"It's all right, dear," the Demish woman said, settling down in front of Horth in a rustle of skirts. An artificial fragrance of flowers wafted off her. "I won't hurt you," she cooed.

Her friends crouched down beside her to inspect Horth.

"Isn't he cute!" exclaimed a woman with an astonishing garden of flowers worked in stiff silk across her bosom. Horth reached out to see what they felt like. The woman giggled nervously at his touch. "Oh, my! They are precocious!"

"He's only curious," said the third woman, and offered Horth the hem of her fur-trimmed cloak to feel. "Aren't you, lamb?"

Horth's brow furrowed as he tried to decode that extraordinary remark. He knew that a lamb was an animal raised for slaughter. He therefore concluded that this was an insult, and hit the women squarely in the nose. He deemed the attack proper because they were both in the highborn challenge class, and since she was so much bigger than him, he didn't understand the resulting fuss.

Father waded into the midst of the row and scooped Horth up, leaving Di Mon to soothe the ruffled Demish who were trying to stem the flow of blood from the injured woman's nose.

Horth felt perfectly safe and vindicated, sitting in the crock of Father's arm, with his legs brushing against the top of Hangst's sheathed sword.

As they approached the entrance to Blue Hearth, Hangst stopped and nodded in the direction of the lavishly dressed man surrounded by admiring courtiers.

"That's the Ava," Hangst told Horth. "He is not what an Ava should be, but the empire is short of Purebloods. That is our excuse for having him produce Amel with Ev'rel, his own half-sister: our excuse for the whole ten-child contract. One down, nine to go." He held Horth a little tighter. "Mine, with your mother, was for three of you."

Horth already knew all of that, but people often told him things he already knew. He relied on it, in fact, since it usually took three or four times before he understood.

Horth pointed at the genotyping machine, which was much more interesting than the Ava.

Father smiled at him. "Right," he said. "Why am I not surprised?"

They went over to Di Mon's *gorarelpul*, Sarilous, a woman with white hair and the wrinkled skin that proved she was not an eternal, like Horth and his family.

Father hitched Horth up a notch against his side. "Open the genotyping unit for my son here, so he can have a look at it," he ordered.

Sarilous obeyed, revealing a series of processing chambers nestled in a mass of *nervecloth* patches with colored, *nervecloth* threads connecting them. It reminded Horth of the intricately woven braid patterns that people wore on their vests to show their lineage.

"Lorel science," said Hangst, when Sarilous had closed up the machine again. "Why do we trust it, I wonder?"

"Do you wish an answer, Liege Nersal?" asked the *gorarelpul*. "One you might be able to relay to your wife, perhaps?"

Hangst frowned. "No answer could satisfy Beryl because she asks no questions. She is merely certain." He reflected on his own words a moment, and added, "It is a refreshing perspective, after living for so many years with your master Di Mon's many complex doubts."

"Monitum has always believed in the power of questions," Sarilous said primly. "And the value of all humans, whether highborns, lesser Sevolites or commoners."

"In their place, you mean?" said Hangst. "Yes, of course, but—"

A scream ripped down Horth's spine.

Hangst spun, putting Horth down behind him. Horth peered around his father's legs as a woman with a mass of black hair tore out of Blue Hearth to hurl herself at the Ava, scattering his courtiers. She was intercepted by the Ava's *gorarelpul,* and raked his face with her clawed hands.

Demish men rushed to protect their Ava, the next moment, and Di Mon seized the mad woman. She fought with a blind, inept fury.

Hara joined Hangst. She had Branst and Zrenyl with her.

"Take them in," Hangst ordered his captain of errants.

"Amel!" The mad woman wailed in a voice like a lost soul. "My baby!"

That was all Horth saw before Hara herded him and his brothers off Fountain Court.

Mother stood in the Entrance Hall of Black Heart with one of her Nesak retainers beside her. Five such men came with her, but Father allowed only one in Black Hearth at any time.

Horth ran straight into Mother's open arms. Branst got a hug next, then Zrenyl.

"Something bad happened!" said Zrenyl. "Avim Ev'rel is screaming about baby Amel."

"I was told to bring them in," Hara told the children's mother.

Beryl rose, holding Horth in her arms with Branst plastered against her skirts and Zrenyl standing beside her. She stared Hara down, but refused to speak to her, as usual.

Hara cursed Nesaks under her breath as she stalked off.

"Hara's all right, really, Mother," said Branst, plucking at her sleeve in an uncertain manner.

"You have no idea what she's like," Beryl snapped. She put Horth down but kept hold of his hand. "Come."

Her retainer, Lywulf, followed like a shadow as they passed through the series of connected rooms, known as the Throat, that divided Black Hearth down the middle.

Branst and Zrenyl both talked at once.

"Tessitatt looked worried!" exclaimed Branst.

"If Father has to duel," said Zrenyl, "can we go back out to watch?"

"Hush!" ordered Beryl. "There is no question here of duels." But Horth felt her grip tighten.

The last duel Father fought had been against a member of the *kinf'stan*. *Kinf'stan* were relatives, on Father's side, with the right to challenge him for his title. They included, in particular, Hangst's adult children sired on his vassals. Which was another reason Mother didn't like them.

At the end of the Throat Lywulf left them. They turned right into Family Hall, headed for the nursery at its far end.

The nursery was the family's place inside Black Hearth and Beryl's sanctuary where no servants, or even noble-borns like Hara, were allowed.

Inside, it was one big room, with a practice floor for fencing, a potted garden with a yard and shed, and one whole side covered in a rope net for climbing between platforms. This was the setting for a game the boys called space war in which the brothers *rel*-skimmed between platforms by swarming over the ropes. When Mother watched, the good guys were the Nesaks, but they switched sides whenever Father was around. Once, when some *kinf'stan* cousins were visiting, a fight broke out over the question of whether Nesaks could be honorable. Zrenyl threw the first punch. Horth and Branst did their best to help their older brother until Hara and her house guards broke it up.

"I bet baby Amel was murdered," said Zrenyl. "I bet Ev'rel got rid of him because he wasn't Pureblood after all and Delm wasn't the sire. A genotyping would have shown it up, so Ev'rel had him murdered. Women do that, don't they Mother?"

Mother gasped. "Not," she exclaimed, "for a reason like that!"

Predictably, Branst took the opposite side from his older brother. "Amel's mother didn't do it," he said. "She was trying to rip the Ava's eyes out!"

Zrenyl shrugged. "Pureblood Ev'rel is a spoiled brat. Even your precious Monatese girlfriend acknowledges that much!"

"Tessitatt is not my girlfriend!" said Branst.

Mother snapped out of the shocked silence inspired by Zrenyl's glib assumption of infanticide on Ev'rel's part, and looked for Branst, who was sitting on a heap of folded gym mats. "Tessitatt?" she asked. "Have you been playing with that Green Hearth nobleborn again, Branst?"

"Not exactly playing," answered Zrenyl. "She was babysitting."

"You take that back!" Branst said, closing his hands in fists.

"Not now, boys!" their mother cried, and collapsed into the armchair where she liked to sit and watch them tend their potted gardens with her indoor greenhouse at her back. Mother required them to make things grow for the spiritual exercise, but only Branst paid much attention. Zrenyl's pots weren't doing so well and Horth's last crop of SanHome bean sprouts had died. Again.

"I don't know how much more I can take of this mad, cruel court, oh my ancestors!" Beryl appealed to empty air, and lowered her face into her hands with a sob.

Horth never knew what to do when Mother cried. He felt it was something Father should look after, even though Father was usually the cause. Horth did not like members of the family crying at all, because it never happened to him. It was another of the ways in which he was different.

Hara said that was nothing to worry about. She said that Vrellish people did not cry. But Horth wasn't sure he wanted to always be the one who was more Vrellish than the rest of the family.

The three boys waited in suspense for their mother to stop crying and look up. When she did, her face was reassuringly composed.

"I suppose we wait," Beryl told her children with a brave smile. "To find out what this latest atrocity is about." She surveyed the state of Horth and Zrenyl's seedlings. "It looks like two of you will be doing some replanting to pass the time. Horth, you have to water seedlings, or they die."

"I forgot to remind him," said Branst.

"That should not have to be your job. Go get us something to eat, will you, Branst, while your brothers put these poor things out of their misery and start over."

"Yes, Mother!" Branst agreed, and scampered off.

"Remember not to let the servants touch what we eat!" Mother called after him, and was answered by a perfunctory one-handed wave.

Zrenyl frowned. He and Horth both knew there was about as much chance of Branst doing his own work in the kitchen as there was of Horth's next batch of seedlings surviving long enough to bear fruit. He always got the servants to do his work for him. But Zrenyl never shared the fact with Mother.

Horth and Zrenyl settled down to work on dumping out their pots and replanting. Branst was back with sandwiches before they were done and helped Horth finish. Then the family picnicked, seated on the coarse brown matting in front of Beryl's greenhouse.

Father joined them as they were finishing their lunch. Usually, he would simply come over and sit down, wordlessly becoming one of them without explanations or any confusing talk. Today, he stopped a short distance from the blanket Mother had spread on the ground, as if waiting to be invited or repulsed.

Mother stopped telling Branst not to play with his food and sat, gathering her courage for a moment. Then she stood up slowly and carefully, her face stiff with injured pride, and turned to face her husband.

"So," she confronted Hangst, "what lurid decadence have your so-called Purebloods indulged in, now?"

Father had looked tired and strained before she lashed out, but the very peevishness of her manner roused him to chide her in his frank, familiar manner. "So-called? You can't begrudge the Ava and his half-sister their blood, my Nesak. Whatever we might think of the wisdom of such souls being eternal, they do possess them — even by your standards. Perhaps it is their upbringing you ought to blame for their bad behavior, as you blame mine."

"You!" Mother said with surprise, and softened. "I have never reproached your behavior with regard to how you lead your house. You are the only decent liege on Fountain Court. As for you being here, instead of where you belong — I know that you had cause to side against us when you threw in with House Lor'Vrel, all those years and so many mistakes ago."

"Threw in with—?" Father shook his head incredulously. "Gods, Beryl! That was Nersal Nesak! Please restrict your criticisms to my current incarnation, whatever may or may not be the history of my soul. Nersal, Prince of Nesak, is my ancestor as far as I'm concerned, and nothing more. This is the only life that I can answer for."

"Then tell me why you serve such a vain and spiteful weakling as your Ava," said Mother as she sat down.

"I told you," Hangst flared. "It is not Delm I care about. It is upholding the empire."

"You admit, then, that you are falsely sworn?" Beryl stayed on the attack. "All this business of the empire is Lorel sophistry straight out of Di Mon's mouth. Trust your instincts, my love! Di Mon is no friend to you, no true *brerelo*. And such a thing as Delm should never last a day as Ava under Sword Law! He would never be *K'isk* on SanHome, that is certain!"

"I know!" Father sighed. "You Nesaks manage things better by lumping all highborns together, instead of wallowing in this Demish trap of insisting that your emperor be a Pureblood. But it is a Demish court! So please," he raised one large hand. "No more, Beryl. Not now."

"Is there going to be a duel?" Zrenyl asked.

Hangst shook his head. "A council of privilege. And after that, a trial of honor."

"But it might end in a duel," Zrenyl held out hope.

Hangst smiled at him wistfully. "Perhaps."

"Is baby Amel dead?" Branst wanted to know.

"Missing." Hangst let out a frustrated sigh. "Come with me to the family lounge, Beryl, and I'll tell you more."

"Without the children, you mean?" she asked, and got stubborn. "No. I want them to know, from your own lips, the truth about the man you call your Ava."

Father grew angry at that. "Amel has disappeared, yes, but Delm is guilty of nothing more than being a silly fool!" Father paused, trapped by his own disgust because it gave Mother weapons. "It was Ev'rel," he said curtly. "She is at fault."

Beryl replied, stonily, "The baby's mother?"

Hangst nodded. "Apparently Ev'rel could not afford to have Fountain Court finding out who really sired her baby. But she tried to make it look as if Delm feared the child as a

rival, in order to blame Delm for the baby's disappearance."
Hangst gave a gruff snort. "How could Delm see his son as a
rival when Ev'rel is the empire's last female Pureblood? Do
they think we would stoop to breeding the son back to his
own mother?!"

"You forced a child contract on half-siblings, didn't you?"
asked Beryl, mercilessly. "You, Silver Hearth, and Di Mon."

"We have to function in a Demish court," insisted Father.

"No," Beryl said simply. "You don't."

"You make it sound so simple," he said, looking away
from her. "It is not."

"How can that be so, husband?" asked Beryl. "*Okal Rel*
demands that a leader have the honor to risk himself in
personal combat, rather than risk destroying habitat in space
wars. That is simple. Now tell me, has Delm ever wielded a
sword in his own cause? *Okal Rel* demands that eternals use
their power to control soulless ones — who lack the hope of
rebirth to restrain them from destroying all they cannot have.
But would Delm hesitate to crack a station or use bioscience
to pursue his goals? Would Di Mon?"

Father stiffened at the mention of Di Mon, and said
through his teeth, "Di Mon is honorable."

Beryl sniffed and shook her hair back. "Well," she said.
"Perhaps you ought to make Ev'rel your Ava. She, at least,
had the sense to deny Delm a child. Is the real father
known?"

"We... think so," Hangst said thickly, looking from her to
their children, who listened with rapt attention. "But it only
gets worse, Beryl. I will tell you when we are alone."

"No. Let them hear it from you," said Mother. "Not from
strangers."

Father unbuckled his sword and set it in a rack by the
chair he used when he spent time in the nursery. Then he sat
down, facing a jumble of ill-tended pots. Beryl's greenhouse
stood at their backs and the remains of their picnic was
spread out on the floor before them.

Horth and his brothers closed in by unspoken agreement.

"How can I explain this to you, Beryl," Hangst began. "I'm not sure if you even understand how different Vrellish women are; if you have ever even heard what highborn Vrellish women can do to a man." He broke off.

Mother wore a brittle, cold look. "I am aware of man-rape, if that is what you are dancing around," she rattled off, making Zrenyl start and Branst looked puzzled. "Are you telling me Ev'rel is guilty of that?"

"Her behavior would seem to suggest she is predisposed. Yes," said Hangst. He added quickly. "It is not condoned, even by the Vrellish. It is considered *sla*. If she is found guilty, she'll be punished." He sighed. "Di Mon is looking for baby Amel. He will find the child if anyone can. But I am afraid the most likely way to lose him would have been for her to order her *gorarelpul* — who is dead now — to drop him down a recycling chute. Her servants have confirmed she gave the baby to her *gorarelpul*, Arous, to smuggle out of Blue Hearth. We are aware of other things, as well. Things that do not say much for her character. In particular," he continued flatly, "it appears that she killed Arous soon after he returned from the job. And killed him with an overdose of the sex drug known as Rush. It is possible for Vrellish women to force an unwilling Vrellish man without Rush." He paused, as if the word made him uncomfortable. "It is less likely to work with commoners, and *gorarelpul* can be rendered impotent by their pain training, which reduces sensitivity in general. Hence, I suppose, the drug. She used it regularly on Arous. Her servants told Di Mon as much."

"Then Ev'rel did kill her own child?" Beryl swallowed thickly, tears of horror welling up in her eyes. "And made a mockery of the most sacred act." Hangst pulled her into the shelter of his arms and she clung. He stood a head taller, with Mother's mass of blue-black hair against his chest and a big hand stroking her back.

Zrenyl gestured towards the door. Branst missed the cue. Horth poked him in the ribs and tipped his head towards Zrenyl who had already retreated to the nursery door. But Branst was riveted. Horth lingered, not wanting to leave without his favorite brother.

"I can't do it Beryl," Hangst said throatily. "I can't send you home. I want you too much. And Di Mon is correct. It will cause trouble, more trouble than it has before."

"I am your wife," she said, listening to his heart.

He shook his head. "No. The contract's done."

"I am your wife," she insisted, and lifted her head to shake out her wavy dark locks. "And your *cher'st*. Your one, true love."

Father's voice was rich with pain, too. "Don't, Beryl."

"Nothing can change that," Mother told him with heartless conviction.

He said tonelessly. "You don't want me to child gift to my vassals, yet you will want more children of your own."

"Of course," she said. "I would fear the anger of the Waiting Dead if we denied them new lives." She stroked his arm.

Father closed his eyes again, as if to shut out the sight of her. But he couldn't shut out her smell or touch.

Grown-ups can be very silly, thought Horth.

"If only I could make you Vrellish," Father muttered.

"Then I would be your *mekan'st*," said Beryl, "and take my children home with me to be raised by my uncles and brothers." Mother drew back to look up. "Is that what you want?"

Father stiffened.

She dropped at his feet without warning, repentant. "I don't want it either! I don't want to leave you, Hangst! But I cannot stop thinking that they must be wondering on SanHome if I've broken faith with them and my mission. You know I could never do that!"

"I know," Hangst said in a drained voice, and extended his hand to her, where she knelt. "It has been a trying day, my Nesak. Please get up."

Mother had lost now, Horth realized. Father was using his formal court voice again.

Beryl got up slowly, looking miserable. Father left the nursery without another word of reassurance.

Mother picked up his forgotten sword and set the sheathed weapon across her lap, sitting in the chair Hangst had abandoned.

Horth considered taking off before she remembered that it was spiritually uplifting for her sons to clean up their own lunch things and tidy up, but her distress prevented him.

"It is the greatest love," she whispered, touching Hangst's sword gingerly with one hand. "The hardest one."

Horth took a step towards her and she looked up.

"Oh Horth, I am living with the enemy!" she cried, and thrust a fist into her mouth as she began to cry.

"Mother, no!" cried Branst, coming back. Zrenyl reappeared, having seen Hangst leave the nursery, and came to kneel beside her.

"We will never abandon you," her eldest son promised.

"Oh, my boys," she cried, and put the sword aside to gather them in her arms. "My own, beloved ancestors made young!"

She hugged them all for as long as Horth could stand before she remembered the lunch things needed to be cleaned up, which felt reassuringly normal, however unwelcome the chore.

* * *

The next day, after morning exercise with Hara, Horth found his brothers sitting on a bed in the room he shared with Branst in Family Hall.

"There's no point asking Hara to explain it to you," Zrenyl said. "Sure, she's Vrellish, but she's only a nobleborn. There are nobleborn Vrellish who deny that man-rape is even possible and the Demish all think it is make-believe as well. But there's *kinf'stan* who will tell you that they do it in Red Reach to captive enemies, to steal their ancestors' souls."

"So Tessitatt couldn't rape a man," said Branst. "Only highborns can."

"Too bad! If you're curious," said Zrenyl.

Branst shoved him backwards off the bed.

"Hey!" complained Zrenyl, climbing back up. "Don't be so touchy, Branst."

"I don't believe man-rape is possible!" protested Branst. "I mean, it isn't as if a man *could* be raped if he wasn't, you know..."

"Aroused?" supplied Zrenyl, with an older-than-you air that made Branst frown. "She eats him," Zrenyl added, leaning forward. "That's how."

Branst's lip curled. "How would that get her pregnant?"

Zrenyl rolled his eyes. "Not like food, you idiot! Female Vrellish have muscles in places that real women, like Mother, don't. But even so, it only works on Red Vrellish men because they're over-sexed to start. Like animals."

"We're Vrellish!" objected Branst.

Zrenyl shrugged. "Not that Vrellish," he said. "We're part Nesak."

Neither of them noticed Horth leave the room.

* * *

The honor trial for Ev'rel came and went with little disruption to Horth's life except for more gossip sessions between Zrenyl and Branst. Ev'rel was found guilty and exiled, but on the day it happened Horth was more interested in the automated watering system he was rigging for Mother. He demonstrated it by flooding the greenhouse floor. Mother told him it was clever before she took it apart and explained that she liked to take her time watering the plants.

It never occurred to Horth that the shameful story of Ev'rel's trial would spread beyond the Ava's court.

Then one morning during breakfast, Lywulf whispered something in Mother's ear that made her upset and excited.

"Kene?" she gasped, and turned to her children. "Go and wait in the nursery."

Father rose abruptly, making Mother start. The tension between them worried Horth as he followed his brothers out.

"Who is Kene?" Branst asked Zrenyl.

Zrenyl said glumly, "A Nesak."

"No!" yelped Branst.

Zrenyl turned on him angrily. "It has to be a Nesak! Mother's three-child contract is up, and Father isn't sleeping with her anymore. They've sent someone to reap the harvest and take us back."

Branst flushed dark red. "I won't go!"

"It's not up to you," Zrenyl told him curtly, and climbed up to the platform in the nursery where they played at keeping the universe safe for the next generation. Branst lodged himself in the rope net at the bottom.

"But we're a family!" Branst cried suddenly, with a convulsive jerk at the ropes in his hands.

"We're not supposed to be!" Zrenyl shot back. "Not like we are. Vrellish parents don't raise children together!"

Branst set his jaw stubbornly. "They could," he said, "if they are *cher'stan*."

"Oh please!" groaned Zrenyl.

"It happens in real life!" said Branst. "Tessitatt's parents were *cher'stan*! That's why her mother had two children by the same nobleborn man and would not give Di Mon a highborn heir to raise in Green Hearth."

"Don't be stupid!" Zrenyl hurled down from his platform.

"Mother says she and Father are *cher'stan*!" Branst yelled back up.

Zrenyl jumped into a block of foam placed for that purpose and hurled himself violently at Branst.

Horth moved between them, blocking Zrenyl's charge.

"What are you staring at, *rejak't*?" Zrenyl snapped.

"Don't call him that!" cried Branst.

"He doesn't care," Zrenyl shrugged off the insult. "He doesn't even understand."

"He does too!" cried Branst, getting worked up. "And it isn't a joke. Hara says that Nesaks kill defective children!"

Zrenyl hunched his shoulders as if he felt cold. "That's right," he said, thunderstruck. "Branst, do you think they'd do that? To Horth?"

"Stop it!" exploded Branst.

Zrenyl lost his temper right back. "Just because you don't want to talk about something doesn't mean it won't happen!"

Branst flew at his larger, older sibling, shoving Horth aside so hard he fell down. Resigned, Horth got up and stood clear to watch.

Zrenyl shoved Branst into a rack of practice swords. But Branst was still fighting mad. He scrambled back to his feet with one of the swords in hand.

Horth frowned. The practice weapons were not sharp near the end like a challenge sword, and their points ended in rubber nubs, but the boys weren't supposed to use them without protective gear.

Branst attacked. Zrenyl blocked the slash at his head with an arm and yelped at the pain. Now Branst had made him mad.

In seconds, Zrenyl had disarmed his seven year old brother and was sitting astride him raining down punches. Horth was afraid Zrenyl might hurt Branst. He scooped up a hard bouncy ball and threw it with uncanny accuracy at Zrenyl's forehead where the bone was thickest. It hit with a loud smack and bounced off.

Zrenyl shot up with a yowl.

"Boys!" Mother's voice made them all freeze in incriminating poses. She was furious, and what was worse, she sounded disappointed in them. "What are you doing!"

"Just... playing, Mother," said Zrenyl, and reached down with one hand to help Branst up.

Branst wiped blood from his mouth.

"Playing?" Beryl Nesak asked frostily.

"Y-Yes, Mother," stammered Branst.

Horth stared past them at the stranger beside Beryl who was beaming at them in amusement.

"Don't scold your boys, sister," said the man with a good-natured laugh. "I would be sorry if I found them embroidering Demish cushions, now wouldn't I?"

Branst and Zrenyl exchanged looks. The ball that Horth had bounced off Zrenyl's forehead ran out of momentum and crawled to a stop. Zrenyl still had a red mark on his forehead where it had struck.

"This is my brother, Prince Kene," said Mother. "He will address you in *rel*-peerage because we Nesaks do not acknowledge birth ranks."

Kene had green eyes like Mother and the same blue-black highlights in his hair. His smile of pleased amusement shed an unconditional blessing on the three of them.

"I'll be staying with you for a while," Kene said, as if it were perfectly ordinary for him to be visiting.

"This is Zrenyl," Beryl introduced her eldest. "The next one is Branst. And this..." she paused just long enough to show discomfort, "is Horth."

"He isn't a *rejak't*!" Branst spoke up, pale from the pounding Zrenyl had inflicted on him except for the bright smears of blood about his mouth. "He understands! He just doesn't talk. I think he gets confused by all the complex stuff like differencing suffixes and he doesn't like to do things he's not confident about!"

"Branst, please!" said Beryl, embarrassed.

Kene knelt down in front of Horth. "We don't think much of Demish grammar ourselves, back on SanHome," he assured Horth. "As your mother said, we have no birth ranks."

"Kene would be a Royalblood by court usage," Beryl interjected. "At least I think he would, since we have the same parents and your father insisted I be genotyped."

Kene gave her a look that made her uncomfortable. "I'm sorry!" she apologized. "I know there is no point in being Highlord or Royalblood or Pureblood. It's a Demish error. I suppose it has becomes a habit, thinking like that."

Kene rose and touched her elbow. "That's why you need to come home, now. You, and these fine sons." He smiled. "You have done well, sister."

Mother kept her eyes down but Horth saw her lids flutter. "Thank you," she said with real pleasure, and looked up at her brother with affectionate admiration.

Kene retrieved the ball used to hit Zrenyl and handed it to Horth. "You got Zrenyl pretty good," he said, smiling. "Was it luck?"

Horth took the ball, pointed at a target and nailed it cold, knocking over one of the pots that contained a dead sprout.

Kene grinned with pleasure. "Not bad!"

"Messy," complained Beryl.

"Women always fuss," Kene told Horth.

Not Hara, Horth thought.

"You're a Nesak," Zrenyl blurted, accusingly.

Kene broke off his one-sided conversation with Horth to face Zrenyl. "Yes," he replied calmly. "I am."

"Did you think I was the only one?" Beryl asked tartly. "Or that my family forgot me when I came here to live at this awful court?"

Kene put a hand on his sister's arm. "It's all right, let the boy be angry. Of course his father's influence has been strong. That is why it is so important you come home now. As soon as possible."

Beryl looked distraught. Branst broke ranks to fling himself into his mother's arms, crying, "No! No!" She wrapped her hands about Branst's dark head and held him against her skirts as he began to sob.

Horth felt numb.

"Why did you look at Horth like that, earlier," Zrenyl asked Kene, suspiciously, "if it wasn't because you were thinking he must be a *rejak't?*"

"Because he is the third child," Kene answered. "And he is already four years old. We had hoped... " He paused to capture Beryl's hand, as if he wanted her to know it wasn't her fault. "We knew it would be too much to expect that one, sweet girl, could convert such a stubborn soul as the one your father possesses. But we had hoped that the marriage would work, and there would be more children."

"He still sees himself as Vrellish," Beryl admitted, defeated. "And so long as he consorts with vassals like Tash Bryllit he cannot be my husband, even if I will always be his wife in my heart."

Zrenyl fixed an angry gaze on Kene, muscles working in his square jaw. "This is all your fault," he confronted Kene. "When I grow up, I am going to challenge you."

"As will be your right!" Kene assured the eldest of his nephews. "The right of challenge is our sacred law as much as it is yours. But the terms of our agreement have expired. It is time to forge a new one, or to take what we have gained and go home. One day you will understand."

Beryl looked up at her brother with glistening green eyes, and Kene seemed likewise overcome, momentarily, with unvoiced emotion at the sight of her surrounded by her three boys.

Then he laughed and took a step back, signaling a change in mood. "I forgot I have gifts to give out. The packages are in my room. Keep the boys here for me, Beryl. I will be back."

Mother said, "Zrenyl, please go with Kene to help him."

Zrenyl hesitated. Branst looked sullen.

Mother touched Zrenyl's shoulder the way she did when she meant one of her sons to mind her, and said firmly, "He is my brother."

Zrenyl swallowed, drew a deep breath, and went to join his Nesak uncle.

"Where are you staying?" Horth heard Zrenyl ask Kene.

"Just down the hall in a guest room. My men are hosted elsewhere, though."

"You've got men with you?" Zrenyl asked, reluctantly becoming interested. "Are you an *avsha*?"

"Two of the men with me are *avsha*," said Kene, amused. "I am an *imsha* — a battlewheel commander." He put an arm around Zrenyl's shoulder. "Or I was, at least, during the war. Such titles mean relatively little now."

The nursery doors closed on Zrenyl's next admiring question.

"Well," Mother broke the awkward silent, brushing her skirts down the way she did when she was nervous or excited, "what do you suppose Kene brought for—"

"I don't care!" Branst erupted. "I don't want it!"

Mother reached for Branst as he bolted but she couldn't catch him. "Branst!" she called again, more crossly, as he tore out of the nursery doors.

Mother went after Branst. Horth followed, and all but ran into her standing still in Family Hall. A commoner maid, laden with clean sheets, stood between her and the first room of the Throat.

"Horth," Beryl said. "Go fetch your brother out of Green Hearth. I am sure that is where he's gone and I won't have it! Not now!"

Horth darted down the Throat, unimpeded by the household staff he dodged past.

The Monatese herald stood outside the open doors of Green Hearth, flanked by errants and talking to Branst. The herald was a commoner, and while her manner and pronouns acknowledged Branst's status, her attitude was nonetheless very much one of an adult dealing with a child.

"But I've got to see Tessitatt," said Branst. "There's a Nesak in Black Hearth and he wants to take us back to SanHome. And I won't go!"

"Master Branst," the herald explained, "that isn't up to us, or Seniorlord Tessitatt, or even our liege, Di Mon. It is your father's business."

Tears stood in Branst's eyes. Horth did not like that. He thought Tessitatt would come out if she was asked, but the herald would not do it for them.

Quick as the thought occurred to him, Horth zipped past the herald and into Green Hearth.

"Drat that child!" Horth heard one of the errants grumble. But Horth was already in Green Hearth's moist entrance hall with its walls covered in climbing vines.

Sarilous confronted him with a cold, calculating stare that made Horth remember his mother's stories about *gorarelpul* who enslaved people with bioscience. *Gorarelpul* exemplified the kind of commoners who had to be controlled by Sevolites. Hara said only the conscience bond that enslaved them to Sevolite masters made it safe for them to study science at all. Without it, they would use their knowledge to poison all existence with their greedy, short-sighted ambitions.

"It's the Nesak brat," Sarilous said bitterly. "The youngest one."

Di Mon appeared behind her, dogged by a couple more errants and wearing his sword. "Horth?" he asked.

"We ought to send him home with something catching, to thin out the population on SanHome before the next wave of them grows up!"

"Sarilous!" Di Mon's anger was biting. "Even meant in humor, that's a vile remark."

She shrugged. "This one doesn't understand. He has a bad case of language impairment. The sort of child Red Vrellish call a *rejak't*, from the English word for something flawed, a child born with nothing but an animal mind. He's all spatial intelligence and reflexes."

Di Mon's lips were compressed in anger. "Leave us, " he ordered the *gorarelpul*. Horth was pleased to see the order had an impact. Sarilous left without another word.

The liege of Green Hearth forgot Horth as Branst arrived, escorted by the herald.

"If Mother goes to SanHome can I stay here, in Green Hearth, please Liege Monitum?" Branst begged.

Di Mon knelt down and took him by the shoulders. "I don't think that would be wise," he said. "But there are many places where a child can grow up safely, Branst Nersal. And when you have the choice, if you come back, you will be welcome here."

Branst's face was contorted by distress. His eyes looked rumpled and his mouth looked as if hard G forces were pulling down on it. But he let Di Mon gather him up with Horth and walk them back to Black Hearth.

Father met them in the Black Hearth entrance hall.

"What will you do, *brerelo*?" Di Mon asked, as Branst and Horth left his side to join their father.

Hangst put an arm around his sons, one on either side. "I do not know," he told Di Mon. "May the gods ignore us, Di Mon, I do not know."

"If there is anything I can do to help—" the liege of Monitum, began, and was cut off sharply by Liege Nersal's curt, "No."

Di Mon nodded, turned, and was gone.

* * *

Dinner was a grim and novel affair.

It was the first time Horth remembered Mother serving dinner in the reception hall at the base of the spiral stairs that led up to the Plaza. She refused to appear at meals served by commoners, and Father refused to let her serve the meal herself when Nersallians were present unless she was prepared to wait on his nobleborn guests, as well.

Lywulf dutifully waited on the guests with her. It was funny to see the best swordsman among Mother's retainers behaving like a servant. But Kene's people asked for things politely, thanked him when he filled their glasses, and generally treated him with respect. It was only Father who ignored him, except for tensing whenever Lywulf passed behind his chair.

Kene had brought a second Nesak with him, named Arn, who was a grim-looking man with tight lips and a cold manner.

"Arn commanded a trio of battlewheels in the war," Kene told Zrenyl. "Now he is a station master based in Red Reach near the jump to SanHome. It's a vital position."

Hangst accepted the next dish that Beryl set before him, sparing her a glance before fixing his eyes, coldly, on Kene once more.

"Kene gave me a sword," said Zrenyl. "It has an insignia on it that stands for the royal house of Sarn."

Hangst sipped his wine slowly, his face composed. "You already have a sword," he told Zrenyl.

"A child's sword," Zrenyl defended his enthusiasm.

Hangst dropped the subject. "SanHome sounds Demish to me," he said bluntly, looking at Kene. "How can you claim you have more in common with we Nersallians, who are Vrellish, than you do with the H'Usian Demish, who reproduce through marriage and treat their daughters differently than their sons."

It was Arn who answered. "House Nersal has been influenced by bad breeding decisions." He raised his glass half the way to his lips. "Nersal Nesak mated with a Lor'Vrel when he broke with his family and splintered a royal bloodline."

Hangst was dryly amused. "Is that an accusatory tone I detect, station master Arn?" he asked. "And should I therefore assume that it is not only my wife — that is, Beryl — who takes it as a fact that I am my ancestor, Nersal Nesak? Tell me, do all Nesaks claim to be clear dreamers, able to recognize old souls in new lives?"

"We are not all clear dreamers," Arn answered stiffly. "No."

"The history of your soul," Kene explained conversation-ally, "was proclaimed by *Zer-sis* Ackal at the end of the war, and endorsed by the council of *zer'stan*."

"Ah, yes." Hangst paused as Beryl collected his plate and replaced it with the next course. He had hardly touched the salad made of vegetables hand-reared in Mother's green-house. Knowing how much Mother cared about her plants, and how precious each harvest was, Horth made a special effort to eat all of his own salad before Lywulf picked his plate up, although he knew that it would disagree with him later. He had trouble digesting high-fiber foods.

"Di Mon believes your *zer-sis* is more politician than mystic," Hangst resumed. "It was a female liege of Vrel who defeated you in Red Reach, although she died doing it: Vretla Vrel, Vackal's mother. You preferred to lay the credit to my account, because you can't admit a woman could be such an able warrior. You needed some theologically satisfying expla-nation for why you had not prevailed. Proclaiming that a great soul — a *zer-rel* — was fighting on the wrong side, was expedient."

"If you are calling the *zer-sis* a liar on the strength of a Monatese opinion," Arn said tightly, "perhaps you had better ask yourself, first, whether you place more faith in Monatese honor than history justifies."

Hangst leaned forward. "Di Mon," he said, "is not a Lorel."

"He deals with them," said Arn. "Through *TouchGate Hospital*."

"Please!" Kene interrupted, flicking his glance towards Horth and his brothers. "If we have irreconcilable differences there are better occasions for resolving them. Let the children enjoy their dinner."

"Agreed," Hangst said, and settled back into the big chair at the head of the table. Arn's lips compressed tightly.

No one drank or ate while they watched Hangst and Arn glare at each other.

It was Branst, to Horth's surprise, who broke the silence. "Do you have children?" he asked Kene. "I mean, since you said Arn is your brother-in-law. That means you're married, doesn't it?"

Kene turned to Branst with a smile. "Absolutely, nephew. A Nesak warrior does not fly, if he can help it, until he's seen a Freedom Price safely born. The more children a man has the more courage he dares to show, because he knows he has a stake in the future that will draw his soul back to the living, if he dies. My children are my greatest joy. I had three before your mother left home. I have seven now, five boys and two girls."

"With the same wife?" Branst asked, mildly awed.

Kene laughed. "Few Nesak men are brave enough to court more than one woman at a time, let alone stray from their marriage oath! Half the Watching Dead are female, you know! I think it would be highly ill advised."

"That does sound Demish," said Zrenyl. "Men who fight and women who look after children at home."

"I do not think the average Demish princess would fare very well as a Nesak wife and mother," Kene said with pride and a fond glance in his sister's direction.

"No, indeed," Beryl spoke up for the first time, apart from giving orders to the retainer enlisted as a waiter.

She had arrived with a dessert tray laden with sweet dishes of prepared fruit, and surveyed the assembled dinners with the no-nonsense air of command that she used when the family was alone. "Nesak women run their households. A Demish princess would perish for the lack of a servant to lift her spoon."

Having said what she wanted, Beryl began handing out desert bowls.

Horth ate his mother's desert with more pleasure than he had the salad, but equal certainty of bad results. By the time the meal was done he was feeling uncomfortable as well as tired, and was glad to leave the adults to their stressful, mysterious talk, filled with hidden threats and awkward silences.

Neither Branst nor Horth slept well in their shared room. Horth's stomach troubled him and Branst tossed and turned in his dreams. Horth dropped off at last, only to be woken by Branst shouting, "Tess!" in the grip of a nightmare.

Horth was on his feet immediately. Branst was sitting up in bed, blinking, his face pale in the dim light from the glow strip along the base of one wall.

"I thought the Nesaks killed her," Branst explained ruefully.

Horth climbed into bed with Branst and both of them slept better.

Hours later, Horth woke to the sound of the bedroom door opening. He saw Father and Kene peek in, keeping it only slightly ajar to reduce the amount of light spilling in from Family Hall. Horth was not afraid. He knew, with the natural insight of a child, that they were being admired.

"There would be one more condition," Kene said, standing shoulder to shoulder with Father in the sliver of light from the hall. "You will have to stay married to my sister. Truly married to her. If I lose, of course."

Hangst said, "I haven't agreed, yet."

Kene said, "I think you have."

Both men withdrew then, closing the door softly behind them, and Horth heard no more.

He slept late the next morning. When he went down to the Octagon to exercise, Hara had already been and gone.

Zrenyl was there, instead, trying out his new sword with Arn.

"Horth!" Zrenyl hailed him. "Do you know what Branst got from Kene? Books! One of them has stuff in it about us! What do you think of that! We get put into books on SanHome."

Horth wasn't sure he was as pleased about that as Zrenyl.

He headed for the nursery, expecting to find his mother there. Instead, he found his own present.

Kene had cleared a space near the greenhouse and erected a three-dimensional frame that was three times as large as Horth. The frame supported pieces of a space-station, in miniature. Kene was still there, working on it. He noticed Horth and stopped in the act of attaching a spar.

"It seems I'll be here for a few days," Kene said. "So I thought I'd show you how to put your gift together."

Horth came forward, devouring the present with his eyes. He'd been to the hullsteel casting fields near Tark, and had a tour of a working space station. He was so excited that he had a tantrum when father made them leave before he wanted to go, but the worst of it was that everything was much too hard to understand. Hullsteel shells were cast in space, all at once. You had to comprehend the whole cast, in one gulp, not put it together in pieces. What he saw in front of him now was a space station that he could assemble.

Kene slid clear of the frame he'd erected and got to his feet. "Beryl told me in her letters that you liked to take things apart. I thought you might enjoy putting something together, too." He gestured at the barely begun structure and the heap of pieces laid out on the floor. "It's a scale model. We use them to rehearse a real job. The frame goes first. That's hardest, because it's built in zero-G conditions and no eternal likes to put up with that! We add spin as soon as we can; then a couple of rim docks on the outer edge with quarters so the crew can stay on board. But in the early stages, all the work is done in zero-G." He smiled a bit ruefully. "Sometimes your head can feel like it's about to explode."

Horth crouched to inspect the pieces on the floor. There were so many! And each one looked purposeful. It was still only a model, but he had the feeling everything would be there; everything would have an explanation; and he

couldn't see how to assemble it, alone. He picked up a particularly complicated looking piece with a moving part. He
would need someone to show him how it all fitted together.

The look he gave Kene spoke volumes. The Nesak took
the piece in Horth's hand from him, held it up against the
frame and said, "This is part of the air circulation system in-
board of the main floor. It has valves, like veins do, to seal
off sections if there's a problem. Let's see. It might go here,
for example." Kene held the piece up in empty air, inside
the bare frame.

The next few hours established a routine that lasted for
the whole three days of Kene's visit. Horth joined Kene in
the nursery after breakfast and they worked together until
Mother came to feed them lunch. One of Kene's Nesaks
usually joined them for the meal, and sometimes Zrenyl
did, too. Everyone talked about the progress Kene and
Horth were making with the station. No one talked about
anything important.

To Horth, the station became the only thing that was
important.

He didn't understand why Branst had torn up Kene's
books and wouldn't speak to anyone, nor why Zrenyl
looked so grim, even though Father seemed more relaxed
now than he had that first day at dinner. Horth didn't
understand why the Nesaks cast long looks at Kene, filled
with tension, or why Mother dropped dishes so often.
When Kene wasn't looking, sometimes Mother stared at
him and began to look anguished. But when Kene looked
at her and smiled she tried to hide it.

Evenings, Mother spent alone with Father. There were
no more meals taken all together.

People said things that Horth tried to ignore. One of the
Nesaks, making small talk about the model station said,
"But will it be finished before..." and stopped when Mother
dropped her watering can. Kene picked it up and held her
hands steady when he gave it to her.

"If you remain here," he told her, "have more children. I will come to you through one of them, I promise." He smiled in his easy, casual way that exuded confidence. "And if you come home, the children you already have will bring his soul back to us." Kene's tone of voice was not the least alarming, but the brief exchange killed all conversation.

Kene stayed later than usual that day, working with Horth on the station.

In the afternoons, Kene worked out on the Octagon with the other Nesaks, but always with screens up. Not even Zrenyl was invited inside to watch. Hara skulked about outside the screens when they sparred, until Father banned her from the Octagon.

In three days, people said, Kene's travel respite would be over.

Horth knew what a travel respite was. It meant that pilots were entitled to rest for three days between arrival and departure. He half expected that the grown-ups had decided he and his brothers would be going home with Mother when the three days were up, and nobody wanted to tell them for fear Branst might try to run away. But the tensions in people around Black Heart told him that whatever was about to happen threatened Father, and Mother spent as much time with his father in the evenings as she did with Kene during the day, although Horth never saw Kene and Hangst together.

The bits and pieces of information at Horth's command would not fit together in a good way, like the model. He preferred to leave them lying on the nursery floor.

On the fourth day, it was much too quiet in Black Hearth.

Mother dressed in a formal, white gown, her long black hair tied at the back. She wore the family crest of the House of Sarn at her waist, above a rectangle of embroidered cloth depicting the *rel* symbol entwined with the Nesak flail and sword. She also wore the dragon of House Nersal embroidered on the long vest that fell to the floor.

"Dress quickly, Horth," she said when she came to wake him up. "We're going to watch a duel."

Horth knew that duels were serious. He dressed fast. But he was so fixated on the station, which was not yet finished, that he fully expected to get back to it as soon as this was done.

Zrenyl and Branst were already down on the Octagon when Beryl arrived with Horth. Father and Kene stood on the Challenge Floor dressed in light shirts and snug stretch pants.

Arn and the rest of the Nesaks, including Mother's retainers, stood about in a clump, outnumbered three to one by another clump of *kinf'stan* that included a robust-looking woman who wore her hair in twisted bands bound tightly to her scalp. Her vest displayed the braid patterns of House Bryllit with liege marks at her collar.

All the screens were down, making one big, open space, with the Challenge Floor surrounded by eight wedges of property belonging to the hearths above them.

There were people on Green Wedge, including Di Mon, Sarilous, and Tessitatt. On Red Wedge there were two dozen nobleborns from Spiral Hall, at Di Mon's invitation since they lacked a highborn. Blue Wedge and Silver Wedge were filled with rows of elaborately dressed Demish — the sword-bearing men standing at the front and women on raised seats behind them.

Di Mon came forward to where Horth's father stood on the Challenge Floor.

"Hangst," Di Mon said, in a firm voice, that was perfectly audible from where Horth stood beside his mother. "Do not do this. Let her go."

Hangst said, "No."

Di Mon sighed. "Very well, then." He stepped back and declared to those gathered on all eight wedges, "You are called here to witness the resolution of a dispute to be settled by a duel to the death, or until one adversary cannot rise again. The stake is one of mutual agreement endorsed by seconds. I stand as heir of Liege Nersal's intentions in this matter; Station Master Arn, of the Nesaks, agrees to support the terms of the duel on behalf of Kene Nesak, Prince of the Royal House of Sarn. The terms are as follows: if Kene wins, he leaves court unmolested with his *full-sib*, Beryl and her sons. If Hangst Nersal wins, Beryl remains here as his ... wife," Di Mon had to push his way past the offending word.

"On the condition," Di Mon concluded, "that they live as man and wife by Nesak standards and continue to have children together."

The watching *kinf'stan* stirred in discomfort, but Di Mon's announcement seemed to be news to no one except Horth and Branst. Branst looked from Kene to his father and back again with an anguished expression, before he began to tremble. Zrenyl watched the Challenge Floor with stoic calm.

Beryl took Horth's hand.

There were a few more declarations, binding the witnesses to observe that the duel was entered into in good faith under Sword Law, and obliging them to honor its terms and to judge whether it was fairly fought. Any *kinf'stan* who wished to oppose Hangst's decision to fight, or the terms he had agreed upon, were invited to step forward to challenge Hangst. The robust woman with the black braids clenched her jaw and work her hand on the grip of her sword. But no *kinf'stan* came forward.

Di Mon retreated off the Challenge Floor and the duel began.

Beryl tightened her grip on Horth's hand. Horth kept his eyes on the duel between Father and the new friend who ought to be helping him finish the space station right now.

Kene attacked savagely. Their blades clashed in tight slashes, and sparks flew from one exchange, startling Horth. Then the actions seemed to come in bunches, as Kene slowly stalked Father. It seemed that Kene wanted Horth's father to thrust his point into his defense, but Father was staying well back. Their faces were taut masks of concentration. This was not practice — Horth grasped the difference. Father was waiting for something.

For what? thought Horth. *For a mistake?* Horth could not decide whether he wanted Kene to realize this too.

Then the mistake happened. Kene committed himself too deeply and had his blade taken. Mother's hand clenched. Horth looked up into her stricken face, to see grief and passion blazing in her eyes.

A thump on the Challenge Floor reclaimed Horth's attention. He looked back in time to see Father standing over his defeated challenger.

At his back, Sarilous hovered with her medical kit in her hand.

"Let the medic help you!" Father ordered Kene. He seemed angry now, no longer cool and calculating.

Kene clenched his failing strength in one surge, the whole side of his chest glistening red from a cut at the base of his neck, and swung his sword up in a slashing arc.

Father caught the slash just above his hilt, and seized the middle section of the blade in his bare left hand, holding it immobile without disarming the dying man.

He muttered, *"Ack rel,"* like a prayer, or a curse, or a farewell, and slashed Kene's throat.

There was so much blood Horth marveled at how it had all fit inside Kene's body to start.

Mother gave a stifled gasp and fell to her knees as they buckled. Zrenyl rushed to support her, displacing Horth.

Father did not look at her. The eyes he sought were those of Di Mon, in his green vest embroidered with threads of red and brown. Di Mon looked back, expressionless.

Beryl got up, brushing aside Zrenyl's attentions. She walked off Black Wedge as if in a trance, and over to where Kene had fallen. The four men of her entourage moved to block anyone from interfering and were joined in their wordless support by Arn and Kene's other two retainers.

Beryl knelt in her brother's blood, making a low, keening sound, and put her hands into the spreading pool surrounding him. The noise she made became a grief song. It was a song she had taught her sons in the nursery. A song that promised to keep faith with honor and reject revenge. It promised to live in wisdom under *Okal Rel*. And it promised to make new children for the mourned one to be reborn so he could fight the just fight of the people once more.

When the song stopped, Beryl raised her hands and stroked her bloody palms over her bare arms and white gown.

A buzz of conversation started, low and urgent, coming mostly from the Demish witnesses. The Vrellish watched in silence from Red, Green, and Black wedges.

Beryl put her hands into the pool of warm blood, again, and this time marked her face with gore. Demish witnesses talked louder. Vrellish ones began to stir.

Horth understood this was grief. It exercised a magnetic pull on Beryl's sons. He thought about joining her, and realized that Zrenyl had already stepped forward.

"No!" Father intercepted Zrenyl, still holding the sword he had used to kill Kene. "Go inside," he told them. "All three of you."

Branst bolted. Horth followed. He was weaving through a loose crowd of relatives just as everyone on the Octagon drew their swords and raised them, shouting, *"Okal Rel!"* in unison, like an earthquake of movement and sound, declaring the matter resolved.

Branst was pounding up the spiral staircase at the back of Black Wedge. Horth caught up. They emerged more or less together in Black Hearth's reception hall where they had eaten dinner with Kene three days earlier. Branst plunged down the Throat, towards Family Hall.

Horth followed.

Inside the nursery, Branst let out a wild cry — half laugh and half shout — kicking things aside as he crossed the floor.

A small, hard ball went flying into Horth and Kene's nearly finished space station. Pieces flew from it at the point of impact, and the whole structure shook, spoiling half a hundred pain-staking alignments.

Branst froze. He looked at Horth as if he had accidentally killed someone.

Horth knelt down, picked up a piece that had fallen to the floor, and remembered how Kene had showed him where to place it the day before.

"Gee, Horth," Branst said, chagrined. "I didn't mean—"

"*Ack rel*," Horth said, and set the piece down.

"What?" Branst floundered, astonished.

"*Ack rel*," Horth said again, and rose, leaving the broken piece behind him.

They were strong words. The same words Father spoke to Kene. Words that acknowledged the pain in any triumph. Words that promised things could matter, terribly, and not bring the world to an end in one fatal spasm. A promise that life could outlive quarrels, even if they had to be fatal for someone.

"You talked!" Branst said, blinking, and blurted a laugh.

Horth frowned. He wanted to share all he felt, but he didn't know how.

Zrenyl came in behind them and Branst turned to him excitedly. "He spoke," Branst told Zrenyl. "Horth said something."

"He did?" the older boy asked, in a daze.

"Say it again, Horth!" Branst insisted.

But to say it again might make it feel less important, somehow. Horth walked towards the damaged model space station. Silently, he began exploring the wound where the ball had struck.

"Horth!" Branst cried, exasperated.

Zrenyl said, "Give it up, Branst!" He lodged himself against the rope wall they used to climb up to the platform that served as a hundred different destinations. The ropes swayed as he got settled.

"It's good Father won, " Branst said momentarily, subdued now.

"Of course," Zrenyl snapped. "I didn't want father to die, you know! I just didn't want—" Zrenyl jerked on a stretch of rope. "It doesn't matter."

Horth spotted a bent spar. Everything would have to be taken apart, to that point, to get at it, but first he'd have to memorize the way the pieces fit together so he could put them back again, afterwards.

"I know what I said, about hating Nesaks," Branst muttered. "But I didn't want Kene to die, either. I mean, I don't see why he didn't let the Green Hearth medic help him."

There was a patch of silence that lasted five breaths.

Then Zrenyl said, in an awed tone of voice, "He knew it would sully him." He paused. "It was something to see, wasn't it? That kind of courage."

"But Di Mon's medic—"

"Di Mon!" Zrenyl said angrily, pulling himself up straight with his hands gripping the ropes on either side of him. "Lorels trained that medic. Lorels trained all of them!"

Branst lapsed into a brooding silence. "I guess. It's just... too bad," he said, at last.

"Well," Zrenyl told him in a grown-up, older brother-tone of voice. "We couldn't go to SanHome and stay here, too. So now it's decided."

"Will there be another war?" Branst asked.

"You heard them shouting *Okal Rel* on the Octagon," Zrenyl said, still sounding knowledgeable. "No war. Besides, if there was, we'd beat them again, no problem. So long as the Red Vrellish stick with Dad."

"And Monitum," Branst added stubbornly.

Zrenyl shrugged. "I don't know whether that's so important. What have the Monatese got left for highborns? Just Di Mon and a couple of *pol* scholars hidden away on their homeworld. Uncle Kene was right about one thing, for certain. Being too scared of challenge rights to breed, like Di Mon, is as stupid in the end as it is cowardly."

Branst began to cry, without warning.

"If you're going to start that— " Zrenyl blustered, and gave up as his own voice faltered. "Oh, come here!" He scooped Branst into a strong embrace and held him.

Horth paused. He couldn't focus on the station while his brothers were distracting him.

Ack rel, Horth told himself again, silently, surprised to discover words could be so powerful. He would practice them with Branst, Horth decided. Just Branst, until he got better. But he knew he must practice no matter how hard it was. He needed to learn a lot more about the things people disagreed about in his family.

* * *

Di Mon, liege of Monitum, sat behind the massive, oakwood desk, in his library, a piece of furniture so old that the trees it was made of had matured on the Earth itself, before war had consumed mankind's homeworld.

He read aloud from a beautifully illustrated storybook in his hands.

> *"K'isk of all the People," said Nersal Nesak, "you
> tell me the Vrellish are animals and have no souls. I tell
> you I have felt their souls in* soul touch. *It is a simple
> matter. Let me prove it to you. Take the test of souls
> with my Vrellish* brerelo *and you will know that what I
> say to you is true."*
>
> *But his father turned his back and said, "No."*

Di Mon looked up. "The rest is torn out."

Behind him, Tessitatt scuffed the toe of her boot on the parquet floor. "Branst was upset about the idea of going to SanHome," she told her uncle.

"That is no excuse for damaging a book," said Di Mon, closing the maimed artifact.

"What does it mean, anyway?" asked Tessitatt.

Di Mon folded his arms. "I expect it is the Nesaks' version of Prince Nersal's defection in minus 610 by the Americ calendar, which would be the year 170 by their own. They count forward from the Revelation. That's what the Nesaks called it when they decided they were something quite different from any of the founding houses of the empire. It was the era of the Purity Wars, when drawing lines around which souls were in or out of which genetic pool was in vogue. Rather than view themselves as Demish/Vrellish hybrids, the Black Vrellish — as Nesaks were known then — decided they were pure Nesak and invented a mythology to back them up. I do not know all of the details. Monitum, itself, went through a civil war not long before and there was some disruption in the logs." He glanced towards the green, leather-bound books that lined his library walls.

Tessitatt made a gesture as if to bat away all the talk of history, which vexed Di Mon. He had planned to be a Sanctuary scholar, dedicated to the study of the Monatese logs. But that was before the Nesak War. And before the disgrace of his predecessor, Darren, who had died in it; Darren, whose children were slaughtered by their Vrellish mother when he was caught having sex with boys. Every time he thought about Darren, Di Mon flinched inside, because he knew that he still shared Darren's affliction, despite a lifetime of denial, and he didn't know if Monitum could survive a second scandal of that magnitude. Sternly, he reminded himself that nothing could go wrong as long as he never expressed his *sla* desires. No one living knew except Di Mon and his bonded *gorarelpul*, and Sarilous was even more dedicated to Monitum's survival than he was.

"So," summed up Tessitatt, "House Nersal split from the Nesaks and inherited the mantle of Black Vrellish, because of a dispute about whether or not Red Vrellish have souls?"

"It would seem so," Di Mon said, mildly.

"What do they believe now?" asked Tessitatt.

"Ask Branst," said Di Mon. "I imagine his mother has taught him a thing or two."

The Green Hearth herald knocked crisply at the library door. Di Mon knew it was her by the knock and had expected to hear from her. He called, "Enter!"

His herald came in and paid her respects with a slight nod. She was a commoner, but well educated, and a valuable member of the household. "Liege Nersal?" Di Mon asked at once.

"In the Azure Lounge," she told him. "Waiting for you."

Di Mon scooped the Nesak book off the desk and headed for the small, private reception room. Tessitatt began to follow but he shook his head and raised his palm, warding her off.

He needed to talk to his *brerelo* alone.

Di Mon's friend and ally waited for him, seated on a couch that looked small and faintly ridiculous when burdened by Hangst Nersal's powerful form. He looked pleased with himself and high on adrenaline, the elation of surviving his damn-fool duel with the Nesak only starting to wear off.

"What is it?" Hangst Nersal greeted his friend's intense expression. "By the look of you, a man would think that you were sorry that I won!" He laughed.

Di Mon opened his mouth to deny that and found himself inclined to punch Hangst instead, right in his broad, grinning jaw. A flicker of involuntary attraction, of the kind he could not tolerate in himself, attempted to assert itself and was aggressively quashed. But it left a sting of lingering self-hatred.

"Of course I am glad you are alive," Di Mon told Hangst as calmly as he was able to. "How long do you think it will last?"

Hangst frowned. "I have more friends than enemies among the *kinf'stan*. Even Bryllit kept her sword sheathed. You saw that."

"I did," said Di Mon. "But I find it acutely uncomfortable that I am likely to agree with the next member of your extended family who carries an objection as far as the Challenge Floor."

"Challenge me yourself then, and get it over with," said Hangst, and surged up, half serious.

Di Mon took an involuntary step back.

They froze that way for a moment: Di Mon ashamed of what he felt, Hangst in complete ignorance. Then he noticed the book in Di Mon's hands.

"One of Kene's presents?" Hangst asked, recognizing the Nesak designs on the cover.

"Branst left it here," Di Mon told Hangst, holding it out to him. "I thought you might want it back."

Hangst took the book into his large, capable hands. "What does it say?" he asked.

"You can read it," Di Mon told him. "It is written in Gelack."

"Don't play games with me, Di Mon," said Hangst. "Tell me what it means and I will listen."

Di Mon warned himself against the seduction of pride, but he was pleased to be asked and to know that his opinion would be valued. He gave in with a thin sigh.

"It's propaganda," he told Hangst. "Stories for children that explain the world view of *Zer-sis* Ackal and his council. You are Nersal Nesak reborn, and the war failed because you are on the wrong side. Your children are a possible conduit for reclaiming your soul for the Nesak cause, and maybe even the soul of San Nersal herself into the bargain — presumably through a female child." Di Mon frowned. "Although I do not understand their reverence for San Nersal, since she was the quintessential female warrior, which is no longer acceptable on SanHome."

Hangst grinned at his friend's serious manner. "You haven't got a drop of mystical blood in your body, *brerelo*. That's your problem." He gestured with his free hand.

"Maybe San had a man's soul in a woman's body. Or she might have been a real Nesak woman, forced to live a Vrellish lifestyle to redeem herself for past transgressions. What you need to understand the Nesaks, my dear Di Mon," concluded Hangst, "is a vivid imagination."

"To understand them," Di Mon said stonily, "or to be seduced by them?"

Hangst lost his good humor. "What, exactly, are you accusing me of?"

"Are you Nersal Nesak reborn?" Di Mon asked. "Has she convinced you of that?"

"Of course not!"

"Why not?" Di Mon insisted. "You believe, very literally, in rebirth."

"I am not a dry-hearted cynic like you, no," said Hangst. "But that doesn't mean I believe priestly lies. Such as nobleborns lacking souls!"

"And commoners," Di Mon added.

Hangst batted aside the qualification with a dismissive gesture. "This is pointless."

"No," Di Mon insisted, "it is not. The Nesaks want one thing from you, and whatever stories they make up, I don't think they'll object so long as they get it. They want to unite Nesaks and Nersallians. And they want to do it because they know they'll never beat the allied Vrellish powers so long as we all stand together."

"All three of us?" Hangst asked, very soberly. "You and me and Vackal?"

Di Mon braced himself for what he knew was coming. It was a sore spot with Hangst that Red Hearth continued to stand empty.

"Any word at all from Vackal?" Hangst prompted.

Di Mon shook his head, tersely. "I've got people looking, but it isn't easy to find Vrellish highborns when they retreat to their cold moons and deep-space hideaways. I've left word with stationers, where possible, asking Vackal to show up or send his heir to occupy Red Hearth more regularly. To remind the Demish we are not the only Vrellish in the empire."

Hangst snorted. "If the Red Vrellish can be said to be part of the empire!"

Di Mon swallowed down a sharp lump of dread. He knew his own fleet would be of only moderate assistance in the next war, because all the *relsha* were nobleborn.

Hangst clapped Di Mon firmly on the shoulder. "My thanks for the book. And for being my judge of honor. We will talk again, later."

Di Mon smiled back, reassured by Hangst's hearty manner and regretting his doubts.

"I should get back to Beryl," Hangst added, collecting his sword from the rack by the door. "She is badly shaken by the death of her brother." He paused before adding, "He was a good man, for a Nesak, Kene Nesak. And I will honor our bargain." He glanced briefly towards the corners of the room, the way that people did when they were thinking of the Watching Dead, and smiled a little.

For a whole minute after Hangst had left Azure Lounge, Di Mon stood frozen, struggling to dispel the chill on his heart. In the end, he managed to convince himself that — contrary to Hangst's opinion — he did, indeed, have too active an imagination. Hangst had lived with Beryl Nesak as his wife for years, and apart from the untimely deaths of a few *kinf'stan* challengers, nothing very terrible had happened.

Maybe this new arrangement would not prove all that different.

Part II

Right and Wrong

(181 Post Treaty)

A girl screamed. Horth was on his feet in a bound and standing in the half-light of the bedroom: a skinny boy of ten with an adult's self-possession, naked from the waist up. He froze to listen.

"What is it?" Branst asked from the next bed. "Is it Mother?"

Horth listened harder. He was sure the scream had not been Mother's even though it had come from the room she shared with Father, and no female Nersallian would scream that way, which meant it was probably a servant, but Mother never tolerated servants near her. She was especially loath to mix with non-eternals now that she was pregnant again, because she was certain she had lost the last child for unnatural reasons, and after five miscarriages in six years even Father was beginning to doubt so much bad luck could be natural.

Branst got out of bed, rustling the covers. At thirteen, he had a man's body topped with tousled black hair, but was filling out in comely rather than imposing proportions, unlike Zrenyl whose physique resembled Father's. Branst was dressed in brown and green pajamas. He wore the same pajamas every night, because they were a gift from Tessitatt.

The two brothers stood in silence for a moment but there were no new sounds. It was Horth who decided to go into Family Hall. Branst followed.

Mother's retainer, Lywulf, came charging out of the nursery fully dressed with his sword in his hand. He had almost reached their parents' door when Hara and two of her errants burst out of the Throat.

Hara put herself in Lywulf's way, flanked by a male errant named Rossen and a woman called Gil.

For a moment, neither Lywulf nor Hara spoke. There were no shared rules of engagement. Hara was a non-eternal from the Nesak point of view, and beneath notice. From the court perspective, she and Lywulf failed to share a challenge class, but as the superior Sevolite it was in his power to condescend to fight with her if he wanted to.

"So be it, soulless one!" the Nesak said through clenched teeth, when he could stand no more. "I will honor you with a quick death, if I must. But I am going through that door!"

"Forget it, Nesak," Hara growled. "I am under no obligation to duel just because it suits you to acknowledge me, now."

Just then the door opened with a bang and Alice, the maid, burst through the bedroom doors sobbing hysterically, although she appeared to be unharmed.

Branst cried, "Alice!" and bolted after the commoner as she disappeared into a servants' passage.

Lywulf seized the opportunity to charge Rossen, who happened to be standing nearest to the door, slashing at Hara's head to hold her off. Hara just managed to draw two thirds of her sword out of her scabbard, in the cramped quarters, and raised it half above her head in an angled prime parry, causing Lywulf's blade to scrape down it and bite into her shoulder. Rossen slammed against the wall, but his partner, Gil, reacted with Vrellish-fast reflexes, darting in to run Lywulf through from the side as he engaged Hara.

Horth witnessed the fight with a deep sense of shock. This was no duel! It was a life and death struggle played out with swords because they were the weapons available. He never forgot the difference. And he quickly decided Lywulf was a fool to take on lesser Sevolites three to one in circumstances that nullified the advantages of being highborn.

Hara hissed in pain, gripping her shoulder, but the bottom two thirds of a dueling sword was not sharp and she was not badly injured. Lywulf himself was down, and bubbling out frothy blood from a punctured lung.

"Get him out of sight," Hara ordered her errants. "Now!"

Horth met Hara's eyes with questions. She only frowned.

Gil sheathed her sword and Rossen staggered up to help her take hold of the wounded man. Lywulf tried to get up and they shoved him down, forcing a moan from the Nesak as he labored to breath through his blood.

"Hara! Are you out there?" Hangst Nersal called from the bedroom.

"Coming, my Liege!" Hara replied and dodged inside. She reappeared supporting the family's *gorarelpul* medic, Narous, whose face was slashed above one eye. Like all *gorarelpul*, Narous did not react to pain like other people. It was merely information to him. But he looked more bad tempered than usual and the whole side of his face was slick with fresh blood.

Sixteen-year-old Zrenyl emerged from his bedroom, belatedly. "What happened?" he demanded imperiously of Hara.

"Your mother happened!" snapped Hara, her respect for Zrenyl's Highlord birth rank restricted to her choice of pronouns. "She attacked Narous and terrified a servant with that Nesak knife she keeps by her bed. She is losing her baby again, and decided to take it out on the people your father asked to help her!"

Zrenyl looked big and solid even in his dressing gown. Such presence should amount to something, Horth felt, but his eldest brother only grimaced, flexed his fists, and strode off. He called back to anyone who bothered to take notice, "I'll be working at the docks."

It was part of an emerging pattern: when things got rough at home, Branst chased women and Zrenyl went to the docks. It felt as if the family was under siege and splintering under the pressure. *Kinf'stan* challenged Father every year, while at the same time a dark and brooding sympathy for Mother built up around the suspicion that something as wicked as a Lorel evil lurked at the root of her inability to give birth to a living child. Zrenyl was constantly in fist fights or arranging first-blood duels with one faction or the other, before he took to the fleet for refuge. He had been shirking his duty as Heir Nersal ever since. He even failed to attend Father's last title duel, which was a serious omission because only Liege Nersal's named heir had the right to reciprocate immediately if Hangst lost. The alternative was to accept the victor as the new liege of Nersal for at least a three day period of respite, and Mother was certain that would be the end of her and her sons. Father didn't think so, and Branst thought Father was right, but the point was Zrenyl ought to attend.

"Why, Kene, why?" Mother's voice pierced the door of her bedroom. "Why won't you come back? Why do you keep dying?!"

Father's voice answered, speaking too softly to be heard but sounding calm and reasonable.

Gil and Rossen reached the nursery and paused to lay Lywulf down while Gil went to open the door. In another moment, Lywulf would disappear inside and probably die.

Heart hammering, Horth stepped in front of Narous and Hara. "Wounded!" he said, and pointed with a stiff arm.

"Yes, I'm wounded," Narous snapped. "Thanks to your Nesak mother! May the gods take an interest in her!"

Wishing the perverse attentions of Earth's dimly remembered, sadistically mad gods on his mother reaffirmed Horth's bad opinion of Narous. But he didn't have time to register his complaint on that front.

Horth pointed down the hall again where Rossen was dragging Lywulf's feet through the nursery doors. "Him," Horth said, in *rel*-peerage, since Lywulf addressed him like that.

"What's the *rejak't* talking about?" Narous asked Hara.

"Gil skewered Beryl's henchman when he tried to get past us," she admitted to the *gorarelpul*, with an uncomfortable glance in Horth's direction. "She should have crippled him, not gone for the torso. Hangst isn't going to be pleased about it."

"Wonderful," Narous said tartly. "All right. I'll see if the Nesak is salvageable." Still dabbing his bleeding eyebrow, the *gorarelpul* stumbled off towards the nursery.

Horth's heart rate slowed. He knew Narous was good at his job. He did not like him one iota more because of that, however. The sour-faced old commoner objected to Horth taking pieces of his equipment to examine. Once, he told Horth not to do it again or he would take out his liver and replace it with an artificial organ that only he knew how to keep alive, the way that the Lorels had done in the times leading up to the Fifth Civil War. Horth did not like the things Narous told Father about his verbal limitations, either. The *gorarelpul* made it sound as if there was something wrong with Horth's brain. He preferred Mother's belief that brains didn't matter, as long as one's soul was strong.

"I want *Zer* Sarn!" Mother's voice wailed through the door. "I want my priest!"

Hangst's voice rumbled back at her, telling her again how Nesak priests did not belong on Gelion and his household could be trusted not to poison her.

"Princess Beryl cries like a Demish girl," Hara said contemptuously.

Horth looked at Hara, hoping she might say more, but she only stayed a moment before heading for the nursery where Narous had disappeared, leaving Horth standing alone outside his parents' door.

Horth decided to go find Branst.

Alice's room near the kitchens was well known to Horth because Alice was a special friend who always did Branst's chores.

Her door was ajar. Horth let himself in without bothering to knock and halted at the sight of Branst leaning over Alice, on her bed. She was lying down with her shoes kicked off. Her legs, clad in the black slacks that were part of her uniform, were all that was visible of her except for her arms that were clasped around Branst's neck. He was kissing Alice, one hand probing under her clothing.

Horth took a step back and shut the door.

He knew what he had seen. It was impossible not to know a lot about sex, growing up in a Vrellish household. The errants indulged with each other, brought in commoner prostitutes, and talked about it a lot. But they were errants. Branst was Branst. And Mother said having sex with a commoner was like breeding with an animal.

Father wouldn't approve either, for Vrellish reasons. At least, Horth was pretty sure Alice hadn't done anything worthy of earning a gift-child from Branst Nersal, which would make her the mother of a nobleborn and be a way for her to gain status.

Horth suspected Branst shouldn't be doing what he was with Alice. But he wasn't entirely sure.

He decided that Zrenyl would know more because he had been trying to find a woman who would give him a Freedom Price so he could start flying combat as a *relsha*. Zrenyl's problem was that Mother and Father could not agree on how that should work: marriage or child-gifting. Horth had heard them arguing about it on more than one occasion. Therefore, he reasoned, Zrenyl ought to know all about fertility manners.

But as Horth was dressing for his expedition to find Zrenyl, the Black Hearth herald stuck his head into the bedroom to interrupt.

"Excuse me, Master Horth," said the herald, expressing his respects through the case and suffixes applied to each pronoun, as was usual in Gelack. "Your father is not to be disturbed and I cannot find either of your brothers, but Liege

Monitum is waiting in the entrance hall. Will you see him on your father's behalf?"

Horth accepted the job with a nod and followed the herald down the Throat.

It wasn't until Horth saw Di Mon, properly dressed with his dueling sword strapped to his right hip, that he realized he was ill-prepared to greet a highborn visitor. A Sevolite should always wear a sword in order to express respect for Sword Law. Even worse, from Horth's prepubescent perspective, his lack of an honorable weapon was a tacit admission that he was still a child.

"Horth," Di Mon acknowledged him. "Are neither of your brothers at home, then?"

Horth shrugged, unwilling to discuss what Branst was up to.

Di Mon's *gorarelpul*, Sarilous, was carrying her medical bag with the snakes on it, coiling around a narrow cross. Horth noted the silver star device on her arm that showed through a gauze patch on the sleeve of her green smock. The stick with the snakes was a Lorel symbol. The mark on her arm meant she had been trained on *TouchGate*, the hospital station that the Lor'Vrellish exiles still ran.

"I heard your mother is miscarrying," Di Mon told Horth. "I am here to offer help if it is wanted."

Horth was sure his mother would not want Monatese help, but was afraid she needed it. He hesitated for only a moment, then led the way back down the Throat to the door of his parents' bedroom. Di Mon and Sarilous followed.

A cry of pain stabbed through the door as they arrived.

Di Mon lowered the hand he had raised to the door's heavy handle and turned to his *gorarelpul*, instead.

"How many miscarriages is this since the duel with Kene?" he asked her as if Horth was not there. "The sixth?" He shook his head. "It doesn't seem likely this is natural."

"Statistically, no," Sarilous told her master. "But it isn't impossible, either. Hangst is 46% Sevolite and Beryl is just barely a Royalblood at 50%. That puts their offspring in the range where the risk of straddling the highborn and nobleborn phenotypes is high. Spontaneous abortions are common in that range because a fetus with only some highborn traits isn't viable."

"Why?" Horth blurted.

Both visitors blinked at him. Without adapting her style to her audience, Sarilous answered. "Highborn syndrome requires a gestalt of interlocking systems. Say, for example, a fetus had regenerative powers but not the regulating mechanism that prevents regenerative cancer; or perhaps the fetus is Vrellish enough for the stress response syndrome called *rel-osh*, but lacks those regenerative powers. There are at least a dozen fatal combinations in offspring more than one third, but less than one half, Sevolite."

"Mother is all Sevolite," Horth told the *gorarelpul* with the snakes on her bag.

Sarilous showed impatience. "No, she isn't. She is highborn, yes, but only about 50% Sevolite. Whether she and the rest of the Nesaks wish to acknowledge it, anyone less than a Pureblood Sevolite makes up the difference with ordinary human DNA — commoner DNA. Just like mine."

"Sarilous," Di Mon cautioned gently.

"Facts are facts," said the old *gorarelpul*. "Nesaks can't change them with superstitious dogma."

Horth frowned. If Mother said she was all Sevolite, he felt that should settle the matter. But Sarilous was talking about numbers, not souls. He let the matter drop for now.

"Horth," said Di Mon. "I want to see your mother. I wish to try to reason with her. Will you show us in?"

Horth weighed his own faith in Di Mon's honor against the nefarious influence of his Lorel connections. He was spared a decision by his father calling out, "Hara? Is that you?"

Di Mon opened the door himself.

Inside, the master bedroom was softly lighted. It smelled of birth and blood. Hangst Nersal's big form was stretched on the bed beside Beryl, who lay curled up against him, limp with exhaustion between her convulsions.

Hangst sat up as the visitors came into the room, reaching automatically for the sword on a bedside table. "What do you want, Monitum," he asked in his deep voice as he rose.

Di Mon stiffened. "Monitum is it? Shall I call you Nersal, then?" he asked.

Father gave his attention to fastening his sword belt around his waist.

Di Mon waited.

"I appreciate you coming," Father told Di Mon when he had the sword belt fastened. "But Beryl assures me that she would rather die than be treated by any *gorarelpul*." Father said this with pride, as well as frustration.

"I understand," Di Mon answered in a neutral tone. "But you suspect something. It is therefore in my interest, at least as much as yours, that those suspicions be proved or disproved. I am not poisoning your Nesak wife," Di Mon said firmly, and added with more kindness. "If someone else is, let me prove it. Or else prove her loss is natural."

Beryl stirred on the bed, reaching out blindly with one groping hand. "Nersal? Where are you, Nersal?"

Father retreated to the bed. "Here," he said, sitting down to take her hand.

"Who's there," Beryl asked distractedly. "*Zer* Sarn?"

"She's delirious," said Sarilous in a cool tone. "I suspect an infection."

"No, it is not *Zer* Sarn, Beryl," said Father, crouching down awkwardly because of the sword he now wore. "There is no priest of your people on Gelion. It is my friend, Di Mon, liege of Monitum, and his *gorarelpul*."

Mother voiced a short gasp of alarm that drew Horth to her bedside. Beryl put her hand over Horth's. Her skin felt hot and damp. A tangled mass of black hair framed her white face. Sweat soaked her brow and her eyes looked hollow.

"Perhaps it is enough," she said, stroking Horth's hand. "Perhaps my work here is done and it is time to go."

Horth's throat constricted and his heart beat faster, making him feel dizzy. He didn't like Mother talking like that.

"Liege Monitum wants to take a blood sample," Father persisted. "He wants to test for drugs that might have caused you to lose this child. Or a sickness that might be responsible."

"No!" Mother gasped.

"Beryl— !" Father tried to argue.

"No!" She shrank away from Father, letting go of Horth, her whole body trembling.

Father rose again to face Di Mon. "I won't force her."

"Have you done any tests yourself?" Di Mon asked.

Father looked away, troubled. His jaw worked. Mother stared out of her large eyes at him like someone waiting for her own execution.

"I gave samples to my own *gorarelpul* on other occasions, yes," Father said adding quickly, "samples of spilled blood."

"You found nothing?" Sarilous asked.

Father shook his head, lips compressed to a thin line. He didn't seem like the man Horth knew from quiet hours spent together. He felt like a liege of Fountain Court conferring with another liege on business matters.

"No!" Beryl wailed, her will lashing out from her tortured body. "Not you! Not— " She clawed at Horth's arm. "Horth! My spirit knife! Give me a weapon!" But the knife was not in the place that it usually was on her dresser. Father must have taken it away after she slashed Narous.

"Beryl stop this!" Hangst commanded, capturing her arms to pull her close against him. "I did nothing to harm you!"

Her hands locked on his forearms. Tangled hair hung in damp coils on either side of her bright green eyes as she looked up at Hangst. "Can't trust... anyone," she gasped. "Not even... my love. "

"No, Beryl! I haven't lied!" Father told her. "I never extracted blood from you and I won't test stained sheets again, either. Not without your consent. I promise. But you must stop this." Hangst squeezed her arms, almost shaking her, and then gathered her against his broard chest as another convulsive spasm struck her.

Over his shoulder, Hangst ordered Horth, "Get them out of here."

The visitors offered no resistance, but they did not go far. They stopped in the first room of the Throat, known as Family Lounge. Since Horth had taken it as his duty to escort them out, he halted as well to wait for them to move on.

Sarilous wore a sneer of contempt. "Next she will be having visions that tell her you are Danseer Monitum of the Fifth Civil War, reborn," she grumbled to her master, "and insist you be publicly eviscerated for your crimes."

"Sarilous," Di Mon said, "that's not helpful." Horth knew Di Mon was always careful to make his corrective remarks to his *gorarelpul* in the form of mere statements, not orders. Tessitatt said that was because a direct command left Sarilous no scope for defending her point of view, and Di Mon valued her most for her willingness to give him an argument. Horth felt that was honorable, since to disobey a bond master's command was fatal to a bonded *gorarelpul*. And yet bonding itself was a Lorel science and felt like something people shouldn't do. Maybe it was all right because *gorarelpul* were commoners who had to be controlled. Horth wasn't sure.

"What do you make of the tests that Hangst spoke about?" Di Mon asked Sarilous, once again acting as if he had forgotten Horth was present. "Does it remove suspicion?"

"As medics, Nersallians make good engineers," Sarilous said with a sneer. "I doubt it was competently executed."

"But they are good technicians," said Di Mon.

"For routine things, I suppose. But the people with the most motivation to sabotage Beryl Nersak's breeding plans are people with access to more than routine resources."

"I suppose you mean the *kinf'stan*," said Di Mon, and frowned. "That would not be like them. If they object to Hangst's deal with the Nesaks, they can take it up by the sword. And have."

"Yes," said Sarilous. "And they haven't done so well, thus far. Honor may tire in the face of so much failure on the Challenge Floor."

It took Horth a moment to grasp she was insulting the honor of his entire house by implying that the *kinf'stan* might be poisoning his mother. Without thinking, he struck out to punish her, and would have connected hard enough to do her frail body serious harm if Horth's attack had not been deflected by Di Mon's right arm. The next moment Horth's access to the *gorarelpul* was blocked by Di Mon's drawn sword.

"I believe that young Horth here understood more than you thought he would, Sarilous," said the wily liege of Monitum, holding Horth's stare with his slate gray eyes. "Apologize to him." He did not prevaricate now — it was an order.

Sarilous bowed in Horth's direction. "Your pardon, Highlord Horth, scion of Black Hearth," said the *gorarelpul*. "My conjecture was merely hypothetical. I accuse no actual member of the *kinf'stan* of dishonorably injuring your mother in defiance of your father's duel-pact with House Nesak."

Horth glared at her over Di Mon's drawn sword, unimpressed by the long, sonorous flow of the words that came out of her. He felt no retraction in her tone.

"My apology as well," Di Mon said as he sheathed his sword. "You speak so seldom, Horth, it is too easy to forget that you can understand." Then he smiled. "Or that you are growing up," he added. "It is going to go fast, from here on. You are more Vrellish than your brothers, if I'm any judge."

"Liege Monitum!" a familiar voice intruded.

Di Mon closed his eyes, very briefly, as Branst rushed over, his clothes still disheveled from his tryst with Alice.

"Good cycle, Branst," Di Mon greeted him civilly. "See me out, will you? My visit here is done."

"Is Tessitatt with you?" Branst asked.

"Alas," Di Mon said with strained patience, "no."

Horth listened to Branst trying to ingratiate himself with Di Mon until the conversation was cut off by the door at the far end of Family Lounge.

Doubly determined to go see Zrenyl, Horth went to fetch a sword. His own was a child's, so on impulse he took one of Branst's and slung it down his back because it was too long for him to wear. He picked a traveling cloak without identifying marks and headed down the Throat of Black Hearth, the borrowed sword bouncing on his back and the borrowed cloak dragging on the floor.

"Where are you going, my scrawny one?" Hara intercepted him before he reached the spiral stairs that led up to the Plaza. "Armed and all!"

Horth scowled. "Docks," he told Hara. "To Zrenyl."

"Not like that you aren't," she said. "At least, not alone." Hara laughed at his serious expression. "I'll take you to find your Nesak brother. I could use the walk. But," she frowned, "leave the sword behind and take that traveling cloak off. Nasty, sneaky habit going about UnderGelion like that. And foolish besides. It is safer to show our dragons. We're Nersallian. People will not lightly mess with us. Besides, that thing will trip you."

Horth shrugged out of the cloak and let it fall to the floor. Some servant, like Alice, would take care of returning it to Branst's closet. He was more reluctant to part with his sword, but when Hara refused to budge he took that off, too, and laid it down.

Hara waved him on ahead of her up the spiral stairs to Black Pavilion. The watch captain began to greet Horth as he emerged, then broke off to salute Hara with the traditional fist-to-heart gesture used by all Nersallians. A Nersallian salute was the net result of an on-the-spot calculation that took account of birth ranks, titles, oaths, and attitudes, culminating in a promise to support the one saluted should a conflict arise. That was useful because people were always struggling over status or deciding how far to assert their own desires, and the watch captain had just told Horth, without any pointed insult, that he ranked second to Hara under the circumstances.

Horth expected nothing else, but it still rankled in a way that was new to him since he had turned ten. He wanted to be the one people saluted, but he knew he had to earn the privilege. People respected Hara because she was captain of errants. Horth was a hearth-son with no special status apart from his birth rank, routinely acknowledged through pronouns, which entitled him to highborn rights of challenge including his membership in the *kinf'stan*; but birth rights conferred no honors beyond that. Horth would have to prove himself in the world.

Once out of Black Pavilion, Hara led Horth through the bazaar of goods and services on the Plaza. Next they passed through the tall arch of the Palace Shell with its rings of balconies for access to the palace, differentiated by birth-rank.

It was possible to see a lot of UnderGelion from the promenade that ran the length of the highborn docks. The city was encased in a hullsteel dome beneath the planet's crust. Without artificial light, everything around them would be pitch black. But being closed in did not bother Horth. He had visited the Nersallian planet of Tark, in Alliance Reach, and knew all about how suns created day and night on green worlds. Watching the whole performance from space made that obvious. But he distrusted weather, and disliked the things in the air on a green world that irritated his nose. Engineered environments felt comfortable.

Horth and Hara threaded their way through the pedestrian traffic on the promenade drawing no more than the occasional second look from other sword-carrying Sevolites. The ratio of Demish to Vrellish pedestrians was roughly a hundred to one, if you included the Vrellish nobleborns from Spiral Hall. It was much worse if you counted only highborns. All the highborn Vrellish in sight were Nersallians. Horth also spotted nobleborns in green Monatese livery, traveling alone or in small groups with packages under their arms, books in their hands, or some servant walking beside them with an air of companionable familiarity. Three times he made out brightly dressed clusters of Red Vrellish nobleborns from Spiral Hall playing physical jokes on one another, entwined in casual embraces, or busy passing small children back and forth between them as if the moving group of adults were a living playground.

Black Gate was the farthest from the Palace Shell along the promenade. Hara was recognized at once and granted passage through the gatehouse. On the far side, she commandeered a car that was powered by a soundless, emission-free battery of the kind that were charged up by pilots as they flew around the universe and exchanged for spent ones at whatever docks they used.

The car came with a driver whose pronouns, as he discussed their destination with Hara, declared him a Pettylord, one of the birth ranks within the challenge class of those called petty Sevolites or sometimes, less formally, simply "near commoners." Hara and Horth got into the back and they set off at a very sane pace for the military stockyard where Zrenyl worked when he took himself off to the docks.

Hara is a rel *woman*, Horth thought, studying her in this rare moment of stillness. She had a strong face and the build of a sword fighter. Her thighs were particularly well-muscled and she had a couple of scars that Horth found fascinating because highborns, like himself and his family, did not scar. It did not occur to him that he should find her unfeminine because of any of that. He could tell by her smell that she was female, and by the contours of her chest and groin. He had been aware of the differences between male and female Nersallians for as long as he could remember. It was Demish women and commoner females, like Alice, whom he did not understood particularly well. In some ways they seemed like his mother, although he knew she wouldn't like him to think of it like that.

A shout drew Horth's attention to see a car pull up alongside them with a pair of Vrellish faces grinning at them from open windows. Horth's window wasn't open but he caught taunts that went with their gestures. They were saying that Nersallians were as slow as Demish farm wagons and they were going to show them up. Then the Spiral Hall nobleborns took off with a burst of speed that made Horth wonder if they had something else besides *rel*-batteries powering the car.

Horth sat forward in his seat, feeling provoked. "Faster," he said to the driver in front.

"Whoa there, hot shot," Hara laughed. "And carry on, Gavin," she corrected Horth's last command. "We're not *so* Vrellish that we have to race bored fools just because they insulted us. I'm getting you there in — what are you doing now?" she interrupted her own lecture.

Horth had noticed something out the window and wound it down to stick his head out. He pulled his head in again and pointed back at a commotion on a Monatese lot beside a bustling, Silver Demish one.

There was a single envoy-class ship parked in the taxiing area outside the Monatese hanger that was drawing a lot of attention. The Monatese were clustering around, but they were swiftly becoming out numbered by the people coming from the Demish yard.

"Interesting," said Hara.

"Might be a duel, Captain," Gavin said with ill-suppressed interest. "And it's on Monatese property with a mob of Demish inviting themselves along."

Hara nodded. "We had better take a look."

Gavin make a sharp turn and sped up. He didn't hit any pedestrians, but he did weave around another car.

"Park," Hara said when the traffic got thick as they approached the disturbance.

Much to Gavin's disappointment, Hara ordered him to stay behind to mind their car.

She and Horth jogged to the edge of the ring around the main event, Hara running with one hand flat against the sheath of her sword and Horth on her other side, feeling foolish and childlike without a sword of his own. He had to admit she was right about leaving the traveling cloaks behind, though. The Demish crowd fell back at the sight of Nersallian dragons on Horth's shirt and Hara's uniform jacket. They had no trouble getting through until they reached the solid mass of people that formed the witnessing circle around the spot where flood lights illuminated whatever they were headed for.

Hara pushed her way in through a clump of petty Sevolites and commoners. Horth followed. They were met by a couple of Monatese docks workers who approached them with the confidence of fellow Sevolites although they were not wearing swords and their leader addressed Hara in grammar appropriate for a commoner.

"It's a Red Vrellish woman, Captain Hara," said the woman, whose name badge read 'Mandy.' "A couple men from Silver Hearth are giving her a rough welcome to court."

"Gods!" exclaimed Hara. "Red you say? What's she doing landing on the highborn docks if she's from Spiral Hall? Unless ..."

"That would be my guess, too," said the bold Monatese commoner. "She just might belong on the highborn docks."

"And we, uh, think she might be space drunk," said the man at Mandy's elbow.

Hara set her jaw and answered their implied request for intervention with a curt nod. The Monatese commoners called out in loud voices for people to make way for: "Hara, captain of the Black Hearth errants!"

Hara was swiftly reinforced by a sword-carrying Monatese watch captain.

"Black Hearth!" he exclaimed. "Glad to see you, Captain Hara. I was not sure what to do."

"Back me up, if necessary," Hara instructed.

As the crowd parted for Hara, Horth saw an almost naked Vrellish female crouched at the center of the thickening circle of witnesses.

Three large Demish men were circling her with their swords drawn, and calling out insults that entertained the increasingly Demish, and primarily male, crowd.

"Careful, Eril, she has space eyes!" one of the Demish bullies called to another.

"And more than one mouth that bites!" an anonymous voice piped up from the crowd.

Eril raised his head to look for who had spoken, looking puzzled, "What is that supposed to mean?" he asked.

His two partners in petty harassment erupted in laughter. "Eril's never met a really Vrellish woman!" one of them gasped out, between roars of laughter.

The half-grown Vrellish female sprang for the man who was laughing the hardest, took him down, ripped his face with her teeth, and sprang back in possession of his sword.

Space drunk or not, which was slang for impairment due to over exposure to *rel*-skimming, the Vrellish woman knew how to use the captured sword. She blocked an attack from Eril and drew blood with a whip across the chest of the third man. She could have killed either one, Horth suspected, watching her with awe. Instead, she seemed to be of the opinion that the whole row was nothing much to worry about.

"Whoever she is," said Hara. "She really is space drunk. And doesn't know a thing about Demish men."

The woman followed up on her victory in an extremely Vrellish fashion. Fighting was fun, she seemed to be trying to convey with her body language, but there were better ways to say, "Hello, and welcome to court." She clamped her thighs over the disarmed man's body and rolled him on top of her, ensuring his body stayed between her and his friends while she tested out his willingness to engage in less aggressive physical sports. The man either misunderstood, or being Demish did not know how to decline with grace, because he reacted with a very inelegant, flailing struggle and a great shout.

One of his friends dove to the rescue, sword out, shouting, "Vrellish slut!"

Whatever the Vrellish female's challenge class, she had tacitly consented to the fight by attacking first. The Demish men were within their rights under Sword Law to take her on — one by one. What tipped the balance for Horth was that two of them attacked her at the same time. That was wrong. But the crowd seemed to be on the men's side despite that.

Or they were, until Hara cleared her sword and shouted, "All right! Back off, or take me on!"

A murmur went through the watchers as people remembered that this was the right approach, and that keeping violence within the scope of Sword Law was supposed to be a witnessing circle's job.

"You back off, she-man!" snarled the man who had called the space drunk woman a slut.

"Make me," challenged Hara in a steely tone.

The man seemed willing to oblige Hara until his friend, Eril, laid a hand on his sword arm. "Ric," he said in a low voice, "that's the captain of the Black Hearth errants."

Horth's heart soared with pride for Hara's reputation as he watched the Demish man falter. It was all the more impressive because the intimidated man was her challenge class superior. Horth wanted to stand beside her with his own sword drawn, to give her some token highborn backup, except — of course — he didn't have a sword.

While the Demish highborn named Ric deliberated, the Vrellish stranger at the heart of all the trouble tossed aside her captive and stood up.

Her lean build was unencumbered by clothing except for a pair of leather flight trousers. Her breasts were not developed enough to be obvious, but the contours of her genital mound were definitely female to Horth. Her black hair was cut in irregular hanks. Her face had a shape that reminded Horth, a little, of the big cats of ancient Earth that he had stared at for hours in picture books that Branst brought home from Green Hearth.

Another disruption in the witnessing circle disgorged Zrenyl. He moved immediately to back Hara, regardless of their differences at home concerning Mother.

The crowd rumbled its disappointment as the Demish trio backed off.

Sword or no sword, Horth was determined to stand by Hara and his brother, and went forward to join them in the short line confronting the strange, Vrellish female.

Their space drunk visitor got one, good look at him, swept aside her stolen sword and relaxed.

"Horth's a Vrellish child," Hara realized. "She can see that. So she knows we are Vrellish, too."

"Vretla," declared the Vrellish woman, slapping her bare chest.

"Vretla!" Zrenyl cried, as if he'd seen a ghost. Vretla was the name of the Vrellish war hero who had defeated the Nesaks in the battle for Cold Rock. They all had the same involuntary thought: this adolescent could be Vretla Vrel the Great reborn.

Zrenyl tried to cover up his spooked reaction with a string of commands. "Hara, break up the witness circle. Tell them there won't be any duel. And you, Horth, what do you think you are doing here, you *rejak't!*"

Horth reacted to the insult with a punch. Zrenyl blocked, letting out an indignant "Ow!"

Vretla Vrel laughed.

"I expect she's used to sib fights," Hara remarked. "Horth, go take her hand and lead her back to our car."

"Do you think that's safe?" Zrenyl worried. "She's space drunk!"

"She won't harm a child," Hara said, and smirked as Vretla proved her right by accepting Horth's guidance without a fuss. "You, on the other hand, Zrenyl, are more of an age to interest her too much."

"Age?" Zrenyl said, sounding puzzled. Then he figured out what Hara meant and added curtly, "I am not interested in bedding Vrellish savages."

"Who said she'd ask you nicely?" Hara mocked his indignation as they headed off. To take the sting out of it, she added swiftly, "Thanks for backing me up there, by the way, Heir Nersal."

Zrenyl grunted, but accepted the change of subject gratefully enough. "I would back up my worst enemy against a bunch of gang-swords!" he told Hara. Gang-swords were people who bullied the unarmed, or tried to start melees for fun.

"Am I your enemy, Heir Nersal?" Hara asked.

Zrenyl stopped. Horth stopped as well, and turned back. Vretla let go of his hand and took a step to the side, sensing tensions. Horth noticed how she automatically positioned herself to be able to see them all at once. He also noticed the way she had said nothing more than her name so far.

Hara and Zrenyl stood facing each other, stares locked.

"Nersal is a Vrellish House," Hara said to Zrenyl. "Are you Vrellish, Heir Nersal? Or Nesak?"

Zrenyl's held his jaw clenched and the muscles of his shoulders bunched. Hara looked relaxed by comparison, eyes hooded and her hand resting limply on the hilt of her sheathed sword. They stood like that for long seconds, the question unanswered.

"I am Heir Nersal," Zrenyl said at last.

"Mm," Hara remarked, as if the matter was entirely casual. "Then you should attend your liege's duels."

Zrenyl swallowed thickly, and scowled.

Vretla turned her head to spit blood from *shimmer*-strafed lungs. She wiped her mouth on the back of her bare forearm.

"You can't take her back to Black Hearth!" Zrenyl protested suddenly noticing that Hara was leading them towards the car. "Not like that!"

"Why not?" Hara asked.

"Because I said so!" Zrenyl battered at her with his deep, angry voice. "Not now, while Mother's vulnerable."

"Fine," said Hara. "I will take her to Green Hearth instead, if that suits you better, Heir Nersal."

"You do that!" said Zrenyl.

Vretla yanked Gavin out of the driver's seat to displace him.

"Oh no," said Hara, "you are not driving in that condition! Horth, take her hand and coax her into the back seat with you."

Horth obeyed with trepidation, and was surprised when Vretla smiled and let him guide her.

"Horth!" Zrenyl cried. "You get out of that car!"

Zrenyl was clearly cranky, which meant he would only rant at Horth and make no effort to be patient with him over his verbal challenges. Horth decided he would rather stay where he was and talk to Zrenyl later about Branst and Alice.

Zrenyl looked exasperated. "If anything happens to you," he threatened, "when mother has just lost a baby—!"

"Vretla won't hurt a child," Hara interrupted, as she closed the front seat door.

"Be careful!" Zrenyl admonished Horth in parting as Gavin pulled out.

Such advice always puzzled Horth. Did Zrenyl expect him to be reckless if not reminded regularly that life was dangerous?

Vretla smelled of stale sweat, fresh blood, and the distinctive sex odor of a Vrellish female. She shifted over to sit close to Horth, taking in his odor and feeling the embroidery on his collar between her forefinger and thumb.

"If she gives you any trouble, hearth-child," Hara called over her shoulder from the front, "let me know."

Horth knew exactly what Hara meant by that, but Vretla made no sexual advances. He slapped her hand to stop her fussing with his blue-black hair as if he were an infant. She chuckled her approval and responded with a playful nudge. Then she curled up on the seat to catch a quick nap.

Back at Black Gate, Hara hustled Vretla out of the car and into one of the anonymous traveling cloaks she had refused for herself and Horth. But Vretla would not wear the cloak, and after the feral girl from Red Reach had shrugged it off for the second time, Hara gave up.

"Fine then," Hara told her new charge, "come as you are and get stared at!"

Vretla resisted only long enough to retrieve her stolen sword from the car. Then she went willingly with Horth and Hara through Black Gate and out onto the Demish-dominated promenade.

A pair of Demish ladies averted their eyes from Vretla's brazen nakedness as their male escort moved to protect them, eyes popping out of his head. They were not the only pedestrians to react like that. Between the ogling bystanders and Vretla's reciprocal curiosity, their progress slowed to a crawl.

One Demish man offered Vretla his cloak to cover her naked upper body. She accepted it for the sake of its silky feel, although she failed to get the idea that it was meant to cover her, and preferred swishing it around. He laughed, and asked Hara, "Are Red Reach women always like this?"

"She is overflown," Hara explained, and then smiled as she added, "that makes her a little indiscriminate."

"Ah," he said, in a good-natured manner. "Meaning I suppose, that she would prefer a Vrellish peer to a Demish inferior, if she were sober."

Vretla terminated the conversation by locking both hands in the man's hair and making her intentions clear with pelvic gestures that were more than either he or Hara were prepared to let her follow through with in public.

The incident made Hara nervous. She hurried their charge past any males who maintained eye contact. Vretla didn't appreciate this interference with her social life much.

News of their passage preceded them. They had barely reached the Plaza when a party from Green Hearth arrived, including Tessitatt, Branst, and a couple of errants led by Di Mon.

Vretla took one look at Di Mon and decided that he was what she really wanted. She handed Hara her sword and went to greet Di Mon with an attitude that Horth would have understood better if the dignified liege of Monitum had been a sumptuous dinner encountered after a long fast.

"Wow," said Branst, staring with frank fascination. "Dad says it's either fight or — well, the other thing — when extremely Vrellish people get overflown. But I never believed him until now."

"Yes, but my liege-uncle isn't much good at being spontaneous," Tessitatt told Branst with laughter in her brown eyes. "So maybe you can help us out, Branst. Make friends, so we get her safely into Green Hearth, fast."

"Me?" Branst blurted.

Tessitatt put an arm around him to help give Vretla the idea, and kissed the side of his mouth as he turned towards her. Branst quickly forgot his surprise and kissed back. That was his downfall. Vretla switched her attention from the unreceptive Di Mon to the good-looking thirteen-year-old with his arm around another woman. Tessitatt smiled to show she did not mind sharing as Vretla extended a hand to touch Branst's hair, watching Tessitatt to make sure she kept looking friendly. It was Branst who flinched.

"She likes you," Tessitatt said, with glee at Branst's discomfort. "Don't be scared."

"I am not scared!" Branst insisted, taking a step clear of Tessitatt's embrace to concentrate on Vretla. "Nice, crazy, much-too-Vrellish person," he said, patting her shoulder.

She patted him back, amused.

"You're sure you want her in Green Hearth?" Branst called to Tessitatt as he coaxed her in that direction.

"Absolutely!" Tess assured him. "We know her — she's Vackal Vrel's daughter by a Red Reach *mekan'st*. Di Mon wanted Vackal to send her to court to act as Liege Vrel in his place, but Red Vrellish clans are pretty fiercely matrilineal concerning children, so it wasn't up to Vretla's sire and her maternal clan is superstitious about Lorel influences. We don't know why she's shown up now, or like this, but we're glad she's here!"

"Unfortunately specific memories won't regenerate along with the brain cells she's burned out," said Di Mon. "We'll probably never know what happened in Red Reach to prompt her to come."

Vretla leaned in to nuzzle Branst. He put up with it until she put a tongue in his ear. "Hey!" He batted at her. "Slow down!"

Vretla thrust a hand under Branst's belt and got rough about expressing her intentions. Horth felt concerned for his brother, since he didn't seem to be enjoying Vretla's advances as much as he enjoyed Alice's. Horth was grateful when Di Mon displaced Branst and took charge.

Vretla did not seem to mind either, even though Di Mon proved much better than Branst at frustrating her attempts to make an exhibition of her Vrellish lustiness in front of Demish spectators.

Relieved of the hazardous job, Branst fell in step beside Tessitatt. Horth noticed Tessitatt take his hand and Branst's close around hers. Then Green Pavilion swallowed them.

Hara stopped Horth from following with a hand on his shoulder.

"Your brother can take care of himself," said Hara. "And if he can't, it's not as if he won't be getting an education." She chuckled.

Horth stared after Branst, still worried. But on the whole it wasn't Vretla who was the danger. It was the way that Branst and Tessitatt behaved together. It seemed to Horth a lot like the way that Father was with Mother. Except Tessitatt didn't get jealous.

Horth returned to Black Pavilion with Hara.

They were greeted at the base of the stairs by an anxious errant.

"Captain!" he said, grabbing Hara's arm. "Liege Nersal's gone!" The alarm in his face made the skin on the back of Horth's neck bristle.

"Liege Nersal was angry about Lywulf," explained the errant. "He dismissed Gil from his service and he sent for the Nesaks. He let two of Beryl's retainers in to stay with her in the bedroom, and took a third one with him to the docks. He said he's gone to SanHome to fetch the priest that she wants."

Emotion pooled in Horth's chest, urging him to action — any action, just so long as there was something clear and obvious to do. But there were only words. Nothing but words, glancing off him, swirling around him.

He decided to go fetch Branst home.

Green Hearth let him in this time without an argument. He found Branst in Azure Lounge with Tessitatt. They were sitting together on a couch with a tray of refreshments set down nearby on a side table. A pot of tea was set out, partnered by mismatched cups of great antiquity that had been mended often. The warm smell of chamomile rose from their cups.

Tessitatt finished a nut she was chewing and took a gulp from her tea cup. Neither she nor Branst were wearing their swords. Tessitatt's stood in a floor rack and Branst's lay on the floor.

"So," Tessitatt said to Branst, with the air of someone resuming a conversation, "if you weren't afraid of Vretla, why be shy?" She cocked her head aside mischievously. "Are you a virgin?"

"I am not a virgin!" Branst protested vehemently.

"But you haven't got a Freedom Price," said Tessitatt.

"Neither do you!" he cried.

"That's different," said Tessitatt. "We Monatese are very picky about who we breed with."

"And Nersallians aren't?" he asked testily.

"Let me think," she said. "The Nersallian *kinf'stan* numbers at least a thousand while at last count the Monatese *kinf'stan* numbers — three."

"You don't have a *kinf'stan*," Branst protested. "That word applies only to Nersallians."

"My point, exactly."

"Now you aren't making any sense."

"That's only because you're ignorant," she told Branst. "*Kinf'stan* is the Nersallian adaptation of 'kin fold,' which is more or less an English word and used to be the general term for anyone empowered by blood right to challenge a liege for her title."

Tessitatt did not actually say 'her.' She did not say 'him,' either. She employed a common gender pronoun used in Vrellish dialect. Horth knew a bit about dialects, but the complexities of Gelack with regard to pronouns of all kinds was one of the reasons he was loath to risk talking in complete sentences.

"These days, of course," Tessitatt concluded, "the Nersallian *kinf'stan* have usurped the whole meaning of the word, because they are the most extreme example."

Branst twisted around in his seat to focus on her.

"I want you to have my baby!" he said urgently.

For three seconds, Tessitatt kept very still. Then she erupted into action to shove him away from her.

"Unlikely!" she snorted.

"Why?" Branst asked. "You like me! And our families are allies," he wheedled.

Tessitatt folded her arms. "Why should I even want the exercise, Branst Nersal? You're only thirteen!"

"But you need a Freedom Price, too, if you're going to fly seriously," Branst said.

"What makes you think I don't have one already?" asked Tess.

"Well," he said, "let's see. You haven't gone missing for months that I'm aware of. Also — no big announcements and genotyping parties. Dead giveaway."

Tessitatt rolled her eyes, leaned over and kissed Branst as thoroughly as Alice had earlier. When she drew back, she said. "Branst, I'll sleep with you. That might be the best way to help you get over the infatuation. But I'm not having your baby. Di Mon would dangle me out an airlock for even thinking about it!"

Branst stiffened. "But how could you ..."

"*Ferni,*" she said, with an effort to make it sound casual. "Monatese take *ferni* to prevent conception. There's nothing wrong with it. And don't give me any superstitious arguments about the Watching Dead. You know I don't believe in that. Not literally." She looked a bit uncomfortable. "My ancestors would understand, anyway."

Branst continued to look dismayed. "Don't you worry it might... that you'll never... or... "

"No," she said abruptly.

Branst swallowed, staring at her with a look of dawning misery.

"Branst," Tessitatt tried again, "you're *kinf'stan*. Having a child with you could mean putting House Monitum within a duel of becoming Nersallian, next generation. You want sex?

Good! It's time we got this infatuation consummated! But stop being so presumptuous about it! I'm not having your baby!"

Branst sprang up. "Come on Horth!" he said, suddenly. "Let's get out of here."

Branst swept up the Throat of Green Hearth so swiftly Horth had to run to keep up with him.

"You'd think being *kinf'stan* was like having a disease or something," Branst grumbled, as they passed onto Fountain Court. "I don't just want sex! I can get that on the Ava's Way with pocket money! I want to mix up our destinies. I want to be reborn Monatese!"

Horth gave up hope of getting Branst to talk with him about anything that day.

*　*　*

Black Hearth kept silent vigil in the reception room beneath Black Pavilion. Errants paced or took turns playing navigational games on a portable *nervecloth* screen that was set up for the occasion. Horth watched for a while, but none of the errants would play with him. They said it wasn't fair since he was highborn. That annoyed Horth. He had enjoyed the thrill of beating his elders at nav-games when he was still young enough for adult nobleborns to find it cute, instead of irritating.

Alice and two other house maids served refreshments and circulated to see everyone was comfortable. Alice hovered near Branst.

Cook declared, "I'm going to bed," twice, and actually did the third time.

No one talked about what might be happening, or what it might mean if Father brought a Nesak priest home with him.

Branst dragged a gym mat out of the nursery and dozed on the floor. Zrenyl left periodically to check on Beryl. Horth circulated restlessly between his brothers and Hara, never speaking or doing much of anything, but unable to settle down.

Eight hours after his departure, Father came down the spiral stairs with his sword on his hip and his face marked by the signature bruise marks of heavy *rel*-skimming.

With him came a man with Kene's black hair and green eyes, but not Kene's open, affectionate nature. This man had a hard mouth and a narrow glare. He wore no sword and was dressed in robes covered in strange symbols.

Relief greeted Hangst's arrival. The errants saluted. The commoners rose to their feet and bowed, the oldest one staggering with fatigue from the long vigil. Branst scrambled up off his pallet. Zrenyl cried, "Father!"

Horth launched himself forward.

Father caught Horth up in his arms and held him up to greet the stranger.

"This is *Zer* Sarn," he said. "Your mother's priest and uncle."

Hangst put Horth down again to clasp arms with Zrenyl. Branst hung back, looking uncertain.

"Your mother?" Father asked Zrenyl.

"As well as can be expected," Zrenyl assured him. He turned to greet their visitor. "She will be glad to see you, Your Highness."

"I go by *Zer*," the Nesak prince corrected Zrenyl. He smiled after he said it, not before or during. "I need no other title."

"Yes, *Zer*," said Zrenyl and lowered his head momentarily in a slow, deliberate nod, so unlike the fist-to-heart Nersallian salute in which both parties maintained eye contact.

Zer Sarn's eyes rested on Branst briefly, then on Horth for a bit longer. He smiled at Horth in the same calculated way he had smiled after speaking to Zrenyl. Then he scanned the room, and said, "The first thing we must do is get rid of the non-eternals."

A chill swept the room, so real Horth could have sworn that he felt the drop in temperature. The faces of the household staff lost color. Errants bristled. Alice shrank a step in

Branst's direction. Zrenyl looked stressed and Branst looked angry. Branst was inhaling to explode into what Horth felt certain would be angry words when Father preempted him, firmly.

"That is not how we do things here," Father told the Nesak.

There was a long, dreadful silence before *Zer* Sarn said, as coolly as if he had not just been thwarted, "Take me to your wife, Liege Nersal."

The word wife made Hara turn and march out. Everyone studiously ignored her departure and kept up the pretence of normalcy, except Branst, who loudly declared that he was going over to Green Hearth to beg for a guest room. But Branst didn't say it until after Father and *Zer* Sarn were out of earshot.

Horth went back to an empty bedroom and lay down, wishing Branst had stayed in Black Hearth with him.

Before he fell asleep, he decided that he wouldn't mind if father had to kill this Nesak relative.

— six months later —

Zrenyl whipped the covers off Horth's bed.

"I wouldn't wake him like that anymore!" said Branst, pausing in the act of doing up the complex lacework of his formal reception jacket.

Horth struck out, making Zrenyl drop the stolen blanket, and sprang to his feet on the bed, man-sized and naked from the waist up.

"Hey!" Zrenyl complained, shaking his stinging wrist. "Don't kill the messenger! It's Dad who wants us dressed for — Branst!" Zrenyl broke off, pointing. "Will you look at that!"

Horth's pajama pants were wet in front.

"So?" said Branst. "You never had one of those dream?"

"But he's barely eleven!"

Branst shrugged. "Vrellish highborns grow up fast. Like Vretla."

"Horth is not like Vretla!" said Zrenyl. "He's just a *rejak't*."

Horth punched. Zrenyl rocked back, but not quite fast enough.

"Why you brat!" Zrenyl touched a bloodied lip. "If you've messed up my formal clothes—!" Zrenyl made a snatch in Horth's direction. Horth rolled across the bed and sprang to his feet on the other side.

"You deserve a trouncing on the Octagon!" Horth's eldest brother threatened.

Branst made a rude noise. "Yeah? By you and which visiting champion? Face it, Zrenyl, Horth can beat you."

"Now I've got to wash and change!" complained Zrenyl. "So you get him dressed for Di Mon's big reception."

"Not happening," Branst told his brother. "I've got more reason to be on time than you do!"

"Tessitatt Monitum, I suppose," Zrenyl said disapprovingly. "She'll never marry you, Branst. She's too Vrellish."

"I don't want to get married!" Branst said, offended.

"Hah!" said. "You would marry her in an instant if she'd let you. Face it bro, beneath the court veneer you are all Nesak!"

"You're the Nesak!" Branst yelled at Zrenyl's departing back. The door closed. Frowning, Branst turned to assess the unwelcome task he had inherited.

Horth got down off the bed to wait for directions. He could dress himself, of course, but not in a manner acceptable for a formal court reception. He was still too childish to master that, although he had shot up taller than Branst in the last month and his bare chest was hard-muscled.

"I will not be late," Branst muttered, unhappily. Then an idea occurred to him. "I'll get Alice to do it!"

"Mother," Horth warned. The strangeness of his new, very deep voice, had set his fluency with words back a year or two.

"What Mother doesn't know can't hurt our character development," said Branst and sprinted out the door.

Alice arrived looking breathless, with Branst's arm around her waist and her hair disordered. Horth could smell her sexual arousal.

"Dress your brother, Master Branst?" Alice faltered, looking Horth up and down with trepidation.

Branst kissed her for courage. "You can do it!" he said, and turned her around to face his looming, 'little' brother. "Oh, I know," Branst admitted. "He looks all grim and grown up, but he's still just a kid. Honest!"

Branst snatched clothes out of Horth's closet. "Skip his shower," he advised Alice, heaping the clothes on Horth's unmade bed. "Just make sure his jacket is laced up and his pants aren't wrinkled."

"I don't know," Alice fretted.

"I can't wait," Branst told her, snatching up the last of his own accessories and buckling on his sword. "Tessitatt's expecting me."

Alice looked as if she were about to cry, even as she hung on every word Branst uttered. The power of her attraction seemed to radiate from her. Branst's hand stroked down her back as he left, and she shuddered.

Horth caught his own breath, shaken by the strange new feelings of excitement that tormented him in unexpected situations. Like this one.

Branst disappeared out the door.

Alice took a deep breath and turned to Horth, the flush on her cheeks still prominent.

Horth only meant to inhale deeply to help him find his balance. He never remembered deciding to do something different. But between one moment and the next, he had Alice in his arms.

She gave a shriek, which bothered him, but she was so easy to control it seemed she didn't mind, somehow. A twist and push knocked her onto the bed beneath him. He knew what he wanted — and it didn't require clothes. He started trying to tear her uniform off.

Alice screamed louder. She pushed her arms against his bare chest without making much of an impression. She felt good and she smelled right. The problem of getting her clothes off became urgent. Horth barely registered her screaming except as an irritation he might have stopped by clamping his hand over her mouth, if his hands were not already fully occupied.

He did not hear *Zer* Sarn come in behind him. His senses were swamped. He did not anticipate a thing until he was yanked up by a pair of strong hands.

Heaved clear of Alice, Horth struck a dresser and scrambled up, ready for violence.

"Vrellish animal!" *Zer* Sarn roared in his sonorous voice. The sound boomed around the room like a gong. "Real Nesaks do not commit the Error of Debasement!"

Horth blinked, too shocked to get air back into his lungs. He was, of course, well aware of Mother's attitude to breeding down. Until that moment, however, he had never thought of the issue as something that personally concerned him. Now he felt ashamed to be caught with Alice by *Zer* Sarn, and distressed by his loss of control. At the same time, Alice's look of betrayed trust condemned him on entirely different grounds. She sat bolt upright on the bed, clutching at her open pants and pale with alarm.

Clearly, he had done something very wrong.

Alice overcame her horror long enough to scramble off the bed and skitter past the glowering Nesak and out the door.

Horth went after her, wanting to fix what had gone wrong.

Mother came out of her bedroom on her way to the nursery to tend her plants and saw Alice streak past. It surprised her to see her youngest son in pursuit, and she cried "Horth!" in the sharp, crisp voice she used when she meant business.

Horth stopped. Between one breath and the next, he suddenly saw his mother as a full-figured woman with a straight carriage, heart-shaped face and wide green eyes. His nostrils flared and his jaw locked, hands fisted. He narrowed his eyes, drawing on other feelings about her to help thrust aside the new, unwelcome awareness.

Mother came quickly towards him, her sharpness derailed by the distress she read in his behavior.

"What is it?" she asked, reaching for him.

Horth flinched away from her.

"Horth?" she said, sounding concerned.

Zer Sarn came out of Horth's bedroom. "He was indulging himself with one of the Black Hearth commoners," he said coldly. "But his soul is in no danger of a bad rebirth. I put a stop to it before it went that far."

Horth barely heard. He was rocked to the core of his confidence. If this was what it meant to be Vrellish, he did not want to continue with his current incarnation. He would not live at the mercy of such a powerful impulse!

Mother kept her Nesak blade by her bedside. She said it was the road to freedom for trapped souls. The knife was as long as a baby's arm with a double-edged blade etched in *rel* symbols, that symbolized the cycle of rebirth awaiting unsullied souls.

He tore into his parents' bedroom with his mother in pursuit. But once he snatched the knife up, he felt better. He could kill himself with it and get reborn again, if necessary. The Watching Dead would understand and forgive him for what happened with Alice. Once he knew it was as simple as that, he felt calm enough to think about it harder.

Mother rushed into the room and froze.

"Horth!" she gasped. "No! It isn't important enough for that!"

She looked so frightened that he felt bad. But he didn't want to put the knife down. Holding it helped him to think better.

Zer Sarn came in behind her. Horth narrowed his eyes at the Nesak priest, his thin nostrils flaring.

Mother turned around. "Please," she begged. "Leave this to me, Uncle."

"I told you that Branst was debasing himself with a servant," the priest reproached her. "And you did nothing. Now the contagion is spreading. You must obtain permission from your husband for them to go to SanHome to find wives as soon as possible. Or their souls will be imperiled."

Mother looked strained. "I am trying to convince their father, honored uncle and great *zer*," she pleaded. "Zrenyl has asked, too. And Hangst has not said no to him, entirely. I cannot achieve more! Now, please, leave me alone with my son. Just this once?"

Zer Sarn glared but she stood her ground. He gave in at last, his face stamped in a pinched expression, and left the room.

Horth relaxed immediately. He was never in a room with *Zer* Sarn without feeling the fine hairs on the back of his neck stiffen.

"Give me the spirit knife, Horth, please?" Mother begged him, extending her slim, white hand.

Horth did not know how to tell her that he just wanted to hold it for a while, so he put the knife down on her dressing table.

"Thank you, my ancestors!" exclaimed Beryl, nearly fainting.

Horth helped her into her favorite armchair, feeling awkward. She used to seem so powerful to him. Now her trembling troubled him. She clasped his corded, man's hand in her own little white one, and held on. He knelt by her knee as he often did when she recited Nesak stories to him and his brothers.

"I have been watching you grow up, Horth," she said. "I've seen what your Vrellish blood puts you through. But remember there is no harm in being Vrellish that can't be overcome. I have told you many times about the Vrellish Error."

Horth nodded. He had memorized a great deal of the Nesak canon, because it was easier for him to memorize and recite words than to produce original sentences. There were four errors. He thought his way through the first three: the Error of Debasement, which meant breeding with commoners; the Lorel Error, that covered putting too much faith in reason as a means to prevent the misuse of banned sciences; and the *Pol* Error, sometimes known as *Okal Lumens*, a Demish branch of *Okal Rel* that worships the *pol* virtues of kindness and compassion, and placed too much faith in literature's ability to guide mankind.

"Tell me about the Vrellish Error," said Horth's mother.

Horth found his place, mentally, and recited. "The Vrellish Error is also known as the *Rel* Error, because the Vrellish pursue what is *rel* and dismiss everything *pol*. Those who stray down this path become Wild Souls who indulge all their lusts. Some Vrellish can even be honorable, in space and in duels, although never in marriage."

Horth noticed Mother look away, and speeded up. "Their bodies suit their passions, making them fierce fighters who are quick to mature. Such souls may live out many lives in this condition, but in the end they exceed the patience of the Watching Dead and suffer soul death if they cannot conquer their excesses in one hard life, and be reborn less Vrellish in the next one."

Beryl stroked Horth's blue-black hair. "You see?" she said. "The Vrellish are redeemable. Vrellish blood can even make you a great warrior. And what harm can there be in any soul as honest as yours?" She touched his face. "Sex is nothing to be ashamed of," she told her son. "It is the answer to death. The way to bring new life to Waiting Souls. Such urges are sacred. You must simply be careful about who you share yourself with, because your soul may follow your error into the next generation."

Horth was not sure he understood but he felt calmer.

"Good," said Beryl, getting up and brushing down the pleats of the dress she was wearing. "Now come along and let me get you out of those pajamas."

Horth followed her back to his bedroom where Mother dressed him with great skill, although she herself would never put on the courtly clothes required for the kind of Demish-influenced event he was supposed to attend at Green Hearth.

"Only eleven," she said when she was finished, and sighed as if she feared the Vrellish Error might prove too potent. Her fingers lingered on the side of his dress jacket that featured her side of his inheritance.

"All Nesaks have some Vrellish blood, you know," she said, tracing a red thread in her family pattern. "San herself was as lusty as any Vrellish woman, but she kept to her husband and bore him the twelve sons who founded the royal lines of SanHome." Her fingers lifted, crossed his chest, and settled on the black and red pattern on the other side of his dress jacket. "There," she said. "Now you are ready for Di Mon's reception."

Horth did not want to go to the reception. Tessitatt would be there, and Branst would be fawning all over her. Di Mon would be trying to get the Vrellish people, like Father, to mix politely with the Demish guests who badly outnumbered them. Zrenyl would spend the whole time muttering things under his breath about both Vrellish and Demish excesses that echoed Mother's stories of the Errors. And all of it would blur in a senseless roar of conversations assaulting him from all directions.

Reciting the Errors was all the talking and thinking he needed for at least another twenty-four hours.

Nonetheless, Horth was striding through the entrance hall, resigned to making his appearance at the reception next door in Green Hearth, when Hara burst out of the errants' barracks on one side of the hall behind him.

"Hor-r-r-th!" he heard her grind out as he spun around. She was flanked by a couple of the errants under her command, the woman smirking and the man looking as severe as Hara.

"Come with me," Hara ordered.

Hara led him through a barrack's door, down a corridor, and into a small common room where six servants were gathered around Alice, who sat huddled in the arms of the Black Hearth cook, crying her eyes out.

"Right, girl," Hara said to Alice. "Tell us what happened."

Alice swallowed, struck mute by the intense attention.

Cook got up, looking shaky, and faced Horth. Her nervousness puzzled him. He didn't see why Cook had any reason to be nervous, unless it was because he had grown so much bigger and stronger since his last raid on the kitchen.

"Master Horth ... tried to rape Alice," Cook declared, stuttering over the words.

Horth frowned. He knew what the word rape meant, and he didn't like being accused of it.

"Hey, and he's only eleven!" The female errant, Kendi, broke the silence, sounding as if she was proud of him.

"That's enough!" Hara snapped. "Horth," she demanded, "what did you do wrong?"

The question engaged Horth because that was exactly what he was trying to figure out. *Zer* Sarn had called him a Vrellish animal. Mother talked about the Vrellish Error. Cook and Hara clearly felt he had messed up, but rape was too severe a charge in Horth's opinion. He would never have hurt Alice. At least, he didn't think he would have.

Suddenly it occurred to him that only one person knew for sure how gravely his misconduct should be judged.

"Ask Alice," he told Hara.

Kendi blurted a laugh. Hara snapped her fist into the errant's face to remind her who was in charge. Kendi staggered into a side table that spilled its contents on the floor.

"Ask Alice, is it?" said Hara. "Good idea. You do that, Horth Nersal. Right now. And you tell him, Alice. Loud and clear. In words — I suggest — of no more than three syllables! Or you can bet it's going to happen again. That is, if you are still around once Liege Nersal finds out you have been sleeping with Branst, which is probably what gave Horth the idea!"

Alice shuddered like a *rel*-ship about to shatter. "Captain Hara, I— "

"Save it for Liege Nersal," Hara rapped back at her with a scowl. "But first, you make it clear to Horth, here, what he's done wrong." She glowered. "Do a good job of that and I'll put in a good word for you, if you think you can remember, in the future, not to seduce hearth-sons you have no right to breed with."

"I— " Alice began, going white, and decided against arguing the point with Hara. "I'll talk to Master Horth," she forced out.

Everyone filed out except Hara who eyed Horth with one of her no-nonsense stares and said, "Hands off! Remember."

Horth nodded, confident that would not be a problem. Alice's distress annoyed him now as much as her antics with Branst had stimulated him earlier. He found himself thinking, instead, about the smirking female errant, Kendi, who had winked at him as she filed past dabbing the blood on her mouth.

Alice sat down again on the couch. "L-Listen, Master Horth," she said, twisting her hands in her lap. "You frightened me. A lot." She gulped.

Horth shrugged. He didn't see how that was his fault.

"I g-guess you don't have, um, a lot of experience? With women." Alice ventured.

"No," said Horth.

Alice giggled a little hysterically. "I'm sorry," she said, immediately. "It's just — you are so frank!" She inhaled, pulled herself together as best she could, and said, "I didn't want to have sex with you."

"You do it with Branst," said Horth, relying on the idiom he'd picked up in the errants' barracks.

Alice turned a fascinating scarlet color. "Oh, gods! And it is going to come to your father's attention now, because of this incident!" She seemed to have tied herself in knots.

Horth wanted to let her know he had not meant to get her and Branst in trouble, but the ideas flew around in his head without an organizing principle to help him get them out. Then it was too late, because Alice was smiling at him, trying to look confident.

"You don't understand much about women, do you?" she said. "I mean real women. Not Vrellish ones like that errant, Kendi, who thinks being over-sexed at eleven is cute! Or — or women like, like —Tessitat Monitum!" Alice burst into tears and had to take a minute to master herself before she could continue. "Ordinary women don't always feel the same way about... well, what you wanted to do with me... as men do. Oh, listen, just don't force yourself on an inferior. That makes sense, doesn't it? Even to someone as Vrellish as you?" She ended in a snappish tone.

Horth nodded. He understood Alice was not willing to behave, with him, the way she did with Branst. That clarified everything. There were things that were reasonable to demand of an inferior and things that were not.

That settled, Horth found himself dejected and completely unmotivated to attend Di Mon's reception. He made his way back to the entrance hall in a brooding frame of mind, got as far as the doors that opened onto Fountain Court, and bolted back into Black Hearth, heading for the Octagon where he could work off his bruised and restless feelings with exercise.

Kendi followed him down there. She strolled onto the practice floor on Black Wedge, watched him work out for a while, then pulled a blunt-ended practice sword off a rack and joined him for a bout.

Horth found himself immediately distracted. She was also an inferior, of course. But there was no doubt in his mind that she was far from unwilling to teach him more than fencing moves.

She probed dangerously with her point at first, which helped Horth to focus. Neither of them had headgear on, which was not uncommon even for friendly sparring matches between Nersallians, but more serious than a straight workout.

She was good enough that he had to pay attention. But when they closed for the first time, blades caught too close to wield, he got a nose full of her sex smell, and he half-forgot what they were doing with their swords. Fortunately, the impact was mutual.

They slid their blades together, up and down, trying to disengage, but as long as they stayed close, the blades were locked. Horth then pushed her blade slowly outwards, to his left, away from both of them, leaving their bodies open and the heat of their attraction pulling them inward like a magnet.

Horth was faintly alarmed at his giddiness, but unwilling to end the good feelings running riot in his spellbound body.

This time it was Kendi who got yanked clear, by Hara. Kendi caught her breath but failed to recover in time to defend herself from Hara's punch. She went down on her bottom with a broken nose. Her sword clattered on the floor and rolled away.

"Think with your head, not your mouth!" Hara told Kendi, using the vulgar word for a Vrellish woman's muscular, lower mouth. "No female errant messes with the sons of her liege house unless she's earned her liege's blessing to breed up!"

Kendi snorted angrily and spat blood, but she didn't get up. "I wasn't going to get pregnant by him!" she defended herself to her captain.

Hara folded her arms. "Whoever plans to get pregnant?" she threw back. "But it's not up to you, is it?" Her expression became unforgiving. "Or are you one of those who thwart the Waiting Dead with *ferni*?"

"No!" Kendi hotly defended her honor. "I just didn't think—"

"Exactly!" exclaimed Hara. Then relented, reached down and pulled Kendi up to her feet again. "Have Narous see to the nose if it's broken," she ordered.

"I didn't do anything," Kendi defended herself, the hand over her nose muffling her voice a little. "We were just sparring."

"Uh huh," said Hara skeptically. "Well, no harm's done so we'll leave it at that. You, however," she said to Horth, "are coming with me. You need an education."

* * *

Hara took Horth to a courtesan den on the other side of UnderGelion, in a freehold district run by commoners who derived their protection from the patronage of important clients.

"Captain Hara," she was greeted by their smiling hostess. "Good to see you again."

"This is Horth Nersal," said Hara, laying her palm on Horth's shoulder. "He's only eleven, but as you can see he is too grown up to remain a virgin without causing trouble."

"I see what you mean," said the woman, acknowledging Horth with an easy smile that was free of the smirking jocularity that made Horth's predicament embarrassing. She eased a sheet of golden hair over one shoulder. "Liz is good with beginners," she decided. "And she copes well enough with Vrellish customers. Third door on the left," she concluded, pointing.

Hara gave Horth a reassuring pat on the back and a slight push in the right direction. "Go on," she told him. "The girl you find inside will make it easy and there'll be no fertility issues to interfere. All courtesans at Eva's are sterile."

Something irked Horth about that idea. He had an instinctive feeling that sex ought to be bound up with at least the possibility of complications, and made an unwelcome but involuntary comparison with herd animals, raised on Tark, that were neutered for the convenience of others.

"Is Terril free?" Hara asked, eyes sheering off to pan the small crowd of about twenty patrons, entertainers and novices on the den's central floor, called the Patron's Round.

"No, I'm afraid he's engaged," said their hostess. "But let me introduce you to an alternative selection."

With Hara gone, Horth decided seeking Liz would be better than standing around looking out of place.

He crossed the Patron's Round in quick strides, went down the corridor indicated and was dutifully headed for the third door when he heard raised voices coming from one of the rooms he was passing.

Horth could tell by the pronouns that leapt out at him that the disputants were Sevolites of unequal classes. The nobleborn woman was Vrellish and the man was a Demish highborn.

He had no trouble identifying the sound of a sword being drawn, either. On impulse, Horth drew his own sword and went through the door. He knew it was stupid, but somehow it felt infinitely easier than solving the social problem of how to relate to a female courtesan.

Inside, Horth found a single Vrellish woman confronting three Silver Demish men, with the courtesan who had been entertaining her cowering well back, out of harm's way. The woman was half dressed, wearing only underpants beneath a loose tunic with a deep V-neck that revealed slices of her small, firm breasts.

The Demish highborn was backed up by a pair of his liveried errants. Both errants had bared their swords, presumably to address the woman's challenge, within challenge class, on behalf of their superior. Except that two on one was not honorable.

The Vrellish woman had shut up and seemed to be having second thoughts about clearing her sword under the circumstances. But the whole dynamic changed the moment Horth entered the room with his sword drawn.

The Demish highborn pivoted, covered by one of his errants while the second kept his attention on the Vrellish woman.

"Nersal?" the Demish highborn said, sounding puzzled. He devoured the details encoded in the braid on Horth's formal jacket in a gulp, and experimented with a friendly manner. "One of Liege Nersal's half-Nesak sons, it would appear. Branst, is it?"

"Horth," said Horth.

"Horth? But Horth is eleven years — uh, well," the Demish man thought better of completing that thought. "In any case, I am Evan Pond, vassal to Liege D'Forest of Lion Reach. My dispute with Liege Thris, here, is a matter of trade business and none of your family's affair. You have no cause to interfere, young man."

"No!" Liege Thris cried excitedly, shifting her feet. The point of her sword twitched back and forth across a narrow field equidistant from the two Demish errants opposing her. The energy she gave off was intoxicating and the cloth of her tunic quivered with her rapid breaths. "Stay!" she commanded him. "If they want a fight, I need a Vrellish judge of honor present!"

"This is ridiculous!" Evan Pond said fussily. "No stake has been declared. No duel is at issue. You drew your sword, not us!"

"Because you meant to have your men here rough me up," said Nanns Thris. "You couldn't bully me in space, so you've decided to take care of it at court!"

"I have never heard such unbecoming twaddle from a woman!" cried Eval Pond, puffing up with indignation. "I sought you out to offer you one last chance to see reason —

short of any kind of violence — out of consideration for the fact you are a woman, even if you are a Vrellish one."

"Ha!" Nanns Thris barked a rude laugh. "Go on! Convince me you would treat me better if I wore a skirt and kept my mouth shut!"

Her vulgar slang choice of the word for mouth made Lord Pond react as if stung by a particularly nasty bug. He went red in the face as he reached for his own sword.

Horth addressed that move with an attack he expected to be blocked by Lord Pond. And it was. But Horth moved so fast that his Demish peer made a rapid transition from fury to white-faced shock.

Everyone froze.

"This is a... misunderstanding," Lord Pond got out, with faltering nerve as he met Horth's eyes over their crossed weapons.

Horth jerked his head in the direction of the door.

Lord Pond took a step and edged around in that direction, deciding not to pursue the argument with swords. "I know what this is about," he blustered. "She's taking advantage of you by making a display of herself."

"I was busy with Terril, here, when you barged in!" Thris interrupted, less nervous and more strident with each retreating step the Demish Highlord took.

Lord Pond looked — involuntarily — at the male courtesan who responded with a weak smile from the back of the room.

"My liege, Prince H'Us, will see your father hears of this!" Lord Pond got in a parting shot at Horth. Then he sheathed his sword with a flourish and waved his errants out the door.

"We are not finished, madam!" he fired at Liege Thris before he swept out.

Horth and Thris remained staring at each other for two seconds. Then they both put up their swords.

She said, "Thanks." Her gray eyes narrowed. "How old did Pond say you are?"

Horth didn't care much for that question. He sheathed his sword with what he hoped was an entirely adult display of no-nonsense competence.

"Will you be wanting me to stay, Your Grace?" the courtesan asked insightfully, and took the answering hand wiggle from Thris as a dismissal. She seemed to have eyes only for Horth.

When the courtesan had let himself out, Nanns This put her hands on her narrow hips and said, "I like your style, Black Hearth. You nearly made Pond mess himself."

Horth indulged in a spontaneous grin. He was noticing something about himself and women. He responded best to the ones who looked like they were interested in sex.

Thris had put her sword away but was still dressed in only her tunic and underwear. She stepped closer slowly, keeping an eye on his reactions in case she had misread his own receptivity.

Horth's pulse quickened. He felt her heat as she slid one foot between his. He was male. She was female. Awareness of that one critical issue soaked his overloaded senses.

He remembered Hara warning him about accepting the advances of social inferiors, but it was like a distant voice crying from a hilltop.

They came together with urgency. His sword belt got in the way. She laughed and waited for him to shed it himself, with less than his usual dexterity, before she helped undress him from the waist down. She had little left, herself, to shed.

Horth experienced sex for the first time in a molten blur too fierce to call pleasure. It was over before he knew what had happened. His head was pounding with the sheer force of his pounding heart that served him well in a *rel*-ship under high G's but was over-powered for the circumstances. He saw spots before his eyes and had to collapse on the mattress embedded in the floor, where they had wound up.

Thris lay on his chest, breathing heavily. Then she started undoing the jacket they had not waited to get off him. She took her time now, caressing him as she went. The sensations were easier to bear and more like pleasure. By the time she got around to suggesting things, physically, that he wasn't sure he wanted to do, he was ready for sex again. But he asserted his preference for sticking to basics with force. She was happy enough to accommodate him. The low sounds she made in her throat as they merged stroked his nerves like myriad electric hands. She wrapped her legs around his back and sunk her teeth into his shoulder hard enough to force him to fight back as they made love.

They rolled back and forth across the sunken mattress, chests pounding hard against each other, boiling in a hot bath of lust. Horth voiced a wordless cry as he climaxed, and was swallowed by close-crowding darkness as his heart seemed to drown him in the pounding of his own blood.

He came to again almost instantly and surged to his feet, panting with surprise and the aftermath of his excitement. Sanity restored, he felt he'd had enough for one session. He needed a moment to sort his reactions out and think about what he'd done. With a shake to dispel the feeling of intoxication that still clung to him, he went looking for his shed clothes.

Liege Thris of Spiral Hall gave a throaty chuckle as she watched from where she sprawled, completely naked, on the mattress of the sunken bed on the floor. She was muscular and narrow-hipped, with smaller breasts than Alice. Her genital mound was more prominent than a commoner's, however, and her anatomy proportionally enhanced. It was widely believed among the Vrellish that the average female could wear out two or three males before she would be sated herself. Horth was more inclined to believe it now, given his experience.

"So," said Thris, while Horth was lacing up his dress jacket with slightly shaky hands. "You are Horth of Black Hearth. The Vrellish one of the Nesak litter, I've heard." She smiled at him smugly. "Bit inhibited like most Nersallians, of course. But worth teaching."

She shifted up on an elbow. "I'm Nanns, Liege of Thris. That's a trading house based out of Spiral Hall. You might have heard of Thris. We're known for our wine exports."

She expected him to be impressed. But the threat of conversation had not dawned on him until now. Panic struck him dumb.

Hara saved him by bursting in the door.

"Gods, Horth!" she exclaimed, with a sweep of her arm that invited the Waiting Dead to share her frustration. "What do I have to do? Supervise you! Courtesan, boy! I said a courtesan."

Thris scuttled to her feet and snatched up her sword, stark naked.

"Don't tempt me," Hara said between her teeth, looking dangerous.

Thris took in Hara's house braid and lowered the sword again carefully.

"Get dressed and go home," Hara told the other woman in a curt tone. She cut an imposing figure, her feet planted wide and her arms set akimbo, the insignia of her captaincy bold on her breast, above the crimson claw marks of the dragon that were known throughout the empire as the symbol of House Nersal.

Thris decided to be nonchalant. "Stay loose, Black Hearth," she told Hara. "I haven't done your liege-son any harm."

Hara made a grunting sound. "We'll see about that, Spiral Hall."

Thris shrugged. She pulled on the bare minimal required for decency, stuffing the rest of her clothes in a pocket of her traveling cloak. The last thing she did was strap on her sword.

"Later," she said to Horth with a smile that he could not help returning.

Hara strode over to Horth when Thris was gone and cuffed him across the temple with a half-fisted hand. "What did I tell you about staying clear of lusty Vrellish nobleborns!"

Horth did not like getting hit. He put up with it because it came from Hara.

"Let's go home before you get into any more trouble," she railed at him, "and hope that glutton isn't fertile!"

Horth had entirely forgotten about the breeding issue. But he felt smugly pleased, at the same time, that it was possible he might have solved his Freedom Price problem before either Branst or Zrenyl.

Despite the smug element to his reaction, he managed to maintain a chagrined silence all the way home. When he got there, he did something unusual for him in the middle of the morning and went back to bed for a glorious nap. He had never slept better.

Hours later, towards the end of day cycle, he was woken by the sound of Branst entering the bedroom.

"You awake?" Branst asked, coming over to sit on the side of Horth's bed.

Horth sat up. He had been warm under the covers, but the air in the room was pleasantly cool on his bare chest.

"Tessitatt spent the whole reception with me!" Branst told Horth in a low voice, pumped full of excitement.

Horth remembered something more important. "Alice," he said.

"Alice?" Branst echoed, puzzled.

"I frightened her," Horth said carefully, in his deep voice.

Branst blinked at him, still puzzled. Then, slowly, he looked distressed. "Is she... all right?"

Zrenyl barged in and turned up the lights with a quick stroke of a *nervecloth* panel.

"You're in trouble!" he crowed at Branst. "Father wants to see you in his bedroom. Right away."

Branst sprang up off the bed and headed out the door, a look of instant dread on his face.

Zrenyl went after him.

By the time Horth caught up, Branst was already confronting both their parents in the portion of the master bedroom where Mother had set up a bit of a parlor. Alice was not there. Neither was *Zer* Sarn, which Horth appreciated.

"Send her away?" Branst was saying, hotly. "Why?"

"She seduced you of her own free will," Father said. He stood very straight, as he always did, as adamant and unmoved as the marble walls of Fountain Court.

"It's not fair!" cried Branst.

"And whose fault is that?" Zrenyl said sternly, "You know how Mother feels about commoners, particularly the risk of having children with them! And you know father doesn't sterilize Nersallian domestics like the Demish do, or indulge them like the Monatese, either. What did you think was going to happen?"

"Alice is pregnant?" Branst asked, looking stunned and baffled.

"The point is," Father said, "that she could have been." He paused. "Couldn't she?"

"Um," said Branst, the anger draining out of him to be replaced by a look of guilty dread.

"Branst!" Zrenyl exclaimed. "You didn't. Not *ferni*!"

"No!" Branst protested and looked down as he mumbled. "There are other ways. Things you can buy on the Ava's Way." He looked up with cheeks burning. "I made sure that Alice wouldn't get pregnant! I wasn't child-gifting without family permission!"

"Oh, Branst," Mother said, in a half-swallowed, disappointed tone of voice.

Branst's bravado wilted. "I'm sorry," he said.

"Will you take responsibility?" Father asked him.

Branst went a shade paler. "Responsibility?" he asked shakily.

"If Alice is to blame," Father told him, "she must leave. If you are, then you must be disciplined."

"Three lashes on Black Wedge with the screens down," Zrenyl told his brother pompously. "In a whipping frame — just like a criminal."

Zrenyl, Horth decided, was jealous because he hadn't had a girl yet himself. Mother and Father couldn't agree on how to arrange for his Freedom Price, and he was too susceptible to Mother's feelings about such things to let Hara take him to a place like Den Eva's.

"W-What would happen to Alice if... " Branst faltered.

"That's not the point," Hangst said firmly. "What matters is which of you is responsible. That person is the one who should be punished."

"Oh please, send the creature away!" despaired Mother.

"Why do you think we have urges?" Zrenyl took it upon himself to lecture Branst. "There's a reason! When you go having sex without even the chance of conception you cheat the Waiting Dead!"

Branst turned on Zrenyl in a temper, "You find me one errant in Green Hearth who doesn't cheat one way or the other and— "

"Exactly!" Mother cried in a sharp voice, as if Branst had hurt her. She rose to her feet in a tower of moral grandeur, her green eyes blazing at her strayed middle son. "Errants! Non-eternals. Soulless nobleborns!"

With that, Mother turned on her heels and retired deeper into the bedroom to go lie down.

Father followed her with his eyes a moment, clearly concerned.

Zrenyl and Branst were still arguing.

"You should never sleep with any woman you aren't willing to sire a child by!" Zrenyl shouted. "It's an insult to her!"

"Oh, and you're worried about me insulting Alice, are you?" Branst hurled back.

"That's enough!" Father exclaimed. "Branst — will you take responsibility or not?"

Branst quailed. He knew he ought to, but he was afraid. Horth could see that. But three lashes on Black Wedge would be better than what Alice would face if she was turned out. Commoners died on Gelion without a family to shelter them.

For a moment Horth was certain Branst was going to spare his back and doom Alice. Then Branst's green eyes met Horth's steady gray ones, and Horth knew his brother could not live with himself if he did that.

"I will take the lashes," Branst said, sounding hoarse.

Father put a hand on Branst's shoulder and squeezed. "Tomorrow," he said. "Now go back to bed."

Father called Horth back as he made to follow Branst and Zrenyl out the door.

Anticipating a sentence of three lashes on Black Wedge for his own misconduct at Den Eva's, Horth waited for his father to pass judgment.

"I have heard about Liege Thris of Spiral Hall," Hangst, liege of Nersal, told Horth in a low voice, and checked over one shoulder to be sure that Mother had not heard before he went on. "Are you taking *ferni*?" Hangst asked.

"No, Father," said Horth.

Father inhaled with a measure of relief and the sense of one danger being bypassed at the cost of running smack into another. "Have you thought, then, about what the woman wants?"

"No," Horth admitted.

"Come with me," said Hangst, and led the way out of Black Hearth and across Fountain Court to Green Hearth, next door.

Di Mon received them in Azure Lounge.

"I'll be blunt," Hangst began.

Di Mon smiled. "You usually are."

Both Horth and his father sat down. Di Mon remained on his feet, but he leaned comfortably against the side of the

couch facing them. None of them were wearing swords. Di
Mon was dressed casually in a quilted jacket for an evening
at home. Hangst's attire was equally casual, and Horth was
wearing nothing over his pajamas but a traveling cloak
donned in the Black Hearth entrance hall. He wished he had
asked for the time to dress himself properly, now. He didn't
like feeling scruffy under the circumstances.

"Horth has just been seduced by a Spiral Hall woman
named Nanns Thris," Hangst began. "A pregnancy is possible." He looked at Horth. "I don't know if an on-going relationship is likely or not."

Horth had not thought that far.

"In any case," Hangst carried on, never surprised by
Horth's silences, "I would like your opinion of the woman's
honor. I do not know enough about Spiral Hall."

Di Mon was silent for a moment. Then he straightened up,
moved away from the couch, and poured himself a drink of
Monatese whiskey before he came to sit down. The drink in
his glass was a dusky green hue.

"Nanns Thris is an opportunistic trader," said Di Mon.
"For eighteen months now, she has been running shipments
of her wine to stations in Lion House Reach that have an
honor bond with Evan Pond. She has no right of trade
acknowledged by the Demish, which makes her a pirate in
their eyes. Silver Hearth took out one of her freighters, en
route, when it refused to turn back, and since the freighter
was destroyed there is an open question — even in Demish
terms — of which side has committed the greater wrong.
Thris tried to appeal to Vretla Vrel at last night's reception, to
take it to a duel on the Octagon. Something," Di Mon added
in a steely tone, "that I will not allow."

"Because your fledgling Liege Vrel is too young?" Hangst
asked.

"Because she is too valuable to risk over every petty
shakeup Spiral Hall stirs up!" Di Mon betrayed his temper
briefly, and put his drink down on a side table. "Gods,

Hangst!" he exclaimed when that was done. "Isn't it obvious what Thris will try to use Horth for? She'll get pregnant first. Then she'll trick Pond into accepting her challenge, out of challenge class, or set him up in some other way that will only work if she can field a highborn champion. Pond will feel complacent and might agree to something unwise to get the question of the destroyed freighter settled under Sword Law. Then she'll substitute Horth, by right of paternity, making sure it is his life that she risks and not her own. She has a keen reputation for trade, but not much of a record on the challenge floor. That's why she tried to get Vretla involved." Di Mon frowned. "All in all, I'd say Thris suffered a very convenient bout of ungovernable lust at Den Eva's."

Hangst looked at Horth. "What Di Mon has just explained," he said, speaking slowly and carefully. "Is that Liege Thris may be trying to get pregnant in order to command your sword on her behalf in a trade dispute."

"The freighter," Horth said to prove that he could listen. He had decided Thris was right. The Demish had no right to shatter her freighter. Although he was dimly aware that his opinion might be influenced by heady memories.

Hangst nodded. "That's right. Horth, I know you want a Freedom Price as much as Branst or Zrenyl so you can become a *relsha* with the fleet. But you are only eleven, despite your maturity in some things. Do not gamble with your life too lightly. If you continue to have sex with this woman, you may face your first serious challenge before you see your Freedom Price born. Do you understand the risk?"

Much too glibly, Horth said, "I understand."

"All right," said Hangst, and stood up. "Understand this, both of you." He looked first at Horth and then Di Mon. "If Horth lets himself be drawn into this challenge, it is Horth who will fight it. Not myself, nor either of his brothers or my fem-kin." Fem-kin was the term for Hangst's sisters, aunts, and their respective broods, which encompassed the more conventional outlines of a family unit among the Vrellish, who were matrilineal. "If Horth insists on provoking adult trouble," Hangst concluded, "he will have to live with the consequences. But," Hangst added fiercely, "if Nanns Thris gets pregnant by my son, the child had better be born alive and stay that way! Or she will answer for it to the *kinf'stan*. And you may advise Liege Thris not to expect me to gift my grandchild to her free and clear, either. Black Hearth will never waive challenge rights. Least of all to her kind. We have nobleborn relations hungry for the sort of territory that Thris owns and better able to help her people fight calcified Demish trading rights, for that matter!"

"Hangst!" Di Mon was aghast. "What are you playing at! Do you want to provoke the Demish and Spiral Hall? Both at once!"

Horth could feel his father's anger lying in wait for the right excuse to fetch it forth: old, compressed, and cold as bedrock. "I want," Hangst said slowly, "to make it clear how dangerous I can be when provoked."

* * *

Spiral Hall was a city in a bottle, and the bottle was the base of the Citadel below the Octagon and Fountain Court. The Citadel was part of the hullsteel cast that comprised the shell of UnderGelion, which meant that living in Spiral Hall was not particularly convenient. It was hard to attach things to hullsteel and impossible to drill holes because hullsteel absorbed stress until it shattered, and very little short of the sheering stresses in a shakeup could accomplish that.

How and why the dominant structures of UnderGelion were made of hullsteel was a mystery, but its citizens coped with what they had.

In Horth's case, that meant he couldn't get into Spiral Hall to visit Nanns Thris the next morning without descending all the way to the Palace Plain and climbing back up, because there were no doors or hatches in the hullsteel floor between the Octagon and the top of Spiral Hall.

After passing inspection by Spiral Hall's guards of honor, Horth found himself looking up at thin towers, heavily interconnected at all levels by an ad hoc collection of crosswalks and ladders. If there were elevators, he did not know where.

He asked for Thris and had a tower pointed out to him. Halfway up was Thris's aerie: an open level supported by pillars at the corners where visitors were received.

Lots of outside staircases, ropes, slides, hoists, and ladders were visible above street level and looked like they might get Horth closer to his destination, but none of them could be accessed without entering a building first. He didn't know any Spiral Hall families well enough to ask for right of passage, so he started out the slow way by hiking up Spiral Coil: a ledge jutting out from the inner wall that ascended at a fifteen degree angle from the bottom to the top.

The path was about two meters wide. In places, buildings encroached so close that Horth could have jumped across if he had been sure of his welcome. In others spots it was necessary to weave around things left on the walk, or negotiate his way past children more intent on their games than avoiding him.

Eventually, Horth had to make his way inward, off Spiral Coil. He studied the three-dimensional terrain ahead, set a course, and crossed over to a building with a ladder hanging down its side. After climbing that, he crossed a long suspension bridge to a public platform that served as a junction for half a dozen paths. A small hoard of children were playing there, ringing a miniature challenge floor where a girl and a boy staged a play duel. The lack of railings around the edge of the platform stirred a dim memory of Tessitatt telling Branst how safety barriers only encouraged Vrellish children to play on them.

Horth reached Thris's aerie via a ladder up the side of her tower. Diaphanous curtains in a medley of pastel colors hung over the opening, a couple of them gathered up in braided cords. Horth heaved himself over the sill of one open side.

He had dropped down on the inside before he realized that Hara had arrived before him.

Hara confronted Thris at a safe distance on the rubberized exercise floor that filled most of the aerie's interior. Neither had drawn her sword yet.

Ringing the exercise floor in a band about two meters wide were various cushions, low tables, and little cabinets full of things stored in drawers. A Vrellish man and woman dressed in open vests and loose trousers lounged on cushions, watching what was going on. A third Vrellish nobleborn was standing on the sill opposite Horth, lounging against a corner pillar as casually as if he was not twenty stories up in a room with four open sides.

"Horth!" Nanns Thris said brightly. "Good to see you."

Hara stood with her mouth locked in anger and her neck muscles prominent. "I am warning you," she told Thris. "Leave him alone."

"Or you'll what?" Thris taunted Black Hearth's captain of errants. "I won't accept your challenge. I know your reputation and I'm not that stupid. There are witnesses here and without my agreement to accept your challenge you have no legal excuse to attack."

"Good with the law, aren't you," Hara ground out. "Coward."

"Well," said Thris, with a sly glance in Horth's direction, "at least I am an honorable coward."

Hara stiffened. "What are you implying?" she demanded.

"Do you really want to know?" Thris asked in an acid tone. "Do you really want me to discuss it in front of one of Princess Beryl's children?"

Something changed in Hara. Liege Thris had scored a bad, internal blow.

"Be careful, Black Hearth," Thris warned, narrowing her almond-shaped eyes. "What I have to lay at your feet is much worse than any charge you've come to lay at mine. So be wise. I'll give your *protégé* an education in the bedroom and if I ask him to take risks for me in return, I will pay him with the Freedom Price that every Vrellish boy desires."

"A child?" Hara tossed back. "With Nersallian challenge entanglements?" She spat on the clean exercise floor. "It may pass Monitum's inspection for paternity by the time you need Horth to risk his life in your quarrel. But I'll wager it won't survive."

Nanns Thris raised her sharp chin in anger. "Are you implying I would kill my own child? What arrogance! We're not as afraid as all that of Nersallian entanglements! Besides, challenge rights cut both ways when they cut at all! Maybe I'll gain a piece of Nersallian property one day, hmm?"

Hara could not take any more. She cleared her sword.

Immediately, the two lounging Vrellish sprang up and the one on the windowsill dropped lightly into the room. They hovered, prepared to interfere if tempers were lost.

"Horth!" Hara said crossly, without breaking eye contact with her rival. "Let's go home! Now!"

Horth said, simply, "No."

Hara shocked him with her look of betrayal. Didn't she want him to act Vrellish? Didn't she want him to be *rel* and take risks on the challenge floor for what he wanted?

"This is not just about you!" Hara ground out.

That was true, Horth thought stubbornly. It was about Thris, too. Giving birth could be as dangerous as any duel, and he needed a Freedom Price as much as he needed sex on terms that were, if not exactly safe, at least mutually acceptable. The trade seemed fair.

"*Ack rel*," he said, aloud.

"The boy has made up his mind, Black Hearth," Thris told Hara. "And so has your precious liege. He's looking for a quarrel with the Demish." She shrugged. "It suits me to share mine. Now get out! Or I'll tell Horth something that he won't forgive you for!"

"No," Hara said, shaking her head. "No, I won't let you blackmail me! I won't put up with it. If you've something to say, say it, you Demish-tongued horror!"

The Vrellish witnesses backed off a little, waiting to see what would happen.

"You would like that, wouldn't you, Hara of Black Hearth?" Thris taunted, getting reckless herself. "You'd like me to say something rash and kill me for it! But I know more than you think! I know more than gossip and rumors! I have proof that I could take to Green Hearth. Now wouldn't that be—"

Hara attacked without warning, drawing and thrusting her sword. Thris sprang back, her fellow Vrellish shielding her. Horth moved in as well, as anyone trained in the etiquette of Sword Law was expected to do. It was he who put himself in Hara's way, ahead of the others, and calmly pressed aside her threatening tip with his right palm. She kept her sword poised, however, half extended, and Horth reluctantly slid his own sword out of its sheath, keeping it low. He stared at Hara intensely. She was breathing too hard.

Safe among her own kind, Thris abandoned the calculating gamesmanship she'd demonstrated earlier and hurled out accusations.

"I know you've been asking after me," Thris accused Hara. "Sending your errants to harass my contacts and pick fights with my pilots. Throwing your weight around to scare me off! Well, I can ask questions too. I'm Red Vrellish, not stupid! Don't mess with traders when you have something to hide!"

Hara lurched back away from Horth, lowering her point. Sensing the changing mood, the Vrellish guarding Thris also drew back, leaving her more exposed. If Thris accepted Hara's challenge, it would no longer be their business to defend her from spontaneous attack. It would be her right, and Hara's, to short-circuit more laborious means of redress for their quarrel.

Hara said stonily, "I have nothing to hide."

"Ha!" Thris cried, her head coming up and her lower lip thrusting out. "What about poisoning Beryl's potting soil from SanHome with Lorel drugs that cause abortion? What about killing Beryl's unborn children? What about that?!"

Horth heard the words and understood them. But they would have meant little if Hara's reaction had not shouted her guilt. Her posture stiffened as she sucked air with a start and expelled it again with a sharp grunt, as if she'd been struck in the sternum.

"It was easy enough," Thris continued, talking so fast Horth soaked in just enough to get the gist. "Years ago, after the duel with her Nesak brother, there were crates of fresh soil for Beryl's potted garden waiting in a Black Hearth warehouse — forgotten in the excitement over the duel. You were in charge of transporting it to Black Hearth. You were in charge of seeing that it came to no harm. When I found out you had also participated in the seizure of a stash of contraband about the same time, I thought to myself, what if Hara had kept a vial or two of childbane that she did not report? The temptation would be great. There you were, seething over Beryl staying on at Black Hearth and determined that she would steal no more Nersallian souls. And you had the means to blight her womb in your hands. It was the perfect poison. Harmless to the boys who were Black Hearth's, despite their mother."

"Your one mistake," Thris told Hara, "was deciding not to handle the childbane yourself, as a woman. So you recruited Rossen, a male errant under your command who hated Nesaks every bit as much as you do. Then you were foolish enough to betray Gil, his *mekan'st*, when your liege sided against her in favor of the Nesaks! You should have stood up for her, Hara. Your henchman would have died before betraying you if you had. Instead, I found him all too ready to talk!"

Horth saw it all in pictures, in his head. Hara palming a vial in the midst of a raid; Hara standing by in the shadows of a warehouse to keep watch as Rossen poured its contents into Mother's soil; the two of them sealing the crate again; Mother working in her garden, poisoned by the soil of her beloved home world.

Horth did not voice his challenge — he felt it. Hara knew. She did not attempt to decline. She turned to face him as the Vrellish nobleborns surrounding them moved clear.

Horth attacked. He had hoped to be quick, piercing her chest before she could react, but he knew instantly that was a mistake. Hara's training was evidenced by the lightning-fast muscle memory in her hand and arm, and she had parried so fast and efficiently that she probably didn't even know at first that she had done so.

Horth twisted away from her automatic riposte, fleching sideways in a great jump, as his scabbard bounced around madly, and he avoided her point, but it still caught in the embroidery of his vest and ripped out of it sideways. Vrellish duels were normally fought bare chested or in light shirts, and Horth silently swore at himself for the complication.

Hara pressed forward, beating Horth's blade away and thrusting in repeated succession. Behind Horth, he knew there was Vrellish clutter: pillows and ornament-filled cabinets on the floor. He broke left, towards the door sill where spectators had lounged moments before. The sill was empty now, their audience all safely inside with both feet on the aerie's floor. But Horth realized he would be partially trapped in the doorway, and flung himself away again, back down to the floor. It looked like Horth was trying to avoid Hara now, and that was partly true. He needed time to think, because at close quarters, with Hara's experience, she would be deadlier than he.

They studied each other in lethal silence, circling slowly now. Their scabbards scudded back and forth around their legs, but they were both trained to avoid tripping on them. Horth was keeping well away but he could not do so forever. At least there was something right about the situation that had been wrong. Thris's accusations had turned Horth's young life inside out. Here, in the midst of the duel, Hara felt like Hara to Horth, once more. Capable. Dangerous. Proud.

Horth's mouth stretched in a feral smile, sharing the purity of her excitement. A testing to the core of teacher and pupil. Hara usually won three out of five of their practice bouts on the Octagon. But now it was different — rarified and sharpened. Intense beyond anything he had felt before.

Hara settled now, squatting deeper, placing more weight on her back leg, and Horth could feel what was coming. It was Hara's trademark, the style he knew so well. She began to envelope him with small beats and cuts, never opening her guard wide, taking away the genesis of any of his own actions by subtle, sharp countermoves, and then flicking at his legs, at his arm, at his chest, keeping her blade a constant combination of offense and defense.

She would smother any attack of his while she prepared her own, and before she finally made a killing stroke.

Hara's face was hot with bitter anger and spoiled affection. She was going to kill him. He did not resent that, somehow, despite his certainty that she was the one in the wrong. But he wasn't going to make it easy for her out of any misplaced sentiments.

As long as he moved away, Horth could avoid Hara's killing stroke, so he kept just out of reach, edging backward and sideways as he tried to find her blade, or avoid it. And then, as Horth allowed his arm to flow mechanically in the exchanges, he saw his chance — a strategy.

But he would have to let Hara get very close to killing him.

His guard became sloppy and tired. His arm became weaker, and Hara's blade began to cut him, on the wrist, on the knee. He could see her confidence build, and he retreated slowly, a beaten man.

The two strategies began to entwine. Horth watched her eyes and her shoulders. There would be a moment different from the rest. His instincts were screaming at him to fight back harder, to take control, but he had to wait. He stopped thinking and watched her, ignoring the bite of her steel as it scraped his flesh. His hand went through its motions without him now, and he felt no pain. And then he slowly gave her the distance, gave her what she wanted, and he watched for the moment. Watched her eyes.

Then it was there. Hara's eyes grew brighter, her shoulder bunched. The stroke was a second intention bind, where she had offered her point to his parry, but immediately took the point back and levered hers down, on top of his, towards his stomach. It was a brilliant move, one which she had set up carefully, and would have been surprising to most opponents. Horth let it happen. But at the same time he detached his own point, turned his body sideways and counterattacked.

It had all happened in less than half a second.

They stood still, locked as if frozen, while both blades seemed to have gone through their intended victims.

Hara tried to suck in her breath, but she couldn't. Her mouth opened. She looked down. Then she stepped backwards, with faltering legs. She let loose her grip, and left her sword sagging from Horth's vest.

Horth yanked his sword out of Hara's torso and she fell. Then he shunted out her sword from his vest with his other hand and tossed it away, striking mutely on the rubber floor. He hardly felt the sliced flesh along his midriff that he knew to be there.

One of the Vrellish darted over, wordlessly offering a seamer for Hara, but quickly saw there would be little the first aid device could do in the case of such a wound.

Hara made a choking sound and coughed blood. "Don't— " she begged Horth, and a hand that was still strangely strong and powerful grabbed his free hand, although the extended fingers trembled. "Don't be a Nesak!"

She made the choking sound again, and her eyes grew frightened. She was drowning in her own blood. Horth felt for ribs with the end of his freed blade and drove the tip into her heart. He believed she wanted him to do that, and, as her eyes closed, her mouth quirked a smile that seemed to tell him he had guessed right. He was afraid her eyes might open again when it was over, and he did not want to see that. Instead, he turned to Thris and found his desire for her broken.

All that he could think about was Rossen. Hara was dead but her accomplice was still alive.

Horth wiped his sword on a pillow, sheathed the weapon and cleared out, leaving Hara where she'd fallen on the aerie floor. Later, he regretted that.

Most of the way he ran. He barged through a Vrellish family picnicking on the sloping path. He kicked aside belongings left lying around without thinking where they might fall. Once, he nearly slipped, and grew more careful after that.

The harder he ran, the longer he could put off confronting what he had done.

At the base of the Citadel he headed up the long flight of stairs to the highborn docks at a run, sweating but comfortable, heart and lungs robust. He ran with his sword belt in his hand, tired of it banging his leg unless he held it with his right hand.

The Demish guarding the Palace Shell did not try to stop him as he tore past, although he heard discussion breaking out behind him as they speculated about why he might in such a headlong rush.

It was not until he saw Black Pavilion that he realized he would have to tell someone what he had done. He slowed then to a walk. His heart adjusted quickly. He was hot, but the main effect of the exercise was to leave him feeling loose and comfortable.

Something about his demeanor prevented the errants on duty from offering greetings or even a salute.

Lywulf happened to be the first member of the household he encountered.

"Horth?" asked the Nesak, immediately grasping there was something wrong.

Horth wanted help from someone older. And Lywulf was Mother's man. "Childbane," he said. "In Mother's soil."

Lywulf believed him. Horth could see it and was grateful. The Nesak's anger rolled out, deep and oceanic. "Who?" Lywulf demanded.

"Hara," Horth said without hesitation.

Lywulf reached for his own sword. "Where is she!"

"Dead," said Horth.

Lywulf was taken aback. "How?"

Horth had no time for that. "Rossen helped," he said urgently. "Hara's orders."

"Blood of the *zer'sis*!" Lywulf cursed in Nesak idiom. "Rossen's gone. Cleared out last night. He must have known."

That made sense, Horth realized. Rossen would have fled after telling Thris what he knew.

People began pouring in from both sides of the Throat.

Lywulf held Horth's eyes long enough to say, "If he is still on Gelion, I'll get him." Then he slid away, leaving Horth to cope again on his own.

Zer Sarn was there, and Father. Mother, as usual, disdained to use rooms frequented by non-eternals. There was someone else there, too. A woman build like Hara, only taller and with thicker bones. She had a majestic, square-cut face and wide shoulders. Her breasts matched her proportions but her jacket bound them snug rather than emphasizing any soft curves. She wore liege marks on her collar and a fleet commander's uniform with braid that declared she belonged to the House of Bryllit, a family Horth knew to be close allies of his Father. In fact, unless the liege marks lied, she had to be Liege Bryllit herself.

"What is it, Horth?" Father demanded. "What's happened?"

The question broke Horth's heart. He undid his sword belt and handed it firmly to Father with both hands.

"I killed Hara," said Horth.

* * *

It was hours before the family had dragged the whole story out of Horth, working mostly through Branst, who had a knack for putting questions in a way that Horth understood.

Zrenyl led a couple of Nesak retainers on a hunt for Nanns Thris, to find out what she knew, while Hara's supporters sought out Vrellish witnesses to hear their versions of the fatal duel.

Hangst convinced enraged Nersallians who called for Horth's blood to wait until he had gathered all the facts, and with Bryllit's help, he organized a trial of honor.

Horth's failure to voice his challenge weighed against him, but poisoners were never popular. If Hara was guilty, Horth would have been justified in killing her even if he had done it at a distance with a hand gun — except that mere possession of that kind of weapon would itself have been cause for summary execution under Sword Law.

Hara's friends insisted she could never have done anything as dishonorable as poisoning a pregnant woman, even if the woman was a Nesak.

By the end of the first day of investigations, one Black Hearth errant died on the sword of another in a lawfully declared duel that played out, on the Octagon, too fast for Hangst to intervene and postpone. The winner upheld Hara's honor.

Six hours later, both *Zer* Sarn and Di Mon independently reported that soil samples from Beryl's garden contained childbane, the contraband drug that could induce miscarriage even in a highborn. The Monatese had a longer and more complex name for it than childbane, of course, but anything Green Heath and *Zer* Sarn could agree upon was generally accepted to be true.

"It was losing its potency with time," Di Mon explained at Horth's trial of honor. "Which is why Beryl's pregnancies were lasting longer. She also spent more time in the bedroom and less in the nursery this last time."

Hangst was devastated. And all the *kinf'stan* in attendance shared the depths of his shock.

Mother's Nesaks looked grim, but their eyes glittered with triumph because Hara's act had proved them right about the untrustworthiness of non-eternals.

Horth sat through his trial feeling too numb to react.

Mother locked herself away in the master bedroom of Black Hearth, where she could insulate herself from non-eternals. Horth did not see Zrenyl, either. His oldest brother seemed to have disappeared. Branst came, but Horth did not want to look at Branst too much. He made a point of avoiding eye contact with people he loved.

It was Father, as liege of both parties, who declared Horth's actions honorable.

Three Black Hearth errants immediately resigned their posts.

Horth knew he had been vindicated of wrongdoing by his liege-father. He also knew a trial of honor touching so closely on Black Hearth's honor was important enough to be a vote of confidence over Hangst's leadership. Hangst would have been challenged if the errants who resigned had been *kinf'stan*. But Horth lacked the will to care as much as he should.

He had killed Hara.

Whatever came next, the world of his childhood was shattered.

The trial broke up in silence, groups disappearing into their respective hearths to discuss the aftermath within their own circles of influence.

"Your mother wants to see you," Hangst told Horth.

Rock steady and coolly indifferent throughout the trial of honor, Horth's hands suddenly started shaking now that it was done. He stopped at the top of the spiral stairs to stare at them in astonishment. But after a moment it became clear he could do nothing to stop the reaction, and he continued down the Throat to his parents' room.

Mother, Father, and Branst were waiting for him at the parlor end of the bedroom. Branst went forward to embrace Horth and it felt good.

Mother stood in the shelter of her husband's arm.

"It is over," Hangst was assuring her. "Horth is cleared, no one challenged. And I will never doubt what you fear again. I swear." The promise made Mother's eyes fill with tears.

There were no servants or errants in the room, only one of Mother's Nesak retainers. The man served up mugs of warm herbal tea, including one for himself, and they all sat down around the little table Mother used for private get-togethers.

"I have sent Zrenyl to SanHome," said Hangst.

Branst shot up out of the chair he had just settled into, crying, "What!"

"Sit down!" ordered Hangst.

Branst shuddered like a struck gong. He stayed on his feet a moment longer, then he dropped into his seat with all the grace of a waxen doll bent at the middle by a child determined to make it join a tea party.

Horth wondered fleetingly what had become of Branst's three lashes, and concluded that his own debacle over Thris had prevented Father's sentence being carried out. Perhaps Branst was hoping good behavior might get him off.

Hangst accepted his middle son's obedience with a sigh. "Even if the *kinf'stan* did not challenge, it does not mean they are all content." He covered Mother's hand protectively. "There is talk — open talk in some quarters — supporting Hara."

Branst's wooden resistance softened with astonishment. "Even though she used childbane?! That's ... *okal'a'ni!*"

"Not necessarily," said Hangst. "An *okal'a'ni* sin threatens rebirth on a large scale, not a personal one. The point is that Gelion may not be a safe place for Horth, despite the trial of honor, while feelings are still running high."

"Horth?" Branst said, surprised. "So why send Zrenyl off to SanHome?"

Mother answered this question. "Your father realized Zrenyl needs to deal, honorably, with his own desires, or run the risk of the sort of trouble you two have inspired over women."

"Horth will follow Zrenyl to SanHome," Hangst told them, once the look of protest died away on Branst's expressive features. "I thought of sending Branst, as well, but he serves a useful purpose for me at court through his ties with Green Hearth. And your mother," he told his sons, with a weary air of mingled resentment and gratitude, "will not go."

Mother gripped Hangst's hand, looking at him across the table with a fixated passion that excluded their children for as long as it burned there. "If you die for my sake, on the Challenge Floor," she told her husband, "do not ask me to wait in this life for you to return. I would rather be a Waiting Soul, beside you, than your widow in a cruel, corrupting world."

* * *

Black Hearth held a quiet farewell dinner for Horth. Branst did not attend. Neither did any of the visiting *kinf'stan*. Instead, the family sat down to dinner with *Zer* Sarn and two of Mother's Nesak relatives dressed smartly in their fleet uniforms.

Mother served them herself. It reminded Horth of the dinner with Kene, seven years before.

After dinner, the six of them retired to Family Lounge, at the deep end of the Throat. Father held himself aloof, but Beryl chatted eagerly, hungry for news of home.

The Nesaks complimented her on dinner and her fine son, by which they meant Zrenyl. It was she who made a point of citing Horth's virtues, although she also warned them about his verbal limitations.

"And you must not forget that Horth is still only eleven years old," she insisted, "no matter how much he looks like a grown man."

"We understand entirely, *K'isk*-daughter," said Arn, executing a slight but very definite bow.

"Your youngest will be safe in our hands," said the more light-hearted of the pair, whose name was Hill. He smiled often, with the sort of good-humored charm that inclined Horth to think of him as a Nesak version of Branst.

But the emphasis on his oddities embarrassed Horth.

The Nesaks called his mother "princess" and "*K'isk*-daughter" with affectionate reverence, but Horth noticed that they failed to take her seriously, somehow. He resolved to prove to them that he was not a child, and that there were more important skills than being able to sustain a conversation.

"Stay, Horth," Hangst said, when people began breaking up to go to bed.

Horth remained behind. His father waited until they were alone before he spoke.

"I have told Zrenyl this," Hangst began. "I will tell you, too." He gestured. "Sit down."

Horth sat. Hangst moved his sword aside to sit opposite him.

"You are going to spend time on SanHome," Hangst told Horth.

Horth nodded.

"It is hard to know how much the Nesaks care about the business of reclaiming my soul line for their own," he told his son. "Your mother believes it all, at face value. Di Mon thinks it is a story made up to save face over losing the war. Either way, Horth, what you do regarding children while on SanHome is up to you." Hangst indulged in a deep chuckle. "I would be a fool to think otherwise, since I could not keep you from Nanns Thris right under my nose, here at court!" Behind the laughter there was both pride and fatherly rebuke for Horth's youthful lack of self-control.

Hangst grew sober once more. "Whatever you do, Horth, I want you to understand the politics involved. Do you understand what I mean by politics, Horth?"

Horth shook his head.

Hangst sighed. "Perhaps I should have let Di Mon play a larger part in the education of my sons." He squared his shoulders and tried to make up for that omission. "Politics, Horth, is about what people want. So is Sword Law, but with this difference. In politics, people do not always proclaim the stake they fight over. And they may not be straightforward about how they get it, either." Hangst paused a moment, studying his son's face for signs of comprehension. "Do you understand?" he asked.

Horth nodded.

"Gods, child!" Hangst exclaimed in frustration. "Say something to prove it to me, will you!"

"Politics," said Horth, very carefully, "are dishonorable."

Hangst's sober face broke out in a wide smile. "That's not a bad start!" he said, and laughed with the first sign of real pleasure Horth had detected all evening.

"Politics are with us, always," said Hangst, "each and every life. But we also have eternal souls. So remember this, Horth. Your children define your soul's future. You may think that you will have a choice when the time comes, but the soul is like a small child. It seeks life where the call of blood is strongest, or simply where opportunity is offered.

Politics should not dictate the life to which your soul may next be drawn. Trust your feelings, Horth. The ones that spring up, wordless, from deep inside. They are the only wisdom that survives from one life to another." He looked down at his open, empty hands; hands that defended his decisions on the challenge floor.

"I used to fear I erred, myself, by letting politics dictate I take your mother as my wife. Now...." He let his hands fall to his lap. "Now I am no longer sure. I think, perhaps, that Beryl is right. We have known each other before. That we are *cher'stan*." He smiled ruefully at that confession. "Di Mon would tell me I'm a fool. But it isn't wrong to be a fool. It is only wrong, in the end, to be dishonorable."

Without warning, Hangst decided they were done, and stood up.

Horth did likewise.

Hangst reached for him and hugged him, once, firmly. Then he let go.

"*Ack rel*, Horth," he said. "May all your choices be honorable."

"*Ack rel*, Father," said Horth, feeling restored. Where there had been hollowness, he now felt courage. He might not understand politics entirely but he knew now to trust his own feelings. And to live by the dictates of his honor.

* * *

Mother was happy and breathless the next morning as she checked through the luggage Horth had packed for himself.

"You won't need your Nersallian dress jacket," Beryl said, taking that out. "You aren't going to stay with strangers. The Sarns will supply you with clothes. Your sword you'll wear, of course, and your new flight leathers." She repacked his shoulder bag, putting aside the long package containing his court clothes. "What else have you sent ahead to the docks?"

"Nothing," said Horth.

Beryl Nesak straightened up. The dark circles under her eyes were harsh reminders of her recent traumas, but she radiated a girlish glee despite that. "Not a thing more?"

Horth had already said as much. He just shrugged.

"You are so like your father!" exclaimed Beryl. "Zrenyl took a couple of trunks worth of stuff."

Beryl fell on Horth's neck then, hugged him, kissed him on the cheek, and straightened his hair. Tears glittered in her green eyes.

"You are a good boy," she told him. "I know that. But please be on your best behavior at Sarn Haven. And don't take things apart unless you ask first. All right, Horth?"

"Yes, Mother."

"And be careful if you go on fleet maneuvers. Remember that you still don't have a Freedom Price, and you are only a child, no matter how grown-up you look. And maybe, with regard to that Freedom Price...." She broke off, looking embarrassed, and fussed with his collar a bit more. "Oh, never mind. It's just — I know they'll take good care of you."

She fixed her hand in his vest at chest height, and spoke to his sternum, unable to look him in the eyes.

"What you did for me, about Hara," Mother said in a voice shaken by too much emotion. "I will never forget that, Horth. Nor must you. All non-eternals are impossible to trust. You must understand that, for your own safety, my true heart. I think, perhaps, you do. Now."

Horth stepped back to look his mother full in the face. He had a warning of his own to impart, and was dreadfully afraid he did not know how.

He looked at her pleadingly, and said, "*Zer* Sarn."

"Yes." Mother smiled. Misunderstanding his intention, she supplied information. "He is one of the Sarns. They are very proud of him and I am grateful that he chose to come, to live with me, at Black Hearth. Arn says he might have been a member of the *zer'stan* by now if he'd stayed on SanHome."

She fussed with Horth's clothing some more. "I am so glad you'll be living at Sarn Haven. It's where I grew up. And I think you'll like Hill." She laughed. "Arn is less fun, I know. Very strictly brought up. His mother is *Zer* Sarn's sister, and my aunt." She bit her lip. "Oh dear, Horth, there is so much that you don't know."

Horth tried once more. "I trusted Hara," he said slowly. "You trust *Zer* Sarn."

"What do you mean, Horth?" Mother asked, looking spooked. "Are you trying to say that you suspect my uncle of robbing me of children, when that's the very thing he—"

"No!" Horth said quickly, afraid his attempt to explain himself was doomed to go wrong. "*Zer* Sarn," he tried once more, desperately, "feels wrong."

"Oh," Beryl relaxed. She stroked her son's arm. "It is because he is a *zer*, I suppose. A Nesak priest, as people say here at the Ava's court. I expect you've heard things about *zers* using drugs, just like Lorels or your father's horrid *gorarelpul*. But it isn't like that. Or perhaps," she smiled, "you find it hard to understand how a man could be celibate, now that you are grown up." She patted his arm. "On SanHome you will learn about all these things, Horth. You can talk to *Zer* Hen. He's the family priest at Sarn Haven and a good, kind man. You might even find a girl who'll help you understand." She stroked his face as she smiled, hope aquiver in her wide, green eyes at the same time as she feared to let him leave her arms.

Horth accepted all the possibilities she offered him with a nod. Then he let Mother walk him to the base of the stairs leading up to the Plaza, where her Nesak relatives were waiting to escort him to SanHome.

Hill smiled. "Ready then, Horth?"

Horth was ready. He shouldered his kit and remembered to say, "Yes."

Hill led, and Arn followed. It felt strange to be leaving Black Hearth, for what could be the last time, in the company of Nesaks. Horth imagined the invisible rebuke of Hara's watching soul, but she had lost her right to influence him when she dropped the shield of honor. He thought of Kene, instead, and believed his uncle's soul would approve.

House errants cast somber, sullen looks at the three of them as they passed through Black Pavilion. Nobody saluted. Arn acted as if the nobleborns were not there, but their glaring made Hill nervous.

Hill's discomfort increased when they emerged onto the Plaza and collected even more stares because of their Nesak attire. When his nervousness became too much for him, Hill talked.

"Arn is a strike force commander, did you know that, Horth?" Hill struck up conversation as they passed through the Palace Shell onto the promenade that ran the length of the highborn docks.

"No," said Horth.

"He's fought the Red Vrellish," Hill continued. "More than once."

Arn caught Hill's eye with an economical gesture and said, quietly but firmly, "Not here, Hill."

Arn was concerned they might be challenged. Concerned, but not afraid. He would be a difficult opponent to second guess in a duel, Horth decided. He had a cool, detached confidence quite different from Hill's charming bravado.

The silence that followed left Horth free to watch the people watching them. He saw fear, resentment, curiosity, and dislike. But people knew what to expect from Hill and Arn because they both wore swords, which meant that they respected Sword Law. They could be trusted that far. And they were here as Black Hearth's guests, sheltered by Hangst's reputation. Even Black Gate passed them through unmolested.

As they got into the car that Hangst had arranged to have waiting for them, Hill asked, "Have you ever been in a shakeup, young Horth?"

Horth wanted to say yes, but he stalled to decide if that was honest. He had flown *rel*-ships, of course. He had learned to navigate using the apparent motion of distant stars displayed, in false color enhancement, on *nervecloth*. He knew how to signal other *rel*-ships, across distances too great for light to serve the purpose, by means of a *shimmer dance* that registered via *skim* telemetry. He had even been involved in an event or two, in space, that involved exerting his will against another pilot, but he doubted any of those was significant enough to be counted as a shakeup. So he just shrugged.

"I have," Hill bragged. "Against the Red Reach Vrellish. I was fifteen the first time. That's not so much older than you are."

"Did you have a Freedom Price?" Horth asked Hill, as Arn guided their car towards a main street and headed for a Nersallian hangar.

"No, but I had one on the way," said Hill. "Now I have four children! But I'm twenty-five now, even if Arn thinks I still act like a teenager." He gave his good-natured laugh. "Arn has grandchildren as old as you, Horth. He fought in the Unification War."

"Unification War?" Horth repeated, not familiar with the reference.

"The war that ended with your parents' marriage," Hill explained to him, as if he were simple.

Horth frowned. "The Nesak War," he corrected.

"Is that what you call it?" Hill laughed, leaning closer in a friendly manner. "We didn't fight it all by ourselves, you know."

Arn spoke up from the driver's seat. "The concept of Unification is hard to understand, all at once. It arises from the story of the Errors, and for each strayed line of Sevildom the journey back is different. But this much, at least, is simple. We are all one blood: Nersallians, Nesaks, and the highborns of Red Reach, too."

"Wild souls," said Horth said, thinking about Mother's warning that the way back for those with Vrellish blood could be hard.

"Princess Beryl's taught you a thing or two, I see," Hill said with approval. "*Zer* Hen will be glad to know that!"

They rode on in silence. There was a small crowd of Nersallians waiting at the hangar they were headed for.

Arn got out first. Hill and Horth followed. The air was crisp with the potential of a challenge. A highborn that Horth did not recognize stepped forward.

"Well met," said Arn, with a nod, and surveyed the other six highborns. "May our souls mix, in death, as our blood has in procreation."

One of the female Nersallians hawked up bile and spat sideways, on the clean metallic floor.

"Not mine," she said. "Keep your blood, and damn your souls!"

Hill shouldered forward. "No one asked you, wild one!"

Arn put his hand on Hill's sword arm.

"Do you honor Sword Law?" Arn asked calmly.

The Nersallian frowned. "Of course."

"Then let us leave," said Arn, "or challenge. But do not goad my junior partner into being a fool."

There was a short, heavy silence. Then the Nersallian opposing them gave in with a nod, and moved aside.

"Take care, liege-son," one of the women among them got in, directed at Horth. He returned her smile with a confused expression, distrustful of her qualifications to wish him well. If Mother was correct, she was the sort of soul who faced an even harder fight to regain SanHome in her next life than he did.

"You'll fly with me," Hill told Horth. "As far as the Red Reach Jump, at least. That's where we pick up the rest of Arn's fighter hand before crossing Red Reach to the SanHome Jump on the other side."

Hill took the pilot's seat and Horth strapped himself into the passenger's side of Hill's cockpit.

Lift-off went smoothly. Horth watched the readings on the ship's console, which had a strikingly different design from a Nersallian one, but was nonetheless intelligible. The biggest difference was the absence of *nervecloth*, because it was made by House Monitum. Hill told Horth that Nesaks lined their hulls with a similar product of priestly manufacture, called *zer*-skin, that responded to voice commands.

"*Zers* learn to sing to their ships to control them!" Hill concluded. "They use pitch, rhythm, and melody to do things you couldn't imagine!"

Horth was daunted by that idea. He focused on the manual controls, instead.

"Intrusion field?" Horth asked, pointing to a likely display. He listened with acute attention to Hill's answers.

The lesson was temporarily interrupted by the G forces that pressed them firmly into their acceleration seats as they climbed out of Gelion's gravity, but by the time Hill was ready to start reality skimming, Horth felt he knew the cockpit pretty well.

"Here we go," Hill said, as he primed the intrusion field. Horth welcomed the feeling of a tug at his heart and a tiny weight on every cell as the ship's phase-splicer engaged. *Rel*-skimming consisted of a series of rapid phase transitions that reduced existence to a stutter punctuated by swallows of *gap*. Pilots tried to describe *gap* in all kinds of ways, from equating it to memories you had forgotten to talking about dimensions lacking space and time. Horth understood it, without fuss or even superstitious dread, as the place where souls waited and watched from after they died. It lurked beyond his powers of perception and attempted to seduce him with its cold allure. But it bothered Horth no more than the risk of a steep fall intimidated residents of Spiral Hall. *Gap* was simply the spiritual dimension of the risk he accepted to cross the vast and lifeless expanses of the universe.

"Mind you," Hill was saying. "It isn't as if we don't appreciate empire products when they can be had. A ship taken in war, for example. We don't trust things the Monatese are willing to sell to us. Nersallians are different. We trust your honor. And you'd be surprised what people will sell to relatives, even if they have been enemies in the past. No one casts better hullsteel than Nersallians."

Horth found Hill's endorsement of Nersallian engineering pleasing. But that work was nearly all done by petty Sevolites or even commoners, because they had greater tolerance for low gravity than highborns. Horth wanted to point out to Hill how the very superiority of Nersallians hullsteel depended on valuing commoners. But he did not want to risk upsetting the companionable feeling that resonated between himself and Hill like a low intensity version of what pilots called soul touch.

Hill felt it too, and because he put everything into words, he began reviewing the connections between House Nersal and House Nesak, repeating stories of a mingled lineage that were carried into Horth's awareness by Hill's easy, shared affection, like a payload.

It was not long, however, before Horth became aware of an old problem that had ended his companionable flights with Zrenyl as he grew up.

Some instinctive part of him wanted to take over from the Nesak.

There was no animosity about it. Horth simply had a hard time keeping his pilot's *grip* politely in check.

Zrenyl had lectured Horth on the rudeness of that impulse, reminding him not to encroach by giving him hard thumps on the chest followed by a brotherly admonishment to "stop fencing me, *rejak't!*" At first, Horth had not understood what Zrenyl meant, because neither of them were holding swords. But he soon figured out that a battle of wills under *skim* could be equally serious.

A *rel*-ship's controls governed its drive and direction, but it took *grip* to resist *gap*. Without it, a ship failed to manifest between one fraction of a second and the next. Instead, it slipped forward in time by absorbing time-debt that was redistributed through the *gap* dimensions.

It was easier to assert your *grip* if you had the controls, but anyone flying at exactly the same mix and vector — which included any passengers — could vie for dominance.

Horth did not want to embarrass himself by interfering with Hill's piloting, of course, but the longer they flew the harder it got.

"Nearly there!" Hill said finally, after an increasingly trying hour in which he had slowly fallen silent.

Horth shared Hill's relief. His hard-to-locate sense of *grip* felt like an over-stimulated muscle, aching to act.

When they cut out of *skim*, Hill exhaled in a forced sigh, wiping his brow with the back of his leather sleeve.

"San's Ghost!" Hill exclaimed, reaching over to give Horth a friendly shove. "You make bad cargo!"

Horth was busy feeling nauseous because they were coasting under zero-G conditions. He kept his teeth locked.

Hill had the same problem, to a lesser degree, and began to cat claw: a method of sipping just enough power from the fabric of the universe for a comfortable one-G thrust in real space without getting ward ships excited. Cat clawing was preferred over the use of other propulsion methods because *rel*-ships had little room for storing fuel and even if they did, spewing out gases would pollute the hard vacuum needed for space lanes.

Their destination was a station near the Red Reach Jump. Hill docked at its rim and showed Horth to a berth where his own *rel*-fighter was waiting for him.

Like all *rel*-fighters, Horth's was spherical with a rotational inner frame that braced the sling-cockpit. The frame was locked down in dock. Once under *skim*, it floated in an energy field that enabled it to rotate relative to the outer hull. The *nervecloth* lining the inner hull was a dull gray in dock. Only under *skim* conditions would it light up with enhanced images of *rel*-ships detected via *skim* telemetry, interspersed with coded warnings representing mass. The ship was a gift from Father. Horth was proud to fly it as an honorary member of Arn's battle hand.

After clearing the station, they took the jump one by one.

Horth had made this jump before with his family, and was able to do it on his own, with the aide of a mental mantra that encoded the trick of survival for him. Jump visions were different for different people. Horth's vision for the Red Reach Jump echoed his memories of a forest fire he had witnessed in childhood, on Tark. Horth remembered sitting in Mother's lap, in an atmospheric plane, feeling safe but curious as he looked out the window at the licking flames and thick smoke. Mother told him the fire was like Red Reach and the souls trapped in Vrellish bodies were like the trees they saw below them, being consumed.

It was comforting to get out of the jump, and exciting to face a trek across Red Reach, where Vrellish pirates came from.

Horth didn't know a lot about such pirates, except that they were without honor and plagued the space lanes in Killing Reach, where Liege Bryllit ruled over a small nation of domed cities on rocky worlds and deep-space habitats. He expected Red Reach itself to be swarming with pirates.

In fact, they did not encounter any trouble on their way across the reach to the jump that would get them to SanHome. Any stations they approached merely sent out their ward ships to make sure they kept going, which was exactly what Nersallian stations would have done.

Horth was mildly disappointed by the untimely determination of the Vrellish to prove perfectly civilized.

Part III

Exile

SanHome

Horth's first impression of SanHome was the double embrace of a crisp breeze and Zrenyl's bear hug. The breeze made him sneeze.

"Allergies?" Zrenyl sympathized with his more Vrellish brother. "It'll pass. It did on Tark, remember?"

Horth's nostrils attempted to pinch closed as he inhaled and his eyes narrowed. The air was peppered with dried leaves, battered to scraps as they tumbled in the wind.

Everything was shades of brown, from the overcast sky to the bare, thorny bushes encroaching on the edge of the landing field.

Hill was greeted by a Nesak woman with a round face and dressed in a light coat that covered her, shapelessly, from neck to ankles.

"This is my wife, Vera," Hill introduced her proudly.

"Hello Horth," said Vera.

"I am positively fantasizing a home-cooked dinner!" Hill exclaimed, taking his wife's hand, and the two of them set off at a brisk walk for a nearby group of buildings surrounded by a wall.

"We're headed for Sarn Haven," said Zrenyl. "A haven is a bit like a hearth, except it is held in perpetuity by something the Nesaks call soulright. We don't have those

because you have to have priests to do it. The *zer'stan* —
that's the council of priests — keep records of everyone's
descent to be sure they know which descendants are eligible,
and then perform rituals to determine if a soul is present in a
new form. Possessions based on soulrights are pretty stable,
because it is hard to get the *zer'stan* to endorse a challenge.
Liferights, on the other hand!" Zrenyl exclaimed. "Now
they're exciting! Men here fight for everything imaginable in
the way of property. And," Zrenyl added with even more
excitement, "I do mean the men! You won't find a Nesak
woman on the planet taking fencing lessons or learning how
to fly, either. We have that side of things pretty much to ourselves!"

Horth listened without grasping all the details.

The path they walked on was flanked by sculpted shrubs
that told stories about evolving shapes, without resorting to
the kind of repetition that would disconcert a pilot with good
navigational instincts.

"Is Horth really only eleven?" Vera asked Zrenyl as they
neared the Sarn Haven enclosure.

"It's the Vrellish in him, " Zrenyl said, sounding awkward.

Horth could tell his brother was trying to make a good
impression and did not want Horth messing that up, so he
forgave Zrenyl just this once. Otherwise, he would have
expressed himself with a punch.

The wall around the Sarn Haven compound appeared to
be for keeping in both domestic animals and the younger
children of the settlement. Horth counted about fifty buildings and estimated a population of a few thousand.

They crossed the compound to the building that Hill
called the Great House, with Hill explaining everything too
fast for Horth to follow, interrupting himself only to extend
cheery greetings to people they encountered in the courtyard.

The front of the Great House had a wide porch, but they
skirted that to enter by a back door. Inside, Zrenyl insisted

they stash their swords and clean off their shoes in a mud-room.

Hustled along by his companions, Horth dreaded the reception to come, expecting it to be like one on Fountain Court. But his next surprise was a good one. Horth's party merely added themselves to the hubbub of people already in the dining hall.

Men were visiting with one another while women put out dishes and dealt with the children. Even among the children themselves, Horth noted that it was the girls who helped with food preparations and the boys who hindered them by getting underfoot.

Zrenyl left Horth's side the moment he spotted a particular girl with a large dish of steaming vegetables and offered to take it from her. The girl, whom Zrenyl addressed as April, wore a floor-length dress of plain material covered with a full, white apron. Her only adornment was confined to the intricate way that her hair was braided, but there was a splash of life about her that made it easy to explain Zrenyl's fascination. What puzzled Horth was that the girl needed no help, whatsoever. Despite this, she let Zrenyl take the dish she was carrying, first blushing, and then murmuring her thanks.

Acting on Zrenyl's example, Horth picked out a stout woman with a sweating face who was carrying a platter with a whole, roasted animal on it that was about the size of a Tarkian dog, and wordlessly offered to carry it for her by lifting it out of her hands.

The stout woman was surprised, but soon grasped his intentions. "Well!" she declared, with her hands on her hips and a wide, beaming smile on her mouth. "Who says court Nesaks have no manners?"

Horth put the platter of meat down where she directed and straightened up. "Not Nesak," he corrected her. "Nersallian."

There was a short, ugly silence shared by everyone in earshot of his deep voice. Then the stout woman spoke up.

"Of course you are Nersallian!" she told him, as if he had said nothing wrong. "And Nersallians are the descendants of Prince Nersal Nesak. Just like I said. Court Nesak." She nodded at the table. "Sit down and be welcome at our table."

Horth cast about for Zrenyl for help figuring out where to sit, but his brother was far more interested in April than he was in Horth.

A lanky girl with large, gray eyes and a wide mouth strode up. She wore a dress very much like April's, but her build was thin and muscular instead of plumb and round.

More Vrellish, Horth decided. She also smelled like a Vrellish female, though the thrilling odor was heavily subdued by a soapy one.

"Is it true that you killed a man at court?" she asked Horth.

Horth shook his head. "A woman."

"Oh." The girl was clearly shocked. Trying to sound worldly, she added, "A Vrellish woman, was it?"

Horth nodded, hoping she would not ask any more about Hara. Perhaps she noticed his discomfort.

"My name's Kale," she introduced herself. "It's a word from the priest-books. A plant word, with a water element. I think I should have been named for the wind, instead, because I don't like water. Do you like to hunt?"

Horth thought about afternoons spent with his brothers on Tark. "Yes," he told her.

Kale lifted her chin towards the roast he had helped the stout woman place upon the table. "I killed that," she told him. "It's a *zer*-pig. *Zer* Hen says the *zer'stan* changed them just enough so they could thrive on SanHome and be useful to us. You have to be careful what you eat in the wild except for *zer*-things. Most of it won't kill you, but it can make you sick."

"Thank you," said Horth, because the warning seemed like useful information.

The stout woman with the sweaty face headed for the far end of the table.

"We'll be starting any minute," Kale said.

Horth looked around while he waited, and saw Hill holding court for a trio of half-gown boys who listened, wide-eyed.

"But can the women really fight with swords?" asked one boy, his voice standing out as the rest of the room grew quiet. "Don't they lose when they go up against men, like Zrenyl? And don't the men feel stupid about fighting women?"

Mothers descended to claim their offspring before Hill could respond.

At the head of the table, the stout woman took off her apron and took her seat beside two empty places, just as her husband, Liege Sarn, and the family priest entered.

Liege Sarn was superficially similar to Horth's uncle Zer Sarn in appearance, but with a less sour and more stately manner. He wore house braid on his semi-formal dinner jacket that echoed elements in Horth's. He was not wearing his sword, but Zrenyl had explained back in the mudroom that this was nothing to worry about.

The family priest was a chubby man with a friendly face, dressed in a robe.

"That's Zer Hen," Kale whispered.

The whole table rose as Liege Sarn and Zer Hen took their seats. Unprepared, Horth shot up with a jerk. Across the table, Zrenyl winced.

"I understand we have a new member of the family joining us today," said Zer Hen, folding his plump hands together as he gave a nod in Horth's direction. "Welcome to Sarn Haven, Horth Nersal."

Horth froze, his heart rate elevated, wondering what might be expected of him. But all that happened was that everyone muttered "welcome" in a perfunctory way that proved they were more interested in dinner.

When they all sat down again and prepared for prayers, Horth looked at Zrenyl for guidance but his brother, who was seated beside April, had already lowered his head.

Kale took Horth's hands and put them together with the left one cupped in the right, and hissed, "For the prayer to dead ancestors." Then she demonstrated a variation with her own hands, in which the thumbs met in front at a right angle. "For addressing a Great Soul," she instructed.

Horth frowned. He knew all that. Mother had taught him. He also knew that Father did not allow them to indulge in Nesak practices at public receptions. But in the end he took his clue from Zrenyl, who had clearly decided to go native.

"My thanks to my good wife and all those who help her to make our home a haven," Liege Sarn addressed the living, followed by *Zer* Hen who thanked specific members of the Waiting Dead for the safe return of Hill and Arn's party, before going on to address San Nersal.

"Bless us with your good will in the bonds we forge here with your children from the House of Nersal in the person of Zrenyl and his younger brother," said *Zer* Hen. "May their lives among us help to reunite all Nesaks in the sacred cause of husbanding life-supporting places in the universe and defending them against *okal'an'i* terror."

"Blessed Life," muttered everyone around the table. Then the mood was broken as the diners dug in, taking food from serving dishes and passing them around.

Horth enjoyed the baked *zer*-pig, but could not do justice to the heaps of vegetables, although he tried to eat some. He partook only sparingly of the dessert tray passed around after the main course, eating a couple of things that looked like large raisins and tasted more like dried plums.

By the time the meal ended, Horth was feeling mildly nauseous from all the fiber he'd ingested, and thoroughly exhausted from trying to track a dozen conversations at once.

Zrenyl noticed, at last, and made Horth's excuses to the company.

Upstairs, Zrenyl showed him around the facilities while briefing him on what he could, and could not, expect the women of the household to do for him. Nesak women were apparently prepared to act like servants but were not to be approached in any way approximating sexual behavior.

"Women here aren't Vrellish," Zrenyl told Horth. "They aren't exactly Demish either, though they may seem more like that. The bottom line is—" Zrenyl made a fist and held it, big and solid, in front of Horth's nose, " — if you do anything vulgar to embarrass me, I'll break your face so badly you'll die of regenerative cancer before it heals up. No sex. Got that?"

Horth frowned. It seemed to him there must be some women on SanHome, Vrellish or not, who needed men as much as he desired women!

"What did you think of April?" Zrenyl asked, grinning like a kid who had just beat his trainer at a sparring bout. "It was a springtime month on Earth, you know," he continued. "It's just right for her!" he finished enthusiastically.

Horth shrugged. Personally, he failed to see what a seasonal variation caused by the axial tilt of an orbiting planet had to do with a silly, blushing girl.

"Oh, what would you know about it, *rejak't*?" Zrenyl said, and stalked off.

* * *

Food became a problem for Horth during his first week on SanHome, but it wasn't until he actually got sick from overindulging in fruit slices that Zrenyl admitted to Mrs. Sarn that his brother had a Vrellish stomach.

Horth went down to the kitchen the next day to be greeted by a grinning Kale who shoved her bowl of breakfast fare in his direction. The bowl was full of shredded meat mixed with lard and flavored with small, dried berries.

"You're not the only one," Kale told him boldly. "Try this. We call it pemmican."

While Horth was digging into the pemmican (which would have been a lot like fleet rations if it had been pressed into bars and desiccated), Kale fetched him juice and a glass of water. He was in the middle of swallowing the last of the juice when Mrs. Sarn bustled in, smiling benevolently.

"I see that Kale has been taking care of you," Mrs. Sarn said to Horth.

Kale gave her a sideways hug, and stayed close, taking her welcome for granted.

"Kale is the only other Vrellish-eater that we have here at SanHome," explained Mrs. Sarn. "But we're no less proud of her because of that." She gave Kale a squeeze as the girl detached herself to go claim her share of their breakfast.

Mrs. Sarn fixed Horth with a serious look, arms folded over her ample chest, before she went on. "Give me your word of honor, Horth Nersal, that you'll behave as befits a son of Princess Beryl, and you may go hunting with Kale today. Just the two of you."

Frequently briefed on the question of women, by Zrenyl, Horth was confident that he knew what was expected of him.

"I will not have sex with Kale today," he gave his earnest promise, rather proud of getting an entire sentence out. "Even if she asks."

Kale burst out in laughter so severe she doubled over at the waist and held her stomach.

"Kale!" Mrs. Sarn admonished her.

The Nesak girl righted herself with an effort. "And I swear," she said with mock gravity, "not to ask you!"

Horth knew when he was being made fun of, but refused to admit his presumptions were unreasonable. Everything about Kale pointed to her being more Vrellish than the rest of the family. She was dressed in trousers today, for example, and her braids were tucked under a tight cap.

"Off you go, then," Mrs. Sarn said, briskly. "And kill us something nice for dinner."

"So," said Kale, once they were clear of the house and headed off across the Sarn Haven enclosure at a brisk walk, "what have you hunted before?"

"Grabrats," he told her. "On Tark."

"You eat those?"

"No," said Horth.

"Then what do you kill them for?"

"They're pests," he said. "They steal from us."

"Sort of like non-eternals are they?" Kale asked. "You leave them alone if they leave you alone, otherwise you clear them out."

Horth shrugged.

Kale took him to a shed where she gutted her catch and kept her weapons. The only weapons he saw were edged ones and hand-operated bows, but he had expected that. Only honorable weapons were used on Tark, even against the pesky native grabrats. It was part of the compromise *Okal Rel* demanded of beings powerful enough to destroy all they depended on for survival — an honorable act of restraint in the conquest of nature that afforded better sport and taught discipline.

"We Nesaks live in harmony with our environment," Kale boasted. "Not like other people in the empire. Oh, you say you do, I've heard that," she reacted to his look of offended honor. "But you don't do it like us. We don't even use *rel*-batteries except a little here and there among the warrior families to show off."

"What's wrong with *rel*-batteries?" Horth asked, finding it as easy to talk to Kale as he did to Branst. As far as he could see, *rel*-batteries were a perfect energy source: charged as a by-product of flying, with no polluting side-effects.

Kale sat down on a stool in her shed with a crossbow across her knees. "What do you know about time slip," she asked.

"Everything," declared Horth.

"All right then, what causes it?"

"Weak *grip*," said Horth.

"No," she said, "not weak — weaker. If no one but you ever reality-skimmed, you would have to absorb your own time debt. Instead, the weaker pilots pay the price for you cheating the laws of special relativity. For every pilot who makes dock successfully, someone else has got to time slip."

Horth held up one hand and wiggled the fingers. "Many, many safe flights," he said, then lowered the first hand and held up the second, balled into a fist. "One pilot — infinite time slip."

"Are you suggesting," Kale said, "that it is all right to fly because only a few people have to experience near-infinite time slip to compensate for everyone else?"

Horth shrugged.

"The fact remains," Kale insisted, "that we are talking about knocking a pilot out of the cycle of birth and death entirely. Not simply killing him. So at the very, very least, we should never fly frivolously."

"Choice," said Horth, having considered this problem himself at length, when he learned what happened when you time slipped. "Pilot's risk. Pilot's choice."

Kale tossed her head sharply. "For you, maybe. I will never get to fly because women do not have to do it. It isn't necessary. So I have no right to force time debt on someone who is flying to keep the rest of us safe from *okal'a'ni* conquerors. It's that simple." She said it so fiercely Horth decided not to argue.

Kale got up and banged around the shed getting ready. She found Horth a crossbow and thrust it at him. "You know how to use that?"

He nodded.

"Good," she said. "Don't make a lot of noise stomping through the underbrush after me."

For the rest of the afternoon he learned a lot about moving through brambles and across squishy marshes without startling *zer*-deer. He also learned how much fun it was to receive a hero's welcome from the women who ran Sarn Haven's kitchens when they came home with dinner.

He and Kale did not discuss the ethics of reality skimming again. But they hunted together regularly.

* * *

Horth got up one morning, months after his arrival, to find the household in a tizzy over a summons from the reigning *K'isk*.

The High Seat, where the *K'isk* held court, was located in a city known simply as the capital, about two hours away by light plane. Zrenyl and Horth were to present themselves in ten days.

Suddenly, the casual rhythms of work and play ended. There were protocols to learn, statements to memorize, and clothes to choose. It reminded Horth of functions held on Fountain Court. Fortunately, here as there, most of the hard work fell to Zrenyl as the oldest brother.

Horth and Zrenyl flew to the capital, with Hill serving as navigator. He was also to act as their guide within the city once they arrived. *Zer* Hen came along to provide any necessary spiritual guidance.

The capital was an ecologically sustainable city of just over a million people, planned around a series of pedestrian-only rings with intersecting roads for vehicles. The palace grounds of the High Seat lay at the center, flanked by the campus of the *zer* seminary on one side and the Temple of San on the other. The surrounding town was divided into sections owned by the different royal families, like the Sarns, who claimed descent from one of San Nersal's children.

The palace itself had a grand façade used for ceremonial departures and arrivals but its most prominent feature was the challenge arena bulging out to one side in an open-air amphitheater.

Hill set the plane down on the outskirts of the capital at an airport named *Zer-pol*.

"What a thing to name an airport!" objected Zrenyl. "A doomed soul — too weak to fight back."

Hill stopped cold and gave Zrenyl a blank stare. Then he slapped his knee and laughed. "Hah! Is that what you Nersallians think of a *zer-pol*!"

Zrenyl frown. "A *zer-pol* proves his enemies *okal'an'i* by becoming their victim," he said stubbornly. "I'd say that's an unlucky name for any dock, even if it is only for atmospheric aircraft."

Zer Hen cleared his throat and spoke up. "Ah, but the thing is, you see, why does the sacrifice have such an impact? It's because a *zer-pol* is loved for exemplifying the *pol* virtues such as cooperation and trust. So you see, *zer-pol* is quite an appropriate name for a shared resource."

"Don't tell me any more," Zrenyl groaned. "It is starting to sound like one of *Zer* Sarn's lectures on the Mysteries and Errors!"

Horth noticed fellow travelers pause to look at him and Zrenyl. Sometimes parents even pointed them out to their children. But on the whole he felt sure that grandsons of the ruling Ava would have commanded more attention on Gelion than he and Zrenyl did on SanHome, which was puzzling given the books Kene had brought to Gelion.

A short drive in a hired car saw them to their lodgings at a place called an Away House, in the Sarn Sector, that was build around a large internal courtyard. It had eight suites, each with an external dining area arranged so residents could take in what was happening on the central exercise floor.

A sort of gymnastic dance was taking place in the courtyard when they arrived, but Horth knew better than to imagine any of the women performing barefoot in long, swishing skirts would be available. He had already learned that Nesaks performed for each other rather than delegating that role to courtesans.

The next morning, Horth, Zrenyl, Hill and *Zer* Hen were picked up by a car and driven to the *K'isk's* palace along one of the radial roads.

They got out at the grand entrance glimpsed from the air the day before, and passed up a long hall with a high ceiling that was lined with Guards of Honor who presented their swords in a ritual gesture as they passed. Horth thought the guards looked odd, because they were dressed in nothing but fighting trunks and sashes that displayed their house braids and colors.

The *K'isk* received Horth and Zrenyl in a huge stateroom surrounded by representatives of the twelve royal families of SanHome. A line of *zers* were also present, dressed in the robes of their various orders that indicated which Great Souls they favored.

The *K'isk* himself wore a heavy mantle of fur and leather over a costume very much like that of the semi-naked honor guards in the hall. Horth thought the *K'isk* had a brash air of youth and reckless arrogance about him for a grandfather, despite the ageless appearance of highborns or as Nesaks preferred to call them, eternals.

They did not stay long in the *K'isk's* presence and nothing was said beyond the phrases Zrenyl had rehearsed at Sarn Haven. Horth found the whole affair worse than a Demish reception. It was on the way out of the audience chamber that he learned something valuable.

"I'm glad that's done," huffed *Zer* Hen, brushing down his robes to dislodge crumbs of pastries he had sampled while waiting in a side chamber.

"It could have been worse," Hill agreed. "The High Seat has passed between the Ko and Sarn lines so often, *K'isk* Ko can't help but view Zrenyl as a title contender. Especially when there are *zer*-factions trying to revive the business of Beryl's children being conduits for the San soul. That sort of thing is bound to attract trouble."

"Indeed," *Zen* Hen said with a relieved sigh. "But not this time."

"What do you mean the Ko and Sarn lines?" asked
Zrenyl. "Isn't the reigning *K'isk* a Sarn? I mean, he is my
grandfather!"

"Technically," said *Zer* Hen, with a sigh of disappointment for humanity, "but biology will out, as the saying
goes."

Zrenyl stopped cold six meters short of the outside
doors. The rest of the party swung about him in a loose pin-
wheel.

"Technically!" Zrenyl bellowed. "What do you mean he's
'technically' my grandfather?"

Hill looked nervous. "Zrenyl, please! Not here! I'll explain it to you on the way home!"

"You'll explain it now!" demanded Zrenyl.

"All right!" Hill snapped, casting a self-conscious glance
at the stone-still guards of honor. "You are the son of Beryl
Nesak and she is a *K'isk*-child. But that was under a different *K'isk*. The title has changed hands since. Lots of times. A
K'isk has to defend his title a lot more often than your father
does. If he didn't the whole system would break down."

Zrenyl looked thunderstruck.

"Look, Zrenyl," Hill said, putting an arm around the young
Nersallian's back. "It doesn't matter if you are descended
from a live *K'isk* or a dead one. You are just as entitled to call
yourself a Nesak prince and challenge for the High Seat if
you want. That's why any reigning *K'isk* calls new contend-
ers to the capital to get a look at them."

"What makes it all a bit more complex, in your case," *Zer*
Hen added, "is the business of your mother being married
to your father to attract important souls back into her line.
There was a Sarn in the High Seat, you see, when that was
done. And there are sympathizers in the *zer'stan* who think
that you, or your descendants, ought to be *K'isk* — even
now. Politics, you know." He smiled. "But let's get back to
our rooms and order dinner. I think that would be the best
thing, just now."

Zrenyl was sullen all the way back to the Away Home.

"I don't know what you are so upset about!" Hill told him, in exasperation. "You are still every bit as much the grandson of the *K'isk* as you would be if the man you met today had been your mother's sire. That's how it works on SanHome."

"It isn't how it works on Fountain Court!" Zrenyl fired back.

Horth said nothing. Ever since *Zer* Hen used the word politics he knew that he wasn't going to understand.

"Just be grateful nothing went wrong!" Hill urged Zrenyl.

But something had.

* * *

A dashing Nesak prince was waiting for them in the courtyard of the Sarn Away House. They came across him chatting with a knot of admirers. He extracted himself from his fans when he spotted his quarry and bounded over to introduce himself.

"Zrenyl Nersal?" he asked Zrenyl, offering an arm to grasp. "I am Prince Corin of Family Sarn, your Uncle Kene's son."

Zrenyl took the offered arm of friendship with hesitance. "*Ack rel*," he said, in a wary tone.

"*Ack rel*," Corin agreed. "May the dead be proud."

Hill looked excited. *Zer* Hen looked worried, which, together with the celebrity attention Corin was receiving in the courtyard, suggested he was well known as a swordsman.

"I am afraid," Corin said, "that you and Horth have been invited to a sporting melee by four of the *K'isk*'s relatives. I took the liberty of telling them I would deliver their challenge card."

Corin produced it with a flourish and handed it to Zrenyl, who scanned it quickly before letting Hill take it from his hand.

"Enard Ko," Hill read, looking paler. "That's bad."

"What's a sporting melee?" Zrenyl wanted to know. "Is it some kind of tournament like the Pan-Demish games on Gelion?"

"I am afraid that ours have rather more fatalities," said Corin. He was dressed in a layered, mauve cloak with a complex knot of tied scarves at this throat, but apart from his dandified clothing, Corin reminded Horth strongly of Kene in the way he conducted himself with quiet courage and an understated confidence.

"Shall we eat while we discuss it?" asked Prince Corin with a nod towards the dining area on the lip of the court-yard.

Hill exclaimed, too loudly, "Yes, sure!" He was still visibly shaken by the challenge card, but seemed equally determined to impress its bearer.

Once the men had settled around the table, a trio of women attached to the Away House came to wait upon them.

"Not too much wine," Corin warned the others when that was delivered. "Not if you fight tomorrow."

"Tomorrow seems a bit rushed," said *Zer* Hen.

Corin shrugged.

The woman who brought the wine settled on a garden seat nearby and was soon joined by two of the women who had danced the night before. Emboldened by the women's example, other guests began to drift in and coalesce around the table to hear more about the proposed melee.

The thickening audience had a pronounced effect on Hill's and Zrenyl's behavior. Hill made efforts to repress his nervousness, and Zrenyl tried not to seem stupid when he didn't know how things worked on SanHome. He tended to accept Corin's lead wherever possible.

Corin spent most of the meal telling them about the four men who had issued the challenge.

"They seem to fight a lot of duels," Zrenyl observed, awkwardly, in a pause.

Corin nodded. "Enard Ko and his team are the *K'isk*'s main sweepers in the capital."

Horth knew what sweepers meant in a space war. They were members of an *avsha*'s hand who ran interference whenever the *avsha* — who was usually the stronger flier — was going for a prime target.

"Melees are typically fought in fours," Corin explained to Zrenyl, "but they are really between the two principals, in this case: Enard and Zrenyl."

"Why?" Horth interjected, like a sword thrust. What was being proposed sounded dangerous. He didn't understand why Hill and Zrenyl seemed so willing to entertain the idea.

Corin answered with patient forbearance. "I know you are only eleven, Horth, no matter how grown up you look." He looked to Zrenyl for guidance.

"I'll tell him," said Zrenyl, emboldened by the audience collecting around their table as the excitement built up. "On the challenge card, Enard Ko claims it is a false hope to expect my blood to be *rel* enough for the San soul to be reborn into our line through my children. He wants me to renounce any claim to that pretension and go back home to Gelion!"

"Enard doesn't think you've got enough experience to realize what you're giving up if you back down," Corin coached Zrenyl. "Or else he thinks you won't be able to raise a good team on short notice. He did this now on purpose, before you had established a reputation."

Zrenyl shoved away his unfinished plate, too worked up to eat any more. "What happens if I decline the challenge?"

"If he wants to remain current, a contender must accept any challenge over grounds that lack unanimous consensus by the *zer'stan*," said Corin. "That's what I meant when I said Enard Ko is a sweeper. However unfair it seems, declining his challenge will cost you the right to contend for the High Seat, now or ever. And that means one less threat to the *K'isk*, his cousin."

Zrenyl held his breath a moment, then let it out in a whoosh, as if he had been winded.

Horth was equally hard hit, but for different reasons! He'd had no idea, until that moment, that his brother had any designs on the High Seat! *K'isk* Ko had not impressed Horth at all!

"Why be *K'isk*?" Horth asked Zrenyl, surprised at the force behind his question.

"Why be *K'isk*!" Hill exclaimed, and slapped his knee. The gesture broke the tension around the table. Women blushed, and all the men in earshot laughed uproariously.

"Why be *K'isk*?" exclaimed a kibitzer. "For the glory!"

"For the women!" said another man, and they all broke out again in choppy laughter.

Grinning like an idiot, Hill leaned towards Horth to explain it to him. "The *K'isk* can marry any woman he wants and she has to have him! Nor can she marry again if she's widowed. She becomes a priestess of the temple and remains the bride of the next *K'isk*, although only children conceived during her husband's reign can call themselves princes and princesses. Children like your mother, Beryl, and Corin's father, Kene."

"You never have to sleep alone if you are *K'isk*!" another man summarized.

"He's commander in chief of the fleet," someone else mentioned. "With many privileges within his gift."

"People flock to see him when he goes on tour!" said someone else.

"And with the right kind of family support," the first spectator concluded, "you can last for years!"

"Family like Enard Ko, unfortunately," Prince Corin reclaimed the floor. "It is up to you, Zrenyl. But I am here to help if you want me to fight on your team. Your father killed mine — but it was done with honor. Kene himself would expect me to extend my arm in friendship to his sister's firstborn."

Zrenyl looked pale for the first time, as if the gravity of what he was deciding had finally sunk in past the buzz of excitement and touched him in a place where he was mortal. He wet his lips.

"I could refuse?" asked Zrenyl.

Corin nodded. "Yes, and go home. I doubt the Sarns would want to offer you a place here if you relinquished the claim that makes you royalty. Not to mention failing to defend your role in *Zer-sis* Ackal's prophecy."

Zrenyl's jaw muscles worked. "I don't know."

Corin smiled, "Of course. Enard and his pack of bullies are not amateurs. The fight is meant to be to first blood, but I'll be surprised if someone doesn't die in this one. You, if Enard can arrange it. It isn't right to bait you like this, if you ask me, when you're here alone except for an eleven-year-old brother."

"And me!" Hill volunteered suddenly, springing up from the bench where he was seated. His face was burning with excitement. "I'll stand with you on behalf of Sarn Haven!"

"Good," Corin said, nodding. "But that still makes only three warriors."

"Don't count Horth out!" Zrenyl said. "He may only be eleven, but he's a natural with a sword!"

The endorsement stirred something profoundly irrational in Horth. He still didn't see why Zrenyl would want to be *K'isk* — except maybe for the bit about the fleet. Women, he still believed, had to be attainable in less prescribed ways. But he was vulnerable to the compliment of being valued by Zrenyl, despite his age and verbal disability.

"San Herself!" Hill exclaimed, drawing his own sword with an exhilarating swish and turning it around to bring the pommel down on the table with a bang. "Let's show House Ko what we Sarns are made of!"

The next thing Horth knew, the rest of them had drawn their own swords and copied Hill's gesture in unison. The sound of the bangs, confirming fellowship, sent a thrill through him.

Only *Zer* Hen muttered unhappily to himself as the evening turned into a celebration of Zrenyl's acceptance.

* * *

The next morning found the team up early, getting ready to go. Corin set the standard for courage with a cheerful, optimistic attitude.

Hill talked *Zer* Hen out of sending word back to Sarn Haven.

"Wise decision," Corin told Hill. "I never tell my wife about a duel."

"I suppose, I suppose," *Zer* Hen fretted. "I still wonder what sort of sense it all makes. *Okal Rel* limits conflicts to the human scale to spare environments. That makes sense. But the number of young men in royal families who do each other injuries because the *zer'stan* can't agree about things... well, that's not the same."

"Don't worry, *Zer*," promised Corin. "I will do what I can to make sure you take all of your Sarn Haven flock home again!"

No one wanted to admit he was scared. Instead, there was so much one-upmanship going on that Horth found it impossible to warm up properly in the courtyard. He was afraid he might forget that they were only practicing if someone pushed him too hard.

Finally, the four of them made their last farewells to a crowd of well-wishers, who were either friends of Hill's, fans of Corin's, or simply the enemies of Family Ko.

Horth was grateful for the silence once they climbed into Corin's waiting car.

A mob received them outside the *K'isk*'s palace. People lined the street and had to be held back from the doors through which they had passed so uneventfully the day before. A holiday atmosphere prevailed despite the gravity of what was going on.

"Corin's popular and Enard isn't," Hill explained, as an attendant directed them down a new passage. "The stands will be full!"

Their destination was a lavish dressing room replete with a wide selection of gear, walk-in showers, and observers acting as a guard of honor. They even had their own first-aid attendant — a low-ranking *zer* wearing a badge that licensed him to practice a limited range of medical arts without giving offense to the Watching Dead.

"All right," Corin told them heartily, "let's suit up. It's supposed to be to first blood, so everyone wears gear."

Protection certainly made sense. But Horth had never fought a serious match with a fencing mask obstructing his vision before.

"You need to wear it, Horth," insisted Zrenyl.

Horth scowled.

"By all the mad gods of Earth!" Zrenyl exploded, snatching the mask from the attendant and thrusting it at his recalcitrant brother. "Put it on!"

"No," Horth declined, afraid of being hindered. Too much of his style was sheer instinct. He was afraid the mask would interfere.

Hill weighed in with arguments, but words were powerless against Horth's qualms.

Time pressed and Zrenyl had to give in before very long. He went off to get himself prepared instead, muttering the whole time about how it wouldn't be his fault if the *rejak't* got himself killed.

"We'll put him between us," Prince Corin said. "That should make it easier to see he doesn't get hit."

Horth was willing to accept that if it made Zrenyl stop fussing about the hated mask, which he now felt superstitiously certain was bound to foul him up if he wore it.

He was happier with the padded fencing jacket that the attendant urged on him. Except the man felt driven by Horth's silence to presume he needed lecturing.

"The goal with a challenge to first blood," the attendant said, "is to nick exposed arms or legs. Your torso is protected by two slash-resistant layers, with a stiffer lining underneath to stop a lunge."

Horth tried the jacket on, decided it was worth the effort of adjusting to it, then turned to the attendant who had put one on himself to model how it should be fastened.

"You see," the attendant said as he straightened up and tapped his middle, once. "Perfectly safe, now."

Horth tested that hypothesis with a jab. He picked a non-lethal target on the right side of attendant's rib cage and he didn't drive as hard as he could, but the Nesak still went down with a surprised squawk, arms windmilling and eyes popping out of his head.

"What was that for?!" exclaimed a second attendant, rushing over to help his fallen comrade.

Horth shrugged. If the Nesak had lied about the jacket's properties, he would have deserved what he got. As it turned out, he had told the truth, and Horth knew more about the body armor than he had before. His sword had torn the two top layers of the fencing jacket. The bottom one deflected the thrust. He also knew how his own sword would feel when striking someone else's jacket, and that there was a risk of it getting caught in the top layer of slash-resistant cloth.

"This way," Corin said when they were all dressed, and led them to a chamber filled with five man-sized tubes. "This is how we get fielded when the time comes," said Corin. "Each of us gets into one of those. There is a lift in the bottom. It goes up at a smart pace, but it's very smooth. There will be nothing around you when you get to the top, but don't step off before it stops or you'll disqualify yourself for making a false start. Once you're flush with the arena floor, wait for a buzzer to sound. That's the signal for the melee to start. Never mind what's happening in the stands — the audience can't hurt you, only the other side can. Size up the opposition, by all means, while you're waiting for the buzzer. Enard is tallest and prefers a central position. He plays his cousins Charl and Devon on either end and his *brerelo*, Mason, on his left side. They're all right handed, like us, except for Horth. Any questions?"

No one spoke.

Corin showed them how to hold their swords, pointing down with the grip in both hands, before they stepped into the fielding tubes. Horth was assigned to the far right, at the last minute, despite the earlier agreement to put him between Corin and Zrenyl, because Zrenyl pointed out that the strongest opponents on the opposing team were the two in the middle: Enard and his best friend, Mason.

"Remember," Hill told Horth for the fourth time as they waited for the lifts to start. "You're out of it as soon as someone bloodies you. Hits made after that cost us the match."

"There're ready for you now," said an attendant, and the lifts began to rise up through the floor.

Despite Corin's advice to the contrary, Horth took note of his surroundings on the way up, but the crowd in the open-air amphitheater did not interest him very much, nor did the boxes occupied by the *K'isk* and representatives of the *zer'stan*. Instead, he took note of the state of the sky, including the position of the sun. There was sufficient cloud cover to mute *SanHome*'s yellow star without being heavily overcast, which was more or less ideal weather for a duel. Horth was reassured by that fact, since he was much more comfortable fighting under indoor conditions.

The floor of the theater was covered in short, green grass. He did not like that, in case the groundcover proved slippery. The grass looked dry but he couldn't be sure. When the lift stopped, he tested it with the bottom of his fitted shoe.

"Horth!" Zrenyl hissed beside him. "Don't move!"

Fortunately, testing the grass did not constitute a false start, because no one ordered Horth disqualified for the move.

Horth took quick note of the judges lining either side of the field, the tracking cameras mounted discretely on the sidelines, and the sense of expectation in the stands. Then he gave his full attention to the opposition's lineup.

Enard's team were dressed in the same masks and body armor as Zrenyl's, except for Horth's omission of the standard mask. As the challenging team they wore black, while white was traditional on SanHome for defenders. Hill had explained all that at some point in the endless talk the night before, and it somehow made Horth feel things were under control to see that it was true.

The presiding judge of honor read out the nature of the challenge and the names of the eight participants, while Horth continued his examination.

He could not make out faces well behind masks, but he had an eye for body language. He saw Mason notice his own head was exposed. Mason turned to say something to the man named Devon, on the end of the line, opposite Horth.

The judge of honor finished. He stepped off the field.

A buzzer signaled it was time to start.

Zrenyl, Hill, and Corin had discussed strategy in a melee half the night and again during practice this morning. None of it seemed to apply now.

Both lines charged toward each other.

Horth's opponent, Devon, was primed to go for Horth's exposed head. Horth decided to let him, trusting he would not get fancy if he thought he had a clear shot. Horth targeted Mason's calf, instead, while Enard's *brerelo* was busy blocking Zrenyl's attack. As Devon's blade went for Horth's exposed throat, Horth dropped to one knee and slashed Mason's leg near the ankle. It was more awkward than he liked, and his footing did slip slightly on the grass, but the utterly astonished yelp from Mason was its own reward.

Unfortunately, Horth had too much to worry about to congratulate himself for being the first on either team to draw blood. If Devon recovered too fast, or Mason didn't stick to the rules, he was going to find himself in an extremely bad position. Horth had to trust Zrenyl to keep Mason occupied if the Nesak decided killing Horth would be worth the forfeit, because Devon was as much as he cope with right now.

Left knee down, Horth had to throw his weight right, very hard, to knock Devon's feet out from under him. There was more luck than he liked in the success of the maneuver, coupled with Devon's almost clownish surprise at his young opponent's novel moves.

Devon toppled right, still without so much as a scratch.

Mason, however, stayed down, too clearly bloodied in the leg to hope it might escape notice. He crawled a meter clear of the struggle before hobbling up and getting help from observers to make it the rest of the way off.

Horth scrambled up on the far side of the enemy line, met Devon's charge and managed to block it. Momentum drove them together, so close Horth could see the other man's angry face through the fine mesh of his mask. They remained that way for the space of a breath, before Horth got himself braced well enough to hurl the Nesak back.

In the respite gained, Horth saw that Hill was bleeding from a wound in his upper arm while his opponent, Charl, was helping Enard gang up on Corin. That left Zrenyl the choice of helping either Horth or Kene's son. Horth grinned a confidence he didn't quite feel at his brother, and left Zrenyl to draw Enard's attack.

Each side had lost one man, so they were still able to match up one on one.

"Kill the Vrellish Error!" Mason shouted at Devon from the sidelines, as he and Horth sized each other up.

Horth charged, unable to contain himself anymore. He drove Devon back towards Zrenyl and Enard, but this time with Devon on their side of the line. Enard realized the danger of Horth coming in from behind and fell back, leading Zrenyl on.

Suddenly, Enard switched partners, shouting something to Devon as he turned to attack Horth. Devon obediently turned his attention to Zrenyl, but Zrenyl refused to be drawn and blocked Enard's slash at Horth's head that might have cost him an eye. The save cost Zrenyl his game, though, when Devon impaled him in the upper arm. Devon tried to drive his sword in farther, through the opening in Zrenyl's jacket, but he didn't get the time. Horth repaid his brother by driving the successful Nesak off.

But they had lost Zrenyl, and were one man short. In the next few seconds Cobin wounded Charl, and Enard caught Cobin on the arm.

Suddenly it was just Horth against both Devon and Enard.

Already in the grip of two attendants, Zrenyl shouted, "Take a safe hit and live, damn you, *rejak't!*"

Zrenyl meant well, Horth was sure of that. But his brother's attempt to advise him seemed ludicrous under the circumstances, because it would require his opponents' cooperation, and neither Enard nor Devon struck him as interested in letting him survive this fight.

He knew that was serious. But it was also no more, nor less, than one piece of the puzzle that he had to solve.

Enard smiled. Then he lunged, or pretended to. Horth was almost irretrievably committed to defensive action when he realized he'd been fooled, and fell back as fast as he could. He learned something vital in that moment because Devon had a chance to go for a flesh wound, but did not. Devon wanted him dead. Horth could use that information.

Balance recovered, Horth engaged Enard in a dance that kept them both busy blocking each other and maneuvering for position. Horth made a point of keeping Devon on the far side of Enard, working for the perfect alignment of both Nesaks.

He was beginning to doubt he could keep it up when he saw what he wanted, at last.

Horth offered Devon a head shot — a fatal one. Devon went for it with an abandon that was all that Horth had hoped for. He deflected the lunge into Enard's chest, knowing the Nesak team captain wasn't too worried about protecting himself there, because of his armor. Devon's sword cut the top layers of Enard's jacket at an oblique angle and snagged for an instant.

In that moment Horth closed with Enard, driving the right-handed fencer's sword clear with his left-handed attack and punching out as hard as he could with the heel of his right hand. His hand hurt where he hit Enard's mask, as Horth knew it would, but he held nothing back. The Nesak's head snapped back. The cloth at the back of the mask did not offer enough resistance to stop it from going farther than it should, and Horth had calculated well for maximum leverage.

Enard's neck broke.

Devon had his sword clear by the time Enard began to fall. Horth ducked, and swept his own sword back to block. Their exchange was fast and furious after that, one on one, but without distractions Devon was no match for the genius of Horth's instinctive anticipation of everything Devon was about to do.

The fight lasted four minutes only because Horth wanted more than first blood, in payment for Devon's own intentions, but the Nesak's body armor and mask offered few lethal targets. As his anger abated Horth gave up and settled for slicing Devon's forearm.

Horth sprang clear. Devon lost control and charged him anyway, with an enraged shout. Horth blocked, and in seconds two burly guards of honor were wrestling Devon to the ground, not only disqualified but guilty of dishonoring his cause.

All at once, like a single, mad being with a thousand mouths, the crowd roared.

Horth was so alarmed he nearly dropped his sword. He had no time to make social mistakes after that, though, because his team rushed back onto the field, some of them still bleeding and others wearing evidence of first-aid attentions.

Zrenyl was hurt the worst, but still couldn't get in enough hugs. "That was brilliant *rejak't*! Brilliant!" Horth's brother kept exclaiming, as he pounded Horth on the back.

Corin's congratulations were equally hearty, but quieter. Hill had lost a lot of blood and had to sit down. Horth began to feel the pain in his right hand where he'd used it to hit Enard, and kept testing it to confirm it still worked properly.

In the end, Corin had to support Hill as they retraced their steps: out of the arena, along the hall lined with guards of honor, and into the hoards of screaming fans who struck Horth as raving mad. A whole troop of Nesaks were necessary just to make it possible for the four of them to get back into Corin's waiting car. Progress along the road back to the Away House was numbingly slow.

Corin and Zrenyl waved to the people out the windows as they talked in loud, excited voices about everything they had done right, and wrong. Even Hill came around and managed to enjoy it all.

Horth sat in the back seat, dumbstruck by the pressing crowd that shouted his name so loudly he could feel the vibration through the car door. He nearly panicked more than once, irrationally sure they would claw their way in with their bare hands.

All he wanted to do when they reached the Away House was to hide in his room. He stayed there the rest of the night, refusing to be dragged out to share in the rowdy celebration taking place on the courtyard. He was grateful to Zrenyl for defending his right to be left alone.

* * *

Hill's story of the way they took out Enard's team at the capital became legend back at Sarn Haven. Horth corrected

Hill at first, when he got details wrong. Horth had not, for example, ever fought more than two of Enard's team at once, and his performance had certainly been flawed. The more he thought about it, the luckier it seemed to him that he'd escaped with his life. There was no stopping Hill, though. Hill even dredged up his memories of Horth involuntarily wrestling him for control in the cockpit on the trip from Gelion, following up his story of Horth's heroism in the melee with remarks like: "And he's got a grip to match!"

Horth found he didn't mind Hill bragging about him quite so much, however, once Zrenyl started saying there was nothing all that special about his little brother, the *rejak't*. The men around Sarn Haven treated him with more respect, and there was one more thing he liked about being the hero of the melee. Whenever any of the unmarried Sarn Haven girls hung on Hill's words of praise, Kale made an effort to be sure she spent more time alone with Horth.

* * *

One morning, weeks after the fight at the capital, while Kale and Horth were out running, Horth found himself struggling with the promise he had given Mrs. Sarn.

Sex was on his mind constantly whenever Kale was around. He was certain she felt the same way, but they had both sworn to behave themselves. So they exercised — a lot.

Much to Horth's disgust, he discovered that arousal hindered him more than it did her, so on top of everything else she beat him more often than she should.

That was why Kale made the crest of a gentle hill ahead of Horth and stood waiting for him there, looking down over a machine yard full of harvesters.

"Look," she said, as Horth caught up. "There's *Zer* Hen."

Horth caught his breath within seconds, but had to give himself a shake, like a farm dog, in the hope that it might sort out his other problem. It didn't, but he was getting used to that.

Trying to ignore the song Kale's very presence sang in his blood, he looked where she pointed. Sure enough, the back end of the chubby priest of Sarn Haven was sticking out the side of a harvester.

Horth had seen machines like the harvester chewing their way across ripe fields all fall, reaping and processing *zer*-barley. A year ago, he would have been interested. Instead, he turned his head to look at the girl beside him.

Kale's chin was tipped up slightly, eyes narrowed against the wind and nostrils sipping the scents on it, which were sure to include Horth as well as the smell of hot metal and old grease from the machine yard below.

Kale smelled female. The April smell that Zrenyl liked to eulogize was more soap than woman, in Horth's opinion. The wind changed with a capricious flicker, delivering Kale's scent to Horth's nose with the impact of a body-piercing stab that utterly murdered his willpower.

The next thing he knew, he had turned and planted himself in front of her, one foot between hers. Kale caught her breath, her braids whipping about her face. Her lips parted. Horth pulled her to him.

The kiss went deep. Her body shuddered, as intensely lost as he was. When she started to panic, she had to wedge both hands between them and shove, hard. They separated with a gasp, Kale looking at him wide-eyed and overcome. Then she seized his hand and tugged him down the slope towards *Zer* Hen at a run.

Horth stumbled on the first step, crippled by his fierce arousal, but the movement helped calm him down. He clenched Kale's hand in return, and ran down the hill with her straight to the priest with his torso stuck into the side of a harvester.

"*Zer* Hen!" Kale all but screamed, still gripping Horth's hand as if she might time slip if she let go.

The priest backed out of his harvester, grunted when he bumped his head, and blinked at them, his forehead smeared in streaks of grime exactly the width of his thick fingers.

Horth noticed the power tool in *Zer* Hen's hand as he set it down. It had a worn and serviceable look with at least six heads that could be selected via a dial. At the moment, the protruding tool was a welding gun and a hot metal tang lingered on the air, strong enough to leave a taste in Horth's mouth.

"Ah," said Hen, taking stock of his petitioners with a worried look. "Is it too late to do anything except set the date for the wedding, then?"

Kale let go of Horth's hand very suddenly.

"No!" she cried. "We haven't — I know I have the red blood, but I am not like that!"

The priest laid a hand on her arm. "There is no shame in desire itself, child," he told her.

Kale looked at the marks his greasy fingers had made on the sleeve of her white shift. The priest withdrew the hand apologetically.

"All the same," he said. "Perhaps you two should think of getting betrothed."

* * *

The betrothal was announced the next day, after dinner.

Horth stood rooted with his will locked on maintaining self control. Kale remained a safe distance away from him, surrounded by women. She had become strangely brittle since their kiss and would not repeat the experiment. He had spent half the day running, trying to wear himself out, and the other half working with *Zer* Hen on harvesters.

"I don't know if marriage is a good idea, for Horth," Zrenyl voiced the sole dissenting argument. "He is awfully young."

"Kale is only fifteen herself," said *Zer* Hen. "But it is no use imagining that they will wait for days, let alone years. It's the Vrellish blood. All you have to do is look at them to see that!"

All twenty adults in the room did exactly that, making Horth's ears burn with embarrassment as hotly as the rest of him burned with overwhelming lust.

"How long do you think they can be kept apart?" *Zer* Hen asked.

Kale kept her eyes on the floor with fierce determination until April giggled; then she burst into action, seizing a pillow off a couch and hurling it at the more Demish-looking girl with such force that April let out a yelp and sat down suddenly on a couch.

Zrenyl sprang to April's side to stand guard.

"As I said... " *Zer* Hen began, trailing off as Kale bolted out the door.

Horth let her go. It was better when she wasn't in the room, although he found — to his great consternation — that the feelings she inspired spilled over into his perception of other women, from stout Mrs. Sarn to Zrenyl's girlish April. He had admitted that problem to *Zer* Hen, and been reassured it was too common a problem, for men, to preclude marriage.

"A betrothal it is, then," said *Zer* Hen when the murmer caused by Kale's departure died down.

Zrenyl looked up from the couch where he sat sheltering April in one large arm. "Is that what you want, Horth?"

Horth cleared his throat and replied in a voice like rumbling gravel, "I think so."

Betrothal, however, did nothing to help with his immediate problem.

Zer Hen recommended cold baths. The whole family conspired to keep Horth and Kale apart while arrangements for the wedding were in motion. Zrenyl made the trip to court to tell their parents and returned with the news that Beryl was again carrying a child.

"Branst says hi," Zrenyl added begrudgingly. "And 'Don't marry a Nesak.'"

Horth also learned his father had been challenged once since Horth had left court. Liege Bryllit had dueled twice, herself, to damp out objections to her steadfast support.

"Mother is a bit worried about you picking a wife as Vrellish as Kale," Zrenyl returned to the subject of Horth's betrothal, and clapped his brother on the back. "But I talked her up for you. Mother will cope."

"Father?" Horth asked.

"He said it's your *rel*," replied Zrenyl.

Horth would have liked a clearer endorsement than the simple recognition that life could offer hard choices, and more than one path might be followed with honor. As a blessing, it was equal parts warning and respectful acknowledgement of Horth's adulthood. It meant too little — and it meant too much.

"Mother approves?" Horth repeated, to be sure.

"On the whole? Absolutely," said Zrenyl.

Horth fell silent, trying to extract a stronger sense of confidence from the fact.

He was glad that his mother was pregnant. But the idea of a fourth child, growing up at Black Hearth without them, felt wrong.

He felt they ought to be together, somehow.

* * *

Arn arrived eight days before the wedding with another member of his fighter hand, named Rad. But it wasn't the wedding they had come for. Something else was afoot, something deeply exciting to every member of Sarn Haven.

Arn spent twenty minutes closeted with Liege Sarn before *Zer* Hen was sent for, while rumors spread throughout the house that Arn was there to raise a fighter for a raid. Then word came down for Hill and Zrenyl to go up. Horth was not invited and it made him restless.

He was surprised when he ran into Kale at the bottom of the stairs, outside the kitchen. They both froze.

Then Kale said, "Arn is going to take a station called *EagleNest* in Red Reach, near the SanHome Jump. He has a writ from the *zer'stan* saying Liege Ky of *EagleNest* has dropped the shield of honor."

Horth's eyebrows contracted at this grave accusation, which stripped the offender of the right to recourse under Sword Law. "How?" he asked, in his deep voice.

"I don't know," she said impatiently. "I'm a woman. I'm not allowed into a council of war!"

Within the Ava's empire it was Fountain Court that took care of punishing *okal'a'ni* behavior. Horth had no idea how Nesaks coped, but it was immediately vital to him that he find out. Kale bristled with the same drive to take action.

"They're meeting in the men's retiring room, upstairs," she told Horth, and bit her lip to stop herself from saying anything more.

Horth took the steps in bounds. He went through the door to the retiring room without thinking and was stopped cold by four pairs of eyes. He recognized Arn, Hill, and Zrenyl. The fourth man had to be the *relsha* named Rad.

Zer Hen was in the room too, but he did not look like he belonged. "Not Horth!" he said at once. "He's too young!"

"His body, perhaps," said Arn. He shouldered past the others to look Horth over in a calculating manner. "But from what I hear, he has a warrior's soul. What do you think," he asked Zrenyl. "Can your brother fly as well as he can use a sword?"

"Horth is not a *relsha*," said Zrenyl. "He's never flown combat."

Horth could see that Zrenyl was excited. If he felt protective of him, Horth understood. He felt protective towards Zrenyl, too. But the price of turning a blind eye to those who dropped the shield of honor meant the end of Sword Law. Horth was aching to go!

"Will you vouch for his honor?" Arn asked Zrenyl.

Zrenyl bristled. "Of course! He's my brother."

"What do you say, Rad?" Arn asked the fourth man.

The *relsha* walked around Horth like a dominant farm dog, on Tark, inspecting a new pup.

"All right," he said at last. "But we leave within the hour or we won't be sure of catching the enemy vulnerable." He turned to *Zer* Hen where the plump priest sat frowning over an official-looking document on his lap.

"Well, *Zer*?" Rad asked. "Will you bless us or not?"

"I suppose I must," *Zer* Hen said, fingers mumbling over the piece of five-sided white vellum bearing the seals and devices of three of the *zer'stan's* five orders. "Strictly speaking, a majority is all that's needed, of course."

"*EagleNest* is held by a female liege, named Ky," Zrenyl told Horth in a breathless voice. "She takes in Nesak defectors. Especially women like your Kale with a strong dash of Vrellish blood. But this time, it was Arn's son, Cobalt. And she's had his child." He glanced over his shoulder in Arn's direction, but the Nesak hand leader betrayed nothing but a cold resolve.

"It's a case of soul theft," Zrenyl concluded with vehemence. "Arn could wind up Vrellish in a future incarnation if he doesn't get that baby back from Ky."

Horth waited for the rest of it, since Arn's grievance so far seemed to be more against his son for being too lax with his favors, than with Liege Ky. No more appeared to be forthcoming, however, which led Horth to a horrible conclusion.

"Man-rape?" Horth asked, and was met with a stir of agitation.

Hill laughed, Arn stiffened, and the *relsha* named Rad looked personally insulted. *Zer* Hen touched his lips with a nervous hand, muttering, "Oh my... " behind his fingers. Zrenyl put his hand over his eyes in a gesture of terminal embarrassment.

Arn snatched the five-sided document out of *Zer* Hen's hands and held it up.

"The point is," he told Horth, "that Liege Ky has dropped the shield of honor, as proved by this document. Warriors do not question what the *zer'stan* chooses to endorse."

"Unfortunately," Rad said in a clipped, economical fashion, "it is not an easy thing to take a station away from Vrellish highborns. Ky normally keeps at least one highborn ward ship out, with others ready to space at the first alarm."

"But we have an ally inside," said Arn. "A Nesak woman who regrets her decision to be Vrellish. We know that Ky has taken her clan off station to help her woo a new ally into becoming her *mekan'st*. The Vrellish do these things with orgies. That's why she's taken all her highborns, leaving *EagleNest* vulnerable. On the other hand, if she wins her new ally, she'll be twice as hard to get at."

"Especially without inviting other members of the family to come along and share the spoils," Hill added, as if that was a good joke.

"Enough talk!" cried Rad. "We have to go — now — or miss our chance!"

"Agreed," said Arn with a nod. "We leave in fifteen minutes. Bring rations with you, since we may not be able to trust any food that the stationers leave for us."

"Let's go!" cried Hill, shooting up. They were all on their feet and astir within seconds.

Zrenyl looked anxious.

"What is it, Nersal?" Arn asked.

"Neither Horth nor I have a Freedom Price," Zrenyl confessed, chagrined.

"*Ack!*" said *Zer* Hen, brightening now that he had something in hand that he could lecture on with confidence. "The need for a Freedom Price is nothing but a Vrellish superstition. We have a way to deal with it here on SanHome. Suppose Horth — for example — was killed. Kale, as his intended, could still bear his child via the rite of priestly possession. All that's essential is that there be a woman designated whom the newly dead soul would naturally be drawn to desire, since a soul must make a dreadful effort to possess the priest assigned to lie with her."

Zrenyl was shocked. "You mean you would make April pregnant, in my place, if I died?" he cried.

Zer Hen flushed and waved a pudgy hand. "Not me! No, no. Of course not! Ordinary *zers* are celibate. Priest possession is a very potent ritual. Only the most holy *zers* can do that!"

"Childless or not, we are proud to fly with you, Zrenyl, son of Nersal, Prince of Nesak," Arn summed up.

Zrenyl had to master his emotions. "And I with you, Arn, Prince of the Royal House of Sarn."

The two men embraced each other. *Zer* Hen got teary as he looked on. Horth met Rad's stare, apparently by accident, but it was not camaraderie that Horth felt from that quarter. He suspected that Rad had his doubts about including the Nersallian brothers: doubts that Horth meant to prove wrong. He and Zrenyl were as good as any Nesak *relshas*.

"Fifteen minutes," Arn reminded his warriors as they broke up.

"Horth!" Zrenyl stopped his brother in the hall as the rest went past.

"We have a special role to play," said Zrenyl. "A role that makes us valuable. Just follow my lead. Do you understand?"

Horth nodded.

"That's the spirit," said Zrenyl, then he dashed away down the hall, no doubt looking for April.

Remembering what Arn had said about rations, Horth headed for the kitchen to collect food. He had actually forgotten all about Kale when he found her waiting at the bottom of the stairs.

The kitchen was deserted, the big stone table where the women made bread and pastries wiped clean and the walk-in pantry at the back swallowed in darkness, like an open mouth.

"Are you flying with them? " Kale asked, her face aglow.

Horth nodded, and then, to prove he could speak, rumbled, "Yes."

Kale swallowed. She wanted to be going with him so badly it was palpable. Instead, she threw herself into Horth's arms.

"I want you," she said, her voice rough with desire. "Now — before you leave. In case you don't come back."

Horth could not find the will to refuse.

Kale dragged him into the open pantry. They were undressed from the waist down within seconds. For the next minute, down on the floor, they needed one another more than either seemed to need air. Kale stifled a cry. Horth climaxed in a burst of sensation so violent that he thought he was going to die. The next thing he remembered was waking up with Kale's anxious face hovering over him.

"Are you all right?" she asked him, horrified.

Horth wasn't sure. He shifted his body and discovered that everything worked fine.

"I know you have to go," she said, and kissed him again, hard.

They could easily repeat what they had just done, but he was leery of it after passing out like that. Nor did he have the time. When he didn't respond, she drew back and sat up cross-legged on the floor, looking flushed and proud and unconcerned about her nakedness.

"That was amazing," said Kale.

Horth grinned at her in answer. Then he scrambled up and left the pantry. He was barely in time to avoid discovery by April, who led the charge of women bustling to put rations together for their menfolk.

Kale hadn't made it out of the pantry, but there was nothing Horth could do about that. With luck, April and the others wouldn't need anything from there to complete their task.

Ten minutes later, Horth was suited up in flight leathers and waiting beside Arn's shuttle on the runway where he had first landed on SanHome.

Hill was the last to report.

"The wife," he said with a sheepish grin as he took his seat beside Horth.

They achieved orbit without incident, each man absorbed with his own thoughts. Everything was ready for them at the orbital station, where they separated to get into their spherical *rel*-fighters.

Horth strapped in and poured over all the controls with a feverish excitement. The *nervecloth* lining of the inner hull rippled with an unblemished gray glow when Horth tested it, revealing no dead patches. He had never felt more thoroughly an adult.

When the order came to launch, his ship shot from the station's rim dock like a stone from a catapult. It was good to be in space, in control of his *rel*-fighter, on his way to do important work. They cat clawed away from the station by drawing power through their phase splicers in tiny sips. The technique was, in fact, a bit like pulling themselves forward by digging virtual claws into the space-time fabric to draw on its binding energy.

Two-Gs acceleration was comfortable for Horth. Cat clawing didn't take too much effort, either. But he was surprised to pick up a tone, like a tuning signal, over the radio. Arn and Rad signaled back.

Then the Nesaks broke into song. They sang one song together, then something more complex with complementary parts.

Horth was astonished. But he knew the song. He had learned it from his brothers, reliving the Nesak War in the nursery on ropes and platforms. The words called on the Watching Dead to help them resist *gap*, explaining that although they went to take by force what could not be settled by Sword Law, it was a much-regretted, necessary act, done to stop the spread of *okal'a'ni* terror.

Horth joined in after Zrenyl, more confident about singing memorized lyrics than he was about conversations. Sharing voices across space made Arn's fighter hand come alive with an electric unity, like a being with a shared will. It was wonderful.

The feeling surged with a great swell of soul touch as they boosted into *skim* together. Radio transmissions were immediately left behind but somehow their souls kept singing, sustaining the link their voices had established.

Horth contributed his wordless strength and fixed determination to be worthy of the men's acceptance. Hill reacted with excitement. Even Arn and Rad seemed impressed. Only Zrenyl's soul touch felt disgruntled, perhaps because he thought Horth was showing off, although details were impossible to pin down. Soul touch was a series of fluttering brushes against raw emotions.

Horth exalted in the Nesaks and his brother. He felt their bravery and their ambition, their camaraderie and willingness to take risks. In all of that, Horth was indistinguishable from them. He felt at peace with the universe and engaged in the righteous defense of its preservation.

The hand ate distance, each pilot nudging up his *skim factor* in a game of friendly rivalry. There was no doubt that Arn was dominant, but through this strange and risky experience of martial soul touch, at an instinctive level Arn recognized Horth as a rival, and bristled.

Horth made an effort to yield to Arn's will, but it backfired when he panicked at the resulting sense of losing his own *grip*, nearly turning a harmonious soul touch into a dangerous wake-lock that could have made one of them flounder.

That was the end of the soul touching. Arn shot ahead and the rest of the hand followed.

They traveled that way in an easy formation for twenty minutes with no sign of encountering a station. Then Zrenyl peeled off and signaled Horth, in *shimmer dance*, to follow.

Horth obeyed, wondering if the special role Zrenyl had spoken about involved a flanking action. Space stations were usually built with large masses or other navigational obstacles at their backs, to reduce the number of viable attack vectors, and his *nervecloth* telemetry was already registering a solar system. He was confident that both he and Zrenyl could fly with enough precision to work between a station and the gas giant behind it. He even felt reckless enough to risk a stray molecule of atmosphere strafing him if some escaped the sweeping action of his ship's intrusion field.

Before long he could see ward ships on his *nervecloth* and primed himself to deal with their reaction once they realized he and Zrenyl were part of a multi-pronged attack.

Two ward ships shot towards them, growing blue on his *nervecloth*, while one fell back, turning red.

But Arn, Rad, and Hill did not appear.

Even more alarmingly, Zrenyl cut speed and began a non-threatening approach — as if he sought dock, not a shakeup.

Horth was taken aback. It was one thing to take out the nobleborn ward pilots of a liege who had dropped the shield of honor, and let Arn demand the station's surrender. It was entirely another prospect to request hospitality! But Zrenyl had told him to follow his lead, so he dutifully cut speed.

Deceleration pressed Horth into his sling cockpit as his heart adjusted effortlessly to higher Gs. Zrenyl continued to show every sign of turning their attack into a docking run!

Perhaps, Horth decided, *they were going to try to challenge after all.* But that didn't seem too smart, given that they were here to punish dishonorable conduct. Besides, he had understood Liege Ky and her highborn relatives were off wooing their counterparts on another nearby station.

Horth wondered if it was going to fall to him to duel, and resented the idea of not being warned. Or maybe their role was to deliver an ultimatum on Arn's behalf, and hope the Vrellish let them leave unmolested. That idea made Horth a bit nervous, also.

The lead ward ship demanded Zrenyl identify himself with a bobbing signal, universal across all of Sevildom.

Zrenyl danced back "House of Nersal," followed by the signal for requesting dock.

For a moment, there was no response.

Shimmer dancing was how ships under *skim* communicated with each other, using direction and the frequency of *shimmer* to create a pattern on other ships' *nervecloth* without moving out of a relatively small patch of space.

It was no good for extended conversations, and beyond the handful of simple patterns, success depended on a shared system of codes.

Horth was not even sure that *EagleNest's* defenders would recognize the Nersallian pattern.

Zrenyl repeated it, followed by a jerk to one side that showed he was a member of the *kinf'stan*.

A ward ship approached after that, testing their sincerity with soul touch. It looped around and matched speed to stroke past Horth, first, and then Zrenyl.

Horth gritted his teeth against the Vrellish pilot's hostile doubts. He caught scintillating flashes of involuntary sexual interest from her at the discovery that he was a highborn, and could not suppress a gut-level response.

But they passed the test. She signaled them to resume their approach. Zrenyl behaved as primly as a Demish lady as he whittled down his *skim'fac*, cut back to cat clawing, and finally coasted into the upright catcher's mitt of a rim dock.

Horth grit his teeth against the head-popping sensation of zero G as he slid into the cup of an adjacent berth. The arm pressed his ship down as the floor sank, and within a minute Horth was in an airlock filling up with breathable air.

He took his dueling sword from the place it was stowed, feeling funny about the declaration of honorable intent that it represented, and swung himself through the struts of his ship's inner hull to slide out the hatch.

Beyond the inner airlock — when it opened — lay a second, larger airlock. Horth strapped on his sword and stepped through.

A bare-chested Vrellish nobleborn dressed in loose trousers and a braided vest was there to greet him, also honorably armed. He was backed up by three stationers armed with either knives or bludgeons. It surprised Horth to see near-commoners armed. The room was warm, and the locals were scantily clad.

"Safe dock," the Red Vrellish nobleborn greeted Horth. "I am Hark. This is Narla." He indicated the woman beside him with a tip of his shaggy head. "She's a stationer." He did not introduce the other two stationers, but they didn't seem to resent it.

"What is your business here?" Hark asked, his grammar acknowledged Horth's superior challenge class but not the finer gradations of birth rank that the Demish insisted on at court.

"I came with Zrenyl," Horth got out, matching Hark's grammar with only a mild degree of uncertainty.

Hark nodded and said, "Come."

The design of the station was identical to Nersallian stations. Outside the rim dock was a platform that connected it to a row of identical docks bracketed on either end by bulkheads. Below, down a steep flight of stairs, was a staging floor lined with stowed gear. An opening in the floor offered a choice of ladders or moving belts with hand- and footholds for descending to the next level.

The locals each selected one of the conveyor belts and Horth did likewise. Riding down between Narla and Hark, his back prickling with an uneasy feeling of danger, Horth wondered again what Zrenyl's mission was and why they had to make themselves so vulnerable. Besides, he had been looking forward to his first serious shakeup. Now he feared he would be stuck on the station when the rest of Arn's hand attacked.

It would be safe enough on the station, in general terms. It was *okal'a'ni* to threaten habitats like space stations with mass destruction. But Horth didn't see the point of testing their hosts' honor quite so rigorously, should he and Zrenyl still be on station when Arn attacked its nobleborn warders.

It crossed Horth's mind that Arn may have wanted to get rid of Zrenyl for some reason. He was glad to spot his brother on the promenade below, surrounded by curious stationers.

The promenade level was lined with cave-like quarters on either side, and heavily populated. At least half of the people showed the evidence of aging that marked them as what Mother would call non-eternals, but it was otherwise hard to tell at a glance which people were nobleborns and which were near commoners. All were brightly clad in shirts, vests, and headdresses, many of them wearing scarves tied about their limbs. Children of all sizes were peppered throughout like seasoning.

"Horth!" Zrenyl greeted his brother in an overly animated fashion, clapping an arm on his shoulder. "You're here."

Zrenyl turned back to a sword-bearing woman wearing a dirty red sash over an equally unhygienic tunic, ripe with the stale smell of body odor.

"Now my brother is here, I will answer your questions," Zrenyl told the woman, speaking down with full, courtly differencing, which Horth found pretentious.

The woman apparently did, too, because she frowned at him sourly.

Horth noticed that a piece of her right nostril was missing, and the lip below it bore an old scar. She was not the only one. Most of the stationers showed evidence of fights they had survived, and all of them could use a bath, in Horth's opinion. At the same time, Horth could not help but be touched by the way the children were an accepted part of what was happening. It was a very Vrellish setting.

"We wish to see Cobalt Tol, son of Arn," Zrenyl declared with forced courage.

"Nesak!" spat the woman with the notched nose, laying a hand on her sword.

Hark shoved her away. "Cobalt is here," he told Zrenyl. "You can see him, but we won't release him. Our liege, Ky, took him in when he fled here to escape some trouble with his father. He seemed happy enough to share her bed and our lives until she had a baby."

"Did Cobalt lay claim to the infant?" Zrenyl asked, showing signs of stress that were less and less understandable to Horth, given how reasonable their Vrellish hosts were proving to be. He was trying to remember what, exactly, Liege Ky had done to earn the condemnation of the *zer'stan*. He had wondered about man-rape but even that was not *okal'a'ni* — just *sla*, the term for dishonorable conduct that was sexually deviant. *Okal'a'ni* sins were of a different magnitude. They threatened rebirth. Spreading disease on purpose, exterminating whole family lines, or destroying habitats were the typical examples.

Horth tried hard to remember what Arn had said about Liege Ky that fitted that description.

"We locked up Cobalt when he started acting like a Nesak," Hark explained, unrepentantly to Zrenyl. "Getting jealous. Threatening to steal Ky's baby. That sort of business. We're not sure what we'll do with him. But it was either lock him up or kill him."

Horth was getting a cold, anxious feeling in his stomach.

To distract himself, he scanned the wall opposite them on the promenade. Its cave-like openings were filled with things like squat tables, mattresses, and hanging bags of belongings sitting just beyond drapes of colorful, if not necessarily clean, fabric. Shapes moved in one of the caves, almost certainly relieving sexual tensions. A pair of entirely naked children played in the mouth of another, tethered to a hook in the wall by sturdy harnesses. Older children scrambled over the rough wall, going from grip to grip and foothold to foothold, in a way that reminded Horth of the rope ladder and platforms in the nursery back home in Black Hearth.

"Of course," Hark was telling Zrenyl, "Cobalt did get busted up a little. He took exception to Ky sleeping with a visiting *sha'st* and tried to put a knife through him from the back. Ky broke his nose, wrist, and collar bone." Hark grinned. "I'm sure you understand. I've heard that Nersallian women are just as much real woman as ours."

Zrenyl swallowed. He was getting angry. He was scared too.

Horth felt something. It was too subtle to say what, but the Vrellish surrounding him sensed it, too. He saw a handful of the nobleborns go still or snatch a breath too suddenly. A child cried.

"Nesak women are the real women!" Zrenyl erupted in a sudden flare of anger. Hark blinked at Zrenyl's vehemence and exchanged a look with the scar-faced woman.

The next moment, Horth's life went terribly wrong.

The whole station quivered. Horth felt it through his feet and in his very soul. It had to be Arn, Hill, and Rad. He almost sensed them: flying in formation, sweeping in too hard for the nobleborns to stop.

They were traumatizing space around the station!

Horth staggered. Shrieks drowned out an alarm. Hark turned to bolt towards the lift up to the docks but Zrenyl drew his sword, his face wild with fear and determination. Horth watched in horror as his brother ran Hark through from behind.

Another, harder tremor shook the station. Bags, bodies, and a shower of smaller objects tumbled out of caves along the promenade.

Narla went down shrieking, her arms waving convulsively about her head. Hark's body bunched up as he tried to rise, bleeding from Zrenly's stab, and slumped again with a groan.

Three quarters of the stationers were on their knees, unconscious, or doubled over throwing up. The attack had felled the lesser Sevolites, separating them from the nobleborns on station in a way that general attire and behavior had not. Most of the nobleborns were running for the docks.

Horth watched a toddler fall from a cave halfway up the wall. It seemed to take a long time. Its little body struck with a soul-sickening crunch.

The nobleborn with the notched nose recovered from her shock enough to snatch a knife from a dazed stationer and hurled herself at Zrenyl with a murderous cry. Zrenyl could never have stopped her in time. He was wrestling another nobleborn, his sword dropped on the floor.

Horth reacted without conscious thought. He body blocked the notched-nose woman, seizing her knife hand.

As the four of them contended, two-by-two, another wave of *skim shock* hit the station. The scream of human protest was less deafening now. The air smelled of urine, the sour reek of vomit, and the metallic tang of blood. Some of the felled stationers were sobbing helplessly on the floor. Those who could were trying to assist loved ones. Somebody was wailing for Ky and the station's highborns.

Arn's strategy was clear now. He was targeting the non-eternals on the station, hoping that it had the structural integrity not to crack! Trusting, if he cared at all, that Horth and Zrenyl, as highborns, would be able to hold out. But for what?

Horth twisted the knife away from his opponent and hurled her into Zrenyl's man. Zrenyl took advantage of the break to snatch up his sword — and found Horth's hand clamped over his wrist like a band of iron.

"You'll get us both killed, *rejak't!*" Zrenyl yelled, hoarse with fear and excitement.

But the nobleborns they had been fighting did not take the opportunity to attack. One stayed down. Notch-nose decided she had better things to do, and staggered off towards the lift back to the docks. Hark was on his feet again and heading there, too, leaving a trail of blood.

"Sarn! Are you Sarns?" A voice pieced the sounds of suffering around them as a wild-eyed woman fought her way past felled and moaning bodies towards Zrenyl.

"Yullie Sarn!" Zrenyl called back, breaking Horth's hold with a violent wrench. "You're the Nesak defector?" he asked her excitedly. "You know where I can find Arn's son, Cobalt?"

Her face was streaked in tears of terror, tears no truly Vrellish woman would be able to cry. But she was highborn. She was still on her feet, and no worse than hysterical.

"The baby!" she shrilled, clutching a bundle to her chest from which a limp, infant leg dangled. "The baby's in a *gap* coma! Oh gods! He won't wake up!"

He and Zrenyl, Horth realized with chilly reason, had docked in order to get Arn's injured son and the female defector off. And perhaps to secure the docks from inside for Arn's arrival.

Horth became aware that he was very, very angry.

"Where is Cobalt?" Zrenyl shouted to the Nesak woman.

Horth bolted for the lift up to the docks.

He heard Zrenyl shout after him, "What are—?" And more frantically, in a panic. "Horth!"

The lift up to the docking floor was motionless. A nobleborn pilot had fallen trying to climb up. She lay moaning at the bottom. Horth stepped over her and climbed swiftly.

The next shock wave hit when he was near the top.

He heard his own voice shouting out in wordless outrage, but he did not black out and he did not stop. His whole digestive tract locked up like a clenched muscle.

No one stopped him from getting into his ship. No one stopped him from launching. No one was capable. Just like one of the station's nobleborn defenders, he shot clear of *EagleNest Station* cat clawing as hard as he dared.

Without warning, Horth's soul seemed to lurch out of his body and then snap back. The nearest of the nobleborn pilots, ahead of him, lost his *grip* and disappeared.

It was terrible sharing the station's helplessness, blind to *rel*-skimming attackers without *nervecloth* telemetry that he could pick up only under *skim*. But Horth could not *skim* until he was clear of the challenge sphere or he would only add to the station's problems.

He clawed harder, accelerating at over nine Gs. He felt instinctively that his heart could cope.

Then he was clear to boost into *skim* and his *nervecloth* lit up.

Three blue spots zoomed towards him, highborn bright, coming in for another pass. Pairs of out-classed defenders targeted each highborn and the Nesaks were forced to veer off. But they regrouped faster than the nobleborn were able to. They went after one Vrellish nobleborn and then the next, cutting them out of existence in a rehearsed, sheering action. Other defenders flocked to help and broke up again as two of them interfered with each other and disappeared.

It was not possible to bring greater numbers to bear very easily. Too many *rel*-ships in one place dissolved space around them, drowning their pilots in *gap*.

Horth charged up from the dark space of the station's challenge sphere looking like another new defender. But he did not stop when his *skim'fac* hit the limits of endurance for a nobleborn. He filled the Nesaks' *nervecloth* in a blue blaze of anger. Furious. Righteous. And unstoppable.

Two attackers fell back. Horth had the momentary sensation of the third wavering, in shock, and caught Hill's feelings of betrayal as the Nesak shot past. Memories of Hill's praise and affection glanced helplessly off the burning anger in Horth's heart.

Arn and Rad came around, trying to catch Horth between them.

On a delta patch of his *nervecloth*, that gave him a rear view on his forward *nervecloth*, Horth saw the ward ships change formation in an attempt to engulf him and two oncoming Nesaks. They hadn't figured out that he was helping them.

Horth dropped hard, his sling cockpit slamming around to match new definitions of up and down. His overpowered cardiovascular system kept pace with new demands. He evaded the misguided nobleborns, but Arn and Rad went after him together, closing ranks.

The defenders regrouped, keeping Hill separate from Arn and Rad. Hill spotted two nobleborn ships making a run for it at the same time as Horth. They were pelting away, deeper into Red Reach, at a punishing pace for nobleborns.

For an instant, Horth assumed they had opted to save their own lives. Then he realized they were going to fetch their highborns.

Distracted, Horth caught a slap of soul touch from Arn as he thundered past, heading in Hill's direction. He feared he must have time slipped for seconds he could not afford, because he surfaced to find everything had moved.

Two highborns were making for the dark space that concealed the station to shake it up again, killing or stunning more of those on board. The third was gaining on the fleeing nobleborns. Horth could stop the run on the station, or he could stop the third ship closing on the messengers.

Or maybe he could do both.

A surge of madness took control. He let the power that bound the universe hurl his tiny ship forward on high *shimmer*, keeping *gap* tight in comparison but still too wide for long-term survival.

Heart straining to keep blood in his brain, he flung himself between Rad and Hill, driving them wide apart. Nobleborn defenders went after each of them. It would not be enough to take the highborns out, but it was enough to hold them off.

Horth shot off in the opposite direction after Arn.

The fleeing nobleborns split up — good tactics when up against a single ship that was more powerful. The Nesak attacker went for one like a dog snapping at a fleeing grabrat. The second Red Vrellish nobleborn probably expected Horth to go after him.

But Horth went for the Nesak, instead, too late to stop him from swamping his first grabrat, but in time to stop him from turning on the second one.

The clash of wills in soul touch jarred Horth to the core. He had expected some consciousness of guilt, or greed, or a drive for dominance. He had not been prepared for Arn's blazing self-righteousness, fierce enough to match Horth's own!

Only belief in the Watching Dead sustained Horth in the face of Arn's disgust. He knew his Nersallian ancestors agreed with him even if the Nesak ones might not. He also knew they couldn't help him right now.

Arn peeled away, heading for the nobleborn signal ship going to call *EagleNest's* highborns home. Horth took off after him and cut him off.

Then he realized he was really in trouble, because the other two Nesaks had followed him out, away from the station. They must have decided that it would be easier to finish the job back at *EagleNest* after reducing his ship to a navigational hazard by shattering it into hullsteel dust.

Horth did not wait to find out. He picked the pilot who felt weakest and attacked.

Hill's surprise, as his *grip* failed him, penetrated where anger had not. But Horth had no time for regrets now.

He had seconds to prepare for Rad and Arn.

Horth threw his *gap* wide, making him disappear.

It was not a move many pilots would risk, since simple death was preferable to becoming Soul Lost. Horth simply felt his *grip* was strong enough.

When he reappeared a quantum leap to one side, he knew he had time slipped longer than before, but did not know by how much. The uncertainty felt like going blind, because timing mattered so much in a shakeup!

Getting his bearings, he saw that the battle had shifted away from the point where he had vanished and the deployment of ships around his position looked all wrong.

With a jolt of recognition, he also realized there were Vrellish reinforcements in the fray now, and his *nervecloth* was streaked with sharp intensities of color that screamed highborn!

Before he could get properly reoriented, someone noticed him, too. Three of the new highborn ships came for him, shifting their formation with an instinct for not fouling each other that most Nersallian pilots had to train to master. People said Red Vrellish highborns were born knowing how.

And he did not think the Red Vrellish where in the mood to discriminate friend from foe. For a moment, Horth considered dropping out of *skim* and taking his chances at getting shaken out of existence while he waited, blind and becalmed, but in the end, the idea was too unnerving.

He slammed his cockpit around and poured on *skim'facs*. It immediately felt like an error. All three Vrellish gained on him steadily.

They shot wide past a sun and its few, bulky planets that registered on his *nervecloth* as obstacles. They were well clear of *EagleNest Station* by now, but Horth's pursuers did not let up.

They shot off across Red Reach, together.

Horth stuck to the route he had traveled on the way to SanHome. He didn't know Red Reach well enough to risk leaving established space lanes. The harder the vacuum the better, when manifesting in it many times a second and flying through a dust field could splatter a pilot on his own inner hull.

Even in hard vacuum, *shimmer* caused internal bleeding at the cellular level, but he knew those effects could be endured for hours. And it was going to take hours to cross Red Reach from one gate to the other.

Horth's other choice was to head for the gate to Alliance Reach, but that never occurred to him. He knew the jump, and might have expected help from the highborn ward ships guarding it on the other side, but he instinctively shied away from the idea of leading a trio of murderous Red Vrellish into House Nersal's industrial heartland.

Besides, it was to Killing Reach that exiles went and surely, Horth thought, he was nothing but a renegade now. He had killed Hill, and he had no idea what had happened to his brother.

Killing Reach was not an easy place to get to, which felt right as well. To get there, he would have to pass through the *Reach* of Gelion and then through Golden Reach, beyond.

Horth was beginning to hope he could make it, when one of his pursuers sped up! Slowly, he was pushed past seven *skim'facs*. Blood vessels burst in his nose, filling his mouth. His will to survive seemed to thin out. Neither he nor his pursuer could sustain this for long!

Desperately, Horth cut back, and noticed with some pleasure that one of the three ships trailing him had dropped out. Only two of the Red Vrellish highborns gave chase now, and they seemed prepared to pace themselves. His pursuers cut speed after another ten minutes of mutual punishment, and Horth gratefully reduced his own mix to five *skim'facs*.

A trial of endurance followed: Horth struggling to keep ahead, pushing his *skim'fac* up when he had to, then trimming it back whenever possible.

He was conscious of nearly overdosing on *gap* during the early part of the run, and adjusted his mix to stress *shimmer*.

Blood in the lungs was a common symptom of high *shimmer*, but he trusted his highborn physiology to cope. He made sure he drank from his cockpit-mounted water bottle, spiked with the proteins and sugars needed for regeneration, since he had no desire to find out if he was Vrellish enough to become *rel-osh*.

He played a game with his pursuers, never going faster than necessary to keep ahead and slowing down whenever they let up.

Finally, the jump into the *Reach* of Gelion loomed up. It glowed on the *nervecloth* lining of Horth's ship in false colors. All a jump was, in reality, was a place where the binding energy of the universe was thin enough to let a ship fall between reaches if it opened itself up to a big dose of *gap*. *Skim*-dependant telemetry could detect the thinness. The glow was an arbitrary choice of how to paint the result onto *nervecloth*.

Stations lined the way before Horth, labeled by signals he picked up from continuously broadcasting beacons. No light-speed signal could reach a *rel*-ship in real time, of course, but many of the stations had been broadcasting for hundreds of years, littering space with signals Horth's ship could sample during its in-phase manifestations. Mobile battlewheels showed up as tiny, nameless lumps. There was no point in a battlewheel declaring its identity by beacon unless it planned to stay in one place for a long time.

Every station buzzed with a complement of ward ships, there to guard their vulnerable habitats from *rel*-ships flying at them like maniacs. Ships exactly like Horth's and his two Vrellish pursuers, in fact.

They attracted ward ships like magnets as they sped past. So long as they kept going, however, the warders let them pass.

The attention seemed to sober up one of Horth's escorts, who fell back to flash a dance to the other one. Horth caught the gist of the *shimmer* dance on a delta patch of his *nervecloth*.

To Horth's delight, what he read in the *shimmer dance* was an order to break off pursuit. He was less impressed when it was utterly ignored. His first reaction as a Nersallian was something along the lines of: *He can't do that!*

Nersallians took orders in a shakeup. Pure Vrellish were notorious for doing what they wanted to do. And this one, apparently, wanted to destroy Horth.

Horth and his stubborn pursuer took the jump seconds apart.

A blazing forest sprang upon Horth's consciousness, challenging him to find his way through. He emerged feeling singed by the experience, the pleasant memories of childhood sharpened to a deadly edge by the pressure of the wild soul in pursuit.

On the far side, Horth dodged saner traffic, picking up ward ships alarmed by the recklessness of his arrival. He and his pursuer were warded all the way along the populated space lane leading from the jump towards Gelion.

Horth headed for the jump to Golden *Reach*, beyond the turn that would have taken him to Gelion. His angry pursuer kept up. As they approached the jump, a Demish battlewheel sent out a fighter hand. Horth's pursuer gave up all at once. He peeled up, cutting *skim'fac*, and shimmered his willingness to back off.

Horth flew on, darting through the Golden Demish formation of slow-flying highborns with his heart in his throat. He plunged through the jump into Golden Reach escorted by three of the Goldens. This jump was one he knew less well than others. He felt himself bombarded with words falling out of heavy books. He heard the babble of Demish receptions on Fountain Court and saw girls and boys in fussy Demish clothing fishing trinkets from a fountain.

Then he was through. Horth gasped with relief at the transition. His brain hurt. He felt half numb. But his Golden Demish escort had stuck close.

Unable to stop now for the sake of pure momentum, Horth endured their soul touch as they swept past. They believed he was a mad Vrellish criminal, run out of Red Reach to make his way into the badlands of the empire where he belonged. He must have felt exactly like that to the Demish, under soul touch.

They escorted him all the way across Golden Reach and, when he hesitated, unsure of how to make the jump to Killing Reach, plunged through it with him to deliver him like baggage on the other side.

Horth experienced this last jump like a plunge from a great height onto a cold gray floor.

When he came to himself in Killing Reach, he was drifting in normal space, alone. The bad feeling of zero G made his head pound. He cut back into *skim* once more and calmed down. But he knew he had to stop as soon as he could. He was exhausted, probably irrational, bleeding internally, and dazed from too much soul touch and *gap* exposure.

But Horth had never been in Killing Reach before. He had no idea which way was safe to fly. He only knew he had to find dock soon, or one way or the other he was going to die.

When two ward ships reared up before him, dancing the familiar codes for "House of Nersal", he danced back a request for sanctuary in their home dock.

Less than an hour later, Horth landed with a stagger on the floor of a Nersallian airlock. He held the middle of his dueling sword tightly in his left hand and shook his head. The head shake made things worse. He did not even realize he had overbalanced until one knee hit the floor with a painful jolt.

His response was to drive himself up again and find his balance. A couple of blinks improved his vision. His nose oozed blood; so did his eyes and lungs. His shirt, beneath his flight leathers, was rank with perspiration. Every muscle ached and his mind was rubbed raw.

He flexed to prove his limbs were still his to command, then slowly and deliberately began to strap on his dueling sword.

A woman watched. She wore a sword herself, which was a good sign. It said that she would not indulge in a dishonorable attack. Her chest braid declared her an *imsha* under Liege Bryllit's command. But her face had a clenched look of hatred, too intense to be anything but personal.

She addressed Horth in an angry bark that struck Horth's ears as nothing more than sounds. He understood her well enough, however, when she drew her sword.

He cleared his own with fatalistic calm.

Another voice bellowed, "Sinka, halt!"

Horth blinked, and looked through bloodshot eyes at a second woman.

Tash, Liege of Bryllit, strode across the docking bay floor to strike down Sinka's sword with her own, rattling off more angry words that Horth could not decode. He could make out no more than a reference to travel respite. Then he passed out.

* * *

Horth woke, twenty-six hours later, to the worst post-flight hangover of his life. Someone was slapping him. He snatched at the offending hand with a snarl, but could not sustain his anger and slumped back. Whoever it was braced him in her arms and poured pilot's nectar down his throat.

"Well, well, young liege-son," said Tash Bryllit, "we thought we might have lost you! Welcome back." She rubbed his throat and ordered, "Swallow."

He obeyed, opened his eyes, and blinked at the wholesome features of the large, confident woman holding him in her arms. After that, he slept again. The next time he work up, Bryllit was sleeping, naked, in the bed beside him with her arm thrown across his stomach.

Horth sat up. Bryllit propped herself up on an elbow. "Feeling better?" she asked. Horth just stared at her.

"I've let Hangst know I've got you," she said, with a broad smile. "He approved of the sleeping arrangements."

Horth felt his brow furrow, trying to grasp what she meant by that. She explained by leaning towards him with unmistakably amorous intentions.

"Let's see if you're up to your father's standard," she remarked.

It was unfair, Horth thought, *to apply that test while he was convalescent.* But at least he understood what he was doing in Liege Bryllit's bed. Horth was, Vrellish fashion, taking over a family obligation. It was something of a coup for him, in fact, since Hangst had offered Bryllit nephews before now, who were turned down. Horth was honored.

He accepted the role with characteristic fearlessness, even though he did not count his performance as more than barely adequate the first time. But he made up for that by the time his three-day travel respite had passed. Bryllit was a perfect match for his straight forward sexual appetite: quickly roused and easily satisfied. What he lacked in experience he made up for in stamina, which any woman as Vrellish as Bryllit appreciated in a man.

On the middle of the third day, Bryllit returned to her quarters from a shift on the bridge, looking troubled, to find Horth working out on her exercise floor.

He was doing a routine Hara had taught him for warming up.

Bryllit unbuckled her sword and sat down to watch.

Moments later, a nobleborn came to lay out a plate of food. Fleet officers used the most Sevolite orderlies they could because it was too punishing for commoners to work on a *skim*-capable battlewheel for very long.

"I'll be sorry if she kills you," Bryllit told Horth when the orderly had gone.

Horth finished the set of movements he was already committed to, stopped, and turned around. He was naked from the waist up and sweating. His skin prickled with the implication he was going to have to duel.

Bryllit tossed him a towel.

"Who?" asked Horth.

"Sinka," said Bryllit. "The *imsha* you met when you first arrived."

Horth sorted through what little he had learned about Sinka, but all he knew was that she was the captain of the battlewheel they were on and it was clear to him that the two women were *brerelo*.

"Why?" Horth asked.

"Because you are Beryl's son," said Bryllit. She took a gulp of strained fruit juice and wiped her mouth on a plain square of towel. "Because of Vrenn, most of all. That's the heart of it." She frowned.

"Who is Vrenn?" Horth wanted to know.

"One of your half-sibs on your father's side," said Bryllit. "And my son." She settled her robust body back in her chair to get comfortable. "Sinka taught Vrenn how to use a sword and bore his Freedom Price. She was Vrenn's mentor and *mekan'st*. She never speaks of him now, except to challenge any Nesak she gets half a chance to take down."

"I am not a Nesak," said Horth. He had shut himself off from that option when he turned on Arn's raiders back in Red Reach.

"You don't have to be a Nesak," said Bryllit. "You just have to be your mother's son."

She leaned forward with an elbow on the table, pushing back the dinner tray. "Vrenn became my heir during the Nesak War. He had to grow up fast. Highborns did, then. He was a *rel* man. Not only an uncanny *relsha*, but a leader. And good with his sword. He did not want peace with the

Nesaks on the terms they offered — he objected to Hangst's marriage. They argued, but Hangst stood by his decision. Vrenn challenged your father. His father, too, of course, but Hangst hardly knew him in that regard. He did not raise his gift children the way he raised you and your brothers. In those days, he still acted like a proper Vrellish man. But he respected Vrenn's contribution in the war, and he respected the fact he was my son. That duel was bitterly hard for me to watch — I was Hangst's heir, Vrenn was mine. I told them I would champion neither one against the other. They would have to settle it themselves, by the sword."

Bryllit paused, but did not look away or by any other gesture suggest that she wished to shy from the facts. Instead, she said starkly, "Hangst won."

"But he did not kill Vrenn," Bryllit followed up. "Perhaps he should have. Vrenn chose to accept treatment from the Monatese and survived. Sinka, for one, would have coped better if Vrenn had died. But he didn't die — he merely lost the courage to duel and turned pirate, here in Killing Reach. Vrenn became no better than one of those Killing War Reetions, prepared to stop at nothing and respecting no law. If he had died, instead, he might have been reborn again cleanly by now."

Bryllit selected a strip of dried beef, coated in a sugary paste with a nutty base, took a bite and waited until she had chewed it thoroughly and swallowed before going on. "I must respect Sinka's challenge. If you wish to live here, on this station, it is her right. If you don't, you may leave, now."

Horth thought about that. He decided there would always be some kind of challenge from someone who did not think he belonged. He felt a little shaky about it, since Sinka was much older than him and a battlewheel captain. But he felt too lonely to give up what he had found with Bryllit, either. He concluded that he may as well face Sinka's challenge, here and now.

He said, "I will fight."

"*Ack rel*, then," said Bryllit with a smile. "We'll make a night of it tonight, but see you get the sleep you need, too."

* * *

Horth faced Sinka the next morning on the docking floor where he had first landed. The location was her choice, to symbolize her refusal to accept him as crew.

They squared off, each dressed in light clothes with their heads exposed. Bryllit stood for both combatants as their judge of honor. About thirty other witnesses were able to squeeze into the room, including half a dozen members of the *kinf'stan*. Whatever happened, there would be reliable reports and stories told.

Sinka's face had the cool, intent look of an experienced duelist. She waited for Horth to attack, expecting him to show impatience. The silence in the room was oddly peaceful. Sinka edged sideways, threatening obliquely. Horth mirrored her. They engaged, beating each other's blades, but Horth would not attack. She had challenged him. He would wait for her to show her temper.

When she did go for him, it was with a controlled and modest test of his defenses. He parried effortlessly and they both backed off, watching and assessing each other.

Sinka was left-handed, like Horth, which was typical for Vrellish Sevolites. She exposed her right side a little, but Horth ignored the invitation. She disliked that. Her lips pressed hard against each other. The next second she attacked in earnest.

A quick exchange followed. Horth easily parried, but Sinka stepped in on his riposte, forcing their blades to lock at the bottom third. Horth swung his sword arm out, pushing her blade away, and they sprang apart once more.

They circled in silence, sword tips testing each other's nerve by jabbing in and out tauntingly. Never committing.

Then she lunged for his heart. Horth parried in a downward arc, but Sinka's point didn't quite clear his nearest thigh, grazing him almost by accident, even as Horth whipped his own blade, back up and around, to pierce her forearm. She grunted, and wrenched her arm back, off his tip.

"Hold!" shouted Bryllit, and half a dozen highborns intervened to break them up before they could regroup to go on.

Bryllit looked from Sinka to Horth and back. Then she said to Sinka, "He is better able to fight with that scratch than you are with that arm. But you took first blood." She waited to be sure she had her friend's attention before adding, "Be satisfied."

Sinka glared at Bryllit, clutching her bleeding sword arm in her right hand. Then she looked at Horth, as he waited, and said, "*Ack rel*, then. Let him be one of us."

Part IV

Falling Out

188 Post Treaty

It was six years before Horth returned to Black Hearth. He exchanged messages with his parents via Branst, and in that way heard news of the birth of his new brother, Eler, and keep abreast of Mother's subsequent pregnancies.

Bryllit had a baby she named Dorn. When Dorn was eight months old she took him to a genotyping ceremony on Tark. Horth was not invited to attend, but he was thoroughly pleased when she informed him that he was the sire. He got Branst to help him write an announcement, for their parents, declaring that he had a Freedom Price.

Zrenyl had survived the *EagleNest* debacle. When Dorn was one, Zrenyl married April, on SanHome. The *kinf'stan* urged Hangst to disown his eldest son, severing him from the right of challenge for the title of Liege Nersal. Hangst refused.

Father was challenged twice, and Bryllit put down another challenger. Branst claimed that most *kinf'stan* were fed up with Nesak encroachments on Black Hearth. But Bryllit told Horth that a growing minority were getting used to trade with Nesaks.

Horth was not surprised to learn his father won his duels with the *kinf'stan*. He expected Hangst to win duels.

"Mother doesn't watch any more," Branst told his exiled brother. "She stays up in the nursery with *Zer* Sarn and little Eler. The runt says he sees it through with her to add his prayers to the Watching Dead, but the truth is Eler's squeamish. And spoiled rotten!" Branst added with a grunt. "Can you imagine you or me or Zrenyl getting away with avoiding a title duel?"

Eventually, the uproar over Zrenyl's marriage ended.

Horth set his heart on becoming a battlewheel captain, like Sinka. To do that, he first had to fly as a *relsha* and then as an *avsha*, a hand leader.

A *relsha*'s work in Killing Reach was dangerous. Persistent threats to navigation lingered, purposefully caused by Reetions in their efforts, two hundred years ago, to stop a Sevolite invasion. They had polluted space lanes with clouds of dust, set loose deadly viruses, destroyed habitat, and generally done every *okal'a'ni* thing imaginable, with no care for future generations. Struggling to set right some small piece of the fallout, Horth was inclined to believe that only soulless beings who cared nothing about rebirth could have been so irresponsible.

After three years, Horth achieved the rank of *avsha*. He met people he had never imagined existed, and he soul touched criminals he wished he had never experienced, but in the cockpit he was always able to wield his anger like a sword.

He saw enough during the years in Killing Reach to harden his early belief in Sword Law to a diamond-hard conviction. Killing Reach offered more opportunities for studies of that nature than anywhere else in Sevildom. Horth worked with engineering crews to clean up shattered stations that were strewn about with flotsam that included bodies. He evacuated starving stationers, cut off from the flow of trade by their leader's treacherous reputation, who got so desperate that they ate their own children. And he witnessed the hideous outcome of struggles that stupidly destroyed the very habitat they fought over.

War in space destroyed the very means of man's survival in a wasteland cold enough to numb the greatest greed, and huge enough to force perspective on the mightiest of egos.

Pilots flew two days on and five off, leaving Horth time for station-side pursuits. He spent most of that time working as a voluntary apprentice with an engineering detail or working on ships in dock. He felt he ought to know as much as possible about battlewheels if he was going to command one.

But though he made a place for himself in Killing Reach, his heart remained on Fountain Court, and he looked forward to Branst's visits.

* * *

Horth was in the officers' gym giving his son a fencing lesson. Little Dorn brought up his shortened sword belatedly. Horth poked him in the chest and the child staggered. Horth took a step back to wait for the four-year-old to overcome his tears. It surprised him that Dorn cried. He had expected any child of his and Bryllit's to be too Vrellish for that.

Dorn quickly mastered the hurt and repeated the failed move, to practice it. Then he nodded to let Horth know he was ready again. Horth repeated the attack, instructively, and this time Dorn parried. Horth rewarded him with a swift smile and Dorn beamed with pleasure.

"Horth!" Branst's voice hailed him from above.

Horth looked up to see Branst standing on the deck of the observation gallery ringing the gym floor.

"I'm coming down!" Branst said and disappeared.

Four-year-old Dorn managed to keep quiet only until Branst burst out onto the gym floor.

"I've got a new sister, Branst!" Dorn announced.

"Really!" Branst exclaimed with satisfying pleasure. "Has Liege Bryllit been generous to the Waiting Dead again so soon!" He slapped Horth on the back. "You must be quite an inspiration, brother."

"No Branst!" cried Dorn. "Not a full sister. A regular ha'sister, on my sire's side. By Captain Sinta!"

Branst raised both eyebrows. "Sinta, no less!" he praised his brother. "Isn't she the one who welcomed you with a duel?"

Horth grinned, as pleased as Dorn about the new arrival. He did not mention that Sinta had threatened to challenge him again if he paid as much attention to her baby as he continued to exhibit towards Dorn. Sinta considered it a Nesak failing that Horth took an interest in the infants he sired. Vrellish men were supposed to help raise the children of their mother's line, not their own.

Over the years, Branst had taken to playing up the Vrellish threads in the braid he shared with Horth and Zrenyl. Now he was blatantly favoring Monatese attire, and had gone so far as to weave green threads into his house braid at the top, as if he could predict his soul's future.

Dorn badgered Branst to let him show off the new move he had just mastered. Branst obliged, donning a safety jacket, and letting Dorn score hits against him. Horth understood that one had to do that with a trainee, but he disapproved of the way Branst encouraged Dorn by feigning surprise when it was clear his brother had purposely allowed a weak effort to get past him. He saw no point in giving Dorn a false sense of confidence.

Branst wrapped up the interlude with a gift of candy purchased on the Market Round in the cosmopolitan city of UnderGelion.

"Do you think you could lend me your sire for a little while, now?" he asked Dorn. "I've come to ask a favor."

"Is it to do with the swearing at court?" Dorn asked, losing interest in his present. "And if Horth is going, can

I come? I want to meet my grandfather, Liege Nersal. Would you ask Mother for me, please, Horth?"

Horth said, "No."

Dorn looked crestfallen. Horth pulled him into a companionable hug, because he understood his little son's frustration. He would have liked nothing better than to take one of his children to court to show off to his parents, but he had no illusions about either of their mothers allowing him to borrow them.

"Next time," Branst told Dorn.

"But I don't want to wait for years and years!" the child protested, threatening to pout.

"You think people only go to court for Swearings?" asked Branst. "*P'rash*, child! There are loads of other reasons. Your mother might take you the next time she goes to clinch a contract, attend a genotyping, or take in the pan-Demish tournament."

"Bet she won't," Dorn said sulkily. "She doesn't like court."

"Well," Branst admitted, "there is that."

One of Bryllit's grandsons, who was ten years older than Dorn, showed up to take him off Horth's hands. Horth gave Dorn a push in the direction of his maternal relative.

With a last, wistful look at Branst, Dorn went off obediently.

"How is Eler?" asked Horth, once they were alone.

"Eler is Eler," Branst said impatiently. "Hard to shut up and happy to be everyone's baby for as long as possible." He laughed. "Sort of your opposite — you grew up fast and never said much."

Horth headed for the changing room. Branst followed, acting fidgety. Horth decided he was nervous about explaining the favor he had come to ask, and would tell him lots of other things first. That was all right. Horth didn't mind waiting.

"Mother's had the baby," said Branst. "It's a girl this time. They've named her Beryllan. Eler spends as much time looking after her as mother does. Uncle Sarn doesn't like it, so I do. Sarn doesn't like anything Eler does. The kid asks too many questions."

"Good," said Horth. He undressed with his typical dispatch in all things practical, and stepped into the hygiene chamber.

Branst paced about the austere, military locker room, working up his courage.

In the hygiene chamber, Horth used the pull-down toilet, sealed it away, covered his eyes with a mask left hanging on a metal peg, and turned on the blast shower. The chamber spewed a fine mist of cleansing fluid, followed by an equally parsimonious rinse and blow-dry cycle. It was less than gentle on one's skin, but it got the job done without wasting water.

"I don't know how you cope without a bath now and then," remarked Branst, as Horth stepped out of the hygiene chamber, opened his locker, and began to put on his clothes.

"I don't know how you cope with the lack of entertainment, either," his courtly brother went on in a familiar vein as Horth dressed in fleet fatigues. "I mean, all there is to do is swap stories about life and death struggles in space over glasses of station gin that taste like recycled urine. Apart from all the sex and duels, of course. What else is there?"

"Engines," said Horth, by which he meant more than simply the phase splicers that let a ship draw power from the binding force of the space-time continuum. He meant everything to do with the operation of the station and its *rel*-fighters. Working on "engines" was like a conversation in which the machinery revealed its function and he taught it how to do its job better.

Branst understood nothing of such pleasures. He preferred to listen to the music of West Alcove courtesans, peruse old books, or debate the rules of rebirth and the whereabouts of Earth over drinks at a cafe on the Plaza — pastimes that would have bored Horth silly.

Branst kept still for a whole minute, watching Horth seal up the jacket of his uniform with the three claw marks of the Nersallian dragon set high on the collar and House Bryllit's emblem over his heart.

"You are coming to court for the Swearing, aren't you?" Branst asked. "As Bryllit's retainer, of course, but you know you could stay with us."

Horth reached for his sword.

"Horth!" Branst caught his arm and met his brother's eyes. "Will you talk to me, please?" Branst let go, looking terribly anxious. "I really need someone I can talk to."

Horth said, "Why?"

Branst sat down astride a bench that was bolted to the floor. "I am scared," he admitted. "I am scared that Dad won't swear to Delm again, like Di Mon wants. I am scared a rift is opening between them. I am scared the *kinf'stan* won't accept Dad receiving Zrenyl at Black Hearth now that he's married to a Nesak."

"Zrenyl is coming?" Horth asked.

"Yes," sighed Branst.

Horth answered with a grunt.

"I'm scared of *Zer* Sarn," Branst continued. "He has so much influence over Mother that he has her all but clear dreaming the future!"

Horth frowned at that last remark. Clear dreamers recalled details from their past lives, to clear dream the future wasn't possible. After some reflection, he decided that was Branst's point. But he still wasn't certain what to make of such a strange assertion. He wished Branst would put things simply.

"And I'm scared for myself," Branst admitted. "Me and Tessitatt."

Horth put a hand on Branst's shoulder. Branst covered it with his own. "I knew you'd understand," said Branst.

Branst was twenty-one and Horth only seventeen, but Horth felt older than his brother. It made sense to him, instinctively, that his soul was the one with more experience, even if he could not access past memories like a clear dreamer.

"There is a child," Branst said, looking straight into Horth's slate-gray eyes. "I have a Freedom Price." He swallowed thickly, his adam's apple bobbing in his smooth throat. "By Tessitatt."

Horth absorbed the fact in complete stillness, aware that there was trouble in it.

"Tessitatt had the child at her paternal grandmother's estate, on Monitum," Branst warmed to his confession. "She hasn't had him genotyped, and won't tell me in so many words that he's mine. But Horth—" He broke out in a smile that dispelled all the anxiety he had been projecting moments earlier. "She called him Branstatt! I don't need to see a geneprint to know he's mine! She did it for me, because she knows how much I want to be reborn Monatese in my next life. Oh Horth, I have to tell someone! I have to say it out loud for more than the Watching Dead. Horth, I love her!"

Horth narrowed his eyes at Branst's choice of a Demish word for love.

"I'm not saying a thing about marriage!" exclaimed Branst. "Tessitatt is not April Sarn! She's Green Vrellish. She would challenge me just for suggesting it, and very likely win the duel! She's the second best nobleborn I have ever had the privilege of losing to in a duel!"

"Hara," Horth said factually. "First best."

Branst fidgeted. "Sorry, I shouldn't have... well, yes."

Horth was not offended. It pleased him that Branst remembered Hara.

Branst's complacency at being beaten by any nobleborn opponent was less pleasing. Branst was *kinf'stan*. One day he might owe his life to his swordsmanship. And Branst had just told him something that might draw a challenge from Di Mon himself.

"I need your help, Horth," Branst told him. "You are coming to court this time, aren't you?"

"I will come," Horth told his brother.

"Yes!" Branst punched air. He gave Horth a quick hug, then stood, gripping Horth by the shoulders and beaming at him with tears in the corner of his green eyes. "Thank you, little brother. Thank you! I know what Mother meant about you when she called you true heart. There's something about you that makes me feel even the most impossible situations might turn out all right if you are there. Something clean and honest that's immune to sophistry. Horth, I so want to be honest myself, about everything."

Horth waited, feeling apprehensive.

Branst let go of him and wandered away, fingering every second or third *nervecloth* panel on the lockers in the change room. Doing something pointless seemed to help him master his emotions. Horth waited. Finally, Branst stopped and turned around again.

"I think Tess and I are *cher'stan*," Branst said thickly.

Horth lifted an eyebrow.

Branst raised both palms defensively, as if to hold off unvoiced objections. "It isn't anti-Vrellish being *cher'stan*! It isn't Nesak marriage. It's a soul bond. Of course I know that being *cher'stan* is rare and almost sacred. I don't mean to be pretentious. But I feel it!"

"Does Tessitatt say you are *cher'stan*?" Horth asked.

"No," Branst admitted, crestfallen, then rallied. "But she has promised she won't take any casual lovers."

"*Sha'stan?*" Horth asked, to be sure, because Branst often meant more than he said when he replaced a well-defined, Vrellish naming word with a fuzzier Demish description. Horth's relationship with Sinka was a *sha'stan* one — casual and intermittent, with no particular commitment in it, but no shame, either. That was not what the Demish meant by "casual lover."

Branst hunched his shoulders unhappily. "Horth, is it so wrong to love the woman who has had your baby?"

"No," said Horth immediately. He loved Bryllit, but he did not know how to adequately qualify the difference between that and the dangerous business of insisting Di Mon's favorite hearth-child was his *cher'stan*.

Branst rewarded him with a sheepish grin. "See you at court," he said, and hurried away, leaving Horth to figure out how to make Bryllit take him with her this time.

His strategy, in the end, was simple. He told her he had to come, and drew his sword to show her how serious he was about it.

"Gods!" she said, throwing up her hands. "Come then, and get killed if it's your *rel*. I can't protect you from Black Hearth embroilment by killing you myself!"

* * *

They dove like birds of prey through Gelion's thin atmosphere — first Bryllit, then Horth, declaring themselves by their very need to work with narrow safety margins. They were *kinf'stan:* no farther than a duel from the title of Liege Nersal.

In some ways, it was truly that simple. In others, Horth was learning that dynamics surrounding the Nersallian right of challenge were as complex as those that Horth had experienced on SanHome. Bryllit kept her finger on the pulse of discontent among the *kinf'stan* families. Many of them trusted her to decide, on their behalf, if Hangst went too far. Others she kept in check at sword point, aided by her reputation and a mob of willing allies.

Their envoy ships raised sheets of fine dust on the runway between dry, reddish cliffs.

Two great tunnels leading down to UnderGelion rushed up. Byllit pulled ahead to enter the highborn chute before Horth. Lights rushed past as they slowed to emerge at a sedate pace on the floor of a great, rectangular cavern.

They taxied to a hangar with an attached hostel that was unimaginatively named Bryllit Hostel in typically blunt, Nersallian fashion.

Moments later, Tash Bryllit dropped out from under her shuttle, sword in hand, and strapped it on, now equipped to negotiate the political scene at the empire's capital. She was a big woman, solid boned and wide at the shoulders, with her braided hair pinned securely to her scalp, the crest of House Bryllit on her breast, and liege marks on her collar.

Horth's build was leaner than Bryllit's, and his facial features sharper, but she only looked more powerful. His strength was just more densely packaged.

Bryllit spoke briefly with the workers who ran to take charge of their ships, advising them of arrangements for the rest of her party who would be arriving soon after. Then she clapped Horth on the shoulder, saying, "This is where we part company, *mekan'st ma*."

Horth did not understand immediately. He had expected that she would come with him to Black Hearth, or at least decline Hangst's hospitality in person.

Bryllit squeezed his shoulder. "Tell your sire I'll be glad to see him if he'll comes to me, here," she told him.

Horth did not relish being the bearer of bad news, but Bryllit left him no choice.

He passed through Black Gate without a challenge, and joined a stream of largely Demish foot traffic on the far side, parting clumps of slower moving blond men or ladies with their retinues.

The moment that Horth saw the matte black fabric of Black Pavilion, a wild feeling of possessiveness ambushed him. He was home.

He recognized only one of the errants on guard — the rest were all Nesaks. He hesitated as he approached, but the errants gave way, allowing him to make his way down the spiral stairs.

The family had been warned and found time to assemble.

Father and Mother stood side by side, Mother with a boy child under one arm and a baby cradled in the other. *Zer* Sarn wore formal robes of a dark purple, embroidered with scenes depicting the Great Errors. Zrenyl stood beside Sarn, dressed like a Nesak warrior.

"Welcome home!" Branst cried, embracing his brother, then turned him around towards their parents. "Look, Mother! It's Horth. Your true heart!"

A struggling, awkward silence followed. Beryl's eye brimmed and she clutched her infant tighter. Hangst's reaction was unreadable, but somber.

Horth fixed his gaze on the wide-eyed boy, about Dorn's age, who stood in the shelter of Beryl's arm.

"Eler," Horth said to the staring child, with a nod of recognition.

The boy swallowed as if addressed by a daunting stranger.

Beryl made up her mind, and with an apologetic glance at *Zer* Sarn, broke out in a smile of welcome. The change in her expression made her face beautiful. Her dress was a fitted shift, suitably practical for tending children, but elegant despite the burping blanket thrown over one shoulder.

"Don't be frightened, Eler," Beryl told her small son. "This is Horth, your brother." She demonstrated her own acceptance of Horth by placing her baby in his arms. "Horth," she said, "this is your sister, Beryllan."

The baby felt so soft and fragile that Horth nearly panicked. Neither Bryllit nor Sinta had allowed him to hold his own infants when they were this young.

This baby is my mother's, Horth reminded himself, and felt entitled. But baby Beryllan began to wriggle, and then cry, because Horth was holding her too tightly.

Eler declared loudly, "I like Zrenyl better."

"You owe Horth your life, Kene-echo," Beryl told Eler as she rescued her infant daughter, smiling at Horth's ineptitude. "He killed the *okal'a'ni* creature who poisoned me to stop me from calling forth your soul into your body."

Eler had clearly heard this kind of thing before and found it redundant. He continued to eye Horth with suspicion.

"I don't think Eler is Kene!" Zrenyl spoke up unexpectedly. "He's not *rel* enough!" He cuffed the four-year-old much as he might have done Horth or Branst when they were little.

Eler swatted back at him, tears in his eyes, and cried, "I am too, *rel*, you big lump!"

"Got a mouth on him, though," Zrenyl admitted as he turned his attention to Horth.

"I hear you are an *avsha*," Zrenyl said to Horth, with a reserved expression. "And have a Freedom Price by Bryllit who is already Eler's age."

Horth nodded. "And a baby girl. By Captain Sinka."

There was a short, awkward silence in which Beryl busied herself with the children while Zrenyl held Horth's stare. Finally, Zrenyl took a deep breath and said, "I have two children myself. By the same woman."

"I still wish you had brought your wife to court," Beryl told Zrenyl with a forced air of simple domesticity. "I could so use another woman's company, and I long to see my grandchildren." The baby fussed, so Beryl bounced it in her arms while keeping her eyes fixed accusingly on Zrenyl.

"I appreciate your interest, Mother," Zrenyl told her kindly. "But it would not have been right to bring my family with me into enemy territory. I have faith in Sword Law. But if something happened to me, how could I be sure that they would get home safely?"

Hangst interrupted them by stepping forward. "Where is Bryllit?" he demanded of his third son. "I thought she would be coming with you."

Horth felt a pain in his chest at this less-than-personal reception, but he rose to the challenge of matching Father's business-first manner. He had already practiced the sentence. "She said she will see you at the docks, if you desire."

Hangst blinked. Then his stern expression softened. "That's quite a speech for you, Horth," he said. Then he added less kindly, "Did she make you memorize it?"

Beryl came up beside her husband to lay a hand on the sleeve of his dress jacket, their baby girl settled in her other arm. Hangst covered her hand with his in an automatic gesture of affection that sent conflicting feelings of warmth, fear, and envy skittering insanely over Horth's heart.

"Branst!" Hangst ordered. "Show your brother to one of our guest rooms."

As the gathering began to break up, Hangst added in a matter of fact tone, "And Branst, we will expect to see you both for breakfast."

Branst talked about politics as he escorted Horth to a guest room on Family Hall, naming *kinf'stan* who might challenge at this Swearing and gossiping about who supported them and who stood opposed. There had been at least six duels between members of the two camps, one of them fatal. Horth got the gist, but the details congealed into word-lumps that only made him tired.

He was glad when Branst left him alone. It was then that he realized what was missing. He had not seen any servants at all.

Once he'd unpacked his few things, he left his room and went into the back rooms, only to find most of them empty. But not all. The sound of quiet voices drew him to a common room where he knew the family servants gathered.

Cook was still there. So was Alice. He recognized another half dozen survivors of Mother's purges, as well.

"My," said Cook, and froze as if she wasn't sure if he was someone familiar or frightening. "Master Horth, isn't it?"

Alice smiled at him with faltering lips, wringing her hands in her apron.

Horth wasn't sure how to let them know how good it was to see them until he noticed the tray of melon slices sitting on a side table beside Cook's armchair.

He stepped over, took a slice, and waited for cook to remember.

The middle-aged woman's eyes filled with tears, inexplicably. But much to Horth's delight, she slapped his hand and said, "You know you mustn't eat those or you'll get a stomachache!"

He was even more surprised when Alice flung herself at him, sobbing. After that, the rest closed around him, emboldened to take small liberties that revived old associations, and for the first time Horth felt himself wholly welcome, without reserve.

* * *

Horth found it hard to eat breakfast the next morning.

Eler wolfed down his food and left as fast as he could. Hangst asked a few polite questions. Zrenyl ate in silence. Branst never showed up.

When she wasn't waiting on the rest of them, Mother picked at her food, casting worried looks in Horth's direction and lowering her eyes whenever *Zer* Sarn addressed her.

Horth stole glances at Zrenyl, trying to understand him as he was now. He wanted to know what Father thought about *EagleNest*. He wanted Mother to be pleased that he had two children.

It was not until *Zer* Sarn finished his meal and excused himself that the family relaxed enough for conversation.

"It is good to see you looking so well," Beryl told Horth. Baby Beryllan was nodding in her lap and Horth wished again that he had his own baby to show off. Preferably with someone else in tow to manage the difficult business of holding her and things of that sort.

"Don't you think Horth looks well, Zrenyl?" Beryl tried to initiate some contact between her grown sons.

Zrenyl looked up from his nearly empty plate of Tarkian farm eggs, beef steak, and fried vegetable mash with an expression as cold as a dead planet. The silence stretched out. At last, to please his mother, Zrenyl said, "How is the weather in Killing Reach, these days, Horth?"

"Bad," said Horth. Weather, among pilots, meant reality skimming conditions and not atmospheric disturbances.

Zrenyl wiped his mouth with his napkin. "All of it inspired by Reetions, two hundred years ago," said Zrenyl. "That's the best you can expect from soulless commoners."

"How is SanHome?" Horth asked in return.

"Better than I ever dreamed," said Zrenyl.

Horth nodded. Zrenyl made his excuses, got up, and left. Only Horth and his parents remained seated.

This was exactly what Beryl had been waiting for. With both *Zer* Sarn and Zrenyl gone, she launched into stories about Horth's new siblings, even drawing stories out of Hangst concerning Eler as a toddler. Apparently, Eler had been a terror ever since he had learned to talk.

"He seems a little shy now," Beryl added, "but I think it's just an awkward phase. He has those, now and then. I wish I could speak with my mother to ask her if Kene went through phases like that."

At the mention of Kene's name, Hangst's expression clouded. "Perhaps you could give me a few minutes alone with Horth?" he asked.

"Yes, of course," Mother said immediately, and bustled out, humming to the baby in her arms.

"She is different," observed Horth.

"It's that priest," said Hangst, and drew a deep breath that expanded his broad chest and straightened his back. "Tell me something about Dorn," he invited. "And your new daughter."

Horth honored the request as best he could grateful for his father's interest. Hangst asked him about his work in Bryllit's fleet and gave every sign of being proud of him for becoming an *avsha*. He also approved of Horth's goal of becoming a battlewheel captain, although he raised the unwelcome difficulty of Horth's communication problems and suggested that he might do better in an engineering career.

"But I am glad you found Bryllit in Killing Reach," Hangst concluded. "And I want you to know I understand why you turned against Zrenyl. I've said as much to Zrenyl. He had no right to squander our family's honor. Di Mon's *protégé*, Vretla Vrel, brought the whole thing before Fountain Court and won an honor judgment against the Nesaks, although there's little can be done to make Arn face her when he answers to the *K'isk*, and not the Ava. The point is, Horth, that even Zrenyl knew it was wrong." Hangst frowned. "Although you wouldn't think so to talk to him now."

Hangst dropped his napkin on his plate, done with breakfast. "You are not remembered kindly back on SanHome," he told Horth. "Arn failed to take *EagleNest* because of you, and neither Rad nor Hill survived the shakeup."

Horth was sorry to have confirmation about Hill. He nearly asked about Kale, and then thought better of it. His memories of Kale were so thickly overlaid with sexual urgency that he didn't know exactly what he had felt about her as a person. He suspected she probably felt much the same.

Unexpectedly, Horth's father laughed. "What really impresses me," said Hangst, "is that you have the energy to spare for Captain Sinta, now that you are serving in my place as Bryllit's *mekan'st!*"

Horth accepted the compliment with a smile. "Is Branst living at home?" he asked.

"Oh yes," Hangst said, and heaved a long-suffering sigh. "He quarreled with Zrenyl before you showed up this morning, and bolted, that's all. As usual. He generally goes next door to Green Hearth when he's in a mood like that." For a moment Hangst weighed what he was about to ask, then decided. "Do you know where he gets to when he goes off planet altogether, for months?"

"Yes," said Horth, remembering Tessitatt's child.

Hangst frowned. "I thought as much." He leaned forward on an elbow. "Horth, I love Branst, but he's trouble. He can't fight well enough to defend his beliefs, but he won't set them aside, either. He may try to draw you into his problem. You know what that means?"

Horth nodded.

Hangst sat back. "*Ack rel*, then, Son."

A brief silence ensued, broken by Hangst's hearty chuckle. "You two always did like each other, hard as that sometimes is to understand!" He betrayed a trace of hope and excitement, steeped in the usual tensions that troubled his peace of mind when Fountain Court politics were involved. "I have an idea or two, myself, concerning Branst's infatuation with Di Mon's hearth-child, Tessitatt. I mean to have it out with Di Mon this afternoon, at the reception on the Octagon for Bryllit." He paused. "Your liege will show up for that?"

"You must ask her," said Horth.

Hangst frowned. "All right. You go fetch your brother back in good time and I will swallow my pride enough to visit Bryllit on the docks. And drag her up here personally, if I must."

"Yes, sire," said Horth, but found the Vrellish approach to acknowledging their relationship too cold and odd. He was entitled to call Hangst l'liege, the short form of "liege of my liege," but that felt equally stilted. "Father," Horth fixed the problem.

Hangst smiled. He got out of his seat, gestured to Horth to get up, and gave him a hard hug.

"Welcome back to Gelion," said Hangst. "And to Fountain Court. You did the right thing at *EagleNest*. You always do." More gravely, Hangst added, "One way or the other, things will change at this reception. And I am not sorry that Branst will have some backup if they go wrong."

Hangst broke off and showed his smile again, one hand on Horth's shoulder. "But I don't know what I am so worried about! I have a reasonable case to put to Di Mon, and reason is the one thing he can be counted on to respond to."

Hangst sighed. "Bryllit may be another matter." In parting, he added, "Don't be late getting back with Branst."

Once they had parted, Horth went out onto Fountain Court and clockwise one establishment to Green Hearth. The herald told him Tessitatt had gone to West Alcove to take in the act of a new Sword Dancer named Von, whom everyone was talking about. Horth decided he would find Branst there, as well.

* * *

"Highlord," Horth introduced himself at the door of Den Eva's, on the far side of UnderGelion. He was supposed to say something that allowed inferiors to deduce his birth rank from his pronouns, but he couldn't think of anything appropriate so he simply declared what he was.

The woman who greeted him accepted his solution with professional aplomb. "How can we serve you today, Your Grace?" she asked.

"Branst Nersal," Horth said, "and Tessitatt Monitum."

"They are here," said the woman, "watching the entertainment." She stepped aside to let Horth pass.

The Patron's Round was much as Horth remembered it, with novices in white togas waiting on Sevolites in a wide band surrounding a central, sunken stage.

A pair of dancers held the room's attention. The woman was a sleek blond with a stately figure. Her partner was a remarkably flawless youth with black hair and gray eyes, who had to be Von. Horth watched just long enough to figure out what made the young man's movements interesting, and decided that it was the way Von's fluid grace masked the strength behind them, making them look misleadingly effortless and casual. The room appeared to be enthralled, but Horth found something irritatingly clever about the way that Von's choreographed moves mocked the violence of a real duel. The props the courtesans used were not real swords, either — only showy replicas.

After dismissing Von's style as vaguely annoying, Horth found himself entranced by the female dancer, whose athletic body was sheathed in a skin-tight costume of blue and silver. He remembered his mission only when Von's body interrupted his view of her.

Branst and Tessitatt were at a table near the dance floor. Horth noted a couple of Red Vrellish nobleborns from Spiral Hall nearby. Most of the other tables were filled with small parties of Demish men. The last one was occupied by a group of Nersallian *relsha*, two male and two female. Satisfied that he had a rough grasp of the surrounding company, Horth headed directly for Branst.

"That's it?" Branst was saying to Tessitatt, with a contemptuous gesture in Von's direction. "You dragged me here to watch him dance? He's not even a grown-up!"

"That's not what his customers tell me," Tess said with a smirk. "They say he's even better *off* the dance floor."

"You haven't—" Branst began and stopped himself.

"What if I had?" she challenged. "It would be good for my reputation. And yours. We're keeping to ourselves too much."

"Yes, but a dancer!" Branst exclaimed, in disgust. "A *child* dancer!"

"Thirteen, in fact," said Tessitatt, choosing that moment to lift her head and say, "Hello, Horth."

"Horth!" Branst gave a start that caught the attention of their Nersallians neighbors. He followed up by pushing a chair out for Horth. "Sit down! Some wine for my brother!" Branst ordered a toga-clad child.

Horth's wine came in a glass horn with a matching metal base for putting it down on the small, round table.

The audience let out a collective "ooh" at something Von was doing.

"Will you look at that!" enthused Tessitatt.

"Big deal," Branst grumbled.

She scowled at him, "Don't be Demish."

"I'm not Demish!"

"But you are jealous."

"You're trying to make me crazy, aren't you?" Branst accused her.

"Here comes the finale!" said Tess, giving Von her full attention.

Branst was equally adamant about not watching. "How did you make out at breakfast?" he asked Horth instead.

Horth shrugged. He had no words to explain what had passed between him and his father.

"Sorry I wasn't there," said Branst. "Zrenyl was saying stupid things about the household commoners, trying to get Dad to evict the few we have left. Then he started telling Dad he shouldn't swear to Delm just to please Di Mon, as if Di Mon actually likes Delm himself! It's got nothing to do with that! Di Mon is thinking of the empire. He'd be as happy as Dad if there was a better choice available for Ava."

"There is Ev'rel," said Tess, without taking her eyes off the young sword dancer wrapping up his routine on the dance floor.

Branst made a rude noise. "Great choice that is! Ev'rel the banished pervert! Where's their kid, the lost Prince Amel, when he could really come in handy? You'd think the Demish could scare up just one more Pureblood, some-where, given all the fuss they make about them!"

Horth glanced over at the nearest Demish tables to see if the occupants had taken offense at Branst's opinion, but the blond men were too absorbed in the show, or the courtesans sitting with them, to pay much attention.

The dance routine concluded in a final pose and the audience exploded in a roar of foot-stomping and whistles. As the commotion died down, the Nersallian *relsha* sauntered over with their female *avsha* in the lead and two men flanking her. Their fourth member went to convey her personal congratulations to Von with the air of someone making arrangements for a private encore.

"You are Branst Nersal of Black Hearth, aren't you?" the *avsha* greeted Branst in peerage.

"I might be," Branst answered in a surly fashion.

"Might be?" The *avsha* pulled out a chair beside Branst and sat down. "That's the trouble with you courtly types — you are never sure of anything!"

"Are you here for the Swearing?" Tessitatt asked one of the male *relsha* as he smiled at her.

"We're not looking for company!" Branst flared.

The woman fixed him with a haughty look, then turned to Horth. "And you are Horth. The one who killed the *okal'a'ni* errant."

Branst stood up, pushing his chair back. "There was nothing *okal'a'ni* about Hara!" he told her fiercely, getting even more agitated.

"Really?" The *avsha* rose to face him. "Then why did your full brother here have to kill her?" She emphasized *full brother* in a way that underscored how unusual that was in Vrellish families.

"It's none of your business!" Branst snapped at her.

"*Kinf'stan* are always each other's business, Branst Nersal," she said, her gray eyes narrowing. "For example, the word is that you've gone the way of your father and full brother Zrenyl when it comes to women, with the sole difference that you prefer the Green Vrellish to Nesaks." She jerked her head in Tessitatt's direction.

Branst went for her. Horth stopped him. It was Tessitatt who voiced a challenge.

"If you're accusing me of man-hoarding," she cried, and paused to clear her weapon, "I will answer. That is, of course, if you will do me the service of overlooking the disparity in our challenge classes."

"Tess! No!" Branst gasped. "She's *kinf'stan!*"

"So are you," Tessitatt said between clenched teeth. "And I can take you."

"I will answer," said Horth, and jumped down lightly on the empty stage floor. People looked. He cleared his sword and waited.

The *avsha* shrugged and joined him on the stage floor with her sword drawn. "I was not really out to start a quarrel," she said.

"First blood?" Horth suggested.

She nodded her agreement.

By now, they had the whole room's attention, including that of the two men under the *avsha*'s command who usurped the empty chairs at Tessitatt's table and settled down to watch in a companionable manner.

"Horth has no business fighting my quarrels!" Tessitatt fumed when she had sheathed her sword and sat down, again, beside him.

"Yes, he does," said Branst. "He's highborn, like her. And I sort of asked him here, for the Swearing, to do just that."

"What?!" exclaimed Tessitatt.

Horth and the Nersallian woman squared off and signaled one another they were ready to start. She lunged immediately, going for a quick jab in the arm that might have caught a novice napping. Horth parried and retaliated.

They enjoyed a furious exchange of free form ingenuity, full of counter-parries and disengages, that lasted a full fifteen seconds. Neither one targeted the other's head or torso.

A touch, scored on Horth's arm, cut his shirt and drew blood.

"Hah!" cried the *avsha*.

Branst looked disappointed.

Horth stepped back. "Again?" he invited.

"Think I got lucky, do you?" his opponent mocked him. "All right!"

She attacked with confidence and lost twice in quick succession. The first time Horth nicked her thigh and the second time he touched her forearm.

They called it a draw at that point.

Both contestants rejoined the table, dabbing wounds to staunch the bleeding. No one clapped, but a fresh round of drinks was delivered courtesy of some admiring Demish patron.

Horth's cut was too trivial to bother with, but one of the *relsha* produced a first aid tool, called a seamer, and used it to seal the *avsha*'s worst cut as she kept her teeth gritted. A courtesan at a neighboring table made a face at the smell of seared flesh as the seamer pressed the edges of the wound together and closed them with a hiss of vaporized blood.

When the ministrations were taken care of, the *avsha* toasted Horth with her wine horn, her criticisms of Branst and Tess apparently forgotten.

"I'm Kega Tark," she told them, and went on to introduce the two *relsha* in her fighter hand, as well as the second woman who had gone down a spoke-hall with the dancer named Von.

The Tarkians belonged to a space-based industrial house with few planetary holdings of any sort. They were here for the Swearing, and to find out if trading with Nesaks might be worth the risk of trusting them.

Branst grew expansive as the drinks flowed, eager to undermine Kega's hopeful avarice with stories of how Nesaks treated non-eternals, all the while vigorously defending his father's essential Vrellishness despite the Nesaks' influence at Black Hearth.

Things did not get tense until Kega objected, rather strongly, to Hangst being married. The reference to his mother made Branst flush.

"That's Vrellish, too," he insisted. "Father is honoring the terms of his duel with Kene Nesak. And it isn't as if we're not honoring old ties, as a family. With Liege Bryllit, for example." He gave Horth a friendly shove.

Kega caught Branst's arm as he drew it back. "And what about you?" she asked, looking into his eyes with the intensity of a mining laser. "Do you keep up old ties with *kinf'stan*, Branst Nersal?"

"He's with me," Tess said in a flinty tone. "Today," she added.

"Don't be greedy, Green Hearth," Kega told her. "Besides, I've got man-kin to share with you. Two, if you're up to it."

Tessitatt inspected Kega's male companions with a calculating eye, but one with less genuine sexual interest than she had shown for young Von, earlier.

Branst's color began to rise the way it did before he said things that he shouldn't.

Tessitatt threw the first punch. She delivered it right across the table smack into Kega's face, following up with a dive into her highborn rival.

The two women fell sideways, their sheathed swords interfering with their movement. Still struggling, they bumped loudly down the long, shallow steps to the stage floor, limbs locked together in a heaving tangle.

One of Kega's male companions was laid out by Horth as soon as he stood up. Branst was having trouble with his man. Horth pulled them apart. He ducked the *relsha*'s punch, caught his arm, and swung him into their table, sending the last wine horn to join the rest in pieces on the floor.

The first man was on his feet again by now, fighting with Branst, who was getting in a punch for each one that he took, although Horth would have bet on the Tarkian in the long run.

"Enough!" Kega's voice bellowed from the dance floor. She followed up with a fruity, tenor belly laugh that made the men stop to figure out what was going on — because on the face of it, Kega had nothing to laugh about. She was lying on her back warding off Tessitatt's fists with bruised forearms.

With a heave, Kega cast her nobleborn rival off and surged up to her feet, grinning.

"Fine, have him!" she said with a hardy clap on Tessitatt's back as she levered herself up beside Kega. "He's yours. And I will never again doubt that Monatese women are as Vrellish as they come!" She paused to spit blood, and added in a more serious manner. "Just remember to pass him around when you're done."

Horth went down to Kega on the dance floor, moved by an instinct he did not try to understand. He wasn't even sure what he meant to do until a smile spread across her wide, sensuous mouth. Then he knew.

He had seen Vrellish patch up quarrels this way before.

Certain of his reception, he slid an arm about her back and went off with her to a guest room amid hoots and thigh-slapping sounds of approval from the two men he and Branst had just been fighting.

Kega's female companion emerged from her own adventure with Von, took in the mayhem around the table, and asked, "Did I miss something important?"

"No!" Tessitatt said grumpily, and swatted Branst for grinning at her. "Nothing at all!"

* * *

Horth woke up beside Kega forty minutes later, acutely aware he was going to be late for the reception. He slapped Kega's thigh.

"Mmph," she said, and sat up rubbing her bruised jaw. Then she grinned at him. "Do you always pass out at the end like that?"

"Reception," Horth reminded her as he yanked his shirt on, not answering the question.

Tessitatt and Branst had already gone on ahead. But he found someone waiting for him with a car.

"Ses Nersal," she introduced herself. "Your brother, Branst, said you might need a lift home. I said I'd take you in exchange for an invitation to the reception. I hear there may be swords drawn. What do you say, *avsha*?"

Horth nodded and opened the door on the driver's side.

Ses Nersal hesitated a moment before she gave in and slid over.

"Real Vrellish, you are," she remarked as she helped him stow his sword in a rack across the back. "A bad passenger."

Horth pulled out and merged with the fast-moving traffic on the Ava's Way, hoping to minimize his lateness.

"They call you the silent one," Ses continued, leaning counter to a swerve as Horth whipped around a slower vehicle. "Some even say *rejak't*. A flawed cast."

Horth hit a clear patch and gave the car full power, with respectable results, but since half the traffic in both directions cruised at top speed, it still wasn't very satisfying.

Ses braced a hand on an overhead bar as she kept up the one-sided conversation. "I enjoy witnessing a good duel," she said, "I admit that. I've taken part in my share as well, of course! And won more than I lost, too. It was a duel that grounded me. A fight with a Demish lout who riled me up with his bragging about how it was always a Demish champion who won the tournaments on Gelion. I told him that tournaments didn't count because Vrellish highborns seldom enter!"

Horth bumped straight over a pile of refuse that had fallen off a vehicle ahead of him.

"Unfortunately," said Ses, "I lost. He got me in the knee, and it hasn't worked right since." She sighed. "What I wouldn't give to be regenerative. But I tell you, it is still a source of great frustration to me that our highborns won't put those Demish in their place at tournaments!"

They skidded to avoid a car that appeared unexpectedly from the dim recesses of an alley between two wayside establishments. Horth's slide sent them into a heap of old crates

set up as a barrier on the other side of the road. They struck
at an angle, shoving two crates full of something heavy for
several meters before Horth regained control.

He turned back into the erratic stream of traffic on the
Ava's Way feeling a little rattled by this last mishap.

"Busy today," Ses remarked.

Moments of clear driving later, she said, "It was the talk
of the garage — that's my business, I run a garage — when
you took down the captain of the Black Hearth guard."

Horth spared her a quick glance.

"Not all of it good talk," she admitted. "We were pretty
proud of Hara! There was a nobleborn who could take any
highborn on their own terms! Except you, apparently. I
liked you a lot better after *EagleNest*, though," she added
cheerily, and put a hand on Horth's thigh.

The resulting wiggle in the car's trajectory convinced Ses
to leave self-expression to words after they managed to survive.

They paid a premium for a safe place to park close to the
Citadel. Horth waited impatiently. When they reached the
stairs, he took them at a run. Ses fell behind at once.

"Wait!" she hollered at him. "They won't let me through
the Palace Shell without you!"

Horth hesitated, wondering what sort of deal she'd made
with Branst and whether he was honor-bound to bring her
along. Irritably, he reversed his steps to reach her, and
swept her up in his arms, sword and all, to carry her the rest
of the way up. She didn't seem to mind, after her initial
astonishment. By the time he put her down at the top, she
had caught her breath.

"I've never been to a Fountain Court reception before,"
she confided with glee, as they arrived at Black Pavilion.

Horth pounded down the spiral stairs to find the main
reception room empty except for few errants and one of
Mother's retainers.

"Everyone is down on the Octagon," said the Nesak retainer, with a glance askance at Ses as she came down the stairs.

"Is there a duel?" Ses asked excitedly.

The Nesak retainer ignored her. "Delm's paladins are trespassing on Golden Wedge," he told Horth. "It has everyone's attention. Both Liege Monitum and your father have repeatedly upheld the rights of the Golden Demish against Delm's claims."

Politics, Horth decided, with an echo of his mother's resentment for Di Mon's ability to embroil Hangst in such affairs.

"Come on," said Ses, "let's go witness."

This time it was Horth who followed her down the next coil of stairs onto Black Wedge.

They encountered more errants on honor guard at the bottom, and beyond them a wall of backs, in something like a witnessing circle, facing out across the Octagon towards Golden Wedge.

"It's that Demish nonsense about Souls of Light — their version of a *zer-pol*," Ses remarked, at Horth's elbow. "Delm claims he is one." She made a rude noise. "So his paladins presume the right to trespass on Golden Wedge, strutting and posing!"

Horth could see three paladins through the crowd. They wore spotless white clothes with golden decorations at the waist and cuffs, their bright yellow hair braided in elaborate patterns. They wielded jewel-hilted swords in a stylized display that reminded Horth of Von, the sword dancer.

"They wouldn't be doing that if Prince D'Ander were here to defend Golden Hearth on behalf of his emperor," Ses muttered. "Not that I normally make a study of Demish champions, but Prince D'Ander has proved himself in high-stake duels. He would make short work of those puppies!"

"I would not discount the skill of paladins too lightly," a familiar voice intruded from behind them.

Horth turned to face Di Mon.

Ses Nersal lost the power of speech upon discovering herself addressed by the liege of Monitum. She began a Nersallian salute, and broke off with a fumbling gesture as she realized that it was not the right one. Di Mon clearly meant something to her. The impression that he made was profound enough to distract her from saluting her own liege when Hangst joined them.

"I wager Ses is right about them being puppies," said Hangst, holding the stem of his wine horn too tightly as he glared at the paladins flaunting their trespass.

"They are trying to provoke us," Di Mon told Hangst firmly.

"Succeeding, actually," Hangst answered, glaring not at the paladins but past them to the place where Delm himself sat watching the scene, ensconced in the midst of admiring princesses and two dozen armed Demish princes.

"It isn't worth it, Hangst!" Di Mon warned. "Paladins may look like fools, but they train hard. And if you take down one, the next will challenge. They are each, officially, the other's heir. Who knows how the Silver Demish princes will react, for that matter! And don't think I'll be fool enough to help you! All we need, before this Swearing, is a melee on the challenge floor to worsen the split between Vrellish and Demish sympathies!"

Hangst said nothing. He just continued to glare in Delm's direction.

"Excuse me," Ses said, looking excited and flustered. "This is out of line, entirely, I realize. But I've always admired your record in the arena, Liege Monitum, when you were younger of course, before the heir problem. I've heard you don't get out much when you are at court, and, well, at the risk of being far too blunt — if you're looking for a local *mekan'st*... I mean, a Nersallian, seeing as there is a bond of friendship between you and my liege—" She stopped with a gulp, belatedly grasping, by Di Mon's nonplussed look, just how far out on a limb she had placed herself. "Well," she finished, and slapped on a wide grin, "I'd be honored."

Hangst looked at Ses, then Di Mon, and barked a curt laugh with no humor in it. "Good idea!" he cried, and clasped Di Mon by the arm. "We must talk now, *brerelo*."

Even Di Mon knew when Hangst would brook no resistance.

"If we must," he said reluctantly.

"Go find Branst and Tessitatt and bring them with you to my study," Hangst told Horth.

As Horth departed on his errand, he heard Di Mon say to Ses, "We'll talk — later."

"Really?" she asked, astonished. And then, with an explosion of pleasure at her good luck, "The gods ignore me!"

It was easy to find Tessitatt and Branst. They were in the front line of the witness circle watching the paladins. Tessitatt was busy telling Branst the names of all the opponents that each of the paladins had killed — probably as a cautionary measure.

"Father wants you," Horth told his brother. "And you," he added to Tessitatt, bungling the shift in pronoun, which made her blink. He was supposed to use *pol* case when down-speaking an inferior. Instead, he had peer-spoken both of them. Horth was fleetingly embarrassed, but as soon as Tessitatt figured out he meant her, she forgot about the grammar fumble.

She and Branst exchanged stares and a bolt of cold shock passed between them. Horth touched his brother's arm to reassure him that he would be coming, also. It troubled him to see Branst look frightened.

Hangst and Di Mon were waiting for them in Hangst's study, off Family Hall. Hangst looked as solid as a hullsteel pillar. Di Mon was pacing. Both of them were still armed.

Branst and Tessitatt sat down on a firm couch upholstered in black leather. Horth took up a standing position near Branst.

"All right, they're here," Di Mon snapped, halting suddenly. "Now what?"

"You and I fought together in the Nesak War," Hangst told his friend soberly. "We have stood together ever since for the Vrellish cause. But today, we must decide to merge— " Hangst meshed his hands " — or go our own ways." He pulled them apart again.

"If this is about me taking a Nersallian *mekan'st*," Di Mon said, very fast, "of course I'll do that!"

"More," said Hangst. He walked over to stand before Tessitatt. "You have a child," he told her bluntly. "I think he is my grandson." Hangst lay a palm over the crossed-hook at the top of the house braid embroidered on his shirt. "If he is highborn, that makes him *kinf'stan*. Even if he is only nobleborn, It makes him blood-kin of a lesser sort."

Di Mon looked stunned, but whether by the fact of the child's existence or Hangst's awareness of it, Horth could not be sure. Di Mon looked at his niece. Tessitatt quailed before the stare of her liege-uncle in a way that Horth had never seen her shrink from anything before.

"I do not accuse your niece of soul-stealing!" Hangst assured Di Mon with energy. "The baby is obviously a love child. An accident of affection, for which my hearth-child is as much to blame as yours! It is done. I say embrace it! Let the blood of Black and Green Vrellish mingle to create one house of courtly Vrellish that is strong enough to stand against Demish corruption. Do not turn away from me!" Hangst interrupted himself to lay hands on Di Mon's shoulders.

Di Mon's chiseled nostrils flared angrily at Hangst's touch, but he suffered himself to be held while Hangst lectured.

"You need the highborn blood!" Hangst insisted. "What do you have left of it on Monitum? One or two indifferent swordsmen and some useless scholars! You hope to woo the

Vrellish, via Vretla, but what good will Red Vrellish ties do you against a Demish Ava? They will never fight unless they are invaded. If a Vrellish power is going to stand against Delm, it must be us!"

"Are you, Hangst?" Di Mon demanded hotly, jerking free. "Vrellish? Are you Vrellish?"

"What?" Hangst was taken aback — and offended. Even Horth felt the urge to reach for his sword. Branst sat straighter.

"Are you still Vrellish?" Di Mon snapped, his own temper clearly lost. "Or turning Nesak?"

"Uncle!" cried Tessitatt, leaping up. "No!"

But the two lieges were fixed on each other, indifferent to the distress of their loved ones.

"I do have Nesak blood," Hangst said in cold anger. "If you fear it, you should know that I fear the Lorel in yours." He paused, his throat locking, and relaxed the muscles with an effort. "Prove to me that you honor Sword Law, Di Mon! Declare the child Branst's. Let there be more. Gods, man! Is it better to let Monatese highborns die out, this generation, than to risk a title challenge in the next one? You are down to a handful of Monatese highborns! And you will not even sire your own heirs on Monatese nobleborns!"

"You know I cannot," Di Mon exploded bitterly. "I am infertile."

"So you claim!" Hangst answered with equal ferocity, and struggled to speak levelly as he continued. "But I have wondered, lately, why it is that you consort with courtesans instead of fertile women. Surely, if you are slow to breed, the more the better! Or are you like Delm — so afraid of challenge-right entanglements that you deny life to your Waiting Dead to protect property?"

Something in Di Mon's bleak expression made Hangst relent with a forced sigh of pent up frustration. "Even if you are infertile," he conceded, "it need not matter! You have kin!

So do I! Tessitatt and Branst will only be the first of many. Join with me, Di Mon, through the mingling of souls. Join with me like a true, Vrellish ally."

"You are asking Monitum to accept becoming Nersallian," Di Mon said miserably. "How can I condone that, *brerelo*? Tell me, instead, that you will waive challenge rights entirely and gift us your half-Nersallian children, free and clear. Tell me you will start with Tessitatt's child, and I will order a genotyping and gladly declare Branst the sire, if it is true. But I do not know that it is true, as I stand here. I swear that much to you. Yes, it could be Branst's child, or it might not. We thought it better simply not to find out."

Branst looked sharply at Tessitatt. She squeezed his hand in silent reassurance.

"The child's soul is as likely to be Nersallian as Monatese," Hangst said stonily. "I cannot refuse to name him *kinf'stan*."

"And you say that I am stubborn!" Di Mon cried.

Hangst inhaled, once, nostrils flaring. Then he headed for the door with decision.

"Hangst?" Di Mon spun around, his anger boiling away in panic. "No!"

Tessitatt got in the way of her liege-uncle as he made to follow. "If he's going to kill himself challenging paladins," she said intensely, "you swore you would stay out of it!"

Horth dodged around them, leaving Branst behind. He sprinted down the Throat to the reception hall and took the spiral stairs two at a time.

By the time he reached the Octagon, his father was already crossing the Challenge Floor towards Golden Wedge with his sword drawn. The leader of the paladins came out to meet him.

Horth halted at the edge of Black Wedge beside Zrenyl. They met each other's eyes, once, and all at once their quarrel over *EagleNest* seemed very far away and unimportant. If Hangst was attacked dishonorably they would join him and make it a melee. Horth had no doubt the rest of the Nesaks and Nersallians around them would do likewise if the Demish princes on Silver Wedge got active.

Beside them, Beryl stood clutching *Zer* Sarn's arm, her face a mask of terror. *Zer* Sarn, himself, looked grimly satisfied.

Across the Octagon from Black Wedge, Demish princes on Silver Wedge fingered their swords, looking apprehensive or excited, each according to his inclinations. The women were hustled up the stairs.

"Liege Nersal," intoned the senior paladin, and flashed a pearly smile.

"I believe you are trespassing on Golden Wedge," Hangst told him, shifting his feet to get ready. "Get off, now. Or die."

The paladin raised one pale, manicured eyebrow. "Why should you defend Demoran claims, and what do you know of them?" The paladin's large, attractive features shaped themselves into a mocking leer. "Or have you taken it into your head to give your oath to D'Ander, this Swearing?"

"No," Hangst said. "Only to instruct you in good courtly manners. Will you fight?"

The paladin glanced back at his two companions, and over at the Demish watching them from Silver Wedge. He looked at the highborns on Black Wedge, as well. Then he shrugged, and said, "Very well."

Horth spotted Bryllit farther down the front line of spectators. She watched the same way he and Zrenyl did — silent and intent.

Hangst and the paladin edged back and forth, calculating, gauging each other's defense with a few quick moves, waiting for an opening. Horth feared it was Hangst whose patience was in the worse repair.

Di Mon, Tessitatt, and Branst came down the Black Hearth stairs and froze there.

Suddenly, Hangst attacked furiously. The first paladin staggered while parrying the repeated blows. The crowd drew a collective breath.

"Gods," Di Mon murmured softly.

Then one of the attacks turned into a feint and disengage, and the paladin was toppling as Hangst yanked his sword clear from the man's chest.

Stillness reigned for a long moment.

Then the next paladin came forward jerkily, driven by shock and anger. This one went down even faster, in his first close with Hangst. Horth had expected no less — the man had been far too emotional.

The crowd seemed to be more surprised as it drew a collective breath. The third paladin was unnerved.

The princes on Silver Wedge swayed and muttered among themselves.

Nersallians and Nesaks tensed.

Whether or not the third paladin meant to drop his sword was a moot point. It might simply have been done out of fear. But he dropped it. And he fled.

A few Nersallians began to laugh.

The Demish raised their voices in a thunderous yell of affirmation for acceptance of the verdict, under Sword Law.

"Okal Rel!"

On the other side of the floor, Di Mon led the answering cheer. *"Okal Rel!"*

The risk of a melee died away with the shouting as everyone lapsed into silence, the two bodies lying where they fell, their clean white clothing leaking red.

Hangst gave his blade a contemptuous shake as if the blood of these enemies sullied it. Then he stalked off the Challenge Floor and back to Black Wedge, drawing Nersallians and Nesaks after him without a word.

Bryllit caught up with Horth as he made to follow his father. "We leave," she told him urgently, "at once."

* * *

Di Mon waited in Azure Lounge for Hangst to take leave of him. Demish callers came, but he lacked the courage to deal with them. Vretla stayed away and he was glad of it. He did not have the patience to explain what had happened to Vretla, yet.

As the hours went by, and Sarilous informed him Nersallian highborns were leaving court en mass, Di Mon began to fear Hangst would leave without a final under-standing reached between them. He even began to dread the unthinkable — that Hangst had somehow found out about his personal affliction, however impossible that seemed.

All Di Mon had said about not daring to overlap chal-lenge rights with the *kinf'stan* was true. But he had other, personal, reasons for claiming to be infertile. Reasons that were reinforced by how he sometimes felt about Hangst, himself. Reasons that would threaten any children he had, if his secret were ever known, and deal a fatal blow to Monitum. Time and again he convinced himself it was im-possible for anyone to guess what he felt as long as he did nothing to act on it, only to have his fears undermine his conviction so he had to do it all over again.

It was eight hours after the bloodletting on the Octagon when his herald finally told him someone from Black Hearth wished to see him.

Di Mon had risen to receive Hangst, but sat down again as if struck in the chest when Branst walked into Azure Lounge.

"Your father is gone?" Di Mon said, when he could draw air to speak.

Branst mustered courage with an effort and said shakily, "He's leaving the servants and a skeleton roster of errants. He's asked me to check in occasionally. H-he said he hoped you would... help. I mean, with keeping Black Hearth open to visiting *kinf'stan*."

"Yes, of course," Di Mon said automatically.

An awkward silence lingered.

"I won't be able to be here a lot," Branst pushed on. "Dad says the Demish would pressure me to swear in his place, if I did. Dad said you could, uh, contact me via... "

Di Mon smiled as Branst began to look embarrassed, thinking about Hangst's sense of humor. "Ses Nersal," he said quietly.

Branst nodded.

"Fine," Di Mon said. It was something, even if it wasn't all he'd hoped for in the way of a sustained connection. He was afraid to ask the next question, but he knew he had to. "Where has Hangst gone?"

As he asked it, Di Mon thought, *Not* SanHome!

To his great relief Branst answered, "To Tark, for the time being."

Part V

Reetions

191 Post Treaty

Horth pelted down the promenade towards Liege Bryllit's quarters after a panic-stricken seven-year-old Dorn who had come to fetch him.

"She's beserk!" Dorn warned his sire as he halted, eyes wide and body breathless.

Horth delayed just long enough to lay a hand on his son's shoulder. He burst in on Bryllit in time to see her hurl a pitcher of ship's ale at the ceiling.

"Watch that!" Bryllit raged at whichever of the Watching Dead she evidently meant to nail with her projectile, and swept up the next thing on the table where she and Horth often had breakfast together.

"Twelve!" she railed, and shook her fist at her disembodied ancestors. "Twelve babies I've given you! Go bless another descendant!"

She was casting about for something else to throw when she spotted Horth.

"You!" she roared, and launched herself at him.

Horth had heard that the hormones associated with early pregnancy could be murderously hard on a woman as Vrellish as Bryllit, whose blood was typically laced with as much testosterone as any man's. But he had not realized until now that the male responsible was the one most likely to get murdered.

Bryllit hit him like a *rel*-fighter doing six *skim'facs*, knocking the breath out of Horth's lungs. They crashed into the low table at the foot of the wide bed where the damage had been done.

Pain stabbed him in the ribs as they rolled over a piece of broken furniture. Horth tried to hang on to prevent Bryllit getting enough clearance to swing at him, or strike him with her forehead. She broke his grip with a roar, reared up, and swung down with a two-fisted blow. Horth heaved her sideways, spoiling her aim, and rolled on top of her.

The next thing he knew, she had her legs locked around his waist and was forcing a kiss on him. Slowly, muscles still straining, he let their body contact transform from violence into passion. He was grateful for the change, but wary of a relapse.

Twenty minutes later, naked and panting with the stress of spent emotions, they found themselves lying on the bed together. Bryllit lay staring at the ceiling with sweat cooling on her limbs and torso.

"It's bad timing," she explained away her earlier outburst heaving herself up and stalking across her living quarters, naked.

She returned with a slim silver box in her hand. It was oblong in shape with rounded edges. Horth could not imagine what it was for.

"Reetion," Bryllit said. "But not an old war artifact. A new thing."

He started as if she had told him it was carrying a fatal virus.

"It has pictures on it," she said. "Pictures of that dancer from Den Eva's, named Von, being molested. I'll show you how it works. Watch."

Bryllit stroked her hand over the box in a smooth motion and its surface lit up, exciting the air above. Images resolved themselves into a solid-looking display.

The technology intrigued Horth, but the images repelled him! He was looking at children in a *sla*-den: the sort of place that catered to abusive fetishes. The children in view were boys being mauled by a man in an unmistakably sexual manner. The children looked no older than Dorn. Horth found himself boiling with anger.

"These things are showing up at the worst sort of trading stations across Killing Reach," Bryllit told him. She tossed the silver box onto their abandoned bed. "But they seem to feature the UnderDocks on Gelion. How could the Reetions have been there? And what do they mean by selling such filth back to us? Sheer mockery? Or is it some sort of vulgar challenge?" She shook her head. "I don't know. But they might know on Gelion. See what you can find out there, and then take word to your liege-father."

She lay her large hand across the flat skin of her belly. "I cannot go myself this early in a pregnancy, not with a clear conscience."

Horth nodded, understanding now why she had been so upset.

"This is not good," she told Horth, her gravity undiminished by her nakedness. "It is not good that there are Reetions in Killing Reach again. We must do something. Hangst must decide what."

Horth nodded. That much seemed obvious, but his limitations as a messenger concerned him.

"Ses Nersal will have called Branst to court," said Bryllit. "Be sure you connect with him. He might have information from the Monatese."

Horth grinned at that idea, feeling better.

* * *

The flying was clear all the way to court. Horth encountered the most traffic in the *Reach* of Gelion, but that was normal because Gelion lay at the hub of a network of reaches.

It was only as his envoy craft reached atmosphere that Horth encountered bad weather — of the planetary sort. But he enjoyed the mind-clearing demands of bringing his ship down through a dust storm of moderate proportions.

When he was hailed by the Ava's Tower, Horth identified himself as a Nersallian highborn.

"Highborn," the male Demish voice responded as if stung. "Which one? We've already cleared Branst Nersal today. Word is the rest of you aren't interested in the Ava's empire anymore because Liege Nersal prefers wooing Nesaks."

Horth cut the channel off without dignifying the Demish man's remarks with a response. He wasn't sure what to say anyway.

He was glad to get out of the storm and into the highborn chute. On the docks themselves, he headed for the hangar he knew Branst preferred to use and parked right outside the wide porch that led up to a long common room.

Horth
had taken six steps from his ship when Branst charged out the doors and down the steps of the porch, arms flung wide.

"Thank you, ancestors!" cried Branst. "It's you!"

Horth dropped his travel bag and sword to greet his brother with a round of back-pounding slaps and hugs. Then he crouched over his travel bag to dig out the offensive little box, stood up again, and handed it to Branst.

"What is it?" his brother said, taking it with a bemused expression and turning it over in his hands.

"Reetion," said Horth.

Branst looked keenly interested now. "Really? Di Mon's got a Reetion here, you know, staying in Green Hearth! And his skin really is brown, just like in the stories from the Killing War." He paused to examine the featureless, oblong shape in his hand. "What does it do?"

Horth lifted his chin in the direction of the porch and headed inside. Branst followed.

A half-dozen curious hangar staff made way for them as they passed inside. Horth recognized a commoner who did maintenance engineering, and nodded to him. He did not understand why the man looked so pleased by the simple acknowledgement, but he didn't waste time thinking about it much.

Horth felt at home inside the hangar. It was well built and practical. Tables and chairs filled one side, and a locker room occupied the other, its open spaces mixed with private cubicles.

A staff member appeared at Horth's elbow and said, "I'll show you to the highborn quarters," up-speaking him four birth ranks. Horth could use a change of clothes after his trip, and a chance to freshen up. He went with her, leaving the Reetion box for Branst to examine. It crossed Horth's mind that if Branst figured out how to make it work, he might be spared explaining anything about it.

Half-an-hour later Horth was back, dressed in casual court clothes he had found in a well-stocked closet, with his sword on his hip. His borrowed attire displayed no markings unique to him, personally, but declared him a Nersallian highborn.

Branst was seated at a table in the dining area with plates of snacks set out. All his attention, however, was fixed on the Reetion box, watching a scene with an expression of mesmerized horror.

Horth turned the box off with a sweep of his hand to announce his arrival. Branst started at the interruption.

"I don't understand," Branst said, blinking at Horth. "These pictures, they were recorded here, on Gelion. If they are real." He paused. "Do you think someone created this to slander the Ava? I mean, because his admiral, H'Reth, is featured in a very bad light! Gods ignore us! The man molests boys!" He paused again, getting agitated. "It looks real! But gods! It shows things I had never imagined possible, no matter how *sla* a den was! Things being done to children! And it all looks as if it takes place through the eyes of that dancer from Den Eva's, Von, who seems to be much younger in some scenes than others. Almost as if these are memories." Branst stopped there, distraught. "What does it mean?" he asked hoarsely.

Horth shook his head. All he knew was that he did not like the silver box. Whether it lied or told the truth, it made a joke of Sevolite honor.

Branst ran stiff fingers through his mop of black hair with a great sigh. "Strange things are happening here, too. You've heard of the Demish rebel, Perry D'Aur?"

"From Killing Reach," said Horth.

Branst nodded. "There's been a horrible transgression, with power weapons, at Den Eva's. Vretla Vrel was wounded! People say Perry D'Aur was at fault. I was going to go find Di Mon to learn more, but he's gone off planet somewhere." Branst nibbled his lower lip a moment before adding, "After he sent Vretla Vrel to *TouchGate Hospital*."

Horth hissed.

"I know!" cried Branst. "But Di Mon did it to save her life! Not to violate her soul!"

Horth frowned, reserving judgment for the moment about Di Mon. He didn't like the way Branst continued to toy with the silver box, as if he meant to turn it back on. Horth was not interested in seeing the vile scenes again.

"Something worries me about this thing," said Branst, as he toyed with the box in his hands. "It could be pure invention. We know that Lorels can do that, so why not Reetions? But if it isn't — and the details are so good! If it is real—" he broke off, looking tortured.

Horth sat down and started eating strips of jerky from a serving tray, dipping them in a thick, gray-brown sauce that he washed down with pilot's nectar.

It was long minutes before Branst mastered his qualms enough to go on. "I saw something once," he said, "in a Monatese library on Sanctuary. Pictures. From a long, long time ago. A time when... " Branst looked up at his brother with a blighted expression. Horth swallowed the jerky he was chewing and put the rest of the stick down.

"The Lorels," said Branst. "They used to use the same technology, on us, that we still use to bind *gorarelpul*. Used it to b-bind the Vrellish," Branst stuttered. "You know how the Lorels destroyed souls?"

Horth had heard those stories. It was one of the reasons why honorable people, like Kene, would die rather than accept Lorel-tainted help. He encouraged Branst with one curt nod.

"The pictures I saw on Sanctuary.... " Branst bit his lip. Slowly, he set his fist down on the silver box. "The Lorels used to do things like this to Demish Sevolites: rape a living brain to harvest its experiences. Oh gods, Horth — that's what these pictures look like! And if it is, then Reetions must be Lorels of the worst sort!"

Horth was stunned.

"Except," Branst faltered. "Von's a commoner. How could he survive? How could it even work?" He spread his right hand over his eyes

They remained like that, in silence, for long seconds. Then Horth put a hand on Branst's shoulder, and his brother looked up with anguish in his green eyes.

"I swear," he promised Horth, his voice quavering. "I swear that I'll stand with the family, even against Monitum, if Reetions use science like that to master Sevolites." He tensed up. "But I can't believe Di Mon would be sheltering a Reetion if they condone things like that!"

Horth frowned. He had lived and worked in Killing Reach. He knew what the world looked like when you let people mock honor. He felt his jaw tighten and his chest swell.

"We had better get to Black—" Branst began, and was interrupted by Ses Nersal barging in.

"Branst!" cried the nobleborn Nersallian. "The Red Vrellish! Two of them have come to court looking for Di Mon!"

* * *

A car from Ses's garage picked them up when they were clear of the docks.

"Di Mon's not back!" reported the female driver, who was dressed in the garage uniform. The man in the seat beside her was fussing over a noisy signal on a shortwave radio console built into the dash of the car.

"Where are we going?" Branst demanded.

"After Liege Sert of Red Reach," said the man, hunting an elusive signal and without turning his head. "Liege Sert went to Green Hearth, apparently out for Di Mon's blood over him sending Vretla to *TouchGate Hospital*. But Di Mon was not there, and she left again with two of the most unlikely people! Di Mon's new *lyka*, Eva, and that Reetion Di Mon is harboring!"

"What's really interesting, though," continued the driver as she turned towards the Demish residential area known as the Apron District, "is that the Demish have gone after them in force! First Delm's last paladin on planet, named Thoth — and then a visiting tournament champion from Princess Reach."

"Hendricks D'Astor!" cried Ses Nersal. "The Pan-Demish Tournament champion."

While they talked, their car made its way past the Apron District, at the foot of the Citadel, towards the streets beyond.

This sector of the Palace Plain was given over to light industry organized into blocks. Each block had its own buildings and area to park. Some had fences around them and some did not. The time of day, in the underground city, was just before dawn, which was generally referred to as lights up for the sake of its suddenness.

They drove in semi-darkness with their car's headlights on, going as fast as the driver dared while the man beside her took directions over a shortwave radio from confederates tracking the Demish cars they pursued. The reception was not good. Radio signals bounced chaotically around the hullsteel shell of UnderGelion. Using short wave overcame that problem, or could have, if rival houses had not made it a hobby to jam each other's signals or to try to eavesdrop, which, together with an ongoing war over standards made communications unreliable.

Nersallians were more persistent than most about countering Demish sabotage and inflicting their own. Many houses simply gave up, unable to invest in the ongoing communications war that had crippled or discredited methods of signaling that did not rely on personal contact or the use of blood ciphers to encode and authenticate them.

The com-man cursed more than once.

"Somebody's flooding our channel!" he griped aloud.

But it didn't matter. They already had their target in sight. Horth gave Branst a nudge and pointed at two speeding Demish cars just ahead of them that bore a Silver Demish crest.

They were driving down a wide street with a central boulevard, approaching an establishment that looked like some kind of food-raising enterprise. The main building was box-like with a fenced-in yard. They were at the back of the complex, so there was no grand entrance or carefully tended lawn. People were trickling out onto the yard to watch what was going on. Demish cars marked with the Ava's rose-and-sword device were parked on both sides of the road.

As Horth watched, Hendricks D'Astor's car pulled off the road ahead of them, disgorging people. The lighting shed by glow plastic on poles along the street was dim, to simulate night, but Horth could make out a stylishly dressed Demish prince.

Their own car drew up near the two filled with D'Astor's people. Branst sprang out. Horth followed him. He could see tanks in the backyard by now, identifying the place as a hydroponics farm.

Delm's paladin, Thoth, was confronting Liege Sert of Red Reach, in plain view on the street. Floodlights mounted on the hoods of Prince D'Astor's cars were turned on suddenly, lighting the area better, but D'Astor made no move to intervene.

Horth guessed the Demish prince was here for the same reason as Branst and himself: to bear witness. But it did not look as if there was going to be a duel. The paladin lacked the nerve. He seemed inclined to talk, instead.

As negotiations began, Horth noticed two people wearing traveling cloaks who caught his attention by bolting off towards the farm building. Horth did not know what to make of that except that it seemed odd.

"Thoth wants D'Astor to fight for him!" Branst hissed to Ses under his breath.

"Uh-huh," she agreed.

D'Astor did not seem interested in taking up the challenge, however. The Red Vrellish challenger concluded that the duel was off, and left the Demish to their argument.

Horth looked to see what had happened to the two people who had run off, but Ses said, "There's a duel pending on the Octagon, over Perry D'Aur." She looked to Branst for a decision. "Shouldn't we be there?"

Branst bit his lip. "I don't know," he said, "but Tessitatt might be at Green Hearth. She'll tell me what's happening."

Branst and Ses talked about bizarre events occurring in UnderGelion as they drove back to the stairs that led up to the Citadel. Horth understood, basically, that there was more than one Reetion box around, causing trouble. A mob had attacked the pregnant wife of Delm's admiral, H'Reth, on the assumption that her child would be tainted by the same boy-*sla* nature that her husband had demonstrated in the Reetion images.

"Why do people believe the pictures are genuine?" Branst asked Ses, nervously. "Gelacks don't trust recordings. They are too easy to meddle with, or just invent."

"There's a rumor that Di Mon is taking the silver box seriously," Ses replied. She indulged in a worried frown. "Di Mon doesn't consider, sometimes, how people interpret the things he does. Like taking that Reetion into Green Hearth. What are Sevolites to make of him harboring the person who, for all we know, could be responsible for that abominable silver box?"

"I still don't understand what the point of it is," protested Branst. "Why go to all that trouble to show us the ugly side of Gelion?"

Ses Nersal had all kinds of ideas about that, but Horth tuned her out. He was remembering the two people back at the hydroponics farm who ran around the building and wondering if he had glimpsed a dark face beneath the hood of one traveling cloak, or if it had merely been shadows.

At the base of the stairs leading up to the roof of the Citadel, Ses halted with a groan and rubbed her leg with the old wound. Horth picked her up without a word and had no trouble keeping up with Branst despite the burden. They did, however, get some funny looks.

"Thanks," Ses said gruffly when he put her down abruptly at the top.

They passed unhindered through a thick line of Demish swordsmen guarding the Palace Shell. Not only were there more of them on guard than usual, but at least six of them were highborns and some were showing signs of nervousness. Horth made one blond prince start just by looking at him, which he rather enjoyed.

"Something's up," Branst muttered under his breath.

They kept up a brisk pace across the Plaza. When they reached Black Pavilion, Horth was glad to see a handful of errants that he recognized. Their leader saluted Branst, avoiding eye contact with Horth.

"Good to see you, scion Nersal!" said their leader.

"Glad I made it in time, Tomin," said Branst. "Can you tell me exactly what's going on?"

Tomin shook his head. "Nothing beyond the obvious. Perry D'Aur has been accused of the *okal'a'ni* attack on Vretla Vrel. Prince D'Ander is supposed to be standing for her, but he's not here yet. Hendricks D'Astor — he's a tournament champion — "

"I know, I know," said Branst. "I'm not Red Vrellish, you know — I pay attention to what happens at court!"

Tomin nodded. "D'Astor is supposed to fight on Delm's behalf."

"There's got to be more to this!" exclaimed Branst, running a hand through his tousled hair as they made their way down into Black Hearth.

Servants came out to greet them within minutes, including Alice, who ran straight into Branst's arms. He treated her with cool affection, letting her shelter there like a child for a moment before moving her firmly into Cook's keeping. Twelve people comprised the entire Black Hearth staff, including the medic *gorarelpul* Narous, a herald, and six nobleborn errants. Horth doubted the errants were even full-time residents. Ses may have called them back to duty, much as she had done with Branst.

Branst greeted each of the errants with expressions of friendship and gratitude, saying things like, "Glad to have you with us." Horth hovered at his elbow.

"I'm going to see what I can find out at Green Hearth," Branst announced when no one had fresh information to offer.

Horth decided not to follow. He was watching Alice. He wondered if she would ever want to throw herself into his arms. The fertility issues still confounded him, but he couldn't help wondering why he found commoners like Alice desirable, if he wasn't supposed to want one to have his baby? Was it his wild Vrellish blood?

He let the question drop when Alice noticed him staring at her and blanched as if she'd been challenged to a duel. He did not like that, and kept his eyes off her after that.

Branst returned ten minutes later.

"Tessitatt isn't home," he said. Then he and Ses went off to find a comfortable place to talk. To avoid Alice problems, Horth tagged along.

An errant came to find them when it was time for the duel on the Octagon.

Branst and Horth went to stand witness, on Black Wedge, accompanied by Ses and a pitiful handful of errants.

The Red Vrellish highborns they had seen outside the hydroponics farm stood on Red Wedge, in Vretla's place, surrounded by nobleborns from Spiral Hall.

Ava Delm himself was on display in the midst of princes and princesses on Silver Wedge. Banks of Demish spectators surrounded him, with more on Blue Wedge.

People took note of Branst's small party, but the Octagon's attention was soon seized by the appearance of a Demish woman dressed in very ordinary-looking pants and top, who was marched out with her arms bound and a gag in her mouth.

Beside Horth, Branst said, "Perry D'Aur."

Horth knew the name. D'Aur had rebelled against Delm in Killing Reach a generation before, and been vindicated by the Golden prince, D'Ander, when the Silver Demish unwisely appointed him as judge of honor. Horth knew no particular evil of Perry D'Aur, but he did not find it hard to believe she might have dropped the shield of honor, because people said that she had small regard for *Okal Rel* in general.

As Prince H'Us of the Silver Demish read the charges, Horth found himself remembering Hara. It was Hara who had taught him that everything worth stealing depended on trust to be created, and therein lay the paradox that honor guarded.

Let others make the mistakes, she had told him, *just like in a duel. And when they do, be ruthless. Take from those who drop the shield of honor. There are more than enough of them for you to gain all you will ever need, honorably, and the struggle will never consume the precious things you fight for.*

Even in a case as apparently simple as obtaining Alice, Horth recognized the truth in it. What would he have if he gained her dishonorably? Not Alice — just a broken spirit in a captive body.

Horth's feelings were so intense and internal, while he worked his way through the pain of unanticipated temptation, that he did not catch any of the details in Prince H'Us's long-winded declarations. But he knew they would be about the charges against Perry D'Aur and the terms of the duel between her defender, D'Ander, and Prince Hendricks D'Astor, acting in the capacity of Throne Champion.

Only the start of the duel snapped him out of it. Even then, Horth watched the two Demish swordsmen with no more than an academic interest as they tested each other, neither one very keen to get serious.

Then the crowd's attention wavered as Di Mon appeared – not on Green Wedge, but Blue.

Di Mon moved quickly through the spectators on Blue Wedge, a girl's voice crying "Von! Von!" from within the ranks of the Blue Demish he left behind him.

The paladin, Thoth, beat Di Mon to Delm's flower-covered seat, carrying a dark-haired boy about two years old. Noticing the toddler's head jerk at the last echo of "Von," coming from Blue Wedge, Horth assumed the unseen woman must be his mother, and his eyes narrowed.

Thoth placed the child in Delm's lap and sunk to his knees before his idol. "Light of Divine Beauty-of-Soul," he implored, "I have heard you accused of seeking this child's death — madness in itself! The reason defies hearing, therefore I beg you to genotype him, now, before Sevildom assembled!"

The paladin went on a bit, but Horth stopped listening. Beside him, Ses Nersal had gone rigid with alarm, her attention fixed on Di Mon. While the Demish babbled, Di Mon kept coming. When he stopped, he shouted accusations in a ringing voice that seized attention.

"That child on your lap is your grandson," Di Mon told Delm, "and even if you break his neck, his genes will still condemn you." He jerked his head in Perry D'Aur's direction. "She is nothing but a scapegoat for what you did at Den Eva's to eliminate a child that Von, the courtesan, had sired. A child you had to kill because you had discovered Von was Pureblood Amel, your son!"

Beside Horth, Branst started with shock. "Amel!" he gasped.

Prince H'Us of the Silver Demish descended on Di Mon. He was a big man, as old as Horth's father and equally vigorous, with thick sandy eyebrows, ornate Demish clothing, and wide shoulders.

"My dear Di Mon," the Silver Demish prince appealed to reason, "you've been flying too hard. Ran into some trouble, I expect, eh? Out in Killing Reach?"

Di Mon narrowed his eyes. "Draw or step aside," he warned dangerously.

Ses Nersal started forward but Branst stopped her.

H'Us leaned towards Di Mon to speak privately. He even clapped Di Mon on the shoulder, making him start violently. There was more talking, and then suddenly Di Mon punched H'Us in the stomach and cleared his sword, all in one motion.

Ses Nersal caught her breath. Branst got out a strangled, "No!"

Di Mon's sword went through Delm's throat despite the devoted attendant who tried to get between them. Delm crashed to the floor. Di Mon went with him. Women screamed. People ran away. Others ran to where Delm thrashed, arterial blood spurting. Someone cried, "Hold him down!" in a panic.

Branst and Ses dashed across the Challenge Floor. Horth followed Branst. The Red Vrellish were already uniting with Green Hearth retainers in a spontaneous show of Vrellish solidarity.

Prince H'Us of Silver Hearth set a sword at Di Mon's throat as his men held the prisoner motionless before him. "You'll die disgraced on Ava's Square for this, you Vrellish animal!" H'Us raged.

Black, Green, and Red — the Vrellish formed a crescent line, cupping the scene.

It was Liege Sert of Red Reach who spoke for them. "You can fight me for the privilege of killing him, later," she told Prince H'Us, "if you're still so inclined, once we know who this wretched child is."

"Show us the child!" Branst exclaimed excitedly. "Now. Or more blood will spill!"

Horth stood his ground, backing Branst up, but he wished the odds were better.

The churning around Delm stopped suddenly. Prince D'Astor came forward, his sleeves soaked in Delm's blood. "He's dead," he said, sounding stunned. "The Ava is dead."

"Genotype the child," Prince H'Us said through gritted teeth, and glared at the Vrellish, whose stand on Di Mon's behalf demanded that much fairness in the process.

Horth was not at all clear about why genotyping the boy was so important except that it had something to do with the lost prince, Amel. He was on the Challenge Floor, quite simply, because Branst was.

Di Mon caught Ses Nersal's eye and spoke, starting a trickle of blood where the sword pressed his throat. "Eva and the Reetion. They're in Blue Hearth."

Ses took that as an order to go fetch them out. Branst nudged Horth to go with her as backup. He followed her up the stairs into Black Hearth and out again onto Fountain Court.

The door to Blue Wedge stood open. The man who had opened it was dragging the unconscious body of the courtesan named Eva, trying to get her out. As he looked up over a shoulder, Horth saw his face was a light caramel brown, and blinked in shock. He had never seen a Reetion before.

Ses gestured, and Horth went to hold off a couple of Blue Hearth errants who appeared at the inward end of the hall. The errants had no right to oppose Horth without Delm's explicit orders, because Horth outranked them, but the situation was fluid enough that Horth was glad to be clear of it without testing anyone's grasp of Sword Law.

Back in Black Hearth, Ses turned Eva over to Cook.

"Would you stay here?" Ses asked Horth. "Di Mon is my *mekan'st*. I need to get back down there."

Horth was worried about Branst, too, but he nodded.

To his surprise, the brown-faced Reetion went after Ses Nersal.

Horth waited in Black Hearth, bewildered by the whole affair. He prowled back and forth between the entrance hall and spiral stairs, feeling like a ward ship guarding two jumps at the same time. He was not aware of how tense he was until things broke up on the Octagon and Branst came flying up the stairs, exclaiming, "Tessitatt's all right, she's just off minding Vretla on *TouchGate Hospital*!" Branst acted as if this had always been the crucial issue.

* * *

It was hours before Horth got the facts straight in connection with the bigger picture. What mattered was this: The dancer named Von was the lost Pureblood Amel, and that gave the images on the Reetion box a new significance.

"A Demish highborn," Branst kept saying, in a dozen variations. "Reetions can extract Demish memories, just like Lorels used to! And if they can do that — does it mean they have the science to control Vrellish pilots as well? Take captives and use our own pilots against us?"

Nersallian tradition was to die before being taken prisoner by dishonorable enemies. Branst's worries gave Horth a whole new appreciation for the reason.

"You've got to take the box to Dad at once!" was Branst's conclusion. "I'd come too, but Tessitatt might need my help with the Red Vrellish when she gets back. They won't like her taking their liege to *TouchGate Hospital*."

Guessing the cause of Horth's dismayed expression Branst set his hand on Horth's shoulder. "The box explains itself," he told his brother. "Just take it, and tell Dad the Reetions can do that to a Sevolite."

* * *

Horth got out of his envoy ship on the runway outside the estate where Liege Nersal was holding court on Tark, in Alliance Reach. He was met by one of *Zer* Sarn's fanatics: a Nesak named Falk with a narrow face and hard eyes that looked out from a soul that must have been so brutally embittered in a past life that it could find no joy in this one.

As he followed Falk off the landing strip, Horth wondered how the Nesaks were coping with the fact that the vast majority of Tarkians were not highborns, and that there were millions of them. Mother and *Zer* Sarn could not empty Tark of non-eternals the way they had tried to do at Black Hearth.

Hangst held court on Tark at a country estate on the outskirts of a city built to serve a major spaceport. Slow trucks, powered by the usual ecologically-friendly methods, dotted a distant road. Beyond that lay a field of solar collectors milking power from the cool autumn rays of Tark's sun. The terrain behind the estate was backed by forested foothills infested by the pesky native creatures known as grabrats.

The thought of grabrats reminded Horth of hunting with Kale on SanHome.

Falk led Horth into a courtyard where three children were at play, dressed up in ill-fitting costumes. Eler was seven now: a skinny, energetic child wearing an improvised admiralty headdress and waving a toy sword in mock combat. The girl he played with was about three. She struggled valiantly to hold her sword steady in front of her.

"I don't care what you think, you vile Vrellish creature!" Eler declared. "I will have a wife if I want!"

The third child was a physically precocious infant. She claimed everyone's attention by falling off the stone bench she was trying to scale, letting out a shriek of indignation as she landed.

Horth scooped her up before Eler got to her. Vrellish mothers said their infants knew a relative by scent. Whatever the reason, the agile baby settled down quickly in Horth's arms. Her reaction pleased him.

Eler was less comfortable with his intervention. He looked to Falk for assistance.

"I will take Sanal," Falk said to Horth, lifting the baby away from him. "Thank you." He gave the infant to Eler. "This way," he told Horth, and led on again.

Horth tried to make eye contact with Eler, but the child avoided his gaze. Reluctantly, Horth followed his Nesak guide across the courtyard and into the estate, to a suite of rooms that Falk explained were guest quarters.

"Liege Nersal will see you at his leisure," Falk told him. "In the meantime, the servants will see to you."

"Servants?" Horth asked, surprised.

"Yes," Falk said with a bit of a sneer. "It is seductive to have soulless ones about in that capacity. In my time here, I've come to understand the temptation that they pose." He left without discussing it further.

Horth unpacked the few things he had brought with him and showered. When he came out of the bathroom, wrapped in a white towel, he found his mother standing by his dresser, staring at the Reetion box. She had managed to turn it on.

Horth noticed at once that she was pregnant again. The next thing he noticed was how bloodless her face looked, and how her stare had a sharp gleam of something brittle about it.

"Horth," she said in a raw voice. Her eyes flickered down to the holographic scene of a girl not much older than Eler who was being sexually assaulted by a cruel-looking man in a room with shabby furniture. The pictures captured little of Amel himself, because they were recordings of his memories: just a wisp of black hair when it fell across his eye and a glimpse of his own blood-smeared hand as he pushed himself up off the floor, setting Horth's teeth on edge for the sake of the whimper that escaped him. That was no way for a Sevolite to face a *slaka'st*!

The child-Amel in the images made a frantic attack. The chaos of the mismatched struggle irked Horth by giving him such detailed information. He would have done better, even as a child against a grown man.

Angry, he took three swift steps to Beryl's side and swept his hand over the box, turning the images off.

His mother stood between him and the dresser where the hated object sat. "I came..." she stopped with a hiccup of pure distress. "I came to welcome you to..."

But her eyes strayed back to the thing that had disturbed her.

"It is Reetion," Horth said. "A memory."

"Of the Reetion home world?"

"No," he said. "Gelion."

Beryl caught her breath.

"UnderDocks," Horth tried to clarify.

The qualification did not seem to matter to Beryl. "Such things happen to children on Gelion?" she cried in a shrill voice, and fled from him.

Horth took a step towards the door and stopped when he saw her run into Lywulf's arms, sobbing. Falk came in, confiscated the silver box from Horth's dresser, and said, "I will see that this is brought to *Zer* Sarn's attention."

Horth shook his head. "My father," he said. "Liege Nersal."

"And the liege of Nersal, as well, naturally," Falk assured him.

Horth paced about his room for long minutes after they had left before deciding that he had to see his father himself.

A Nersallian honor guard stopped him outside the main house where Hangst was living. He contemplated challenging their captain. It was much more straightforward doing that with fellow highborns than it was with a nobleborn honor guard, who ought to yield automatically in theory, but often chose to claim they were empowered to act, en masse, on behalf of a highborn liege. But Horth did not want to kill or be killed over whether he saw Hangst now, or later.

Instead, he went back to his room to wait for Hangst to summon him.

Kega Tark brought his breakfast tray the next morning, instead of the servant Horth had sent to fetch it for him.

"What's the matter?" she asked, putting the tray down. "Don't like eating with the rest of us?"

"Nesaks," Horth tried to explain his discomfort.

Kega shrugged sturdy shoulders. "You get used to them."

Horth was glad to see Kega. Their encounter at Den Eva's three years earlier qualified her as a *sha'st*. He assumed that was why she had substituted herself for the servant he sent to fetch him breakfast, and she proved him right.

The physical comfort of sex was welcome. But she indulged in conjectures about the Reetion box afterwards.

"Amel is pathetic, of course, but he is Sevolite for all that!" she said, offended. "And Reetions are commoners." This pointed seemed to bother Kega. "Of course, Amel is Demish," she continued. "Some sort of Demish icon, in fact. A kind of *zer-pol* for those guilty of the *Pol* Error. Maybe the insult is intended for the *Okal Lumens* and not all Sevildom."

Something about her analysis bothered Horth, but he didn't realize until after she was gone that it was her matter-of-fact reference to one of the Nesak Errors. He wasn't sure how to put his discomfort with that into words the next time she visited.

He also found out Kega had been promoted. She was no longer an *avsha*, like Horth, but a command officer on a battlewheel and entitled to the military title of *imsha*. That placed her firmly on the career path that Horth coveted, and he did not want to make a bad impression.

* * *

It was six days before Horth saw his father.

He passed his time watching Eler and their sisters from a distance, or training from time to time with Lywulf, who assured him that Beryl was as well as could be expected given the difficulty she was having with her latest pregnancy, which obliged her to rest often.

"Your mother is distressed because she does not want to return to Gelion," Lywulf told him. "But we must go back to Gelion to satisfy the *kinf'stan*. Many won't renew their oaths while your father keeps his back turned to the Green and Red Vrellish, and we cannot begin Unification by fighting those who should be allies. On that point we are all of one mind. What we do about the Reetions, we will do together."

The next day, Horth had unexpected visitors. He had gone for a long run that morning, and returned feeling empty of anxieties to do with Reetions.

A woman in a plain, full-length dress of gray wool leaped to her feet from a stone bench outside his guest suite as he came around a corner. It took Horth a moment to recognize Kale, from Sarn Haven.

Zer Hen came jogging back from where he had been taking tea with Beryllan and two other little girls dressed up in clothes that were too big for them.

Kale looked strong but careworn, with tension in her brow and a downward bias about her mouth as if it were an effort to maintain a neutral expression.

"There you are!" *Zer* Hen said. "Good! Good! Could we come inside?"

Reluctantly, Horth let them into his rooms. The servant assigned to him was not there. Horth decided that was just as well. The visitors settled on the couch and chair available in the sitting area while he retrieved his sword from the rack just inside the door and strapped it on over his jogging clothes. He wasn't quite sure why he did that, since neither Kale nor *Zer* Hen were what the Nesaks would call warriors, but it felt right to him somehow.

"We've come a long way to see you," *Zer* Hen stated the obvious.

Horth waited.

"We heard you were here, you see," the priest went on, "when word came about the Reetion abomination."

Horth was starting to feel concerned about Kale's subdued behavior, and was worried he was going to get blamed for having sex with her before he left, even though — as he remembered — it had definitely been her idea. As far as *EagleNest* was concerned, he had no doubt he had done the right thing. And it had been impossible for him to go back to SanHome, after.

Zer Hen stood up again, uncomfortable sitting while Horth loomed over him and his female charge. Kale stayed seated, her eyes downcast.

"The thing is, Horth," *Zer* Hen rambled on, the way some people will when confronted by silence. "Our Kale here has had a bad time of it. She told us, in the end, about what happened in the pantry before you left."

Horth saw Kale tense, as if that passionate indiscretion had haunted her ever since, like an angry ghost. That bothered him.

"There she was," *Zer* Hen continued, "living in the house that had taken you in, living with Hill's grieving widow." *Zer* Hen failed to overcome his own grief on that score and felt driven to add, "Hill praised you so, Horth, for your showing at the capital! He liked you!" *Zer* Hen shook his head, making his cheeks wobble. "It is hard to understand."

"*Ack rel,*" Horth said bluntly. "I liked Hill, too."

Kale looked up. *Zer* Hen froze.

The priest wet his lips and fidgeted. "I had reservations, myself, you know — if it had been a planet, of course, out of the question! But the *zer'stan*... and the only residents all non-eternals..." *Zer* Hen broke off and straightened up. "But we aren't here to dwell on the *EagleNest* incident. We are here to find out if you'll honor your promise to marry. It is Kale's wish. She finds it hard to live among us now, under the circumstances. But with Unification coming, the family felt it was worth finding out if she could be one of you."

When *Zer* Hen stopped, Horth put a hand on his back and pushed him steadily but firmly out the door. The priest resisted at first, calling "Kale? Will you be all right, Kale?" over his shoulder, but when she did not answer he let himself be mastered rather than oblige Horth to get forceful.

Horth found Kale on her feet when he came back from that chore. She was looking at him frankly. He preferred that, and rewarded her with a grin. Then he pulled her down on the couch beside him, hindered by the sword he had put on, and held both her hands.

Kale's face was animated by a disturbing amalgam of fear and hope.

Horth looked straight into her eyes and said, "No."

The hope and fear collapsed with a jolt. "You won't... marry me," she got out in two disconnected gasps.

"No."

Kale tried to lurch up. Horth held on. She looked wild for a moment, and Horth thought he would have a fight on his hands. She was too Vrellish to cry.

He said, "Fly with me."

"Wha-what?"

Horth stood, drawing her up after him. "Now."

He led her step by wooden step out of his rooms. She gave *Zer* Hen a look of stark confusion as they went past, but she did not ask him for rescue and the mild-mannered priest let them go.

Kale was no more dressed for reality skimming than Horth was, in his sweat suit, but Horth was too impatient to waste time hunting up flight leathers. He marched her out to where his ship was parked and bundled her into the pilot's seat despite her dress.

"I don't know how to fly!" she cried when she realized what he was doing.

"Learn," he said, and showed her how to start.

They started with a nasty lurch and nearly hit a parked space-to-orbit shuttle before making it through a very bumpy take-off.

Kale let out a cry of excitement as they pierced the first bank of clouds.

Horth taxed his powers of communication to coach her in the minimal piloting skills she would need to control the *rel-ship* under *skim*. She had to know at least a little before he dared engage the phase splicer.

"I've flown before, of course," she told him as the moment to begin reality skimming grew closer. "To get here, I mean. As a passenger."

He waited for her to raise the immorality of needless trips, but she never broached the subject.

When the time came, Horth made Kale take over. She gripped the controls, poised herself, and then hesitated, drawing up her hand to hover over the lever that unleashed the phase splicer, as if it was too hot to touch.

"Do you really think I can?" she asked in a crisis of confidence. "I could kill us both, or worse! The Lost are not reborn."

Horth closed his hand over hers and pulled.

Gap washed through them both. It felt like being forced underwater and refusing to strike for the surface, but Horth held back. He felt her grasp their peril. Then the sound of Kale's wild laughter filled the ship as Kale flew.

They very nearly had an accident with a ward ship in the next few seconds, but they made it down to the planet again in the end without suffering more than an hour's wear and tear and a half a day's time slip.

* * *

Hangst sent for Horth the day after Kale's first flight. They met in the family's private rooms, in a space that reminded Horth of Black Hearth's nursery because, in addition to a comfortable sitting area, it contained a playhouse, a jungle gym, and *nervecloth* toys that could be retrained to change their interface protocols.

Eler sat reading in a corner. He looked up when Horth came in, and buried himself all the harder in his book. Beryllan was napping on a mattress at one end of the room, curled around a doll.

"I did not want to keep you waiting," Hangst told Horth as they sat down. Beryl sat beside her husband, looking drawn.

"I understand, from another envoy, why Bryllit was unable to bring me the Reetion box herself," Hangst opened, and gave his son a wry smile. "Congratulations — again."

Beryl shifted away from Hangst at the mention of Bryllit and picked up her sewing from where she had set it down beside her.

Baby Sanal scrambled onto Beryl's lap. Hangst lifted his youngest daughter away from her mother's stomach and put her back down on the floor, saying, "Eler, come entertain your sister."

Eler slouched over with a sulky expression.

"Do not take Eler's attitude too personally," Hangst told Horth, when the children had moved to the far corner of the room. "He has a hard time accepting Zrenyl, as well."

"He seems to like Branst well enough, though," Beryl spoke up, and went back to her sewing. She was making a miniature vest, complete with house braid, that was the right size for Beryllan's doll. "Eler is a sensitive child," she remarked. "Horth can seem a little threatening, that's all."

Horth remembered her pleading with Hangst not to take him to the reception for Amel, on Fountain Court, and cast a wistful look in Eler's direction at the realization he had been replaced.

"Horth," Hangst broke the silence. "I want your help."

Horth nodded.

"First," Hangst said, "you ought to know a few things. Amel is in Killing Reach with Perry D'Aur and apt to stay there for the time being. D'Ander means to use him as a puppet Ava. Di Mon supports his mother, Ev'rel, as do the Silver Demish. So Killing Reach is full of Demish ships, partly to keep an eye on Amel while D'Ander negotiates, and partly to make sure the Reetions stay on their side of the jump. Di Mon is attempting to maintain communications between the Reetions and the Silver Demish. The Golden Demish, under Prince D'Ander, are making sure they stay between the Silvers and Amel. They won't move Amel to court until the stakes of the duel concerning him are guaranteed. And who can do that for a dispute between the Demish powers of Fountain Court, except the Vrellish lieges? Di Mon needs Black Hearth to pull off any deal. And, as you know, I am not there. So, they are stalemated over the Amel affair, but I am talking to Di Mon about it to find out what he knows about the Reetions. And he knows a great deal. He has made a friend of a Reetion named Ranar — the same you saw on the Octagon, I believe. Di Mon asked you and Branst to fetch him out of Blue Hearth along with Di Mon's *lyka*, Eva."

Horth said, "I remember."

Hangst sighed. "I need to know more than Di Mon is telling me about the Reetions. I need to know the jump into their territory. Di Mon knows the jump, himself, but he won't share it with me. In fact, he has convinced the Demish to stop anyone who tries to hitchhike through with a Reetion pilot."

Muscles worked in his father's jaw as he explained this last piece of what he seemed to view as a betrayal on Di Mon's part. He inhaled after a pause and squared his broad shoulders.

"Apparently Amel knows the jump, as well," said Hangst, "but I may as well wish to learn it from the Golden Emperor. Amel has too many keepers to lay hand on him. So something else must be done."

Hangst leaned forward, elbows on his knees and large hands folded quietly together.

"I want the Reetions to stay in Killing Reach," he told Horth. "I want them to keep bringing in pilots and building the station they are constructing on our side. I want them there because I need to learn the jump, one way or another. I do not want Reetions knowing how to get into Killing Reach when we do not know how to follow them back out."

That made good sense, militarily. It was important to know jumps. Horth nodded.

Hangst sighed as he sat back. "The Silvers would prefer the Reetions went away. I don't blame them. But that solution isn't permanent. It was the one imposed by Ameron two hundred years ago and it has failed. I want to be able to chase the Reetions back through that jump, into their territory, to establish a base there. That's the only way we can be confident of containing them."

"What do you want me to do?" asked Horth, slowly and deliberately. "Steal the jump?"

Hangst shook his head. "No. That's too dangerous. If the Demish warding it don't get you going through, they will get you coming back out. Even if you succeeded, it would start trouble before I'm ready. No, this is what I want." Hangst instructed. "I want you to join Branst on the Demish battlewheel named *Quicksilver*, where he went to be with Tessitatt. Di Mon makes every pilot arriving from the Reetion side dock there, so he can be sure that they are Reetions and police knowledge of the jump. I want you to get a look at them, so we'll know which ones are pilots when the time comes. And I want you to get a good look at the Reetion station — up close. I want you to think about it from the point of view of how we'd take one, given that they do not honor Sword Law and their stations appear to be more fragile than ours because they have no hullsteel."

Horth thought about that and found the request reasonable. It was important to be prepared for trouble. Only one thing puzzled him.

"Branst is there," he said, hoping his father would deduce his question. "Already."

Hangst nodded. "That's why you will be welcome. I hope. But I can't rely on Branst to give me information himself. Branst is our son," he said, taking Beryl's hand as he spoke. "And I know that he would never betray us. But I am equally sure that if I asked him to do this for me, he would argue. And he would tell Di Mon what I want."

Horth nodded, and got up.

"Eler!" Beryl called sharply, and watched as the boy's head rose slowly over the arm of a nearby couch. "Were you listening?"

"It doesn't matter," said Hangst. "Branst will not be visiting here again before Horth gets back. I don't expect we'll see him until we go back to Black Hearth."

Beryl stopped sewing to look at them both. "Why, yes," she said, and smiled. "We'll all be together there at last. I hadn't thought of that!" But she reached for her husband's arm immediately, dread on her face. "Why am I so afraid of it then, beloved?"

Hangst covered her hand with his, keeping his eye on his youngest son. "Eler," he cautioned the child. "Branst trusts the Monatese more than he should. You understand?"

"Yes, Father," the boy said, looking miserable.

"Eler hates the fact we can't all get along," said Beryl.

Hangst laughed. "I think," he said, "you overestimate the *pol* side of young Eler's character."

* * *

Father was probably right about Eler having more *rel* about him than *pol*, Horth decided, because he caught the seven-year-old trying to stow away on his envoy ship when he left the next morning.

Horth had to drag Eler out of the cargo compartment behind the cockpit, screaming, and hand him to Lywulf.

"It's wrong to lie!" Eler yelled at Horth. "It's wrong to lie, especially to brothers!"

"Strange sentiment coming from a master of lies," said Lywulf.

Kale was there, too. Horth wished he could convince her that it was honorable to become *mekan'stan* even if they couldn't marry, but he hadn't had any luck on that front. He had arranged with Kega to take over Kale's flying lessons, in the hope that Kega might recruit her as a *relsha*.

Kale gave Horth a wide smile as he got into his envoy. "Good weather," she wished him. "Fly well!"

The flight to Killing Reach began to get sticky in Golden Reach. Horth was herded into dock by three highborn ships and wasted a whole day waiting for officious Golden Demish functionaries to clear him. By the time it was over, he wished he had taken the chance of ramming through instead of putting up with the intimidation. He hated being bossed around by Goldens.

Killing Reach itself offered surprisingly clear weather on the end that connected with Golden Reach. But as he moved across it, towards the jump that led to Reetions, the display of moving *rel*-ships on his *nervecloth* grew alarmingly dense.

There were battlewheels everywhere, most with a hand of *rel*-ships buzzing around them, and some of them *rel*-skimming themselves at a sedate half a *skim factor*. Now and then, satellite *rel*-fighters danced signatures to identify themselves.

Prowling every access to the Barmi II system, where D'Ander has stashed Amel, were Golden Demish defenders, while the Silver Demish barricaded the jump itself.

The sheer number of ships under *skim* at any given time made Horth feel like someone walking on thin ice that gave a little with each footfall. It was irrational to have so many ships in the area.

Horth located the *Quicksilver* and signaled "House of Nersal" very carefully before dropping out to boost himself along by cat clawing. He even stopped that early, and endured more zero G than he wanted to, coasting in without acceleration.

"Horth, born of Black Hearth and sworn to Liege Bryllit," he announced himself when he was hailed on the radio. "Here to see Branst Nersal."

Horth was more than surprised to be met in the airlock not only by Branst, but also the brown-skinned Reetion named Ranar.

"Horth Nersal," the Reetion greeted him in Gelack, and proceeded to further surprise Horth by using pronouns appropriate for a peer, not a commoner. "I did not get a chance to thank you properly, on Gelion."

"It's not an insult!" Branst said fast, watching Horth bristle. "It's called peerage of convenience. Ameron used it behind closed doors. Di Mon thinks it helps with diplomacy."

Tessitatt fixed Horth with a steady gaze. "Who sent you?" she asked.

"Tess!" Branst objected to her rudeness.

But Horth answered factually. "Father," he told them.

It was the Reetion who stepped forward. "I understand," he said, "that Liege Nersal supports our goal of establishing an embassy station on this side of the jump. Please tell him we are grateful."

Except for his general good health, Ranar was physically unimpressive. But he had an aloof self-possession that Horth did not expect in commoners, unless they were *gorarelpul*. And his brown skin made an interesting visual contrast with the rich blue of his tunic and matching slacks.

"Fine," said Tessitatt. "You came, Ranar said thanks — how about you leave again?"

"What?" Branst cried, and rounded on her. "Tess, that's Horth!"

She inhaled to argue with him and just tossed her head, instead. "I wish Di Mon were here," she said.

"I don't," Branst said cheerfully. "Because then you would have to switch places with him again, and we'd be flying back to Gelion. I want to stay put for a few days. I think my gums are still bleeding from the last switch that we made!"

"For a highborn, you are such a whiner," Tessitatt admonished him.

* * *

Horth stayed for a full three-day travel respite, but Tessitatt made a point of keeping him away from any Reetion pilots. There was always someone keeping an eye on him. But since Tess had no Green Hearth staff with her on the Demish station, she was sometimes forced to let Branst do it.

That was how Horth and Branst came to be sparring on the grand challenge floor of the Silver Demish battlewheel, directly below the rim docks. The floor underfoot was covered in tightly fitted wood, and the witness stands were hung with drapes that had long silver tassels.

When they were finished, they deposited themselves in two plush seats up in the stands. Each man pulled off his protective mask, borrowed from Demish lockers, with an almost identical gesture.

Branst laughed first, but Horth saw the joke, too, and joined him.

"The Reetions think we're crazy to use swords to settle quarrels," Branst volunteered, unexpectedly.

"Why are they still alive?" Horth asked what was, to him, the logical follow up question.

"They control themselves in other ways," Branst told him. "Ranar says they use things called arbiters. He says a rogue pilot couldn't make a Reetion space station surrender, because the arbiter on board would not accept a threat as a legitimate argument! Isn't that funny?" He grinned, then shrugged. "I'm not entirely sure of all the details. But the thing is, it's the arbiter that makes them stick to their laws, and their laws say nothing can be taken by force. Nothing!"

"Arbiter?" said Horth.

"That's right. A kind of living computer. I haven't seen one because they don't have one, yet, on *SkyBlue Station* but Ranar says they look like foggy crystals with faint scintillations moving around inside called the cognitive core, which is alive but doesn't have a personality." He flinched. "That part is creepy. Anyway, Reetions house them in blocks of the crystal stuff, all around their stations, and talk to them through outlets they call stages. And nothing can intimidate them into doing anything!" Branst laughed. "I rather like that idea, really."

"Do they fly?" Horth asked, thinking with cold fear of a fleet of soulless *rel*-ships loosed upon the empire.

"Not even as well as a commoner!" Branst assured him. "The Reetions have tried it, apparently. But *gap* blanks out an arbiter. They can't make a stitch without disappearing. They don't even make decent passengers except in a sort of embryonic form or as something called a nav-persona, which is a kind of temporary subroutine. Reetion pilots fly with what they call subarbitorial crystronics on board. All the same, arbiters are amazing. The Reetions depend on them so heavily that they wouldn't know what to do on an average day, without their arbiters! I wanted to go see a Reetion station that was up and operational, but Tessitatt wouldn't let me come." He scowled. "She doesn't trust me knowing the jump. But one day she is going to really trust me." He brightened up. "Gives us something to work on! Like the next baby."

Horth said — and did — nothing to let his brother guess what he had just told him about Tessitatt.

* * *

Days later, back on Tark, Horth struggled through telling his father about arbiters, and that Tessitatt Monitum knew the jump into the Reetion territories. Hangst took in the information thoughtfully. So did *Zer* Sarn, who stood beside him.

All Hangst said was, "Thank you."

Then there was more waiting, with messengers arriving almost daily from everywhere in the empire, as well as from SanHome.

"Your father is persuading the *kinf'stan* to unite with us against the Reetions," Lywulf told Horth. "But they all say the same thing. They will decide on Black Wedge, nowhere else. And not until Bryllit is able to stand for them if they decide against your father."

Horth could not remember when he had come to realize that Unification was going to take place over the conquest of the Reetion territories, but he was not immune to the excitement trickling through the ranks of those who gathered about Hangst in hope of favors. Whole planets awaited, people said, with no one to defend them except commoners. Nersallians talked about fields and factories populated by brown-skinned workers, while Nesaks talked about the problems of depopulating their new territories so they could stock them properly with immigrants from SanHome. But the worst tensions were over nobleborns, not commoners.

One evening, in the great hall where Hangst's guests took dinner together, a Nesak shoved a nobleborn. The nobleborn pulled a knife and killed the Nesak. By the time the resulting melee ended, eighteen people were dead and twice that many injured. Horth heard about it the next morning, from the servant who brought his breakfast to his guest suite.

Not all interactions were fatal ones, however. Much to Horth's surprise, sex made inroads where blades failed, in the form of female nobleborns intent on seducing Nesaks to commit the Error of Debasement.

Not every Nesak succumbed to these temptations, but Kale was aghast at how many did, given that every one of them had a wife back on SanHome.

Nersallian women sobered up after the first dozen found themselves grounded by pregnancies, and business picked up again for male prostitutes in the nearest town, much to every Nesak's apparent disgust although some of them snuck off to tag along with the Nersallian men who visited the commoner women at such brothels.

Horth was beginning to wonder how long they could keep waiting, with Nesaks and Nersallians living in such close quarters, when word of the *zer'stan*'s decision about the Reetion box arrived in the person of Ackal, himself, the *Zer'sis*.

* * *

Every Sevolite at the estate gathered at an outdoor amphitheatre to hear the *Zer-sis*.

Horth was down the front with his family. Even Zrenyl was present, although he stayed on the far side of their mother and her younger children.

There were also a dozen broadcast crews present, Nersallians being less strict than the Demish about keeping impersonal forms of communication to a minimum, especially as Tark was free of the endemic interference and meddling suffered within the hullsteel shell of UnderGelion.

The mood in the amphitheatre was expectant. The *Zer-sis* represented all *zer-pol* souls among the Waiting Dead, although why a *zer-pol* would desire rebirth was beyond Horth. He could not imagine willingly stepping into a life that was destined to be strewn with shame and defeat, no matter how much he might desire to warn the living through the nastiness of his sacrifice. The whole idea of *zer-pol* put Horth off. He would prefer to take direction from a *zer-rel* — a strong leader who emerged in troubled times. He thought his father might be a *zer-rel*. He knew his mother thought so and he wanted, very badly, to be sure himself. He hoped that might be what *Zer-sis* Ackal had come to tell them.

The *zer-sis* was a tall, thin man with bony hands and hollow eyes. He opened his arms like a bird of prey, spreading wide a cloak full of symbols.

"Nesaks, and no less our cousin-Nersallians!" the high priest cried in a sonorous voice that filled the air. "Rejoice! For you are lucky to be living in a great age. You are privileged to be the generation to achieve Unification!"

A cheer greeted this opening. Eler jumped up and down excitedly between his younger sisters.

Zer-sis Ackal went on to recount the story of the last war, and how it was misguided. Beryl's face glowed as he told the story of her marriage, naming all the children, but dwelling on Zrenyl in particular and how he had become a Nesak warrior.

The *zer-sis* moved on to the things that still divided Nersallians from Nesaks: differences in how women behaved and differences in how they viewed the non-eternals known as nobleborns.

"How, then, shall we deal with these differences?" asked the *zer-sis* in a voice that mesmerized the audience.

"Remember, first, how Nersal Nesak was lost to his family over a similar question. 'The Vrellish have souls,' he said, 'and in soul touch it can be proved.' But his father would not listen." The *zer-sis* paused. "Now Nersallians tell us there are nobleborns with souls among them. Well," he paused, as if weary. He lifted his head. "Is that strange? Is it impossible? When nobleborns have highborn ancestors?" He raised his hand immediately as the crowd inhaled. "The *zer-stan* has deliberated and this is what it has decided: some nobleborns may have souls. It is possible."

Ackal let the crowd rumble a moment before he overcame them, once more, with his outstretched arms.

"Let us unify against the Reetions! Let us smash the threat they pose to *Okal Rel*. Then there will be time to test who has a soul and who does not, through soul touch. But in the meantime, let it be proclaimed that it is possible!"

A murmur of indecision stirred the audience. Quickly, *Zer-sis* Ackal progressed to the next challenge.

"Nersallian women!" Ackal cried. "Are Vrellish women. They struggle, in this life, to be redeemed. Many men among the Nesaks struggle, as well. We rebuke them, yes! But they are still members of our family. Let us not dwell on differences such as these. And let us not forget that *SanHome*'s founder, San Nersal, was the greatest warrior of her day, although, of course, she honored marriage in the Nesak fashion."

This time the crowd's restlessness was punctuated by laughter and a few jeers.

Zer-sis Ackal raised his voice again, stilling the restless among them.

"Enough of differences! Let me speak about a thing that unites us. A terrible thing. And a thing of beauty. The *zer-stan* has consulted, and declared that we live in a time of dire threat to *Okal Rel*!"

"Reetions have Lorel technologies, able to steal memories from a living mind, and they have used them on a Sevolite.

But what is this boy, this lost Prince Amel, who the *Okal Lumens*, in their misguided usage, term a 'Soul of Light'? What is he but—"

Ackal broke off, as if he had arrived too fast at his conclusion. He gave a sort of laugh. A sound like grief, but rich with love.

"It moves me to know the thing that I must tell you," Ackal said. "It moves me with elation for the gift of suffering — the gift that instructs by its sacrifice. It moves me to fear, as well. Fear that even this gift, this suffering, will not be enough to move us. That it will be wasted. Fear that you may not believe, as I do."

He strafed the group in front of him with his stare. "Amel was mind-raped by the Reetions and his suffering spewed across the universe by them. Amel is called a Soul of Light by *Okal Lumens* — or at least by those with enough courage to contemplate the horror of so much suffering befalling someone so gentle, so compassionate, so—"

"*Pol!*" Falk shouted in a hard bark from just behind Beryl.

"*Zer-pol!*" others took up the cry, here and there.

Suddenly, there was shouting all around Horth: a tidal wave of voices merging into one to chant, "*Zer-pol. Ah-mel. Zer-pol. Ah-mel.*"

Horth looked at his father. Hangst looked back at him, untouched by the hysteria surrounding them. He detached himself from Beryl and moved behind the family to reach Horth. He touched Horth's back. Horth leaned towards him to hear, above the shouting, what his father said.

And in Hangt's deep voice, with its ripple of humor, Horth heard distinctly, "Whatever works."

* * *

Horth was moved and excited to be included in his father's war council on the eve of their departure for Fountain Court.

The meeting took place in a small, stately room above Hangst's living quarters. The walls were wood lined and the table at the center was made of the same stuff. *Gorarelpul* oversaw security, scanning guests discretely for any undesirable technology, and the guards of honor at the door were highborns.

Horth joined a group of *imsha* waiting for Hangst to convene the meeting. Kega was there, and a half a dozen other commanders, both Nesak and Nersallian. Horth was the only *avsha* in attendance.

He felt his junior status all the more acutely when Zrenyl appeared, dressed in the uniform of a Nesak arm commander in charge of three battlewheels. Zrenyl spared his younger brother a single smug smile and made a point of socializing with his military rank peers.

Hangst got the meeting started by hanging his sword belt on a peg along one wall. Everyone else did likewise, then they seated themselves around the table. Four of the twelve people present were women, and the rest men. The imbalance gave Horth a faint feeling of uneasiness, but he told himself it was only to be expected when half the people in the room were Nesaks. He counted Zrenyl in that subtotal.

"Horth is here as Bryllit's representative," Hangst explained, noting the looks cast in Horth's direction. Kega caught Horth's eye and winked at him, earning a disapproving look from the Nesak across from her. She either did not notice or did not care.

"These are the issues," Hangst got the war council off to a brisk start. "First, we must know the jump into the Reetion territories. Bryllit's people have been looking for stray Reetion renegades in Killing Reach, but so have others, it would seem. The supply has dried up. I have delegated *Imsha* Zrenyl the task of arranging for a Nesak priest to steal the jump. The Nesaks have also claimed responsibility for a backup plan in case the priest fails. So we will count that problem solved."

"The second problem," said Hangst, "is a harder one. My son Horth brought me information about Reetion stations that I have since confirmed through other channels. First, unlike hullsteel stations, Reetions stations will crack almost immediately if anti-personnel tactics are employed against them. Second, Reetion command is mediated by a machine that will not make deals. We could win hands down and still be denied dock. Apparently, we could even achieve occupation and not gain control but be treated, by this thing the Reetions call an arbiter, like mere criminals."

Kega leaned forward on an elbow. "From what you related of Horth's intelligence, my Liege," she addressed Hangst, "these arbiters have an even weaker grip than commoners. Might even the slightest bit of shaking solve the problem?"

"Disable the arbiter?" Hangst said, and frowned. "Possibly. But only at the risk of cracking at least some of the stations they inhabit and even if we did succeed, it is unclear that Reetions will behave like ordinary commoners. My information comes to me indirectly, via contacts I still have on Gelion, but Di Mon thinks that Reetion stations can't be captured."

One of the Nesak said bluntly, "Then we take the stations out — all of them. Make them dust."

"That will make for bad weather!" cried Zrenyl, straightening up as if stung. Everyone looked at him. "I mean," Zrenyl continued, "wouldn't it be better to just crack them gently enough they break in big pieces? Dust is... well, it's dust. You can't fly through dust. And it spreads out..."

"I believe we are all familiar with the navigational hazards," said Hangst in a tight tone. "Is there any other objection?"

No one spoke. Kega fidgeted. Most of the other Nersallians and one of the Nesaks looked uncomfortable.

Horth found his voice without knowing he was going to speak until he did:

"It is *okal'a'ni*."

"Yes, it is *okal'a'ni*," said Hangst, and relaxed.

A babble of voices ensued, with everyone speaking for or against station-cracking tactics without listening to what the other said.

Hangst stood up, wide-shouldered, large, and angry. "Enough!" he cried.

The war council fell silent. Hangst sat down again. "Other ideas," he invited.

"Not hullsteel," said Horth. "Punch holes."

Hangst gave him a rare smile. "Yes. The fact their stations aren't hullsteel makes that possible. But our *relsha* are not trained for tactics like those. It would require an assault force working out of *skim*, in zero G, inside the station's challenge sphere and possibly under fire from light-speed defense weapons if the Reetions use them. Lacking hullsteel to protect themselves, they well might. They did two hundred years ago in Killing Reach."

"Use Nersallian commoners," Horth said.

A Nesak got up, stiffly. "To arm the soulless, Hangst Nersal, is to empower short-sighted wantonness. No, not even to conquer the Reetions. It is better to destroy their stations utterly."

Hangst leaned forward. "Better to crack stations than risk planets? Is that it?" he asked the Nesak. "Are you that sure? Are you prepared to stake your soul's next rebirth on it, Frankin?"

The Nesak arm commander addressed as Frankin drew himself up. "I will send to the *zer'stan* back on SanHome for an answer. *Zer-sis* Ackal himself can take it to them. We will bring their judgment to you, on Fountain Court. But whatever answer they return, you had better be prepared to decide if you want Unification as much as you would like to make us think!"

The Nesak and his following extracted themselves from the table and left. Zrenyl looked at his father anxiously for direction. Hangst waved at him to leave and he did, with a grateful expression.

After that only the Nersallians remained.

Kega turned to Horth. "What does Liege Bryllit say? Is it right to crack stations when the inhabitants are *okal'a'ni*?"

"Bryllit will come to Fountain Court," Hangst answered in Horth's place. "She is my First Sworn and my named heir. She has Nesak blood, like most Nersallians, but she is everything the *kinf'stan* honor: a warrior, a breeder, an *imsha*, and an Old Sword whose reputation is without flaw. A veteran of the Nesak war, herself, and one who knows better than most what kind of mess the Reetions leave behind them and the corruption they spread. I will make my decision, and Bryllit will endorse or condemn it there."

Hangst got up, signaling the end of the meeting.

People began to leave swiftly. Hangst raised his head and called, "Horth? Stay."

Horth walked back join his father.

Hangst straightened and smiled, looking less burdened. "I have a commission to offer you," he said. "A battlewheel, the *DragonSon*. One of the three in my arm. I would like you to captain her. I'll discuss it with Bryllit, naturally — I know you are sworn to her. But we are about to have a Swearing at which that could change." Hangst smiled broadly. "Will you fly with me into this Reetion hell?"

Horth had not hoped for so much, so suddenly. He was sure his face said all he felt, because his father laughed and clapped him on the shoulder.

"I'll take that as a 'yes,'" Hangst said, and laughed again. He went to collect their sword belts from the rack on the wall.

"Of course," Hangst added, handing Horth's sword to him. "We'll have to find you some nobleborn orderlies who can learn to interpret your silences." He laughed again in a lighter way, and put his palm in the middle of Horth's back. "In the meantime, start eating with us. And if Eler is rude, just sit on him. That was Branst's solution."

* * *

Di Mon *shimmer danced* a code. *Dot dash dash dot.*
Dash dot dot dash, the Demish ship *shimmered* back.

If there was one thing the Demish could be trusted for, it was observing protocols, no matter how complicated. A Vrellish blockade would never have lasted this long, let alone put up with pass codes that required them to memorize a rotating schedule of transformations.

Di Mon could make his point now without fear of starting a shakeup. He had identified himself as part of their blockade.

He flew in a broad arc, watching for the Reetion ship he stalked to commit to the jump. Then Di Mon dove at a punishing six *skim'facs*. He braked just as hard to match mix with his prey as he plunged into the jump with him, catching the man's alarm in soul touch.

Di Mon knew the Killing Jump. The Monatese had known it for two hundred years, although they never made it except to teach new members of the ruling family so that the knowledge would be preserved. But if he had not known the jump, he could have learned it just now. That was the point he was trying to make — that jump stealing was possible for Sevolites. And that it was very hard for a surprised pilot to overcome his instinct to survive in order to take the hitchhiker into oblivion with him, instead of through the jump to safety.

They burst out together on the other side in the stretch of space the Reetions called the Reach of Paradise. Di Mon turned, and dove right back into Killing Reach again.

He attracted anxious Demish ward ships who were following his own directions to prevent hitchhikers making it out of the jump again. Even his *shimmer-danced* password did not reassure them entirely. A couple dropped out of *skim* to dog him in real space, but at that stage he was able to make radio contact and explain.

Quicksilver's grand Challenge Floor lay between the rim dock Di Mon favored and the quarters he and Tessitatt had been allocated. Their rooms served as a sort of Green Hearth embassy for the duration of the blockade, although the two of them were seldom present at the same time. One had to be at court as much as possible.

The Demish had rolled out a high-traffic carpet to protect the Challenge Floor, and locked up the fencing gear, as well, after Branst Nersal's sparring bout with his brother Horth. Apparently Demish cooperation did not extend to damaging the plush seats or scuffing the wood inlay on the Challenge Floor unnecessarily.

But it wasn't the Demish who were irritating Di Mon the most today. His little demonstration of jump stealing was an act of desperation to make the Reetions see they shouldn't be here. Ranar was waiting for him near the far end of the Challenge Floor.

"Do you feel better now?" the Reetion asked, in a tone more like that of a perplexed parent than a suitably impressed commoner.

Di Mon halted, ground his teeth, and waited until he could draw a steady breath before retaliating. "Do you feel safe?" he demanded.

Ranar sighed. "I told you, we know we put ourselves at risk by being here. But what is the alternative? Waiting on the other side of the jump, in ignorance?"

"Yes!" Di Mon exclaimed. "Because every day you stay here, you risk starting a shakeup that will do untold harm!"

"The buildup out there is about Amel. Not us," Ranar insisted. "Why don't you go convince D'Ander to transport Amel to Gelion and settle things the way you want?"

"I can't!" Di Mon said bitterly.

Ranar relented. "Yes," he said with sympathy, "I know. You can't resolve the conflict over Amel because the Goldens and the Silvers do not trust each other enough. You need your friend, Liege Nersal, back on Fountain Court to reassure them both that the challenge will be fairly fought." Ranar touched Di Mon's arm. "I do understand it complicates things for you to have us around. But just like you, there are things that I can do out of friendship and things that I cannot. We are here because we have to know what's going on. That is as basic to our culture as honor is to yours. Reetions will never trade safety for ignorance."

Di Mon met the Reetion's eyes directly. "But you, yourself," he said, "could go home."

Silence greeted the suggestion.

They spoke in English, a dead language that Di Mon had learned as part of a classical Monatese education, and Ranar had learned because he studied Gelacks. In English, the question of whether or not to address Ranar in peerage, as a diplomatic gesture, was moot. But somehow that also made it too easy to get personal.

And Ranar mattered too much to Di Mon.

Particularly since Hangst had left Fountain Court, Di Mon had been starved for the kind of company he found in Ranar: a willingness to entertain ideas in perfect trust. But that was not the worst. He loved the stubborn Reetion man in a way that he could never have dared love his Vrellish peer on Fountain Court.

Di Mon wanted very much to stuff the Reetion in a ship and fly him home. He suspected the Reetion had guessed that, however, because Ranar had made him promise not to do exactly that. And somehow the Reetion managed to extract such promises in a way that committed every fiber of Di Mon's personal honor, as well as his maddening, impossible love.

Di Mon said, "Ranar, I don't know what to do."

"I know," the Reetion said. "I'm not sure, either."

They were interrupted by Branst Nersal, dressed in flight leathers, who came charging in from the far end of the Challenge Floor, nearest the docks.

"It's happening!" Branst exclaimed, in Gelack, as Di Mon was turning around.

Branst crossed the floor at a run and grabbed Di Mon's forearms. "You have to do something! Father is summoning the *kinf'stan* to court for a Swearing. He is going to ask for their support to take out the Reetions! With the help of the Nesaks!" Branst paused to catch his breath and swallow. "Father thinks he can work with them! He's won concessions: tolerance for female warriors, a gesture in the direction of nobl,eborns being redeemable." Branst was shaking with outrage all at once. "Redeemable! Tolerance!" His eyes filled up with tears. "I can't believe my father can accept that!"

Di Mon detached Branst from him. "Sometimes," he said, "people risk too much, to keep what they love."

"Mother?" Branst asked, painfully. Then he rallied. "Then why doesn't he protect her from *Zer* Sarn? He is making her crazy! Talking as if what happened to Amel could happen to Eler, Beryllan, and Sanal if she doesn't convince Father to do whatever *Zer* Sarn wants him to do next!"

"I do not believe," Di Mon said, with a heavy feeling of unwelcome truth, "that your father can be led anywhere he does not want to go, even by your mother's influence. Or that he can wean your mother from Sarn. Your parents matter to each other. But they act out of their own, deep motives: Hangst to forge a Vrellish power able to overthrown the Demish court, and Beryl to unite Nersallians and Nesaks in one great cause." Di Mon sighed. "The tragedy is that the two have come to overlap. And that, I fear, is my fault."

Ranar raised a hand to touch Di Mon's arm, making him flinch away with a look of thunderous affront. Had the Reetion no sense! To betray familiarity like that in front of Branst!

Branst missed any suggestion of intimacy in the aborted act. He said instead, with grim humor, "You could lose a hand that way, Reetion. Or worse."

"Yes," Ranar said awkwardly, realizing his own mistake at last. "Of course." He did not even bother to assert peerage of convenience by correcting Branst's choice of pronouns in Gelack.

"I cannot return to court now," Di Mon decided on the spot. "Even if I did, there is nothing I could do but observe, and Tessitatt should already be there by now, to witness for Green Hearth. What of you, Branst?" Di Mon asked, careful to maintain a neutral tone. "You are *kinf'stan*. Will you heed the summons?"

Branst looked torn. "I-I have to," he stammered. "But you have to talk to Dad! He listens to you!"

Di Mon shook his head, grimly. "Not anymore."

"But—"

"Branst!" Di Mon snapped with a flare of impatience that showed the red depths of his anger. He grit his teeth, mustering self-control. "I have been out-maneuvered. There is nothing I can do. I know your father's long-term agenda. But in the short term, he has bought the Demish by promising to ensure a fair outcome in the duel brewing between the Silvers and the Goldens over Amel, which is really over the throne. He asked, in return, that they refrain from barricading the Killing Jump — which is how the Silver Demish and I would prefer to solve the Reetion problem. And the Reetions have not helped by refusing to go home."

"Contact is inevitable one way or—" Ranar began, and was silenced by Di Mon's raised palm.

"You know what he wants the Reetions here for, don't you Branst?" Di Mon asked. "You know why he sent Horth here, too. To learn the Reetions' weaknesses, and how to gain the jump. Would that I knew what intelligence he took back!"

"No!" Branst protested with vehemence. "Not Horth! Horth is honorable!"

Di Mon sighed, but he liked the young man despite his foolish hopes. "Hangst can offer your brother everything he wants," explained Di Mon. "Sometimes, when there is that much to be gained, all honor requires is an excuse."

"No!" exclaimed Branst. He shook his head. "You don't know. You don't understand us as well as you think you do."

"Us?" Di Mon asked mildly. "And who is that? You and your brother? Your family? The *kinf'stan*? Or all Nersallians, perhaps? Where, exactly, does honor reside?"

"Bryllit will stop it!" Branst said adamantly, and nearly choked as he realized what that implied.

Di Mon said, "Perhaps." He had never imagined he would be hoping for Hangst to lose a challenge.

Branst tore away from them, heading back to the dock where he'd left his ship, one level up.

"Branst!" Di Mon shouted after him. "Rest a day before you fly!"

But it was no use. Di Mon turned back to Ranar, hoping his Reetion confidante had grasped the gravity of his people's situation at last.

But Ranar looked as stubborn as ever. "They cannot attack us on our own territory as long as they do not know the jump."

Di Mon opened his mouth to remind the Reetion of his little demonstration, but just closed it again. *Inevitable*, Ranar would say. *Contact was inevitable.* Reetions would not hide or wait for it to happen on someone else's terms.

Instead, Ranar surprised him by adding, "But I'll get on the radio and see what I can do to convince them to evacuate nonessential personnel."

Ranar had been at that, unsuccessfully, for two hours when an arm of Nesak battlewheels showed up.

* * *

Quicksilver's captain, Prince H'An, greeted Di Mon's arrival on the bridge with a frosty look. "We have no orders to fight in defense of the Reetions," he reminded Di Mon. "If any fighting starts, we'll pull back."

"I understand," Di Mon said automatically, and turned his back.

A composite image loomed on a panoramic *nervecloth* screen, beyond the communication's console. One layer showed the deployment of stationary objects, including the Killing Jump. Another showed the last reported locations and trajectories of *rel*-skimming ward ships. Since that data could be collected only under *skim*, it was necessarily out of date. A number in one corner of the screen changed from 30 minutes to 10 as Di Mon watched, indicating a change in the update interval. That meant Prince H'An's ward ships had to drop out of *skim* more often to communicate with the stationary *Quicksilver*.

A typically Demish decision, Di Mon thought, *trading flexibility of response for more information.* He added dourly under his breath, "They ought to get on well with the Reetions."

"So far, the Nesak commander has done no more than deploy wards ships with due notice and consideration for the other traffic in the area," said Prince H'An, stuffily, as if three polite Nesak warships were far better company than a handful of Vrellish visitors who scuffed up *Quicksilver*'s Challenge Floor.

Di Mon displaced the officer at the com station to open an internal channel to Ranar, who was back in his embassy rooms. "We have Nesaks on watch for an opportunity to steal the jump," he informed the Reetion. "Let your people know not to send any pilots across. Starting now."

"It's too late," Ranar said. "We have one en route, taking the question of withdrawing back to synch with the arbiter net, for a broader vote."

Di Mon cursed under his breath. Then, despite the impossibility of the timing, he bolted for the docks.

* * *

Security was tight on Gelion. The new Ava, Ev'rel, installed by Di Mon, had palace errants and throne *gorarelpul* out in force. That was partly due to feelings running high over Amel, in all directions; but it was also due to Hangst's proposal of a war alliance to subdue the Reetions.

Ava Ev'rel had declared the question of Unification a Nersallian affair, and wished it settled as expediently as possible so that the Demish could get on with the duel over custody of her son. She had, however, made a point of disagreeing with *Zer-sis* Ackal's proclamation that Amel was a *zerpol*. The Inner Circle of the Golden Demish reserved judgment on Amel being a Soul of Light, as well. One way or the other, the talk in highborn receptions was of little else but Amel, while in less privileged quarters of UnderGelion, people united in a show of righteous passion in support of *Okal Rel*.

From the meanest commoner on the Palace Plain — where terrible memories of Lorel plagues still harvested lives in children's nightmares — to nobleborn Demish families whose plans for increasing their riches were threatened by the thought of fouled space lanes, the population of Gelion stood firm in opposition to the willful disregard that great people could inflict on less important ones by waging war.

People greeted each other with *"Okal Rel,"* like a prayer. Gangs raided freeholds run by people rumored to be nonbelievers. Self-declared clear dreamers, able to remember past lives, got up in public places to proclaim cautionary tales in which those who violated *Okal Rel* were denied rebirth into the world they had seen fit to damage to gain their ends.

Settle by Sword Law! the people of Gelion demanded of their betters. *Or be damned*. They wanted no space wars within the empires.

What happened at the edge of the empire, with Reetions, they found harder to understand. Many thought contact should be cut off again, as it had been 200 years before, while others liked the idea of quick extermination before something catastrophic went wrong, and questions were asked about why the Monatese appeared to like the Reetions.

One day on Gelion was enough for Horth. He chose to wait in orbit, instead, on his new battlewheel. Kale was assigned as a cadet on its sister ship, the *DragonDaughter*, and visited Horth a few times. He was glad to see her doing well as a Nersallian woman, even if she remained stubbornly Nesak about sex. Her appreciation of his new status as captain was more gratifying. She wanted to know everything he could tell her about it.

DragonSword was the flagship of the trio. When the Swearing was done, Hangst would take command of it himself.

* * *

The day before the Swearing, Horth found Bryllit in his quarters.

"I guess I should have offered you a battlewheel sooner," she remarked on his good fortune. "But it's just as well. You and I are much too fortunate a combination for the Waiting Dead."

"The child?" he asked.

"A fine girl," she told the sire. "Dorn is very pleased with her."

Horth grinned back. It was likely to be the most direct chance he would have to bask in paternal feelings towards this second child by Bryllit, so he made the most of it. But he was less happy about the suggestion that their sexual relationship was going to end.

Bryllit sat down at his eating table and pulled over a disk of snacks. "You are still my vassal until tomorrow's Swearing, however," she told him. "So tell me: what is Hangst playing at with this Unification idea?"

Her uncharitable tone gave Horth a chill. He did not like to think that she and Hangst might disagree. He knew all too well what that would mean.

Reluctantly, Horth sat down opposite her. "I do not explain well," he said.

Bryllit wagged a protein stick in his direction. "Exactly why I want to know what you think. Tell me straight. What's the worst we're looking at here?"

"Deaths," Horth said. "Many of them."

"Reetions?" Bryllit remarked, around a mouthful she was chewing.

"Reetions," he confirmed, "and the stations that they live on. But it is not necessary," he added, surprising himself.

"Oh?" she encouraged him.

Horth began to get excited, and felt relieved of a burden at the same time. He could tell Bryllit what he had been thinking but unable, until now, to put into words. She would tell Hangst when they met before the Swearing.

"No need to crack stations," Horth told Bryllit. "Isolate them instead. No Sevolites to duel," he acknowledged that drawback. "Gain surrender with food. Other necessities." He shook his head. The ideas were coming out more jumbled than he meant and Bryllit was frowning at him. If only he could explain properly!

He knew that force was necessary to control the *okal'a'ni*, and he saw nothing wrong in those who took the risk of stopping them being the ones to gain territory in exchange. But he was disturbed by the idea of cracking stations, even if the inhabitants were Reetions. *Okal Rel* endorsed war against leaders, not people.

Even more significantly, he did not see how they could ever teach the Reetions to live within the limitations set by *Okal Rel* if they started by breaking their own laws to conquer them! The Nersallians and Nesaks ought to use their strength to gain control, instead, and work on more difficult problems from a position of moral strength.

Desperate to convey all that in words, Horth tried again. "Cracking stations is *okal'a'ni*," he said.

Still frowning, Bryllit nodded. "I share your discomfort there," she said. "I wish I knew more about this *zer-pol*, Amel."

"Not a *zer-pol*," Horth insisted. "Just *pol*." Put that way, being *pol* was an insult, not something that elevated vulnerability to a higher plane. Horth was sick of all the talk about Amel.

"If he isn't a *zer-pol*," Bryllit said in a hard voice, "then we could be about to imperil our souls."

She did understand, Horth decided, and she would explain it to his father.

He got up, feeling reassured there would be no station cracking now, however the *zer'stan* ruled on it.

* * *

Di Mon was not in time to stop the Nesak going through the jump with the Reetion pilot but he was in time to see three Demish pursuers balk shy of a jump they did not know.

Maybe I should signal them to follow me, Di Mon thought, and then rejected the idea. The Demish set like concrete once they took over anything, and however little they wanted to do with the Reetions right now, Di Mon feared to put temptation in their path.

He took the jump alone and emerged on the Reetion side in clear space, in the Reach of Paradise.

Nothing but a faint flicker of *skim* activity registered between Di Mon and the station named *Second Contact*, the original base of Ranar's mission. There were no ward ships visible, but Ranar had assured him that Reetions didn't use them. They used a medical technology related to the one used to extract memories from Amel, which was able to ensure that all pilots were trustworthy before they got into a *rel*-ship. The idea raised hairs on the back of Di Mon's neck, but according to Ranar it worked.

No ward ships, however, meant no outlying ships to communicate with via *shimmer dances*, and no way to know what to do next. And where were the Nesak and the Reetion pilot he had hitchhiked through with? It was situations like this that could make reality skimming situations so maddening.

Di Mon was fairly sure he had not time slipped. So he decided the Reetion and his Nesak hitchhiker must have, and would shortly emerge. Unless they were lost. The problem was how long to wait. And what to do while he did.

Two dim *rel*-ships appeared after a few minutes, coming towards him from *Second Contact* Station. Their faint wake signatures tallied with them being commoners, probably sent out to investigate.

Brave, Di Mon thought with grudging respect. *Or stupid.*

Probably both, he decided, thinking of Ranar.

He forgot the Reetions the next instant, as the Nesak and his prey tumbled out of the jump together. The Reetion pilot promptly dropped out of sight on *rel* telemetry. Di Mon went for the Nesak.

He caught him with a fly-by before the hitchhiker got oriented, then coiled around and went for a wake-lock with his next pass.

The resulting soul touch was illuminating. The Nesak was a *zer* and a strong pilot, but he had been entirely unprepared to experience soul touch with a commoner. His faith was perturbed, and with it his self-possession.

Di Mon took control of both their vessels, through the wake-lock, and hit the Nesak with as much *gap* as he felt his own convictions could weather without leaving him too badly stunned.

To Di Mon's elation, the Nesak dropped out of *skim* like a wounded squirrel dropped by an avian predator of native Monatese origins upon discovering it did not like the taste of Earth-derived blood.

What to do next was a problem. Fishing for ships in real space under *skim* was like trying to find a dropped coin in an ocean. If the Nesak wasn't dead, he was out of Di Mon's reach for the moment. But he couldn't go anywhere without betraying himself, either, and if Di Mon got lucky he might wipe him out with a close fly-by without even knowing it. Colliding with the becalmed Nesak during in-phase manifestation would be a whole lot uglier, but Di Mon would have to be astronomically unlucky to do that, even if he criss-crossed the area trying to pick up the tiny point of mass during in-phase sampling.

Di Mon was circling, watching for his prey to bolt, when he realized the Reetions from *Second Contact* Station had their own ideas.

Fascinated, but unable to communicate without shared *shimmer* codes, Di Mon watched as the Reetions came on steadily.

Whatever they were doing seemed to take forever, in part because they dropped out of *skim* from time to time themselves. He decided they must be using sensors that depended on being in real space to detect the becalmed ships. They certainly did not seem to be prepared to stop because of Di Mon's presence, however alarmingly he must have registered on their own *rel* telemetry equipment. Finally, the Reetion ships split up to go after the Reetion pilot and the Nesak one.

Di Mon watched the one headed for the area where the Nesak had dropped out of *skim*, searching his memory for anything Ranar might have told him when he wasn't quite listening about how Reetions conducted themselves in space. He retrieved the idea of an ambulance ship, with pilot and crew able to work in both *skim* and zero G, and with a hold big enough to swallow a one- or two-person *rel*-ship.

When the ambulance ship near the Nesak disappeared, Di Mon made up his mind and dropped out of *skim* to communicate, bracing himself for the unpleasantness of zero G.

"Reetions," he hailed them in their language, learned from Ranar, feeling mildly foolish not to have a better salutation ready. "This is Di Mon, liege of Monitum. The pilot you are retrieving is my prisoner. You will take him through the jump back into Killing Reach, and dock with the *Quicksilver*, over there."

A frustrating silence followed. Then a female voice answered, "We are a medical rescue ship, uh, Liege Monitum. Forgive me if I don't know how to talk to you, I'm not an anthropologist. Our mandate is to return to *Second Contact* with anyone requiring our help. We are not authorized to surrender any patient, especially not to someone with, ah, well.... To someone calling him a prisoner."

Di Mon grit his teeth, allowing himself the pleasure of imagining, for an unworthy moment, a joint strike force of Nesaks and Nersallians sweeping Reetions pilots out of space.

"*Rel*-capable ships do not carry arbiters," he told the Reetions to prove he knew something about them. "You can make up your own minds."

There was a pregnant pause. Then a second voice cut in, belligerent and male. "You misunderstood our chief medic, I think," the voice said. "What she meant to say was — we don't take orders from Gelacks. Is that clearer?"

Gods, Di Mon thought, *give me patience!* He was barely able to stand zero G as it was, even without the rising blood pressure this pointless banter was causing him. Red blotches danced before his eyes.

"Get through that jump ahead of me," Di Mon ground out over the radio, "or stay here and be shattered with the creature you are sheltering! That is your choice. Nothing else."

He didn't wait for an answer. He couldn't stand a moment more of zero G. He boosted to *skim* and circled around the Reetions in tightening circles, watching for them to appear on his *nervecloth* as a *rel*-skimming ship again.

Much to his fury, they did not oblige him immediately.

* * *

It was hours later when Di Mon joined Ranar at the embassy suite on *Quicksilver*, after checking to make sure his Demish hosts had the Nesak *zer* he'd captured locked up securely in their brig.

The two medical Reetions from the battered ambulance were resting on Di Mon's bed, one male and one female. Both were dressed in blue uniforms and slack on the *klinoman* administered by the Demish as a first-aid measure.

The Reetion pilot lurched out of the chair where Ranar had been ministering to his nose bleed. The pilot's eyes were bloodshot. His face was darker than Ranar's and his hair was fuzzier. He was also a larger, more strongly built man, as tall as Di Mon.

"You Sevolite primitive!" the pilot shouted, fisting his hands in rage. "I'll kill you!"

"Don't say that," Ranar urged, getting between them with the bloody cloth he had been using still in one hand. "He'll take you seriously."

"Well he should!" raged the Reetion pilot, and was forced to pause to snort blood.

"This is more than a broken blood vessel," Ranar worried. "He's also coughing blood."

"We have got bigger problems," Di Mon told him coldly.

The big Reetion pilot shoved Ranar to one side and swung a fist like a mallet at Di Mon's head.

Di Mon swiveled, snatched the commoner's arm at the wrist as it shot past, and backhanded him across the jaw with his other hand. It felt much, much too good watching the Reetion go down.

"Will you stop that!" Ranar shouted, losing his temper. "Law and Reason, Mon! You have already done these people serious harm!"

"You look after them then!" Di Mon shouted back. "I have things to do."

* * *

When Di Mon got to the bridge of the *Quicksilver*, he went over to the com station and ordered, "Get me the Nesak commander!"

Prince H'An was in the captain's chair at the center of the circular room. He bristled at his visiting dignitary's presumptions, but something about Di Mon's demeanor made him give up and confirm the order with a nod, instead.

"Remember, we are not getting into a shakeup with those battlewheels for you," Prince H'An reminded Di Mon.

"Strangely," Di Mon said, "I haven't forgotten."

Zrenyl Nersal appeared on the com screen in front of him, giving Di Mon a shock. He immediately realized that it shouldn't have. But he remembered Zrenyl growing up, on Fountain Court.

"I am not glad to see you here, Liege Monitum," said Hangst's son.

"I am not glad to see you in a Nesak uniform," said Di Mon.

"It suits me," Zrenyl answered.

Di Mon said, "I have something that belongs to you. A Nesak. He tried to steal the jump. You may have noticed that the Reetions have stopped sending pilots across. That is not an accident. Our liaison here, Ranar of Rire, convinced them it was unwise — at last — and the Demish have taken any pilots left on the unfinished station into their protective custody here. You will have a long, long time to wait if you mean to try to steal that jump again."

"Maybe," Zrenyl said. "Or I might be able to persuade you to give *Zer* Kal back."

"I can't imagine how," said Di Mon.

"Because," Zrenyl said, "I have someone else with me who knows the jump. But she's being uncooperative, so I think a trade might be desirable for both of us."

As he said this, he reached to one side and pulled Tessitatt into the picture, looking bruised from hard flying and unsteady on her feet.

"Tess!" Di Mon gasped.

* * *

Horth finished dressing for the Swearing, and thought of Alice as he noticed a pulled thread in the patterns on his vest. He fingered it slowly, remembering he had not seen her since their return, nor any other servants, either. He frowned. It was an unimportant detail at the moment.

Beryl appeared at the door of his bedroom holding her latest baby, born just weeks before they traveled. Her haunted look had grown worse since they had moved back to Black Hearth. She kept four-year-old Beryllan and eight-year-old Eler close to her all the time. She tried to do the same with Sanal, but the one-and-half-year-old girl was too Vrellish and agile. Beryl was frequently forced to send Eler after Sanal to collect her.

"It will be over soon, won't it?" Beryl asked Horth, or perhaps she meant to ask the Watching Dead. Horth could not tell.

He saw her draw Beryllan closer against her skirt, and wanted to assure her that whatever happened on the Octagon, the children were safe. Nersallians did not kill children.

But he could not believe that there was going to be a duel. Bryllit shared a fundamental solidarity with Hangst that had survived watching their son, Vrenn, challenge him and lose.

Horth closed his eyes to see if he could grasp why he was thinking about things that seemed irrelevant. Alice was a commoner. She used to live in Black Hearth. She'd been sent away. Vrenn was Bryllit's son by Hangst. He had been Bryllit's heir, as well. He'd challenged Hangst about his Nesak marriage and failed.

Horth gave up and dispelled the fragmentary ideas. When he opened his eyes, his mother had gone away.

He wished his brothers were there. Branst was supposed to be. Someone said they'd seen him at Green Hearth. It seemed impossible he wouldn't stand on Black Hearth with them when Hangst called for challengers. Horth knew why Zrenyl wasn't present. He was with the Nesak fleet, waiting for them.

He missed Bryllit, as well. But he knew that she had spoken with Hangst the day before, when they arrived. She would be waiting with the other *kinf'stan* down on Black Wedge.

Horth checked his sword belt to be sure it felt right and could be unclasped easily in case he was called upon to fight, although he could not imagine the Swearing turning into a melee. Nersallians took protocol seriously. Hangst would declare himself for Unification as a means to strike the Reetions. If any member of the *kinf'stan* wished to challenge, they would fight immediately. If Hangst lost, it would be Bryllit, as his named heir, who was entitled to challenge the victor immediately to retain Hangst's title for him if he survived, or claim it for herself if he did not. If there were multiple challengers, they could sometimes fight each other for the privilege of taking on Liege Nersal. But in none of those scenarios should Horth be called upon to act for his father, liege, and admiral.

Shaking his apprehensive feeling off, Horth went to join his family at the spiral stairs. Hangst looked hale and well. He smiled at each of them. Then he took Beryl in his arms, held her firmly for a moment, and relinquished her into *Zer* Sarn's care.

Eler said, "Father, I'm scared."

Hangst went down on one knee, took his eight-year-old son by the shoulders and looked him in the eyes. "*Ack rel*, my mischief," he said and smiled. "The *kinf'stan* are family, as well. They must have their chance to object by the sword. That is *Okal Rel*."

He said it much too lightly. He was not afraid.

He has worked it out with Bryllit, Horth decided, trying to feel relieved. *They have reached some acceptable compromise.*

Suddenly, it was time.

Hangst led the way down the spiral stairs. Horth followed. Next came the family errants. Lywulf stayed to guard the entrance to the Throat that led to Family Hall, where Beryl would be waiting in the master bedroom with the children and *Zer* Sarn. Falk would bring her the news when it was over. He came down with Hangst and Horth onto the Octagon.

The Octagon was decked out as it always was on important occasions, with tier upon tier of Demish witnesses. There were some Red Vrellish from Spiral Hall, surrounding a subdued Vretla Vrel. The young Vrellish liege, not long returned from *TouchGate Hospital*, observed with a sullen air, as if she was only half interested.

The new Ava, Ev'rel, was on the wedge that had been Delm's and was now hers. She was surrounded by retainers of mixed blood from her possessions in the reaches called the Knotted Strings. Horth had never seen her before. She did not wear a sword like a Vrellish woman, but she did not dress like a Demish one, either. She wore dark slacks and a long vest stiff with house braid. She wore her dark hair pulled back from a beautiful but calculating face, and there was a dagger on her slim belt. Her teenage son, D'Therd, flanked her, and a sprinkling of Vretla Vrel's nobleborns from Spiral Hall, as well.

Branst was with the nobleborns on Green Wedge. Horth could not stop staring once he caught sight of him. Branst looked agitated. He wore his sword uneasily, as if it frightened him. He was also the only highborn with the Green Vrellish. Di Mon was nowhere to be seen. Tessitatt Monitum was not present, either.

As Horth watched, Branst abandoned his position on Green Wedge and started towards Black Wedge. Suddenly

Horth had a new fear, but for the moment, at least, Branst issued no challenge. He just kept walking towards his blood kin, leaving his adopted house behind him.

Two dozen *kinf'stan,* representing all the families of House Nersal, waited in a clump on Black Wedge: all hard-eyed men and women who had the right to kill or be killed if they could not follow where Hangst led.

Bryllit stood off to one side as Hangst's First Sworn and named heir. She nodded to Horth when she saw him, then her attention flickered back to Branst again, as he stopped at the edge of the *kinf'stan* and stood, trembling visibly.

Hangst refused to give Branst his attention. He placed himself at the edge of the Challenge Floor and turned to address his gathered vassals.

"I have heard from the *zer'stan* concerning the question of how to deal with Reetion stations that oppose us," Hangst told them. He spoke in a voice that carried effortlessly.

Horth forgot Branst for the moment to listen.

"You know why we must conquer the Reetions," Hangst continued. "They reveal themselves through their use of Lorel science to extract memories from a Sevolite, like Amel. This is true whether or not you believe, as the *zer-sis* has decreed, that Amel is a *zer-pol.*"

A stir greeted the use of this emotionally explosive term. The Demish on Silver Wedge broke out in a rash of overlapping objections, creating a babble. Their leaders silenced them with reassurances that what the Nersallians did or did not think about Pureblood Amel was of importance only to Nersallians and after a ruffled minute of disruption, everyone calmed down again.

Horth was more interested in noting which members of the *kinf'stan* looked skeptical, and how many, including Bryllit, looked grim.

In fact, the look on Bryllit's face gave Horth a strange sensation, as if he had overlooked something important about the floor on which he fought a duel and stumbled over it.

Branst pushed his way forward unexpectedly. "Where is Tessitatt Monitum, Father!" he shouted at Hangst Nersal.

Their audience was shocked. Members of each house appointed to act as guards of honor glanced at each other, wondering if they should intervene. But Branst was *kinf'stan,* and a child of Hangst's hearth on Fountain Court. They weren't certain.

It was Hangst who responded first. "This is not the time, nor the correct way, to confront me about anything," he told Branst. "Go home. Or go to Green Hearth. We will talk when this is done." It was generous. Hangst could have ordered Branst arrested with a gesture, instead.

Branst didn't care. "I want Tessitatt back!" he shouted even louder, and he reached to draw his sword.

Branst was shaking so hard that the thought of him dueling anyone was absurd! Horth sprinted the short distance between them to wrest the weapon out of his brother's hand. The struggle ended as Horth was joined by two other members of the *kinf'stan.* Together they disarmed Branst and dragged him towards the base of the spiral stairs on Black Wedge.

"Horth!" Branst appealed in desperate confusion, trying to grab at Horth's arm as the other two *kinf'stan* forced him along. "I can't believe you are with them! The Nesaks! The Nesaks kidnapped Tess! Forced her down in Killing Reach on her way back. And I told you she knew the jump, Horth! It's my fault!"

Horth stopped, staring after his hysterical brother as Branst turned his head to shout, as loud as he could, "Nesaks do what they want and have priests make up excuses. *Okal'a'ni!* They are *okal'a'ni!*"

Without Horth's protective influence, one of Branst's handlers hit him in the stomach, and he shut up as he tried to double over.

"Take him to his mother," Hangst said.

Torn between the ritual still playing out on Black Wedge and his brother's outburst, Horth wavered near the bottom of the stairs as Branst was taken up them. He heard Lywulf receiving him, above. Finally, after seconds that seemed to last forever, he turned back.

By now, Hangst was firmly in control once more. Horth calmed himself to listen.

"I know that many of you, among the *kinf'stan*, are conflicted in your feelings about joining with the Nesaks, even in so just a cause," said Hangst. "I understand. We are not Nesaks. We're Nersallians." He looked at each face in turn. "You fear the doctrines of the Nesaks may dominate our own beliefs." He stopped again, looking powerful and adamant. Then he made a promise. "It will never happen."

Father sounded so certain. Horth frowned in confusion.

"It will be the other way around!" declared Hangst.

"Think about it!" he challenged them, and waited for a moment before adding, with a rich vein of humor in his commanding voice, "which house is it, so far, that has issued proclamations of compromise?"

A ripple of surprised laughter bubbled through the *kinf'stan* at this reminder of *Zer-sis* Ackal's concessions over female warriors and the possibility that nobleborns might have souls.

But not Alice, Horth thought, suddenly realizing why he had been thinking of her as he got dressed.

How many like Alice live on Reetion space stations? he wondered. Not perpetrators of mind control over Sevolites, but ordinary people: the kind that *Okal Rel* was sworn to protect.

"The greater question," Hangst continued, "is how we can fight these Reetions at all! They scorn Sword Law and surrender their decision making to lifeless things of science they call arbiters."

The *kinf'stan* shifted in discomfort. A few looked directly at Bryllit, others at Hangst or about the room to see how the rest of Fountain Court in attendance was reacting.

"We know how Reetions fight when they are dealt with honorably," said Hangst. "We know what they made of Killing Reach two hundred years ago, when we first encountered them. No one knows better than Liege Bryllit, who has spent decades in Killing Reach living with the consequences."

Hangst turned to Bryllit. "You have been my *mekan'st* and you are my heir. We have lived through terrible things together, and shared triumphs as well. Last night I told you what the *zer'stan* have decided about the measures we plan to take to defeat the Reetions, swiftly, before they can use science against us in ways we cannot even anticipate."

He waited for her to nod.

"Tell the *kinf'stan* what you feel," Hangst invited her.

Bryllit inhaled so deeply it felt as if she might take all the air on the Octagon into her lungs before she committed herself.

"We stand between two evils," she finally declared. "I have no use for Nesaks. Their compromises—" She turned her head to spit on the floor. "Pah! They do and say whatever gains what they desire." She tipped her head towards Black Hearth's spiral stairs. "In that, I do not disagree much with Branst Nersal, however addled he's become."

"Reetions can destroy our way of life," Bryllit returned to the main thrust of her argument. "So can the Nesaks. It comes to this: someone must decide which threat is greater. Someone must take the burden on his soul of being right — or wrong — in making this decision; and it is a bitter one, because an error of such magnitude could damn the soul forever. To ignore the warning of a *zer-pol* on the one hand. To condone *okal'a'ni* acts on the other."

She turned to Hangst, then. "I am sworn to Liege Nersal. I say, let him decide."

In the perfect silence that followed, Hangst touched
Bryllit's arm in thanks. Then he told the *kinf'stan*.

"I have decided to extend to Nersallians the same exemp-
tion that the *zer'stan* have allowed their warriors, for the
greater good of all Sevildom. We will crack and cripple every
Reetion station. We will rebuild our own, in hullsteel, once
we take their worlds. We must act against *Okal Rel*, temporarily, in order to save it and extend it afterwards."

The reminder of what conquerors could gain was not lost
on his audience. Some faces told Horth they did not care that
the means of achieving new lands would be *okal'a'ni*. They
were the real threat. Horth saw it so plainly it stunned him.
Okal'a'ni lust wore many disguises, and argued its case in
many languages. But it stood naked before him, in those few
faces untroubled by the compromise that tortured Bryllit.

Horth's father ceased to be his father in that instant. He
was just a leader, poised to make the wrong decision. Hangst
was nothing but his father the next instant. A man about to
foul his soul with a terrible error.

Horth hardly heard his father speak the mandatory invitation to challengers.

He hardly knew who he was as he stepped onto the Challenge Floor and drew his sword.

* * *

"You aren't serious?" Ranar demanded.

Di Mon finished checking his fencing shoes and straightened. He was dressed lightly, in a sleeveless green tank top
and stretch pants. He would be inspected by the Demish before facing Zrenyl on the Challenge Floor. So would Zrenyl.
Neither would wear any protective gear.

"Di Mon," Ranar choked out, and paused to swallow. "I —
I can't believe this is happening."

"It is," Di Mon told him. He did not put on his sword belt.
He would be given a sword identical to Zrenyl's by their
Demish guards of honor. It was all settled and agreed to. The

Demish held the stakes, as well: Di Mon's niece and the Nesak *zer* named Kal. Both went to the winner.

"This is no way to settle a... a reciprocal kidnapping!" cried Ranar, clenching his hands and then hugging his arms about himself, as if he had to do that to stop himself from laying hands on Di Mon.

It was that slip sideways into anguish that touched Di Mon. He spared the Reetion, with whom he shared an impossible friendship, one last long look. He did not even think of touching him. They were probably alone, but they were on a Demish station. The stigma of being exposed as boy-*sla* was the very last legacy Di Mon wanted to leave behind if he had misjudged the match between himself and Zrenyl.

"Do not worry so much, Reetion," Di Mon told Ranar. "It is Zrenyl who is the fool here, for letting me manipulate him into this agreement." Di Mon smiled thinly, without pleasure. "Rising too rapidly in life can go to people's heads. Zrenyl would like to be remembered as the righteous Nesak who destroyed the Lorel-tainted Liege Monitum. But it is I, not he, who is the Old Sword. Zrenyl's a child!"

"I thought," Ranar said shakily, "that anything could happen in a duel."

Di Mon shrugged, but stayed no longer to debate the matter. Partings of this kind were best done without thinking about them too much.

* * *

Horth registered his father's startled look as he stepped forward. Hangst did not understand at first. Bryllit did. Horth heard her suck her breath in.

No one else breathed hard enough to be heard.

Horth stopped. With his sword gripped in his left hand, he unclasped his belt with his right and threw both belt and sheath clear. He waited. Hangst's lips parted as if he meant to say something, but he stopped. He could see the decision in Horth's face.

"*Ack rel*," Hangst said simply, instead, and cleared the regret off his face as he drew his sword.

They faced each other, crouching slowly into their fighting stances, but both kept their points lowered. They stared.

Horth knew his father was fiercely aggressive as a fighter, as well as technically precise, but Hangst knew that his son had become an expert at defense, largely due to his uncanny sense of body language. The other's confidence gave each of them pause.

But it was more than that. There was the finality of it. There would be no room for error in this challenge and Horth knew it must be to the death to achieve its purpose: Hangst's death, whether or not he survived himself. Whatever happened, wherever Hangst's blade went, Horth must find his father's heart.

Hangst took a deep breath, and flicked his weapon up. Horth lanced in at the same moment with a single, straight thrust to Hangst's check. Hangst instinctively drew his right hand across his body in a tight, perfect parry, and stepped back. But Hangst never felt Horth's blade connect, and still waited to parry it as Horth angled his sword a further 45 degrees backward with his wrist, jutting around Hangst's blade, and thrusting into Hangst's ribs, batting Hangst's point away from his face with his right hand.

Horth was lucky that his point did not lodge in his father's ribs. With the reverse angulation of his wrenched wrist, and stretched out to make up the distance, he could neither push the tip as hard as he wished, nor recover if Hangst made his own thrust or slash. But he was lucky. His blade pierced flesh and went deep. Horth sheared away, off balance.

Hangst stepped back, faltering, Horth's sword still sticking out of his chest. Hangst gripped the blade of Horth's sword in his left hand. He pulled it out with a grunt, looking strangely thoughtful, as if he intended to re-enact the action.

Mercifully, Horth never met his eyes. It was Bryllit that Hangst looked to as his knees buckled. She ran out onto the floor and dropped at his side, taking him in her arms as his wounded heart pumped blood out of his chest.

It was like that, in silence, that Hangst died.

Horth felt nothing about any of it yet. He knew he had won. He felt that was important. He had almost forgotten why.

Bryllit got up, stained with Hangst's blood, and confronted him. She was his father's sword heir. It was her right to challenge him if she so wished.

Behind them, Falk sprinted up the spiral stairs to tell Horth's mother that her husband was dead.

The Nesaks in the audience, on Black Wedge, looked paralyzed.

"Challenge!" a voice rang out from among the *kinf'stan*. It was not Bryllit, but one of those in whose faces Horth had seen an avarice willing to accept any compromise with *Okal Rel*, and now saw that greed frustrated. If Hangst had won, no second *kinf'stan* could have claimed the right to challenge again, immediately. But as House Nersal's new liege, Horth must accept. He picked up his sword from where his father had dropped it, making certain not to look at his handiwork.

That was when he heard the thin sounds of screaming coming from the spiral stairs, muted by intervening rooms and distance: the high, piercing voice of a child.

"Go," Bryllit said sharply, scowling as she stepped between Horth and his challenger.

"I was his father's First Sworn and heir," she told the challenger. "I'll be his, as well. The decision is made. One way or the other."

Horth left her to deal with any disappointed *kinf'stan* and bolted for the spiral stairs.

* * *

When Falk came to tell them that Father was dead, killed by Horth, Eler couldn't believe it.

Beryl Nesak shot straight up, dropping her newborn. He hit the floor hard, on his head. She stared with wide eyes at the messenger. She didn't seem to notice anything else.

Beryllan shrieked, "Mother!"

Eler clutched a struggling Sanal. Mother had told him to keep hold of her. She had told him they all had to stay together in the bedroom with *Zer* Sarn and the spirit knife she had set out on her dresser. His heart was racing hard enough to dizzy him.

Beryl formed the word "Hangst" with numb lips. But no breath passed through them. She stared as if her soul had left her body.

"It will be swift," *Zer* Sarn promised. "If we act together."

Mother looked at the spirit knife on her dresser.

Branst came unstuck from where he sat, staring in disbelief from the chair where he had been deposited. Falk drew his sword to attack Branst, filling Eler with sick dread. This was his family! This wasn't possible. But mad things kept happening.

Beryllan made a dash for comfort towards their mother. Beryl received her with the spirit knife in her hands. She clutched her daughter to her. She sobbed. And she slit Beryllan's throat so fast it was over even before Falk intercepted Branst.

Falk's sword went through Branst in the next instant, but Branst turned enough to deflect it a little.

Sanal bolted. Eler screamed. His mother was coming for him. Uncle Sarn was trying to catch Sanal.

Branst buckled to his knees as Falk went to the door to lock it, carrying his sword under his arm.

"Hangst!" Mother wailed like something supernatural, no longer merely human. "Wait! We're coming!"

* * *

Lywulf stood at the top of the spiral stairs as Horth charged up them. He looked almost as spooked as Horth felt. But Horth didn't know if he could trust him. All he knew was that Eler was screaming. He struck the Nesak aside with a blow that numbed his own arm.

Horth charged down the Throat through open doors, left that way thanks to Branst's struggling passage through them earlier. In their rush to return to the Octagon, the *kinf'stan* who had escorted him had apparently not taken the time to close them again. Horth was grateful.

He ran with all the strength his heart could muster, carrying his sword backwards in his right hand for speed.

The screaming began again as he set foot in Family Hall. Eler was shrieking in wordless terror.

Horth burst into his parents' master bedroom, knocking Falk away from the door hard enough to buy an instant to take in the mayhem, even as he switched hands on his sword.

He saw bodies on the floor. He saw tiny Sanal evade *Zer* Sarn's attempt to grab her. He saw Eler staring, frozen, as Beryl walked towards him with a blank expression, holding her spirit knife in a hand already crimson. He saw Branst drag himself up off the floor, holding his stomach.

Then Falk attacked him.

Horth beat off the Nesak's blade and put his own sword through Falk's shoulder, immediately pulling it out and drawing it across the Nesak's neck in a vicious flourish.

Sanal got caught. She twisted in Sarn's gasp like a grabrat, but it was no good. He would break her neck in a moment. Branst staggered to intercept Beryl. Horth made his decision.

Zer Sarn roared when he realized he was going to be interrupted. Horth put his sword through the hated *zer*'s chest with his left hand as he clamped the hand holding Sanal in his right one. *Zer* Sarn had his hand around Sanal's neck, her tiny fingers tugging at his large ones. She was doing her best to bite, as well, and kicking furiously.

Horth squeezed to make the dying man release her and succeeded with a final jerk, letting her use his body to break her fall.

He turned to see Branst sink down Beryl's side, still trying to clutch at her with one bloody hand. Beryl stabbed at him wildly. Fresh blood flowed from his flank and arm. She tugged free, breathing in gasps, and staggered towards Eler.

Horth saw that Eler would not move. Could not move. Could not even scream any longer. Beryl lurched to plunge her knife in the eight year old's body, Branst still clutching at her from the floor. Horth flung himself towards her, thrusting his sword through her rib cage from the side, feeling it grate along the bone. Then he wrenched it out and spun around in front of her, body checking her away from his terrified little brother behind him.

It was only as he watched Beryl fall that Horth recovered the complexity of thought to see her as the mother who had sent him off to SanHome, taught him how to pot plants, and served them picnics in the nursery.

He did not know what to do with the information.

Instead, he let her die, and went to see if Branst was still alive. Branst felt cold as Horth rolled him over to look at him. His eyelids fluttered.

"Tessitatt," he said, and raised a palsied hand streaked with crimson. "S-Save her!"

Branst's heart gave out in Horth's arms. Horth set him down swiftly. He focused on Eler and Sanal, who had united in a clump behind him. He stood to defend them against whatever came through their parents' door next.

But it was only Bryllit, backed by half a dozen of the *kinf'stan*.

She looked around the room and muttered, "Mad gods."

"Mad Nesaks!" exclaimed one of the *kinf'stan* with her, in bitter satisfaction.

Horth was glad to see Bryllit. He knew she would take care of his surviving siblings.

He lowered his sword and shouldered past her, out the door.

She turned and followed him for several paces.

"Liege Nersal!" she halted him with a cry, when it seemed clear he wouldn't stop otherwise.

A shiver went over Horth. He cast about him spiritually for his father, before he realized his error. He turned back to Bryllit and waited.

"Where are you going?" she demanded.

He said one word in answer: "Zrenyl."

* * *

Di Mon faced Zrenyl Nersal across a couple body lengths of hardwood on *Quicksilver*'s Challenge Floor.

It would be a nice place to die, he decided. He could not afford to do that, however. Not with Tessitatt in the balance. He knew that she would never voluntarily teach Nesaks how to get into the Reetion Reach of Paradise. That left her two choices: to die or be broken. He did not relish either. And there was that pesky *zer* who stole the jump from the foolish Reetions to consider, also.

So he simply had to win the duel.

It is lovely, Di Mon thought, *when life becomes so simple. Even for a few minutes.*

Zrenyl was young and impatient. Di Mon let him glimpse a few chances, and drew him out expertly.

After the first exchange, they maneuvered around each other for nearly half a minute. Di Mon toyed with possibilities, smiling as he watched Zrenyl start to go for them and change his mind.

"Hangst taught you well," he said, spontaneously.

Zrenyl didn't say anything. That was wise — it was better to concentrate.

Di Mon's own concentration may have lapsed while he thought such things. Whatever the reason, he caught his breath with a gasp when he realized he was in the middle of a furious and fatal attack.

Instinct and experience took over. Circle, counter, slide, and know the distances to a hair. It felt strangely like a dance that had already been choreographed.

He felt Zrenyl's sword enter his body and tear sideways. It tore free instead of penetrating because Di Mon had killed Zrenyl first, with his own hit.

They staggered apart. Zrenyl fell. Di Mon wondered what the Demish would do if both of them died and half laughed at the idea.

Pain clutched him with a hundred small, insistent fingers, that fired to a roar as he took a step and pressed his right hand over the gash above the deeper puncture. He was wounded in the liver. He knew just enough about the kind of Sevolite medicine practiced on *TouchGate Hospital* to imagine his highborn Vrellish physiology reacting to the grievous insult: clamping off blood supply where possible, fuelling regeneration where essential, breaking out emergency stores of essential chemicals. He was not going to die immediately, not if he could shut down the bleeding. That's what seamers were for. Sadly, he had forgotten to bring one to the duel.

Oh well, Di Mon thought, and sank down on one knee. It felt more comfortable.

He heard feet running towards him. Ranar was beside him the next moment. But to Di Mon's immense relief Ranar did nothing demonstrative. Instead, he had brought one of the Reetion medics with him. Di Mon thought the woman looked the worse for wear, and doubted that she understood his bullying, earlier, had been in the interest of the greater good. Even if she did, people could hold a grudge.

He flinched away from the woman's attempt to inspect his wound.

"Don't be stupid!" Ranar cried. "You could bleed to death!"

A six-guard of their Demish hosts were approaching, no doubt with seamers.

Di Mon glared at Ranar, who expected him to trust an unknown Reetion he had recently injured, and then at the woman, who looked annoyingly earnest in her professional concern.

"Can you be quick?" Di Mon asked curtly in Reetion, the pain doing nothing to improve his diplomacy.

A trio of Nesak observers was approaching.

She nodded. He lowered the arm shielding his wound with trepidation. The Reetion's hands were shaking, but she cut away the sliced and sodden cloth over the wound with satisfying speed, slapped on something that stung like mad, covered it with a strange device a handspan in circumference, and whipped a band around the whole affair as wide as the first-aid device and tight enough to hold it snug. The band sealed and tightened with magical dispatch. A coolness spread where the first-aid disk was doing things Di Mon was loath to know about. It felt as if the side pressed to his skin was full of tiny sweeping tentacles, for a start. It also oozed something that sealed off the bleeding.

Trying to ignore the thing, Di Mon forced himself to his feet with enough vigor to make the medic gasp. She did not seem at all pleased by a patient with an independent agenda. As he turned to face the Nesaks and the Demish, Di Mon heard her babbling dire warnings to Ranar, who tried to explain in terms that included the words "Sevolite" and "highborn." Di Mon was somewhat irked to hear the Reetion word for "idiot" as well.

Did Ranar imagine he was at leisure to lie down and be ill when there were still three Nesak battlewheels on their doorstep? It was not as if he would mind! If he was going to die of his wound, he'd rather do it lying down shot up on *klinoman* than like this!

He greeted the Nesak who had just succeeded Zrenyl
with a cynical sneer. The Demish had brought Tessitatt and
the Nesak *zer* with them.

"According to the terms of the duel," Prince H'An said
with an officious air, "you have custody of the Nesak hitchhiker and, of course, your niece."

Tessitatt moved silently to Di Mon's side.

"That looks bad," the Nesak remarked, nodding at the
wound high in Di Mon's abdomen.

The Reetion first-aid thing must have contained drugs.
Or else it was combining with Di Mon's own physiology to
strange effect. He suffered a wave of giddiness as he answered almost jauntily, "Feels worse."

On the crest of that disconnected feeling, he turned to the
Nesak *zer* who stood waiting tensely, his hands bound
behind his back and his feet hobbled. "Jump stealing is typically punished by those that you offend against," he said,
testing the grip on the sword he still held, naked, in his left
hand. "But I don't trust the Reetions to show sense."

Without waiting for anyone to raise an objection or alternative, Di Mon whipped the sharp third of his sword across
the prisoner's throat, opening his jugular.

The Reetion medic yelped a cry and fainted. That kept
Ranar busy, fortunately.

"This isn't over, Green Hearth," said the new Nesak arm
commander, glaring bitterly at Di Mon. "The Nersallian
fleet will be here to join us any moment. Then we'll see how
this is resolved." He narrowed his eyes. "Hangst Nersal
may decide to start with those who protect Reetions." He
glanced at the alien-looking dressing on Di Mon's chest.
"And are fool enough to trust their science."

Di Mon was ready to agree with him about that. The
Reetion first-aid disk was seriously upsetting his compo-
sure. It was all he could do to keep still as the Nesaks collected their dead *zer* and withdrew towards the docks, shad-
owed by a Demish honor guard. Sweat began to pop out on

Di Mon's brow as his giddiness progressed to a rising sensation of burning, centered on the wound. His insulted, aggressive immune system was fighting back.

He swayed, and toppled into Tessitatt and Ranar's arms.

"Get it... get it off," Di Mon said.

The Reetion medic was conscious again but in no condition to be useful to anyone. She wasn't used to watching people being murdered in front of her.

Tessitatt did what Di Mon asked. After that, one of the Demish volunteered a seamer. Ranar turned away, looking faint, as the Demish man seared Di Mon's wound closed, penetrating deep enough to cauterize internal bleeding as well. What they did would kill a non-regenerative human. It was crude, but it left Di Mon quasi-functional once he recovered from the agony enough to stand up.

A foreign, acid smell of burned Reetion sealant accompanied the more familiar reek of burned flesh and blood.

"That wound is bad," Tessitatt fretted at him, helping him stand.

Di Mon kept his teeth gritted against the useless groans of pain that would only upset her and Ranar more, thinking angrily to himself, *I know that!*

Why wouldn't anyone focus on the war that was about to happen? Why did he have to worry about it, in his condition?

"We have to get him to *TouchGate Hospital*," said Tessitatt.

"Get me to the bridge," Di Mon said angrily. "I have to be there when Hangst shows up. I have to talk to him. Try... somehow."

"I don't think that's going to work," said Prince H'An, in an interested but detached manner, as if the whole thing was a particularly excellent Demish play. "You just killed his son."

Good point, thought Di Mon. But he didn't know what else to do.

Ranar argued with Tessitatt about the merits of disobedience all the way up to the bridge, but he helped support Di

Mon's weight on the other side. They set him down in a chair at the com station.

Tess stayed with him. Ranar agitated for another channel to call the Reetion station nearby.

"What for?" Di Mon cut across the Reetion's negotiations with the Demish.

"You need medical help!" Ranar snapped, his usually relaxed body was electric with emotional alarm.

"Not Reetion help!" Di Mon answered just as furiously, sweating from his feverish response to Reetion drugs. "I've tried that."

"But — "

"*TouchGate Hospital!*" insisted Tessitatt.

"All right!" Ranar snapped right back. "But I'm going with you!"

"You can't—" she protested.

"Why not?" argued Ranar. "You won't be flying very hard, I think, with him in that condition!"

No one is going to TouchGate Hospital, Di Mon thought with exasperation, beneath a haze of mild delirium. *Because the Nersallians are going to show up and start a major war.*

"We've got battlewheels incoming," a Demish officer called, picking up the latest data dump from *Quicksilver's* wards.

Di Mon closed his eyes.

Tense minutes later, the next dump arrived, and the officer amended, "They're fielding wards and dropping out of *skim* themselves." He laughed a bit hysterically. "Good thing. We're tight enough to split space at the seams around here."

"I've got an electromagnetic signal," said another officer. "A request to communicate on an audio-visual channel. From Liege Nersal."

Di Mon sat forward painfully, not sure which he dreaded most: the disaster that lay ahead when the Unification alliance took out the Reetion station in frustration over the jump, or facing Hangst with Zrenyl's death on his conscience.

Odd, he thought, *how relationships skew things so out of proportion.* But he couldn't help it. This was not how his friendship with Hangst Nersal ought to have ended: not just with disagreement, but with hatred. To balance his feelings, he reminded himself Hangst must have known what had befallen Tessitatt, even if he had let the Nesaks do the dirty work. Hangst needed that jump to make the Nesaks and Nerallians come together.

Maybe Ranar is right, Di Mon thought sadly. *Reetions will have to deal with us eventually and we with them. All I've done is put off the inevitable.*

He still doubted that his Reetion friend grasped the enormity of a Sevolite invasion on the scale that had emptied Killing Reach of his ancestors and left it spoiled for *Okal Rel*. At least they had averted that for the time being. He wondered if Hangst would be canny enough to take the Reetions on the half-finished station prisoner in the hope of netting pilots, which reminded him that he still had a Reetion pilot on board the *Quicksilver*. Perhaps he ought to kill him.

The com display in front of Di Mon switched on, revealing a head-and-shoulder visual to complement voice communications.

Di Mon started at the sight of Horth Nersal. He was about to ask where Hangst was when he noticed the liege marks on Horth's collar.

"Tessitatt," Horth Nersal requested.

She moved to share the visual with Di Mon. "Here!" she told him. "Horth, what's happened?"

"It is *okal'a'ni* to crack stations," Horth said flatly. "Even with the *zer'stan's* approval."

Such few, simple words, thought Di Mon. Such important words. Words he had no difficulty translating into what must have played out between Horth and his father on the Octagon.

"I am... glad we agree about that," Di Mon said, finding it hard to breathe properly. "*Ack rel.*"

"*Ack rel,*" Horth answered automatically.

Di Mon forced himself to remember the Reetions, even as he thought, *Damn the Reetions!*

"What will you do now?" he asked Horth.

"What would Branst do?" the new Liege Nersal asked Tessitatt.

Tessitatt began to look anxious. She put a hand on the console, her fingers slowly curling into a fist.

"Horth," she said carefully. "Branst? Is he—"

"Dead," Horth said. "Trouble. With Nesaks."

Tessitatt stopped breathing, as if she'd been winded.

Mad gods, Di Mon thought, wishing suddenly that he had taken the time to understand Hangst's silent child better. *What goes on in that head of his?*

Tessitatt gripped Di Mon's arm as she struggled for self-possession. "I think— " she said, and faltered on a grief too fresh to manage. "Horth, I think Branst would have wanted the Nesaks to go back to SanHome."

Horth nodded. Then he grinned at her suddenly, shockingly, making her eyes widen. "Branstatt," he declared.

Tessitatt's nails bit into Di Mon's bare forearm. Her throat worked. "Yes?" she answered, tentatively.

"To you," said Horth. "For Branst. No right of challenge." He paused, aware the sentence wasn't well formed. He made up for it with extra finality as he said, "Granted."

An infinitely fragile silence followed, in which Di Mon dared to hope for a saner tomorrow.

"Horth," Di Mon said, almost kindly, touched by grief and pain and miracles. "Thank you, but you must know — the *kinf'stan* — you'll be challenged."

"*Ack rel,*" said Liege Nersal.

Our titles are available at major book stores and local independent resellers who support Science Fiction and Fantasy readers like you.

Alphanauts by J. Brian Clarke - (tp) - ISBN: 978-1-894063-14-2
Apparition Trail, The by Lisa Smedman - (tp) - ISBN:1-894063-22-8
Black Chalice by Marie Jakober - (hb) - ISBN:1-894063-00-7
Blue Apes by Phyllis Gotlieb (pb) - ISBN:1-895836-13-1
Blue Apes by Phyllis Gotlieb (hb) - ISBN:1-895836-14-X
Children of Atwar, The by Heather Spears (pb) - ISBN:0-888783-35-3
Claus Effect by David Nickle & Karl Schroeder, The (pb) - ISBN:1-895836-34-4
Claus Effect by David Nickle & Karl Schroeder, The (hb) - ISBN:1-895836-35-2
Courtesan Prince, The by Lynda Williams (tp) - 1-894063-28-7
Dark Earth Dreams by Candas Dorsey & Roger Deegan (comes with a CD)
   - ISBN:1-895836-05-0
Distant Signals by Andrew Weiner (tp) - ISBN:0-888782-84-5
Dreams of an Unseen Planet by Teresa Plowright (tp) - ISBN:0-888782-82-9
Dreams of the Sea by Élisabeth Vonarburg (tp) - ISBN:1-895836-96-4
Dreams of the Sea by Élisabeth Vonarburg (hb) - ISBN:1-895836-98-0
Eclipse by K. A. Bedford - (tp) - ISBN:978-1-894063-30-2
Even The Stones by Marie Jakober - (tp) - ISBN:1-894063-18-X
Fires of the Kindred by Robin Skelton (tp) - ISBN:0-888782-71-3
Forbidden Cargo by Rebecca Rowe - (tp) - ISBN: 978-1-894063-16-6
Game of Perfection, A by Élisabeth Vonarburg (tp) - ISBN:978-1-894063-32-6
Green Music by Ursula Pflug (tp) - ISBN:1-895836-75-1
Green Music by Ursula Pflug (hb) - ISBN:1895836-77-8
Healer, The by Amber Hayward (tp) - ISBN:1-895836-89-1
Healer, The by Amber Hayward (hb) - ISBN:1-895836-91-3
Hydrogen Steel by K. A. Bedford - (tp) - ISBN-13: 978-1-894063-20-3
i-ROBOT Poetry by Jason Christie - (tp) - ISBN-13: 978-1-894063-24-1
Jackal Bird by Michael Barley (pb) - ISBN:1-895836-07-7
Jackal Bird by Michael Barley (hb) - ISBN:1-895836-11-5
Keaen by Till Noever - (tp) - ISBN:1-894063-08-2
Land/Space edited by Candas Jane Dorsey and Judy McCrosky (tp)
   - ISBN:1-895836-90-5
Land/Space edited by Candas Jane Dorsey and Judy McCrosky (hb)
   - ISBN:1-895836-92-1
Lyskarion: The Song of the Wind by J.A. Cullum - (tp) - ISBN:1-894063-02-3
Machine Sex and other stories by Candas Jane Dorsey (tp) - ISBN:0-888782-78-0
Maërlande Chronicles, The by Élisabeth Vonarburg (pb) - ISBN:0-888782-94-2
Moonfall by Heather Spears (pb) - ISBN:0-888783-06-X
On Spec: The First Five Years edited by On Spec (pb) - ISBN:1-895836-08-5
On Spec: The First Five Years edited by On Spec (hb) - ISBN:1-895836-12-3
Orbital Burn by K. A. Bedford - (tp) - ISBN:1-894063-10-4
Orbital Burn by K. A. Bedford - (hb) - ISBN:1-894063-12-0
Pallahaxi Tide by Michael Coney (pb) - ISBN:0-888782-93-4
Passion Play by Sean Stewart (pb) - ISBN:0-888783-14-0
Plague Saint by Rita Donovan, The - (tp) - ISBN:1-895836-28-X
Plague Saint by Rita Donovan, The - (hb) - ISBN:1-895836-29-8
Reluctant Voyagers by Élisabeth Vonarburg (pb) - ISBN:1-895836-09-3
Reluctant Voyagers by Élisabeth Vonarburg (hb) - ISBN:1-895836-15-8

Resisting Adonis by Timothy J. Anderson (tp) - ISBN:1-895836-84-0
Resisting Adonis by Timothy J. Anderson (hb) - ISBN:1-895836-83-2
Silent City, The by Élisabeth Vonarburg (tp) - ISBN:0-888782-77-2
Righteous Anger by Lynda Williams (tp) - ISBN-13: 978-1-894063-38-8
Slow Engines of Time, The by Élisabeth Vonarburg (tp) - ISBN:1-895836-30-1
Slow Engines of Time, The by Élisabeth Vonarburg (hb) - ISBN:1-895836-31-X
Stealing Magic (flipover edition) by Tanya Huff (tp) - ISBN:978-1-894063-34-0
Strange Attractors by Tom Henighan (pb) - ISBN:0-888783-12-4
Taming, The by Heather Spears (pb) - ISBN:1-895836-23-9
Taming, The by Heather Spears (hb) - ISBN:1-895836-24-7
Ten Monkeys, Ten Minutes by Peter Watts (tp) - ISBN:1-895836-74-3
Ten Monkeys, Ten Minutes by Peter Watts (hb) - ISBN:1-895836-76-X
Tesseracts 1 edited by Judith Merril (pb) - ISBN:0-888782-79-9
Tesseracts 2 edited by Phyllis Gotlieb & Douglas Barbour (pb) - ISBN:0-888782-70-5
Tesseracts 3 edited by Candas Jane Dorsey & Gerry Truscott (pb) - ISBN:0-888782-90-X
Tesseracts 4 edited by Lorna Toolis & Michael Skeet (pb) - ISBN:0-888783-22-1
Tesseracts 5 edited by Robert Runté & Yves Maynard (pb) - ISBN:1-895836-25-5
Tesseracts 5 edited by Robert Runté & Yves Maynard (hb) - ISBN:1-895836-26-3
Tesseracts 6 edited by Robert J. Sawyer & Carolyn Clink (pb) - ISBN:1-895836-32-8
Tesseracts 6 edited by Robert J. Sawyer & Carolyn Clink (hb) - ISBN:1-895836-33-6
Tesseracts 7 edited by Paula Johanson & Jean-Louis Trudel (tp) - ISBN:1-895836-58-1
Tesseracts 7 edited by Paula Johanson & Jean-Louis Trudel (hb) - ISBN:1-895836-59-X
Tesseracts 8 edited by John Clute & Candas Jane Dorsey (tp) - ISBN:1-895836-61-1
Tesseracts 8 edited by John Clute & Candas Jane Dorsey (hb) - ISBN:1-895836-62-X
Tesseracts 9 edited by Nalo Hopkinson and Geoff Ryman (tp) - ISBN:1-894063-26-0
Tesseracts 10 edited by Edo van Belkom and Robert Charles Wilson (tp)
    - ISBN-13: 978-1-894063-36-4
TesseractsQ edited by Élisabeth Vonarburg & Jane Brierley (pb) - ISBN:1-895836-21-2
TesseractsQ edited by Élisabeth Vonarburg & Jane Brierley (hb) - ISBN:1-895836-22-0
Throne Price by Lynda Williams and Alison Sinclair - (tp) - ISBN:1-894063-06-6

EDGE Science Fiction and Fantasy Publishing
P. O. Box 1714, Calgary, AB, Canada, T2P 2L7
www.edgewebsite.com
403-254-0160 (voice)
403-254-0456 (fax)

WHAT SHOULD I READ NEXT?
Selected books published by EDGE . . .

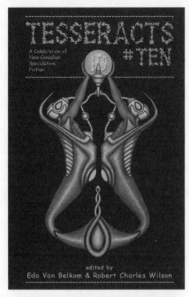

Speculative Fiction - Short Stories

Robot Poetry Collection

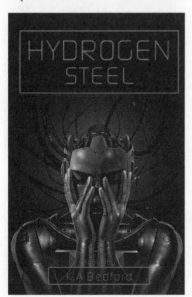

Science Fiction

Science Fiction

WHAT SHOULD I READ NEXT?
Selected books published by EDGE . . .

Science Fiction

Fantasy Short Story Collection

Science Fiction

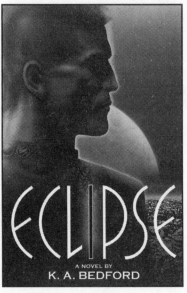

Science Fiction Mystery

WHAT SHOULD I READ NEXT?
Selected books published by EDGE . . .

Science Fiction

Speculative Fiction Short Stories

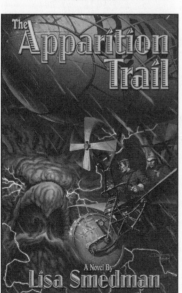

Historical Science Fiction

High Fantasy

WHAT SHOULD I READ NEXT?
Selected books published by EDGE . . .

Science Fiction

Science Fiction

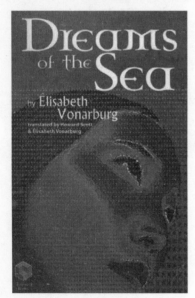

Science Fiction

Science Fiction

WHAT SHOULD I READ NEXT?
Selected books published by EDGE . . .

Science Fiction

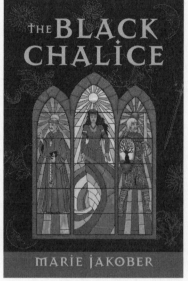

High Fantasy

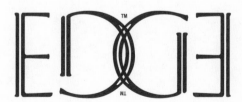